Thunderhead

TO: David

From grandma

On 10th birth-
day before
she past
away!

Also available in Perennial Library
by Mary O'Hara:

My Friend Flicka
Green Grass of Wyoming

Thunderhead

Mary O'Hara

Harper & Row, Publishers, New York
Grand Rapids, Philadelphia, St. Louis, San Francisco
London, Singapore, Sydney, Tokyo, Toronto

A hardcover edition of this book was originally published in 1943 by
J. B. Lippincott Company.

THUNDERHEAD. Copyright 1943 by Mary O'Hara. Copyright © renewed 1971 by Mary O'Hara. All rights reserved. Printed in the
United States of America. No part of this book may be used or
reproduced in any manner whatsoever without written permission
except in the case of brief quotations embodied in critical articles
and reviews. For information address Harper & Row, Publishers,
Inc., 10 East 53rd Street, New York, N.Y. 10022.

First PERENNIAL LIBRARY edition published 1988.

Library of Congress Cataloging-in-Publication Data
O'Hara, Mary.
  Thunderhead.
  1. Horses—Fiction. I. Title.
[PS3529.H34T5   1988]   813'.52   87-45653
ISBN 0-06-080903-5 (pbk.)

95 96 OPM 12 11 10 9 8 7

Thunderhead

1

Within the firm walls of flesh that held him prisoner the foal kicked out angrily. He did not want to be born. The violent constrictions of the walls of his house, which came unexpectedly, disturbed his long peaceful growth and put him in a fury, and he unfolded himself and kicked again and again.

He wanted no change. Here was quiet darkness—nothing to prick and tantalize his eyes. Here was security—no possible harm could reach him. Here was food without effort or even knowledge on his part. Here was the softest floating bed to buffer him against shock. Here was warmth that never fluctuated. Here was—(in some dim way he felt it)—love and protection from his mother's heart. He would not be born.

Twice before he had foiled the labor pains, and his dam had resigned herself and had continued to carry him. (She was the handsome sorrel mare called Flicka, belonging to young Ken McLaughlin of the Goose Bar Ranch.) She had stood patiently, not moving much, up in the Stable Pasture just beyond the corrals. And it had become the habit of everyone at the ranch, Rob and Nell McLaughlin, and their two boys Howard and Ken, and Gus and Tim, the hired hands, to walk out to see her every day, to note how patiently she stood, getting larger and larger, her bright and lively nature changed to sombre brooding. If anyone went near her hindquarters she kicked at them.

Visitors to the ranch went out to inspect her too. One

1

said to Nell McLaughlin, "That's the hugest mare I ever saw."

"She's not so huge," said Nell. "It's just that she's carrying a colt that should have been born in the spring, and here it is, nearly time for the boys to go back to Laramie to school, and still she hasn't foaled."

They all agreed that now and then such things happened to mares and everyone could tell of a case. There was much curiosity as to what the colt would be like. He surely ought to be a good one, big and strong and well developed.

The laboring mare lay down on the ground. The foal, impose his will as he might, was helpless. The violent surges continued, coming at regular intervals, and he was being turned this way and that as if by intelligent hands, until he took the position of a diver, front hoofs stretched out and his little muzzle resting on them. Then he felt pain for the first time and would have struggled and kicked if he could have, but he was held in a vise and could not move. Pressure was strong against him on all sides. There was the sensation of movement through a passage and suddenly a jar as he slid out to the earth.

For a moment he was sheltered from the air and the light by the envelope of membrane in which he was enclosed; then the mare gained her feet and whirled around and her teeth and tongue stripped him of the membrane and he began to breathe.

From that moment on all that he knew was pain, for the breathing hurt his lungs, and opening his eyes, they were stabbed by blinding flashes of light. Terror came when his ear drums were hammered upon by crashes of thunder, and he reacted by giving little choking bleats and trying to sit up. Icy rain sluiced upon him. The hard ground upon which he lay was running with water.

His mother licked and licked him. This warmed him and brought the blood to the surface of his body. He yearned to be closer to her and struggled to rise but had not yet the strength.

There was no mercy for him in the skies. It was the

2

collision of several storms that had ridden up from the lowlands to this high peak of the Wyoming Rocky Mountain Divide. Clusters of purple thunderheads struggled mightily, hurling themselves against each other with detonations that shook the ground. Wide bands of intolerable light stabbed from zenith to earth.

But there was mercy for the colt closer by, and he knew it. His feeble struggles to rise became stronger. His mother's licking tongue encouraged him. The yearning to reach the warmth and shelter of her body grew to a passion—he must, *must* get to her.

And so, long before the storm was over, the foal had found his feet. The teat, hot and swollen, was in his mouth. He was safely anchored; and because of the danger and pain so lately experienced, his awareness was sharpened. Warmth and milk were more than food—they were an ecstasy.

Ken McLaughlin was hunting his mare.

A thin, twelve-year-old boy, with a shock of soft brown hair falling over dark blue eyes that had a shadow as well as a dream in them. He stood looking at the place near the corrals where Flicka should have been and could hardly believe that it was empty, for more than once a day all through this last month since he had stopped riding her he had been out to see whether she had foaled, and she had never been far from her feed box. This afternoon she had been near the spill of fresh water that ran out of the corral trough, but now there was no sign of her.

This meant, Ken knew, that her time had come, and his heart beat a little faster. She had hidden herself away, as all animals will if they are free, to give birth to her foal with no one to witness her labor and pain and victory.

As the boy hesitated there, his eyes scanning the pine woods that edged the pasture, his wits were at work. If *he* had been Flicka and had wanted to hide, where would *he* have gone? And immediately he turned to the woods. Those woods, spare and free of underbrush, covered the rocky shoulder of the Stable Pasture where it sloped away, north, to the little stream called Deercreek which

3

bounded it. The hill was so precipitous in places that it formed low cliffs overhung with twisted pines. At the base of them were caverns. Ken and Howard knew every foot of these terraced cliffs. They had been there on foot and on horseback. Flicka and Highboy—their saddle horses—knew them too, and had become accustomed to the steep paths down which they must slide on their haunches with the boys clinging to their backs like monkeys; or the scramble up, during which the boys kept from sliding off backwards only by tangling their fists in the horses' manes.

Flicka might be on any one of those narrow shelves or pockets, or hidden in one of the little dells at the base of a cliff. She knew them all.

Ken darted toward the woods. It had just begun to rain. The boy cast a careless glance at the sky, refused to accept the warning of what he saw there, telling himself that it would be just a shower from which the trees would shelter him, and began his search.

Occasionally he stopped and called her, "Flicka! Flicka!" and then stood listening to that peculiar state of tension which everyone feels when they call and are not answered.

The daylight on those September evenings held until after eight o'clock, but this evening there was a murky gloom, and under some of the trees there were already pockets of darkness into which Ken stared for minutes before being sure that no living thing was there.

The rain pattered like shot on the ground, and presently Ken heard the long familiar roll of drums in the sky. Suddenly a wind was roaring. The mass of dark clouds sank toward the earth, then opened and poured out torrents of rain. Lightning blazed and thunder crashed.

The boy, crossing an open dell, caught the full brunt of it and dove under a projecting, shelf-like rock, which had left a shallow cave beneath. A small cottontail was sitting primly there for shelter. As Ken shot in, the cottontail shot out, and the boy, panting, drew up his knees and

4

clasped them and sat looking at the spectacle of the storm with an expression of exultation on his thin eager face.

Such torrents of water were coming down that presently the earth was covered. Running streams tore between the trees and shot off the cliff-tops. A good-sized rivulet swept under Ken's sheltering rock, and in a moment he was immersed and drenched. He rolled out from under and stood choking and laughing, shaking the water out of his eyes. Then, since he could be no wetter, he decided to ignore the storm and continue his search for Flicka.

Either the wind was getting colder or the rain was turning to hail or snow, for his wet jersey was like ice against his skin as he trotted in and out of the paths and trees. Often in September there were snowstorms on the top of the Divide, and it seemed to him one was coming now. Up here in the high altitude one day it was snowing and the next like summer.

Ken came upon Flicka in a little dell at the foot of a cliff, cut by the narrowest thread of a path. She stood under an over-hanging tree, but even that could do little to protect her against the rain. When he saw the foal beside her, he stood staring. There had never been a white foal born on the Goose Bar Ranch before. He could hardly believe it. There came a dry fullness in his throat. Flicka—Flicka's foal—her first! And not only off color, but *white!* A throwback! It was a shock to him.

He called her name quietly. She turned her head and he went to her.

She looked anxiously at the foal. Ken stood staring down at it in the gathering darkness. White and narrow and with head beaten down by the pouring rain, tilted toward its mother—it looked as though it might fall over any minute.

Flicka gave a little grunting whinny. Ken could understand her talk, and he knew she was cold and miserable and worried about the foal. They should both of them be in the barn, and Flicka should have a good pail of hot

5

mash. He wondered if the foal could follow her up that thread of a path, and coaxed the mare to try the ascent.

She would not move. Ken put his belt around her neck and led her up. The little one, coming after her with wavering steps, struggled but could not follow. Flicka, turning, saw it halted there. She balked. Ken slipped the belt off her neck and she backed down to the foal and licked it.

Somehow the foal must be got up the path. Ken wondered if he could drag or carry it. Often he and Howard, wrestling with the little foals as they trained them (part of the work of their summer vacations), would clasp their arms around them, lift them off the ground. One little fellow Howard had carried all around with its long legs trailing. But this was an unusually big colt—Ken was doubtful.

With his hand on Flicka's neck he sidled toward the foal, speaking soothingly. "There, there, little fellow—wouldn't hurt you—don't be frightened—it's all right, Flicka—wouldn't hurt your baby—you know I wouldn't—"

The mare was excited and anxious and the foal, as Ken's hand touched its neck, squealed and tried to struggle away. Ken put both arms around the wet slippery body and held tight, but lifting was a different matter. Still talking to Flicka, who was nickering nervously, Ken exerted all his strength. Suddenly he had a little kicking fighting demon in his arms and the foal bared its four baby teeth and bit his arm.

Ken dropped it. Flicka whirled close and stood protectively over it. Ken, scolding under his breath and holding his forearm that the foal's teeth had pinched, realised that he must get help.

He leaped up the pathway.

Gus and Tim, immediately after the supper dishes had been washed up, had taken the pick-up and driven over to the Saturday night dance in Summervale's barn at Tie Siding. Ken's mother and father had gone in to town to dine with Colonel Harris. There was no one but himself and Howard on the ranch, and the responsibility was his own because Flicka was his mare. Besides—this little foal—this particular foal—at the thought of all that depended on him, Ken's feet flew faster, and his eyes, made keen and knowing by his life on the ranch, gazed at the sky and the clouds, gauging the storm—

The wind was changing, veering around to the east, and, yes—what he had suspected was happening. Every raindrop now had a body to it, a little core of slush—it was changing to snow. It beat on his face and nearly blinded him. The wind changed its tune, it rose to a howl, whipping the branches of the pine trees.

But Ken was not cold. The excitement in him made him hot and swift. He reached the corrals, ran down through the Gorge to the house, and burst into the warm kitchen where Howard, who was interested in increasing the size of his muscles, was reading in a droning voice from a "Hercules" pamphlet.

"Flicka's colt's born! You've gotta help me get it in! It's down in the Stable Pasture. Down at the foot of that red cliff—the one you and I ride up and down!"

Ken paused for breath and Howard stared at him.

Howard always took his time. He glanced down again at the page opened on the table before him and finished reading "I'll alter your life—success depends on your bodily development—"

"Gee, Howard! Come along!"

Howard closed the pamphlet and got up from his chair. "Won't it follow Flicka up the path?"

"It can't. It's too steep. It tried but it can't make it."

"Jiminy Christmas!" said Howard, "what'll we do? It might die if it stays out in this storm all night."

"We'll carry it!" cried Ken impatiently. "Come on! That's what I came to get you for. We gotta—"

Ken rushed for the door, but Howard yelled, "Say! Wait! You're soaking wet. You change your clothes first."

"Aw—there's not time," cried Ken at the door. "Come on—what if I *am* wet—"

Howard went calmly back to the table. "Nothing doing.

7

If you don't change your clothes I won't go. I'm not gonna be bawled out for you catching pneumonia again."

Ken looked at him despairingly. Howard meant what he said and was actually sitting down and beginning to study the knotted body of the magazine Hercules again.

Ken rushed to the middle of the floor and began tearing off his clothes. He left them there in a heap and ran stark naked from the room. Howard heard his small bare feet thudding on the stairs. He presently tore down again with an armful of clothes and a bath towel. Standing before the stove he rubbed himself dry, pulled on sweater, pants, boots—and was ready to go. Their slickers and sou'westers hung on the porch.

The two boys ran up the Gorge. Passing the stables, Ken hesitated. "He's a regular little kicking devil," he said doubtfully, "maybe we'll have to tie him—" He headed into the stables.

"Bring a lantern!" shouted Howard, and Ken emerged with two halter-ropes, a halter and lead-rope for Flicka and the stable lantern.

The temperature was falling rapidly. Ken's face flamed and burned from the heat within him and the stinging cold without but he didn't notice. All he could think of was the white foal—*white*—!

They slithered down the steep path, not much more than a gully cut by the rain in the cliff, and saw the mare and foal just as Ken had left them.

"White!" exclaimed Howard, halting just as Ken had done.

"Come on," said Ken impatiently.

Trained never to frighten animals, they slowed their pace and spoke soothingly and quietly to give the mare confidence as they approached. Her eyes were frightened and anxious. But when Ken went to her head, she pressed her face against his chest—that little gesture she had just for him, to tell him that she relied on him and trusted him. And he held her and told her that they had come to take her to a warm bed in the stables—her and the foal too—and that no one would hurt him.

8

Ken slipped her halter on and dropped the rope. Then the two boys together tried to grip the foal but he squealed and bit and seemed to have a dozen thrashing legs.

Suddenly Howard slipped and sat down. The colt, too, lost his footing and fell and Flicka whirled nervously and stood over him. Ken threw himself on the foal.

"Here, Howard!" he said, keeping his voice calm, "while I'm lying on him—tie his hind feet together, can you?"

Howard accomplished this, then Ken rolled over and the two boys tied the front feet and stood up, panting, while Flicka grunted anxiously over the prone body of her bleating foal.

"We can't ever carry him up that path," said Howard, lighting the lantern. "He weighs a ton—never saw such a husky colt. And is he strong!"

"He sure is," said Ken proudly, "ought to be—he's been in there two months more than a year—just growin' and eatin'—look Howard, we'll have to get him up on Flicka. She'll carry him."

"He'd fall off," objected Howard doubtfully.

"I'll ride her too and hold on—you can lead her."

"How'll we get him up?"

"Lift him."

Howard hung the lantern on the bough of a tree and the two boys lifted the struggling foal in their arms and hoisted him onto the back of his dam.

Flicka stood with her head turned, watching them, but she seemed to know the moment her foal was across her withers, and though she kept her head turned to see what the boys would do next, she became quiet.

"Gimme a leg up," gasped Ken, leaning against her side, holding the foal in position. And Howard placed his knee and hand and Ken scrambled up behind the colt.

"Can you hold him?" asked Howard.

"Yep. I think so—" Ken leaned over the colt, grasping Flicka's mane.

9

Howard took the lantern, picked up Flicka's lead-rope, and went ahead.

Flicka knew now just what she had to do. And the little procession wound its way up the cliff, pausing occasionally for a breath, or for Howard to lift the lantern high and pick out the way in the smother of snow which was beating against them.

The foal lay like a sack of meal across Flicka's withers.

The first part of the journey was the worst. When that was accomplished they were on level ground, going rapidly toward the stables. Flicka whinnied with joy as the familiar smell reached her nostrils. And when she was in her stall, and the boys had untied the colt and lowered him to the floor, she stood over him and smelled and licked him and gave the deep, soft, grunting whinny by which a mare reassures her little one. The foal struggled to its feet, staggered about uncertainly, shook itself, then hunted for the teat. Finding the bone of the thigh, instead, it gave a savage bite at it and kicked out in anger.

"Gosh! Look at it!" exclaimed Howard. "What a mean little devil!"

Ken said nothing but watched anxiously. The foal found the teat at last.

"You stay here, Howard, will you?" asked Ken. "I'll go down and make her some mash. You might give her some clean straw."

"I'll rub her down," offered Howard generously, and as Ken left the stable he got a dry sack and rubbed her steaming back and flanks and neck.

A half hour later the mare and foal stood content and dry and comfortable with a deep bed of dry straw under them and a pail of mash for Flicka in the feed box.

"She's all right now," said Howard, at the door of the barn. "Come on—"

Ken pretended to be casual and offhand. "I want to wait till she's finished her mash. You go on down, I won't be long."

Howard still hesitated, eyeing his younger brother where the boy stood leaning on the rail of the manger,

10

almost under the mare's head. "Well—I'll go ahead. I'm goin' to make some hot cocoa—want some?" Howard was handy at making chocolate and flipping eggs and giving his mother a hand with the cooking.

"Sure!" said Ken. "You bet!" But he sat still on the manger rail, watching his mare, and Howard went out, closing the door behind him.

2

Ken stood listening to Howard's retreating steps. He heard the rasp of the corral gate being opened and closed again. Now they were alone, the mare, the foal and himself. In the stable was a sweet quietness and the smell of hay and horses.

Ken sat on the manger rail close to the feed box in which he had placed the bucket of mash, and the mare dipped her muzzle into it, ate hungrily, then lifted her head and chewed, looking at Ken, her long ears pointed forward. She had gentle golden-brown eyes with a seeing expression in them. Looking at Ken, her intelligent face was not a foot from his. He straightened the flaxen forelock that hung between her eyes, murmuring her name now and then. She swung her head around to look at the sleeping foal. The lantern, hung on the corner post, only half lit the stall.

Ken too looked at the foal. Now that he had it safely in the stable, the surprise and worry that he had felt when he first saw it took possession of him again. What a to-do this was going to make! A white foal out of Flicka! A white foal on the Goose Bar Ranch where everyone knew Ban-

11

ner, the big golden sorrel stud that sired the yearly crop of colts.

Ken's uneasiness was linked to a series of nearly disastrous events of past years in which he and a certain line of horses had been involved. This train of events led directly to the small white foal lying there so innocently on the clean hay, and it had begun long before, when a wild stallion of the plains, called the Albino because of his white color, had stolen a mare from the Goose Bar Ranch. She was the thoroughbred, Gypsy, one of Rob McLaughlin's foundation mares. He had bought her when he was a cadet at West Point and used her for polo. When he graduated and then resigned from the Army in order to go in for horse-breeding, there were three of them that came west together and settled down on the Goose Bar Ranch, Rob McLaughlin, Nell, his young New England wife, and the black mare, Gypsy. Rob bought more mares and built up his foundation stock. Then, one spring, Gypsy disappeared.

The McLaughlin ranch was not the only one in that section of Wyoming from which a fine mare disappeared. There began to be talk of a white stallion, "a big ugly devil but a lotta horse," who had formerly ranged the open land of Montana, had come across the border during a drought, and had gathered a band of mares in the open land of Wyoming, stealing from ranchers, tearing down fences, fighting and even killing other stallions.

He reigned for six years. Then a number of ranchers banded together, held a round-up, and caught the Albino and his mares, finding brands from all over the state on the hides of the stolen mares.

Gypsy of the Goose Bar Ranch was there with four beautiful colts. Rob McLaughlin was delighted with their looks and speed and outstanding personalities, and took them home with him, feeling that Gypsy's philandering might contribute valuable qualities to his polo stock.

But he found it impossible to break and train the colts. Even though the fillies were bred by Banner, the Goose Bar stud, than whom no horse could be more intelligent or better mannered, yet the offspring showed the outlaw strain.

He explained it to his boys, "Colts learn from their mothers. They copy them. That's why it's practically impossible to raise a good-tempered colt from a bad-tempered dam. The colts are corrupted from birth. That is the rule. There are, of course, exceptions—we have some very striking exceptions among our own horses. Here is Gypsy, the best-mannered mare in the world—with a bunch of wild hoodlum colts—absolutely unbreakable."

"Is it because they were born and brought up with that gang of wild horses?" asked Howard.

"It's because of the prepotency of the stallion," said Rob grimly. "His wildness outweighs all her gentleness and that of her long line of aristocratic forebears. Some stallion!"

But all of this was an old story to Howard and Ken. They had grown up on the Goose Bar Ranch, familiar with talk and speculation about the near-mythical personage, the Albino, and witnessing their father's struggles with the outlaw strain which, through Gypsy, had been introduced into the breeding stock.

Ken's actual involvement in this tangle was of more recent date. On a day a little more than three years ago he and Gus had been working in the meadow, and came upon a new-born foal and its dam.

"Luk at de little *flicka!*" exclaimed the Swedish ranch hand.

"What does *flicka* mean, Gus?" asked Ken.

"Swedish fur leetle gurl," explained Gus.

And when, a year after that, Rob McLaughlin told Ken he could have for his own any colt on the ranch up to one year of age, Ken chose that same little golden filly and named her Flicka.

Flicka was out of Rocket by Banner. And Rocket was, by common consent, the wildest of the offspring brought home by Gypsy from her sojourn with the Albino.

Rob McLaughlin was exasperated. "I was hoping you'd

make a wise choice, son," he said. "You know what I think of Rocket, of that whole line of horses—it's the worst I've got. There has never been one amongst them with real sense. The mares are hellions and the stallions outlaws. I'd have got rid of this whole line of stock if they weren't so damned fast that I've had the fool idea that someday there might turn out one gentle one in the lot and I'd have a race horse. But it's not going to be Flicka."

But Ken had fallen in love with her and could not give her up.

That summer one nightmare disaster followed the other. Flicka, as wild as her wicked black mother, fought beyond all reason when she was roped and brought in. When she could escape no other way, she made a suicidal leap into the high barbed-wire fence, and there ensued her long illness from the infected wire-cuts, terminating in McLaughlin's command that, next day, she should be shot and put out of her misery. Ken spent that night with her, sitting in the stream where she had fallen, holding her head in his arms. Gus came looking for them in the morning, and carried Ken, helpless with cold and exhaustion, up to the house.

This caused Ken's long and severe attack of pneumonia, during which, miraculously, the filly recovered.

At the end of the summer, there was one triumph which made up for everything. The filly loved Ken as dearly as he loved her, and he was able to say to his father, "She did get gentled, didn't she, Dad?"

And Rob McLaughlin answered, with a softer note than usual in his voice, "Gentle as a kitten, son."

And now here she stood in the stall, a husky three-year-old, docile, gentle, beautifully trained, resting her liquid, trusting eyes on the face of her young master.

But the foal! That all-conquering prepotency Rob McLaughlin had spoken of! After all the trouble Rob had taken to rid his stock of the hated blood of the Albino, here it was cropping out again. This foal was unlike its dam, unlike its sire, unlike any horse on the Goose Bar Ranch. It resembled only one—the Albino. It was almost

14

like having the Albino right there in the stall! Was the power and ferocity of the great outlaw enclosed within that mottled baby hide of pink and white? This thought made shivers go through Ken.

Flicka had finished her mash. Ken lifted the bucket down and went to the door of the barn. He swung the top half open and looked out. It had stopped snowing. The wind had reversed itself and had blown the storm back into the east whence it had come. There was a riot of scudding clouds in the sky with big stars close and bright, going in and out between them. It was much warmer.

Ken folded his arms on the bottom half of the Dutch door and leaned there thinking.

There were still other shadow-shapes woven into the aura that encircled the foal like the predictions of a fortune-teller.

That word Rob McLaughlin had dropped so casually into Ken's thoughtstream that day—*race horse*—

Race horse. It could not, of course, be Flicka, owing to the thickened tendon which was the result of her infection. But why not a colt of Flicka's? With a sweet and tractable mother to teach him manners, with the power and speed which came down to every one of the Albino's line—why not? It had been Nell who had first made this suggestion. Since then it had not been out of Ken's mind.

Ken turned from the barn door and ran his hand down that right hind leg of Flicka's. It was his fault—that thickened tendon—because he had made them catch her for him.

"But you're not sorry, are you, Flicka?" he whispered, going to her head, "because now you've got me—"

Her face, leaning against him, was very still and contented.

The foal—the little race-horse-to-be—lay with his back curved, his feet and nose drawn together like a greyhound asleep. Perhaps he was dreaming of his great future—to redeem the ranch from debt and failure, to deck Nell out in jewels, to make his young owner a hero—

15

Ken bent over him again. His name—what should his name be? Something to sum all that he was and might become. Ken could think of nothing fine enough. His mother would name him—probably as soon as she laid eyes on him. She had a way of doing that. Some words would spring to her lips and out of them the name would come. That would be tomorrow morning.

Ken took the lantern, gave one last look backward, and then left the barn, closing the door tightly behind him. He ran down through the Gorge.

In front of the rambling stone ranch house were several acres of lawn, called by his mother, the Green, after the neat little village Greens of New England where she had spent her childhood. It was covered with a thin sheet of snow. Ken ran across it to the house, and, in the warm kitchen, took off his slicker and sou'wester and drank the hot chocolate Howard had made.

While they sat drinking, the two boys engaged in one of the wrangling, incomprehensible and wholly oblique discussions which made adult listeners conclude that the constitution of boys' minds, and their language, have nothing to do with reason, logic or natural facts.

3

"Promise!"

"Let go of me!"

"But he's mine!"

"My tongue's not yours."

"Prom—" Ken's voice rose.

"Sh—sh—sh—" hissed Howard angrily. "If you wake

Mother—" He squirmed and struggled to loosen Ken's legs which were locked around his waist. "Get off my back, darn you—"

"Promise not to tell!"

In furious writhing silence Howard tried to remove Ken's arms from where they were clasped under his chin. The two boys rolled and bumped about on the floor of Howard's room—their faces scarlet.

"Promise!" exclaimed Ken even louder.

"Sh—sh—sh—" warned Howard.

But Ken was conscious of being in the right. If their father heard the noise and discovered it was because Howard wouldn't promise not to tell about Ken's colt before *he* had a chance to, Howard would get it in the neck.

"Promise. Promise! *PROMISE!*"

"All right, I promise. Get off my back."

Ken loosened his arms and legs and the boys untangled themselves. In complete amity, their faces recovering normal color, they straightened their clothing, slicked their hair, tip-toed downstairs, and burst out into the day.

Bound for the stables and the colt, they paused behind the house at the sight of two strange cars. Visitors. Visitors brought home to the ranch from the dinner party last night. They recognized the cars. The blue one belonged to Colonel Morton Harris, an old classmate of their father's at West Point, now Colonel of Artillery at Fort Francis Warren. The gray one belonged to Charles Sargent, millionaire horse-breeder, owner of the famous racing stud, *Appalachian*. Sargent had his home ranch not twenty-five miles from the Goose Bar.

"Charley Sargent and Mort Harris," said Howard airily. "That's keen. No church today."

But Ken stood looking at the cars and thinking. Charley Sargent, tall and thin as a beanpole in his narrow Cheyenne pants—always kidding and clowning—his long brown face under the wide-brimmed western hat looking as Gary Cooper's might when he got older—it was always fun when Charley Sargent came to visit, and he might talk about his race horses. Ken's heart felt a

17

little flutter of excitement. He wanted to know all he could find out about race horses. And Appalachian, the big black racing stud—he—

"Come on!" said Howard, heading for the barn.

Ken walked slowly after him, wondering if the presence of visitors would interfere with his own surprise. Should he tell them at breakfast? It had to be arranged so that the impression was favorable. They had to be glad and proud that it was white, as he was himself. That wasn't all. He had really to act so that no one, not even his father, would suspect that he was hiding anything. That was going to be hard. It was hard to keep any sort of secret—harder still if you felt the least bit guilty about it—

When they reached the corral they saw that Flicka and the colt were both out, enjoying the early morning sunshine. Gus and Tim were watching, astonished and amused.

Ken rushed at Gus and grabbed him. "Don't tell anyone, Gus—they don't know yet. I want to s'prise 'em— promise—"

"Yu cud knock me over with a feather, Kennie," said the old Swede, with his slow smile. "But white horses is gude luck, they say."

"Never seen no such colt on *this* ranch before," added Tim. "What'll the Captain say?"

"Don't tell him until I have a chance to," insisted Ken. "Promise, will you?"

"Sure. You can tell 'em, Kennie," said Gus. "She's your mare, and your colt too, I guess."

Ken opened the barn door and called Flicka in. The colt did not follow but stood blinking in the sunshine. Gus and Tim shooed it gently in. Ken put them both in the farthest stall and he and Howard stood for a while watching them.

But Ken had important business on his mind, and presently ran down to the house and found that his mother was making breakfast and his father upstairs shaving.

18

Ken leaned against the bathroom door and called gently, "Dad!"

"Hullo there!"

"Say, Dad—would you tell me something?"

"Depends."

"Well—if you had money enough, what kind of fences would you have on the ranch?"

"Well—if I had money enough, I'd tear out every foot of barbed wire and put in wooden fences. Good solid posts about ten feet apart and four feet high. Even one line of rails on top of that would keep horses in—that is, if it was solid enough so they couldn't rub them down with their fannies."

"Would it cost much, Dad?"

"You can get the poles for nothing up in the Government Reserve, but the cutting and hauling would cost money—that's work. I wouldn't have time to do it myself."

"Even if it costs *lots* of money, Dad, it wouldn't matter."

Rob's answer was smothered in the sounds that go with shaving, and suddenly he began his favorite shaving song:

"K-K-K-Katy! Beautiful Kay–ty—"

It didn't seem as if he was paying a great deal of attention to the important news.

Suddenly the door burst open and he strode out in riding breeches, boots, singlet, and a very gay good humor. His black hair was rough, his eyes very blue, and all his big white teeth showing. He almost rode over Ken and the boy felt overpowered by the impact of his father's personality. With the door closed between them, it had been less potent.

"I'll be waiting for you a-hat the kitchen door!"

roared Rob, stamping down the hall toward his room. He stopped at the head of the stairs, looked over and shouted, "Say, you fellows! Mort! Charley! Are you still asleep? Flapjacks comin' up!"

There was an answering shout from the terrace at the front of the house, "We're way ahead of you!" and Rob hurried into his room to finish dressing.

Outside, Nell and her two guests were being entertained, as was usual at the Goose Bar Ranch, by the antics of assorted animals. Chaps, the black cocker, and Kim, the collie, were chasing each other on the Green as if nothing were needed for exuberant happiness but to have been shut up for a night and then let out again.

All traces of snow had disappeared. There was intense sunlight breaking everywhere into the colors of the prism. There was a boisterous wind bending the pines and making Nell's blue linen dress flutter.

"What do you think of him?" she called to Colonel Harris, who stood near the fountain inspecting Rob's work team. They were huge brown brutes. "That one you're looking at is Big Joe," she added, "the pride of Rob's heart."

"I should say," said the Colonel in his cultured, precise manner, taking off his glasses and polishing them, "that he is a pure-bred Percheron, sixteen hands high, and weighs thirteen hundred pounds."

"Just about right," said Nell, picking up her cat, Pauly, who was begging beside her. Pauly, a sinuous, tortoise-shell angora with long topaz eyes and a little siren face, slipped one arm around Nell's neck, hung on, and tried to lick her mouth.

Nell tapped the tiny coral sickle-shaped tongue and laughed.

Charley Sargent's lanky form hovered over her. "You're lookin' mighty pretty this mornin'—how do you get those pink cheeks?"

"You forget I've been slaving over the kitchen stove getting breakfast for—let's see—five male men—" She buried her face in Pauly's soft brown fur. Charley Sargent always embarrassed her with his flattering eyes and flirty ways. He made her feel about eighteen.

20

"Isn't this a day!" she exclaimed. "Who could believe it was snowing last night! That's Wyoming for you!" She turned her face up to the sky. There were magpies and plover and chicken hawks gliding on steeply tilted wings against the blue, and now and then, when the wind veered, came a breath of snow from the Neversummer Range in the south.

"Last night," said Charley, still hovering, "was a mighty nice party. But I'm afraid to face Rob. He bawled me out for dancin' with you so much."

"This other one," called Colonel Harris, "is not pure-bred, is he?"

"No," said Nell, running down the steps to join him. "That's old Tommy. He's our bronco-buster. Whenever Rob has a young horse he wants to take the ginger out of, he harnesses him up with Tommy."

While she chattered she was remembering how furious Rob had been last night when Charley Sargent had waltzed with her and spun her around and around so fast that her long blue dress had stood out like the skirt of a whirling dervish. All the same—it was fun.

The Colonel looked down at Nell with pleasure. His manner was punctilious. "You appear to be fond of cats."

"I am. Very. At least, this cat."

"More than dogs?"

"I've got it all figured out about cats and dogs. Dogs are like lovable children. But cats are entirely adult."

"What about that one over there? She doesn't look very adult."

"Oh! That yellow one! That's Matilda. She's just a kitten, but she's really something! She's Pauly's daughter—you'd never think it, would you?"

"I certainly would not."

"Well—it was after Pauly had a visitor. A tall thin city cat with long straight legs—nothing like our cats—they're like weasels, you see. He was yellow. She usually has litters of four or five, but this time she had only one kitten and it was enormous. It evidently got all the nourishment that four should have had and it turned into a

21

regular tigress. It took possession of Pauly and the ranch and everyone on it. It explored every cranny of the house, the sheds, the roofs, the chimneys, and it grew like Jack's beanstalk. Rob tells people, if they hear a horse galloping on the roof, not to be surprised—it's just Matilda."

Matilda, at this moment, began to take an interest in the Percheron, who had drunk all he wanted on the fountain and was wandering toward the flower border.

Nell shooed him away. He paid no attention. She clapped her hands and stamped her foot at him. "Get away from there, Big Joe!"

Big Joe stood his ground.

Matilda took a hand. She advanced toward Big Joe belligerently, not too closely—just there to the point of his nose—then dashed away again to a spot four feet distant.

"What's doing?" asked Rob, coming through the door.

Charley Sargent laughed. "That little yellow devil is teaching the Percheron his place! Look at her!"

Matilda proceeded to do her stuff. She flung herself on her back before Big Joe, tossing a pebble between her paws.

"See that?" she said to the big brute who was watching her, astonished and fascinated. "See that? If you were this pebble, this is what I would do to you!" She smacked it from side to side. She chased it when it rolled away, then fell on it and rolled on it. She bit it. And last and most insulting, she went over on her back, held it in her front paws and disembowelled it.

Her audience roared with laughter.

"Look at Big Joe!" exclaimed Rob. "Look at his face!"

The Percheron was hypnotized. He hung on every motion of the little yellow ball of fur. Tentatively he reached out his nose and sniffed, took one slow step. Matilda turned inside out, lit on the Pergola, in one more leap was on the roof and galloped thunderously away.

Breakfast was noisy. There were flapjacks, thin and brown and light with slightly crisp edges. Piles of them, piping hot. A bowl of brown sugar was on the table and a jug of maple syrup. With her flapjacks, Nell liked marmalade, melted and thinned and hot.

"By Jiminy, I'll try that!" exclaimed Charley, taking the pitcher.

All the time, the thought of his colt was never out of Ken's mind. Even while he was watching and listening to the others, he was trying to figure out just how he would tell it. The build-up he had attempted with his father hadn't come to much. Ken wanted, too, to talk to his mother about the things she would like to buy when his colt was winning money on the race tracks. Dresses and velvet things with fur like the General's wife wore, so that they would all fall in love with the colt the moment they saw it because of all it was going to do for them.

But as the hilarious breakfast progressed through grapefruit and flapjacks and sausages and pots of coffee with thick yellow Guernsey cream, and Rob got up again and again to go to the kitchen, and Howard carried piles of plates in and out, Ken became convinced that this wasn't the time to tell it. They wouldn't pay attention— would just say, "Oh, a new colt? Flicka has foaled at last? Fine—pass the syrup, will you?" After all, there were so many colts born on the Goose Bar Ranch.

A car drove up and stopped behind the house. As Rob returned from the kitchen, Colonel Harris said, "That's probably the sergeant and orderly with my mare."

"What for?" asked Nell.

Rob explained. "Mort wants to have his saddle mare bred by Banner, so I told him to send her up today."

"It's late for breeding, isn't it?"

"Yes," said Harris, "it is. I thought she was bred, but she isn't after all, so we're going to try again."

"Why don't you have her bred by a real stud!" said Charley. "You don't happen to be ignorant of the fact that my Appalachian is the finest racin' stud in horse history, do you?"

"But think what you charge as a stud fee," said the Colonel. "Two hundred and fifty bucks! That's too much for a poor soldier."

"What I charge is one thing and what I get is another," growled Charley, rolling and lighting a cigarette.

"Run out, Ken," ordered his father, "and tell the sergeant to drive up to the stables and put the mare in the little east corral. She can wait there until I get Banner in."

"Gee!" exclaimed Howard. "Getting Banner in!"

Ken went out and saw a car and trailer, two uniformed men in the front seat and a blanketed mare in the trailer. He gave the message and returned to the dining room.

"Besides," Colonel Harris was saying, "your Appalachian is as pampered and petted and sheltered as a movie star, with his special pasture and meadows and feed and stables for every sort of weather and season—he don't have to think any more—everybody thinks for him."

"Pampered!" roared Charley indignantly. "Pampered so that he produces one winner after the other! Country Squire, who won at Tia Juana in 1934! Spinnaker Boom, who won the handicap last year at Santa Anita, and a filly—Coquette—in the two-year-old class—"

"I know, I know all that," said Colonel Harris. "He's a good stud for racing stock. But this tough fellow of Rob's here—Banner—that's the sort of fellow for my money, thinks for himself, takes care of his mares on the range in all sorts of weather, knows what Rob is thinking and doing a mile away—lives like a robber baron up there in the hills with his harem—"

"Talk about robber barons," said Rob, "remember that stallion they called the Albino? There was a robber baron for you—reigned like a king, no one to think for *him!* Robbed, pillaged, helped himself to whatever he wanted—"

"What became of him anyway?" asked Colonel Harris. "Haven't heard anything about him for years."

"I'll wager he's around somewhere, lusty and wicked as ever, with a band of mares picked from all over the state," said Rob. "And the finest! He sure knew how to pick 'em! You know, we had him in a corral once."

24

"Pity someone didn't have sense enough to keep him," said Charley. "If I'd been there—"

"If you'd been there," said Rob sarcastically, "it might have been you he ran down and damn near killed instead of me."

"Ran you down, did he?"

"It isn't often a horse will really attack a man, but he sure did me. We had him in the corral, and the whole bunch of mares, including my Gypsy and her four colts. He never let go of the mares—kept rounding them up, milling them around, heading them in one direction and then the other, until he saw he was licked—they were caught and would never get out. Then he decided to save himself. He went right at one fence—crashed the top bar and was in the wing. I had dismounted—I had a hunch he'd crash the wing fence too—and I ran to head him off. You know if you jump in front of a horse and wave your arms you can deflect 'em, nine times out of ten. Crosby was coming on his horse as fast as he could, swinging his rope. But that's when the Albino ran me down. He couldn't jump the wing fence, but he charged it and just kicked it to pieces. And God! How he did go—we just stood there and watched his dust!"

"Hurt you any?" asked Colonel Harris, and Rob leaned forward and parted the black hair on one temple. A short white scar showed. "I dodged him at the last minute, but he left me a keepsake—one of his front hoofs."

"Gee—ee—ee—" said Ken.

"And I'll never forget the look of his eyes," continued Rob. "I saw them close—too close—a wicked eye."

"What kind of an eye, Dad?"

"An eye like Rocket's. Charley, remember that fast black mare I had that you almost bought?"

"You mean, that I bought and you almost delivered," corrected Charley.

Rob grinned and turned to Mort Harris to explain. "He bought this mare from me for five hundred dollars provided I could deliver her safe and sound. She was a hellion, one of the colts out of my mare Gypsy, sired by the

Albino—and she had that same wild, wicked eye of his with the white ring around it—well, I got her in the truck but when we went under the sign out there by the highway, she reared up and brained herself against it."

"Dad," said Ken, "if the Albino was white all over, how could you see that there was a white ring around his eye?"

"In a horse, the pupil of the eye is very large—usually fills the space between the lids entirely. If there's a white ring around it, it is because the eyelids are stretched a bit too wide open—that shows the white eyeball all around and gives that wicked crazy look—and it always means a bad 'un. Everybody hates a horse with a white-ringed eye."

"And you've heard about my Mohawk," roared Charley, "out of Stole-Away by Appalachian—won everything there was to win at Saginaw Falls two years go! I tell you, Mort, Appalachian—"

Mort Harris put up his hand. "Charley, I don't want a race horse. I'm not going to run away from the enemy. I want a horse like Rob's, trained in the hills and high altitudes. I want endurance and good wind and a heart for anything. I want to know when I start out on him that he'll bring me back. Stand up under any condition. Besides—Appalachian's black. And I want a sorrel."

"And you'll get it from Banner," said Rob. "He breeds true. Occasionally I get a black colt—his dam was a black Arab mare named El Kantara—but mostly sorrels, one after the other, as like as peas in a pod."

Hearing this, Howard and Ken looked at each other, Ken blank and disconcerted, and Howard making fantastic faces of alarm and concern. He mouthed silently, "When are you going to tell?" And Ken mouthed savagely back, "Shut up!"

The boys saw their mother's eyes upon them and stopped their face-making.

Ken was very thoughtful. The morning was going to be crowded with excitement. Bringing Banner in. Breeding the Colonel's mare. He began to feel worried. Events

26

always got themselves tangled around you so that things came out wrong. Perhaps it would be better to save his surprise until all this other stuff was over.

Rob added, "And you're right in wanting a sorrel, Mort. A sorrel's the hardest of all to break and train, but when you've done it, you've got a horse." He pushed his chair back. "What about you fellows riding out with me to get Banner and the mares?"

"The mares?" repeated Harris. "Why bring in the mares? Banner's the one we want."

Rob looked at him, an odd quizzical gleam in his eye, and Charley Sargent drawled, "You don't really understand our western broncs, Mort. They're so damn affectionate. Take Banner now—this tough boy you've been bragging about—why it would just about break his heart to be separated from his harem. Rob wouldn't have the heart to do it, would you, Rob?"

Harris grinned. "Well—sure. I spend my life on horseback anyway, and now that I'm off on a little visit for a bit of relaxation, I suppose the thing to do is ride some more. I hope you can give me a good mount."

Rob turned to Howard. "What horses are up in the corrals now, Howard?"

"Taggert and some geldings, Bronze—Shorty—Highboy—"

"Run up there, Howard, and tell Gus to saddle Taggert and Bronze and Shorty."

Half an hour later they were in the corrals ready to mount. Charley Sargent, as always, in his long Cheyenne pants and wide-brimmed hat, and the Colonel as neatly turned out in breeches and boots as Rob himself.

"You can have your choice," said Rob generously.

"Which do *you* ride?" asked Charley suspiciously.

"This blood-bay Taggert—you can have her—you never felt such gaits."

Sargent removed his big hat and scratched his head reflectively. "She looks a dandy—and I'm sure obliged to you. But a mare—no, I think I'll take one of the geldings —you take the mare, Harris—"

27

"What a grand horse," said the Colonel looking her over with interest. "All right, I'll take that big mare." He mounted her and settled himself in the saddle.

Charley mounted Shorty and Rob Bronze, and the three men rode out of the corrals together.

4

Nell stood at the edge of the old sheepfold looking for mushrooms. In the spring she had picked lamb's quarter there, fresh young greens which, when cooked and chopped fine with salt and pepper and garlic and cream, were more delicious than any spinach. It grew where sheep had been. There were sheep on the ranch now. Rob had leased out some grazing and here was where the fold had been in the spring, a square place, bare of grass, fenced around with wire. When the sheep were there, lanterns hung on the four corners to scare away coyotes, but now the sheep had gone up to the back range and grass has grown over the fold, and often mushrooms grew there too. She quickly filled her basket.

When she got back to the kitchen she made the stuffing for the ducks. Four of them. She was glad she could use up some of the young ducklings—they were so much better right now at about six months of age than later. The four small yellow corpses lay on the drain board of the sink. Tim had plucked them but she must look them over again. With the point of a sharp knife she dug out the pin feathers.

She peeled potatoes, drew cold water and put them in, murmuring to herself, *plan for two o'clock*. She had a great deal to do and hurried around the kitchen, her brown sandals light and quick on the green-painted floor.

Pauly sat in the middle of the room, from which spot she could, by turning her head rapidly, keep Nell in sight. Occasionally this made her so dizzy that she fell over sideways with a little thump. Then she would pick herself up with bewildered shaking of her small head and again take her seat and resume her adoration. Often, her eyes on Nell's face, she purred and kneaded the wooden floor under her paws. She was waiting for that moment when Nell, passing her, would suddenly stoop, sweep her up, hold her in front of her shaking her a little, talking to her, then cuddle her a second and put her down and go on with her work. Pauly knew when these moments were coming and as Nell approached her, she would run to her, stand upon her hind legs and reach her arms up with sharp cries of ecstasy.

Nell glanced at the clock and wondered where the men were. Whenever she thought of Rob she could see him in her mind's eye and could sometimes almost feel his force. She saw him now, riding, head up, frown between his eyes. Suddenly she felt compassion for him and fear— the life here so dangerous for everyone—cliffs and mountains, horses, weather— She braced herself, her lips closed firmly. *Happiness hangs by a hair.*

She went to the spring house carrying a yellow bowl and a dipper. She removed the cover from the jar in the shallow tray of running water and dipped out the cream. So much for the mushrooms—so much for the apricot Bavarian cream—easier to make than ice cream and just as good. Coming out of the spring house she stood a moment, her eyes wandering over the blue hills of the far range and the slopes of tawny grass near by. All the hardships of her life at the ranch were mitigated by the natural beauty around her. It was like an ever-present, harmonious accompaniment, with which, when she wished, she could fall in step and be comforted.

A streak of heavenly color cut the sunny air over the Green—a bluebird, with the light metallic on its wings.

29

It perched on the tip of one of the cottonwood trees, swinging in the breeze. Nell had to smile, watching it.

She turned her head to the Gorge again and listened. The wind was coming down from the stables. It might carry the sound of a voice, Rob shouting, or a dog barking, the whinny of a horse, but there was nothing. She went on to the house.

When dinner was ready, all but the roasting of the ducks, she sat down sideways in a chair by the window, folded her arms on the back, bent her head upon them and rested. Pauly sat close behind her.

She was remembering how, as he left the table that morning, Rob had laid his hand for one moment upon the top of her head. It was so gentle a touch that not one hair of her shining cap was disturbed. She knew what the caress meant. He hated to leave her with all the work to do and blamed himself. There was always that hidden sweetness he had for her underneath the shouting and blustering. But not so often now as it used to be.

She raised her head and looked out at the Green. Still the windy blue of the sky with the chicken hawks tilting and swinging. A file of red-gold horses was walking slowly through the pines opposite. The sun touched their shining coats. There were vertical bars of gold flickering, alternating with bands of shadow.

She bent her head and listened again. Still no sound from the stables.

Rob—was he all right? All right in himself? All right about life? All right toward her?

There was that thing he never ceased worrying about —if he had done right in bringing her here to the West, away from everything and everybody she had grown up with.

Just the other night they had been talking about it after the boys had gone to bed. Taking his pipe out of his mouth, the smoke wreathing around his finely modeled dark head, he said, "I should never have brought you out here."

Looking at him, she saw behind him across the Green,

30

the dark pines with their jagged outline against the placid, star-filled sky. "Why not?"

"There's something about the life here that's pretty hard to take, isn't there?"

"I guess there's something pretty hard to take about life wherever you are."

"But this is downright primitive."

Nell said dreamily, "I remember, when we used to go to California in the winters, crossing the plains I would look from the train windows and see all the uninhabited land, with here and there a pitiful-looking huddle of buildings against the sky—all their lines off the square, and looking as if they were about to collapse—usually clinging to the side of a windmill. And it gave me the most terrible feeling—despair really—at the thought of such a life for anyone; just winds and emptiness and un-measurable miles, and a crooked, tumble-down jumble of boards, *home*, in the midst of it. Such loneliness! I could almost taste and smell it—right there in the Pullman looking out the window! And now—here I am! And now I know that very likely some of those buildings I saw were the center of a ranch of anywhere from two to ten thousand acres; and that in the middle of the jumble of corrals and fences and out-buildings and crooked walls, was a real house; weather-tight and cosy inside, crowded with homely furniture, red-hot stoves in winter, big families, clustering children, old people, booted men, noise, food, good cheer. I've been in many of them. They aren't lonely and forlorn at all."

Rob was aggrieved. "There isn't a single wall off the square on this ranch."

"Oh, Rob, I didn't mean *our* home. This is beautiful. You made it beautiful. I couldn't have a lovelier home."

"Honest?"

"You know it."

He puffed in silence for a few moments. "And yet, Nell—it could have been in the East. Will this ever be home to you?"

"Rob if you go away from your own place and people—

the place you spent your childhood in, all your life you'll be sick with homesickness and you'll never have a home. You can find a better place, perhaps, a way of life you like better, but the *home* is gone out of your heart, and you'll be hunting it all your life long. You must feel that as well as I."

Out of a deep silence his answer came. "I do. It makes me quite desperate sometimes."

"And so—" she had leaned to him and slipped her hand in his. "Here—this—your hand, is home for me."

He had clasped her hand with sudden violence.

Rob's hands— They were big, square-fingered hands, the veins standing out full and hard so that you thought of the blood pushing within them and the bounding pulse. For all their size and hardness they were finely drawn hands; significant. Hands a sculptor would choose to hold a torch. Hands a horse would choose to bridle him. Thinking about them, she saw them detached from Rob. Two little persons, moving about of themselves with a will and brain of their own, always doing something; carrying tools, pieces of metal, odds and ends of machinery or leather or wire; making the terrace, laying the low stone wall which held it; planting the flower border beneath it; making the stone fountain in the middle of the Green; planting and watering the cottonwood trees—

He spoke again out of the darkness but she had gone so far away in thought, knowing nothing but the clasp of his hand and the smell of his tobacco-scented nearness that she drew herself back with difficulty.

"But the boys, Nell."

"Yes."

"This is home for them."

"Oh, yes!"

"But will they stay here? Or wander away as we did? And then be homeless too?"

She answered passionately. "As long as they live they'll never forget these skies and storms and rainbows and storms and fiery elements."

"That's just it. We were born and brought up in the

32

cities—and escaped. To this. It will be just the opposite with the boys."

"It's that way with everybody nowadays."

They had mused and talked about the poetry which is the pulse-beat of the living earth. Here, on the ranch, one lived right on the naked body of nature. In the cities, nature is encased in a shell. One cannot feel the warmth, the blood; one almost comes to doubt its life. In cities, indeed, one can be utterly lost.

For an hour they had talked, their hands clasped, the warmth of palm against palm, an hour of closeness and agreement and understanding. Such hours came more and more rarely.

This troubled Nell. Why should it be so? Because Rob spent his days fighting. Horses, men, weather, the elements—and the *bank balance*—Mostly, he wore an armor of defiance and stubbornness. From out of this he glared and shouted and cracked the whip at everyone— often at her too— Again—why? The bank balance.

She hated to think of it. She leaned closer to the window and looked out, watching a flock of small birds tossing high in the air above the Green. The sun was striking the underside of their bodies and they looked like silver butterflies.

Bank balance. Long ago she had come to the conclusion that the horses would never pay. Why didn't Rob see it too? And she didn't dare hint it to him. Was she being cowardly? Was it her duty as a wife? But Rob—he wouldn't be able to take it. Not Rob. As much as Kennie, he set his heart on one thing, and could not give up. That was childish, really. A grown man should be more fluid— able to change and revise his opinions and change his plans. But not Rob— Oh, never Rob—

Yes. It was impossible that the horses should pay. The ranch was too far from the markets. And buyers demanded size. Without making an enormous outlay you couldn't raise a big three- or four-year-old in Wyoming, owing to the hard winters, lack of help, equipment, buildings, shelter. And what was that thing the income-tax man had told Rob once? No ranchers in Wyoming made money except dude ranchers.

Raising costly, pure-bred horses here just wasn't indigenous to the country. It was a country for—let's see—what did go well here—? The railroad, and raising sheep and beef (when the markets were good) and some mining. Small ranchers ran a little beef, butchered it themselves and often peddled it in neighboring towns; and caught and broke and sold a few mustangs.

Just two things she couldn't face. The bankruptcy and destitution that they seemed to be headed for. And Rob's despair. For it would come. If one came, the other would follow. Already, every day, more harshness in his voice. More bitterness about his mouth. Less of the tenderness and humor which had made their youth together long and sweet. What did a woman do when that went away— Oh what? Oh, Rob—

She bent her head again on the back of the chair. She had faced all this often before and her habit was simply to push it all to the side of her mind and think of other things.

There was this beauty amid which she lived. The open prairie; the calm blue days; the wideness of the plains— elbow room and to spare. Think of that. Think of the boys. Happy. Well. Growing in strength and intelligence and character.

And think of that other night—that hour of companionship between herself and Rob—and this morning at breakfast when his hand had touched her head in passing, saying so much.

Sitting there in the kitchen chair she put her hand up to smooth the hair on the top of her head as if to meet his hand there.

At the screen door Matilda was demanding entrance with peremptory screeches.

Pauly looked up at Nell. "Shall we let her in?"

Nell went to the door and opened it and Matilda galloped joyously in, enveloped in a pungent atmosphere of skunk.

34

Neither shouts nor the clappings of hands, nor ener-
getic pursuit, nor the waving of a broom persuaded her to
go out. She leaped upon the cushion of Nell's chair and
sat licking the smell of herself with amorous delight.

Nell showed her a cracker. Matilda was very fond of
butter crackers. She made a leap for it, but Nell was too
quick for her; she ran out of doors closing the door safely
behind them both, then stooped and offered the cracker
to Matilda. Matilda could never behave like a lady. She
stood up on her hind legs, boxed at the cracker with both
paws, knocked it out of Nell's hand, seized it and fled.

5

Banner searched the wind.

The mares and colts were grazing in a saucer-like depression of the upland, the stallion a little above them
cropping the sweet tubular grass along the edge of a ridge
in the hillside. Suddenly he flung up his head and stood
alert, his compact red-gold body gathered and twisted to
face the alarm, his legs thrust out against the irregular-
ities of the rocky ground, his red tail and mane flying in
the wind.

For a few seconds he stood motionless, then moved
into action. At a swift trot he circled the mares, his nose
lifted, nostrils vibrating for the scent. It came now and
again—just the faintest tang—

He swept in widening circles, reaching his nose higher,
his eyes and ears wild and eager.

Up above him rose the pinnacle, topped with a craggy
outcrop of rock. This was the highest point for miles

around. From here his long-range eyes could see the farthest moving speck and his razor-keen sense of smell
catch and identify all that was on the wind. He went up
the steep sides without variation of pace or action, the
long smooth muscles under his shining coat rippling ef-
fortlessly.

He stood on the peak, forefeet planted on the topmost
spur of rock, his body sloping down. He lifted and swung
his head, but he didn't get the scent. He went down
again and began circling, nose pointed straight up, tail
high and pluming over his haunches. Above him the
deep blue sky bent low and the solid white cumulus
clouds hurried across it as if they were squeezed between
earth and sky.

The mares and colts grazed placidly.

The movement of a stallion's head when he is searching
the wind is something to see—never still a moment.
Swinging, lifting high, higher—even straight up to the
sky, the nostrils wide and pulsing. He covers the ground
at a swift, effortless trot or canter, always in a circle, so
that he misses no inch of the field of scent.

At last Banner, on one of his wide circles, caught the
unmistakable scent of his master, halted, swung around,
and headed for the approaching horsemen, but wide of
them and behind, so that, as Rob kept glancing backwards and to the sides, well knowing what to expect, he
suddenly saw the stallion in pursuit of them, coming
more sedately now, cautious, with his high springing trot
and his steady eye fixed on them.

He was full of questions and looked to Rob for the answers. What was up? Was he to bring the mares in? Was
the band to be moved to another pasture? Or was it to be
just an exhibition?

The men drew rein and turned to meet him. Both Sargent and Harris had seen the horse on former occasions,
but it was impossible not to feel excitement and to respond with altered expressions as the intelligent animal
drew near, taking in the group with pricked ears and an
investigating curiosity.

Rob had often wondered how the stallion read his thoughts. Possibly by the swing and tilt of his body as he rode. Close observation will disclose how continuously the body, by a hundred little movements, indicates thoughts and intentions. Or possibly, it was by the direction of his glances. To a certain extent, of course, by his words and the tone of his voice and definite signals.

"Look at him!" exclaimed Charley Sargent. "The son-of-a-gun!"

"Some horse," said Harris. "Came up behind us—"

Rob said, "His mares are probably back yonder." He gestured over his shoulder. "No oats for you today, old boy—" Banner knew that already. There were never oats when his master came a-horseback—only when he came in the automobile. Rob added, "Where's your family?" and, turning slowly, caught sight of the band of mares a mile away. He touched spur to his horse.

"There they are! Want to see them, Mort?"

"I sure do."

They cantered over the range, the stallion following, running in half circles around them, crowding close, sniffing at each of the horses.

As they drew rein near the band of mares, Charley's gelding swung around to face Banner and they spoke— half-squeal, half-grunt. Both of them reared and suddenly Charley was having trouble in keeping his seat as the two began a playful fight, striking at each other with their forefeet, nipping over the head, trying for the neck.

"They're old friends," said Rob, grinning.

Charley leaned out and made a swing at the stallion. "Get away with you, you brute!"

Banner gave a great start and bounded away but in a few seconds was back again, this time sniffing at the mare Harris rode, sidling up to her, crowding close. Suddenly he lunged at her.

Colonel Harris drew her away and shouted at the stallion. Banner circled, came back with head low, snaking along the grass, and Rob and Charley grinned, pulled up their horses, and watched.

37

The mare was receiving commands from two quarters. From her rider, who held her forcibly back and commanded her to cease her play with the stallion and to stand still—from Banner, whose single lunge had been enough to tell her what he wanted, and who now followed it up by nipping her hind legs.

Frightened and helpless, she obeyed the stallion. In vain Colonel Harris tugged on the reins. In another second Banner had forced her into a gallop, driving her straight into his band of mares. Rob and Charley followed slowly, broad grins on their faces.

"You wouldn't think that a man who had spent his life on horseback would be apt to get a brand new ridin' experience, but it looks to me like that's what's goin' to happen to Mort," said Sargent joyously. "I'm just as glad I'm not on that mare!"

Taggert and her rider were lost in the group of mares, which closed up when Banner gave the command. He circled them rapidly, head down, teeth bared, mane tossing over his eyes.

Rob took a whistle out of his pocket and blew it. The stallion and all the mares halted and looked at him. Rob turned and began to trot back toward the ranch. He held one arm high. *"Come on, Banner! Bring 'em in!"*

He broke into a gallop, Charley following close.

The stallion wheeled and began the round-up of his mares.

Rob spurred his horse to a faster pace, saying, "I'd just as soon keep ahead of them!"

But it was impossible. Long before they had reached the bottom of the slope the band of mares with the stallion driving them and Harris hopelessly caught in the midst of them were abreast of Rob and Charley, leaping gullies, plunging down hills, sliding the drops, crowding each other. A spirit of wild fun infected the band. They broke out sideways kicking and bucking. The lead mare kept her place, neck stretched out and jealously crowding any mare who challenged her. The colts were three or four months old now and had had many such runs. They

38

were fleet and sure-footed; leaped the ravines, tossed their heads, squealed and played.

Rob and Charley caught sight of Harris's white face and the sound of a single profane shout as he swept past them. Leaning back like a steeple-chaser, he kept his seat and his knee-grip, allowing his body to whip pliantly from side to side. Any guidance or control of his mount was out of the question and he did not attempt it—merely held the reins and let her go.

Charley Sargent chuckled. "Even an artilleryman don't often take part in such a charge as that."

The mares disappeared over the crest of a rise and then, for a few moments, all that Rob and Charley could see was a cloud of dust above the mountainside.

Howard and Ken had the gates to the pasture open. The mares knew the way. As Banner got them close he slowed up. They made the turn. Presently the stable sergeant and the Colonel's orderly burst into exclamatory and profane speech which expressed their admiration and astonishment at the sight of the red stallion bringing the band of mares and colts at a headlong gallop down through the pasture and into the corral.

Gus closed the gates.

Only then did the two soldiers see that their Colonel was in the band. He was dismounting from Taggert, straightening his hat with a hand that trembled slightly. His face was very white. Gus took the mare's bridle.

"Some ride!" he remarked, brushing himself off, for he was covered with dust and foam and bits of gravel. The orderly presented himself and saluted.

"Where's the mare?" asked Harris.

He might have saved himself the question, for Banner was already rearing and pawing at the gate of the eastern corral.

The men opened the gate and the stallion went in.

Charley and Rob rode down to the corral with innocent faces, and the Colonel met them, impassive, thoughtful as ever, his eyeglasses neatly on the bridge of his nose.

"You yelled something as you passed us," said Rob. "I didn't quite catch it."

The Colonel grinned. "You may not have heard—just as well you didn't. But you knew what I was saying all right. However, it's over now, and it's all right—it's all right—" he turned away grinning. "Quite an experience. I wouldn't have missed it."

"Makes you feel good now, Mort, don't it?" said Charley, "to be standing here in the corral, all safe and sound and on your own two legs, nice sunshine—dinner comin' up—"

"Dinner comin' up in more ways than one to judge by the look of him," grinned Rob.

"I must have been asleep at the switch when I let you two hand me that mare."

Ken and Howard arrived at a gallop and flung themselves off their horses. The Sergeant and orderly were blanketing the mare again and Banner was put back with his own mares by Tim.

Gus and Tim filled the feed boxes which stood on the ground near the corral fence with oats and the mares and colts began to feed. There was nipping and kicking and some scrimmages. Rob supervised the process, his harsh voice quelling the disturbances. He had Banner's share of oats—a generous half-bucketful—in his hand, and the stallion would put his head in cautiously, his eyes looking up over the edge into Rob's face, then withdraw it and chew the oats, turning his head to watch the mares, then dip it in again and take another mouthful. The process of covering his eyes and nose—upon which depended the safety of his mares—outraged his every instinct and he shook all over. Only his trust of Rob made it possible.

At last Rob dropped the bucket and told Tim to open the corral gates. "That's all," he said to Banner, "there isn't any more." He gently raised his arms and advanced toward the mares, as it were, pushing them before him.

"Take 'em back, Banner," he said to stallion.

The band drifted slowly out through the gates and

began to graze on the long lush grass beside the little stream.

"What'll they do now?" asked Harris.

"They'll hang around the corral for a while, grazing and thinking about oats. Then they'll work up through the pasture to the country road gate. It's open. They'll go through it and on up to the range again. Banner'll hold them together. Tim, keep a lookout. When they've all gone through the county road gate, close it."

"Yes sir."

Ken saw his mother approaching. Now is the time, he thought—everything over and everybody here together—

The men grouped around the trailer, loading the Colonel's mare. The sergeant and orderly got into the front seat of the car and drove away with her.

The men stood watching a moment.

"Dad," said Ken.

"Well, son?"

"I've got a surprise for you."

"Sure enough?"

"I've been saving it since last night."

Everyone turned to look at him. He had their attention at last.

"It's in the stable," he added. "Come and see it." He seized his father's arm and urged him through the corral gate.

Suddenly Rob guessed. "Not Flicka's colt?" he asked.

Ken nodded, beaming, his blue eyes shining with excitement. "Yep!"

Rob explained to the others. "Ken's saddle mare should have foaled in the spring. She's been up here in the pasture all summer like Sitting Bull, waiting for the event, swelling up like a balloon. It must be fourteen months—"

"You wait here!" said Ken excitedly when they were all in the corral. "I'll bring them out. They're in the stable."

In a moment the stable door opened, Flicka trotted out, then, for a space, nothing. Flicka turned and looked

41

back and nickered. Still nothing. At last an angry little squeal was heard and Ken appeared, shoving the white foal before him.

Absolute silence greeted this apparition. Rob's jaw dropped. His eyes popped.

Nell was the first to speak. "Why, Kennie!" she exclaimed, "a white colt!"

Charley Sargent found his tongue and with delight in his eyes looked at Rob. "I suppose this is an example of Banner's true breeding. I remember you said, *one sorrel after the other—as like as peas in the pod—*" He turned to Mort Harris and said sadly, "I sure do sympathize most deeply with your bad luck, Mort—Your mare—"

Harris gave a howl and turned and looked in the direction the car and trailer had gone, then seized his head and pretended to tear his hair.

Ken was caught in one of those agonizing moments of life where extravagant hopes and deep despair were somehow reconciled by wishful thinking. Also, he was trying with all his wits to think of a way to suggest to them this was a happy event. Also, he was on the watch for anything his mother would say, for, from out of her first words, the colt would be named. Also, he must keep his guilty secret.

"Isn't he a beauty?" he cried happily, "and a white horse is good luck, you know. Everybody knows that!"

Rob's face was convulsed. He took his hat off and wiped his forehead. "My God, Ken—" he began, but there was nothing to say.

Flicka nickered again for her baby. It started to run toward her, saw Highboy standing against the fence with reins loosely thrown over a post, and ran to him instead and tried to nurse on him. A shout of amusement and incredulity rose from the spectators. Highboy, annoyed, moved away from the foal, turned around and butted it gently. The foal stood, bleating, then it ran to Cigarette and tried to nurse on her. Flicka called it unavailingly.

42

When it passed near its mother it seemed to recognize no difference in her from the others.

Nell's face showed horror. "Why—it doesn't know its own mother!"

The foal surged about the corral.

"A white horse is good luck," repeated Ken desperately. "Gus said so. Everybody knows that."

Rob found words at last. "A throwback!" he exclaimed disgustedly.

He looked at Ken—one of those blasting looks which Ken could not meet. Somehow, it was his fault.

Nell was studying the foal. It did not look like the Goose Bar colts. A newborn foal of pure breed is built on the perpendicular, its little back so short that all four legs seem to be in a close group underneath it—and the neck continues the perpendicular line, carried straight up to a small inquiring head like a sea-horse's. But this foal was built on the horizontal like a full-grown horse. It had a repellent look of precociousness and maturity, with its heavy neck and the big knobby head on the end of it, the large mouth with thick, rather loose black lips, the short, uneven legs—

"Why," she exclaimed in a shocked voice, "it's a goblin!"

The blood rushed to Ken's head and made him dizzy. He went to the corral fence and took hold of the rails to steady himself.

No one spoke for a moment.

Goblin. She had named it.

"Goblin," shouted Howard. "Goblin, Goblin, *Goblin!*"

But Ken was not licked yet. He turned to his mother. He would pretend it was just a word. He would pretend that she hadn't named it.

"Mother, would you think of a name for him?" he pleaded, "something about his being white—and—and —about his going to be a wonderful race horse—"

"Race horse!" The exclamation was a chorus.

Suddenly Ken's face flamed. He looked at his father.

43

"You said—*there might be one gentle one in the lot and you'd have a race horse!* And Flicka did get gentle. I gentled her. As gentle as a kitten. You said that too. And then, because of her bad leg, she couldn't be a race horse and it had to be her colt instead of her. And here he is. And he's a horse colt. And he's big and strong. And he's got her blood and her speed. And the speed and spirit of all the Albino's colts. And his mother will teach him manners because she is gentle so he can be schooled and trained for a race horse—he won't be hard to handle even if he has got a white coat from the Albino!"

"The Albino was his great grandsire," explained Nell to Sargent.

"And Banner's his sire," drawled Sargent. "Now what about all Rob's theories of line breedin'? He bred Flicka back to her own sire, and look what he got!"

But Rob was looking at his small son standing there red in the face and with fire in his eye, fighting for his foal! And the anger went out of his heart and a silent cheer was there instead, *Good for you, son!*

"Name him, Mother," insisted Ken desperately. "Give him a name that will be right for a big winner of races. And something about his being white."

"Cottage cheese!" yelled Howard derisively, and then, mincing about delicately, "or Cream Puff!"

"Pearl of the Harem," joshed Sargent.

"Mooley Cow!" exclaimed Howard and cantered awkwardly across the corral.

"Somebody stop that guy or he'll go on forever," said Rob, making a pass at Howard.

Howard ducked but fell into the arms of Sargent who grabbed him and clapped his hand over his mouth.

Nell had not spoken. Ken watched her. "Mother," he urged her, "go on, Mother—"

Sargent let go of Howard who, casting a glance at his father, decided he had gone far enough.

There was an ache in Nell's heart. She looked at the foal—that stubbornness, the mulish head, that stupidity, trying to nurse on every horse in sight, not knowing his own mother; and its anger—it ran across the corral head down, kicking out with one hind leg—it seemed full of hatred.

"Mother!" insisted Ken.

In despair Nell raised her eyes and saw, up behind the line of the green hill, a great thunderhead pushing up into the dark blue of the sky. It was so dazzling white it half blinded her.

"There," she said calmly, "see that? A thunderhead. And it's pure white. We'll call him Thunderhead, Ken— and that's a fine enough name for any race horse."

No one spoke. The silence was like a cool shadow on a hot, dusty day.

Ken stood quiet, feeling weak—the name was so beautiful. Thunderhead. He looked at the great cloud, and turned away so that the others could not see his face. Thunderhead. That would carry the colt to glory. With that name what horse could fail?

The colt, still making little rushes about the corral, kicking and bleating, came up against the group of people by the fence. He had no fear of them. An ordinary colt would have veered away but Colonel Harris got it by the neck and was nipped and let it loose.

Nell put out her hand. The foal careened against her and for a moment its face was hidden and there was darkness—that welcome and familiar darkness of all the long months inside its mother. He pressed closer and stood quiet.

A strange feeling went through Nell. He was ugly, and she had miscalled him, and they had all laughed at him, but here he was turned to her, and a rush of protective compassion went through her. She put her hand on his neck and stroked him. Panting slightly, his sides going in and out, his chunky legs splayed out comically, he leaned against her, hiding his eyes from the world and from people.

45

6

They went down to dinner.

When Rob added a bottle of Burgundy to the meal, even Charley Sargent abandoned his wisecracking on the subject of the white foal and gave his attention to the roast ducks and mushrooms in cream.

Ken was in the seventh heaven. After all, it had gone well—better than he had dared to hope. *Thunderhead!* What a name! And his father had stopped Howard from making fun of it— He glanced at his father and found the penetrating blue eyes fixed on him in a very thoughtful manner.

The look made pins and needles go through him. It was the look by which his father ferreted out what he had been doing, where he had been, even what he had been thinking. Time was when Ken would try to keep his secrets, but he had found out it was never any use if his father actually put him on the witness stand.

Ken dropped his eyes and busied himself with the fat drumstick. He took it up and picked it, glancing at his mother for permission. It helped hide his face, but his cheeks were hot and his father was still looking at him. He didn't want to look back. He determined not to. He held himself from looking until all his body felt strained and anguished. Then he looked. His eyes met his father's. And after a second, a little smile appeared on his father's face, as if he had got what he wanted.

After that his father didn't look at him any more and when Colonel Harris asked, "What I would like to know is, why did you bring all the mares in just because you needed Banner? Was it just to give me that ride of the Valkyries? If it was, many thanks. I wouldn't have missed it. A little more and Taggert and I would have gone sailing right off the earth. I was hearing music already!"

Rob laughed and said, "Howard, tell Colonel Harris why we brought the mares in with Banner."

Howard found it difficult to answer so simple a question. "Because he wouldn't have come without them, sir."

"You mean," said Harris, astounded, "you can't take that stud anywhere without all his mares?"

"All his mares and all his colts," answered Rob calmly. "Twenty mares, more or less, and twenty colts. That's his family. When he moves anywhere forty-one of him moves."

"Anyway," said Howard, "you see, if he did come alone, how would he know that he'd ever see them again? Who would protect them? They're his responsibility. so he's got to take 'em along."

"And when you want one of the mares?"

"We bring them all in," said Rob, "corral the mare— then Banner knows she's safe and being taken care of and held for him—and drive the rest out."

Ken contributed nothing to the talk that followed. He was lying low, anxious for the meal to end as quickly as possible.

When at last it did and his mother had prepared the big pot of coffee and placed it on the tray with cups and saucers to be taken out to the terrace, he was about to dash off to the stables. But his father's voice called him back.

"Stick around, Ken—I might want you."

Ken sat down on the edge of the stone wall which supported the terrace, his legs dangling over the flower border, and his back to the group on the terrace. They arranged themselves around the low wooden table and poured their coffee.

Ken often sat this way when his parents had guests. You could hear everything they said if it was worth listening to, and if it wasn't, there was plenty to watch on the Green and in the pines on the cliff or in the sky. Today his back was tingling because it was turned to his father, but he tried to forget what was coming and interest himself in something else.

Down there by the fountain a big robin was intent upon getting a worm. He sat over the worm-hole—turning one ear to the ground—listening, Ken always thought, for the movements of the worm to betray its exact position by some squeak or rustle. Then the sudden plunge of the beak and out it came holding one end of the worm, and the robin backed off—pulling—pulling—the worm stretched like elastic—Ken was fascinated! Two inches of worm—four—still the robin backed away—the suspense was terrific—

"And now," said Rob genially, "Ken's got something to tell us. He's going to tell us who is really the sire of that white foal up in the corral."

Ken had thought he was prepared for it, but it was a shock all the same, and unpleasant feelings went through him. He couldn't find words. His mind was in a fog.

"The sire!" exclaimed Harris, astonished. "Why, what's this? I thought Banner was the sire of all your foals."

"Not that one," grinned Rob. "Your mare is perfectly safe, Mort. You'll have a fine little sorrel colt—dead ringer for Banner—when she foals next summer. I told you, Banner breeds true. Sorrels. Like as peas in a pod."

"Hah!" exclaimed Charley. "You're crawling. Just because you've got a throwback, you're going to disown it! Didn't think it of you, Rob!"

"Come on, Ken," said Rob, "who is the sire of that little goblin up there?"

Ken, without turning around, jerked his head and elbow in the direction of Charley Sargent. "That big black stud of his!"

"Whose?"

"Mr. Sargent's."

"Ouch!" shouted Sargent. Then, "Do you let him tell whoppers like that, Rob? Or is he given to pipe dreams?"

Rob was as astonished as anyone. "Appalachian, Ken?"

"Yes, sir."

"Why, he doesn't even know Appalachian," shouted Sargent. "Ken—did you ever see him? He's never been off my ranch, and that's twenty miles away."

Ken answered, "He's that big black stallion with three white socks and a white star between his eyes. He hangs out in that little draw by the quakin'-asp and the box elder where the fence crosses your line. Twenty miles away by the highway, but about eight miles of straight riding across country. Only one gate to go through, and your buck fence to take down."

There was a shocked silence. Then, as Ken's words sank home, Charley Sargent jumped to his feet. His long brown face was serious for once, his big hat a little awry, a frown between his brows.

"I don't believe it! It couldn't be! Why—that little misbegotten pup up there—son of Appalachian!" In two strides he reached Ken, seized him by the shoulder and yanked him up. "Stand up here." He set the boy on the low wooden table facing them all.

Ken's face was a little pale, but his dark blue eyes looked at his father without flinching.

"Come on, Ken," said Rob, "let's have the story. I'll begin it for you. A year ago last spring we decided Flicka should be bred."

"No, sir, it was the fall before that. About Thanksgiving time. You and mother said we'd breed Flicka as soon as she was old enough and get a foal."

"That's right. I remember now. You and Howard were home from school for the Thanksgiving week-end."

"Yes. And when we went back to school, all winter long I was thinking about that. And when I came home for the spring vacation at Easter, you remember you let me start working with Flicka and riding her a little, because she was just exactly two years old and strong and well-grown. And you said I was light enough so it wouldn't hurt her back any. And I worked her out with the blanket and surcingle and began to ride her. And during that vacation do you remember the time you took me in to town with you and we met Mr. Sargent and had dinner with him at the Mountain Hotel? And he was talking about his stud, about Appalachian. And bra—well, praising him and praising him. And then he got to brag—well, praising all the colts he had had from him—"

Ken paused, looking interrogatively at his father, and Rob grinned. "Yes, I remember. He praised 'em. It's a habit he's got."

Harris laughed and Sargent's hand pinched Ken's shoulder a little harder and he said, "Get on with your story, young man."

"Well, so you see—when I went back to school after that Easter vacation I was thinking about Appalachian."

Rob groaned. "And when Ken begins to think about something, I don't mind telling you, it's a single track mind."

"So," said Ken doggedly, "when I got home in June that's what I was thinking about. I rode over several times on Cigarette to look at Appalachian."

"The hell you did!" said Charley. "Well—" with some eagerness, "what did you think of him?"

"Oh," Ken's voice rose in enthusiasm, "just what you did! I agreed with all the proud things you said about him!"

"Thank you for that, son!"

"And what then, Ken?" asked Rob.

"Well, that was about the time to breed Flicka. And you told me to see to it."

Rob's eyes narrowed and glanced away as he tried to remember. Nell nodded. "I remember that, Rob. You had moved Banner and the brood mares up onto the Saddle Back. There were just the saddle mares in—Flicka and Taggert. And you told Ken it was his responsibility, and that when she came around he was to take her to the stallion."

Rob nodded. "I remember. Well, Ken?"

Ken's words came with a struggle. "Well you see, I had been thinking and thinking about Appalachian, because we wanted Flicka's foal to be a racer, and Banner was never a racer. And when I remembered all Mr. Sargent had said about him, and every colt he had got by him, why then—why then—"

"Well?" prompted Charley.

"Well, when she came in heat, I just rode her over there one day—it took me most of the day—and put her in the pasture with Appalachian—and when she was bred I rode her home again. That's all."

There was silence for a moment as Ken finished his recital. Suddenly Harris burst out laughing. Howard stared in open-mouthed awe at his younger brother. The stunt itself was nothing to the secrecy with which it had been concealed for more than a year. It was a faculty Howard was envious of—to do unusual things—and then keep them entirely to yourself.

Rob said, "You took that long, sixteen-mile ride on your mare?"

"Yes, sir. I got off and rested her now and then. You were letting me ride her because you said she had grown so well and I hadn't."

It was true. Ken was still no larger than he had been at ten.

Rob thought again. "You must have been away most of the day. I don't remember it."

Ken said, "It was a day when you and mother had been in town. And you stayed there for lunch and you didn't get home until late in the afternoon." Ken was keeping his biggest punch to the end. "Anyway, I can prove it to you, Dad," he added.

"How?"

Ken stepped down from the witness stand and vanished into the house. They heard his steps going upstairs. He returned holding a paper, folded and wrinkled and soiled. He handed it to Rob who opened it a with a mystified air and read it silently, then passed it to Charley.

Sargent stared at it a long time, then read aloud slowly, "FLICKA TO APPALACHIAN, 12:30 P.M. JUNE 28th."

Sargent flung down the paper, sprang to his feet and

51

shouted, "I don't believe it!" then, with one long leap over the flower border, turned his back and went striding up to the corral.

"This beats me," said Rob. "I didn't dream it was Appalachian. I knew it wasn't Banner. What I thought was that the Albino was somewhere in the neighborhood again and that he had got to the mare—or perhaps that Ken's mind had been working overtime and cooked up some crazy scheme and that he had taken her out to him."

Charley came striding back. "Gimme a drink, Rob—if this is true, it's a terrible blow."

"It's true all right," said Colonel Harris. "I watched Ken's face when he told it. His face was straight and the story's straight."

Charley gulped down the drink Bob poured for him and as Rob filled the other glasses, held his out again.

"Hope this won't make you take to drink, Charley," said Harris dryly. "Brace up! Lots of people have family secrets to hide!"

"We won't give it away, Charley," chuckled Rob.

Charley didn't even hear them. He threw off his hat and ran one hand distractedly through his hair. "Maybe it didn't take," he exclaimed suddenly. "Maybe, later on in the summer she was bred by some other stallion. That's it!" he said excitedly, "you *said* the colt came months later than you expected!"

But Ken shook his head. "She was never out on the range again. You see, that was the first summer I had been able to do much with her or ride her at all. She was a two-year-old. And I had her down here in the stable or the Home Pasture all summer so that she would be well schooled by the time I had to leave the ranch in the fall. And there weren't any other stallions around."

Nell nodded. "That's true. She was underfoot all summer. Ken did everything but have her in the kitchen."

"I *did* have her in the kitchen, Mother! Remember the time you put the oat bucket in the kitchen sink, and I called her in, and she walked right in and went all around

52

the kitchen, looking at everything and smelling it, and then ate her oats at the sink?"

"Look here, Ken," said Rob, "do you realize that you *stole* that service? You heard what Mr. Sargent said at dinner—that the stud fee for Appalachian is $250.00."

Ken's mouth dropped open. All the rest he had been prepared for, but this— He was always coming up against money. He made no answer, but turned to look at Charley Sargent with the face of one condemned to the gallows.

"I've always told you, Ken," his father rubbed it in, "that you cost me money every time you turn around."

"Cost you money!"

"Well—you owe that money to Charley here and you can't pay it, can you?"

"No, sir."

"Someone's got to pay it."

"I should say-ay-ay not!" exclaimed Charley. "If that's the Appalachian's foal, you owe me for nothing. On the contrary, I owe Ken an apology. And the nice little mare too."

Ken began to breathe again and glanced at his father to see if there were to be any penalties from that quarter.

"If Mr. Sargent forgives you the debt, Ken, I've got nothing to say."

"Here comes the Goblin now!" exclaimed Howard.

Gus had let the horses out of the corral to pasture and Flicka and her foal and Taggert and the geldings were coming to water at the round stone fountain in the middle of the Green.

The men and boys went down to look at them more closely.

"You'll just have to face it, Charley, it's a throwback all right. Throwback through Flicka to the Albino. And your stud's blood wasn't strong enough to outweigh hers."

"My stud's!" groaned Charlie. "It isn't his blood alone but sixty generations of the finest racing blood—and this mare of Ken's outweighs them all—and throws back to that wild mustang!"

The colt, as usual, was not following his dam but wandering here and there as he felt inclined. Flicka turned her head and nickered for him, then dipped her nose into the fountain and drank.

"That's a beautiful mare," said Charley, looking at Flicka's glossy golden coat, her full, flaxen tail and mane, and the gentleness and intelligence in the golden eyes she turned to them. She mouthed the cool water, letting streams of it run from her muzzle, then turned her head to her foal again.

"Dad," said Ken miserably, "is he—really—so awful?"

Rob hesitated. "Well, Ken, nobody could say he has good conformation. He is shaped like a full-grown horse, a bronc at that. He'll have to change a good deal."

"But he will, Dad! He'll grow!"

"He'll have to grow in some spots and shrink in others. That jughead!"

Ken looked at the head. It was certainly too large. It had a terribly stubborn look.

"Hi, fellah!" said Charley to the foal, then turned to Ken. "Well, you win, Ken. I believe your story. Your Goblin is by my Appalachian, and if you want papers, you can have them."

"I can only have half papers, sir, because Flicka only has half papers."

"You oughtn't to have any papers at all with a stolen service, Ken," said his father.

"I'll waive that," said Charley. "Do you realize, Rob, that this little Goblin has Appalachian for a sire, Banner for a grandsire, and the Albino for a great grandsire? That ought to be enough T.N.T. to bust him wide open."

Harris said quizzically, "And the greatest of these is the Albino."

Matilda came dashing out. She charged at the colt, who was standing with legs braced, head hanging a little. He poked his nose at her and did not flinch. Matilda swerved, sprang up onto the coping of the fountain, ran around it, jumping off again just before she reached Flicka's nose. Highboy swung his dripping muzzle out

54

over the grass and took a long step toward the cat. She crouched, lifted a paw and tapped him smartly on the nose, then as he advanced again, she dashed away, sprang up the trunk of one of the young cottonwood trees and hung out on a branch, long yellow tail and one taloned claw hanging down—waiting her chance. Goblin watched it all.

Rob was still speculating. "Maybe your stud isn't so much after all," he suggested. "I presume all these winners you've been bragging about—ahem! Excuse me! I should say, *praising so* (that's a good word, Ken)—had fine blooded mares for their dams?"

"Well, sure."

"Perhaps their racing successes came from their dams and not from Appalachian."

"A little more of this and I'll be going home to shoot him!"

"Have another drink, Charley!" said Colonel Harris. "And calm yourself. Ever read *Three Men in a Boat?* Well—it's *your* shirt now—that's the only difference. One good thing," he sipped his highball, "this clears Banner."

Ken stood looking at the foal. His confidence had been whittled down by the many contemptuous comments about it. The name of *Goblin* had stuck—not the other. Even he himself was thinking of it as Goblin now—where was the beautiful name and all the pride and glory?

The foal turned and looked at him. The pupil of the eye was dark. The edge of the lids and the eyelashes were dark too. Between the pupil and the lids was a ring of white eyeball. A white-ringed eye! That was why the foal had that wild, furious look! Ken felt, suddenly, completely beaten.

A car drew up and stopped at the end of the terrace and there descended from it several visitors.

As Nell went toward them and the salutations began, Ken fled into the house and out the back door. He had had all he could stand, and now it would begin all over

55

again. About the white foal. And Appalachian. And what he had done. It was publicity he was running away from, the blistering heat of it—the inescapability of it—the way you had to stand and take it—and take it—and take it! Oh, when would it end? How long would it be before all this was forgotten and they could think of it calmly as if it were unimportant? When could he be unimportant himself again?

He ran up the hill at the back of the house and in amongst the trees. Then he began to cry. It was because he suddenly knew that there wasn't going to be an end to it at all. Not with the Goblin. Not with that furious jug-headed throwback with the white-ringed eyes, who was destined, by him at least, to be a great racer and had the ancestry for one! In fact, it was all just beginning, and it was he himself who had started it and he would have to go on taking it for a long time. And what at the end of it all? Would Goblin be a great racer? Probably not. Probably nothing. That's what they all thought.

He threw himself face down on the pine needles. He was crying because he had got himself in such a mess and couldn't get out again. You couldn't undo the foal. But deep down he knew he didn't want to. Mess or no mess, he was crazy about the Goblin. It was Flicka's—her first. The great destiny had been planned by Nell long ago and everything had been done to bring it about. Half of his sobbing was because of this love that was bursting his heart for the ungainly little creature that had turned away from him and looked at him with a resentful, white-ringed eye.

He was crying, too, from disappointment. He had taken it for granted that Flicka's foal would be a beautiful black, aristocratic and long-legged and fine-headed with three white socks and a star on its forehead—or, perhaps, a golden sorrel with flaxen tail and mane like its mother.

And some of the tears were pure relief; that the year-long deception of his father was over and his conscience clear at last.

When the weeping was over he turned on his back and let the wind dry his eyes and his cheeks.

He was beginning to be happy again. Peace had come into him. Bit by bit he was accepting all that had happened and all that lay ahead. Whatever it was, he could get through somehow.

And the foal—

Absent-mindedly Ken's eyes were outlining the shape of a great white cloud in the sky. It was one of the solid ones, as if it were carved out of marble, dazzling white. Suddenly he recognized that cloud. It was the thunderhead that had given the foal its name. The cloud had pushed slowly up over the horizon to the zenith. Other thunderheads crowded it from the rear and the sides. The shape had changed a little, but it was the same—the same! And like an old friend to Ken. More than that, like a renewal of the promise and the hope.

Blissfully, he flung both arms out on the ground—his face turned up to the cloud.

7

When Goblin was two weeks old he accompanied his mother, ridden by Nell, up to the Saddle Back.

Nell made the ride bareback without even a blanket because she intended to return on foot. She sat, relaxed and comfortable, across Flicka, her feet in their Congress gaiter boots and small chainless spurs, hanging straight down. They started out of the corral at a walk and continued up through the Stable Pasture.

It was a cold day and already there was the taste of

winter in the air. The sky came down in gray and white billows, sweeping the sad brown grass of the September plains. Nell was in black gabardine jodhpurs and gray tweed coat, a red woolen scarf knotted around her throat and a visored cap pulled over her eyes. Her face looked a little pinched and bleak, facing the wind, facing the mountains, facing the long winter.

She tried to keep her eye on Goblin but this was not easy to do. He did not run close to his mother's side as most foals run.

An observer, watching a wild mare and foal being rounded up and corraled, might imagine that the umbilical cord was still there, invisible to human eye, and that the foal was fastened by it to the mother's side, so exactly does it parallel her every action. Turn to the right, dead stop, rear and wheel, plunge to the left, complete quick turn, straight-away dash—in every maneuver the colt maintains its place as close as a Siamese twin.

But no umbilical cord bound Goblin to Flicka, hardly even a spiritual tie. He knew her as the source of nourishment and made peremptory demands upon her when he was hungry or thirsty. And in a rather vague manner, he accepted her as a port in a storm, although really preferring to fight his own battles. She was not his life. He made his own.

In these first weeks his development had been rapid. Abnormally large and strong to begin with, he grew as if he intended to catch up with the colts who had been born in the spring.

Howard and Ken had been working with him, anxious to get the first training accomplished before they left for school. They had penned him, brushed and handled him, lifted his legs one by one, put the halter on him, led him around. He had accepted all this without much struggling. It was a good beginning. They had found that he was not stupid, merely different. There was about everything he did a quality of independence and aggressiveness. Whether he ran at his mother's side or stood far away in the corner of the pasture he did it of his own will—not because she led him or called him. Sometimes he wandered alone for an hour or two, then returned to nurse, then went away somewhere and lay down to sleep.

In a fashion that was uncanny in so young a foal he took interest in everything he saw, every other horse, every person. It was all his business. He had to investigate, frequently to interfere, which he did by using his teeth and his heels. When he was standing with a group of horses it annoyed him if his mother moved away or was called elsewhere. He would at first refuse to follow, then would gallop after her angrily, wheel, and lash out at her. If this did not make her return, he would gallop to the others, then after a few moments back to her again. He wanted them all together in one place. And if Flicka continued on her course and the distance between them grew wider his gallops back and forth would get more frantic, punctuated by furious squeals.

The gallop of most young foals is indescribably light and airy. At birth their legs have almost the full length of the mature horse, and it is these long spindly legs which carry the small bodies over the ground so swiftly. But Goblin's legs were not thus. Both in proportion to his long body, and actually, they were short. And when he laid himself out in a run he was so close to the ground that Howard invented a special name for this peculiar gait—*scrabbling*.

When he scrabbled madly to and fro between his mother and the other horses, his big white head stretched out on its long neck, the sight was so funny that beholders were convulsed with laughter. Even Nell had to wipe the tears from her eyes although with a sort of pang. You didn't like to laugh at animals, not even the Goblin. Besides, she suspected that he loved her. There was not much ground for this, merely that, looking at her, there seemed a sort of recognition. Merely that, when he was by her and she put her hand on him, he did not move away. Occasionally he watched her as she moved about. And now that the boys had gone back to school and Nell had charge of him, he accepted her.

The Goblin disliked having anyone ride his mother. It was apt to interfere with his demands upon her. He knew, the moment she was under the command of someone else, and he fought it angrily, even when it was Nell.

He came rushing back, now, from where he had been wandering alone in the farthest corner of the Stable Pasture and lined up alongside Flicka to nurse. Flicka kept moving right ahead. As soon as Goblin got the right position and had had one or two swallows of milk, the teat was jerked out of his mouth and he had to try again.

In less than a minute his patience was exhausted. He wheeled, backed, and lashed Flicka's side, aiming particularly at Nell's leg hanging down; then he turned around and bit it.

Not once only, but for minutes this struggle went on, Nell pushing his head away as well as she could, or swinging her leg up on Flicka's neck. The ferocity and determination of the small creature were astonishing.

"You—are—just—a—little—fiend!" exclaimed Nell, laughing as, once again, she rescued her leg from a savage nip.

This time she snatched off her hat, made a big swing at the foal with it, and touched Flicka into a gentle trot. Goblin galloped away.

At the County Road gate Nell dismounted, opened it and led Flicka through, then waited for Goblin to follow. He showed no signs of coming. He was sulking way off in the corner.

She called him, "Goblin! Goblin! come along, boy—come along!"

The Goblin headed in the opposite direction.

Nell hitched Flicka's reins to a post on the County Road and walked back to get the colt. It was interesting to try to understand him. He was always up to something. Now he was standing alert, his ears pricked, eyes directed over the fence. Nell called him again. He turned and saw her and started to gallop toward her. Just short of her he brought himself up, braking on all four legs, and stood for a few moments in a funny way he had, head reached out and hanging a little, eyes rolling. Obviously the sight of Nell on foot surprised him. Where was his mother? They had been together. Now here was Nell, two-legged, on the ground; and his mother nowhere. His thoughts were so apparent that Nell was amused. She called him again, but at that moment Goblin spied his mother and started to her at a dead run, his small hoofs thundering on the ground. Almost reaching her, he stopped with stiff legs sliding in the dirt and looked back at Nell, then turned and scrabbled back to her. Then again to Flicka—every run accomplished with the utmost violence. Nell laughed so that she could hardly walk.

Finally all three were through the gate. Nell closed it, mounted Flicka again and started up the Saddle Back.

Riding slowly up the long gentle slope, she was wondering where Banner and the mares would be. Not too far, she hoped. She didn't want a long walk back. On a cloudy day like this night would fall early.

Idly her thoughts played with Goblin's situation. Here was Flicka going into the band of brood mares with a foal by Appalachian. How would Banner take it? Would he feel differently toward this foal than toward his own? Would he know it was not his? Yes, probably, but he wouldn't care. He never paid any attention to the foals anyway. Well—that wasn't quite true. When the first snow came and the colts looked at it forlornly, not knowing where the green grass had gone, the stallion pawed up the snow to show them the grass beneath. It was even richer and more nourishing now that it was dried. And of course, if anything attacked a colt—a wildcat or timber wolf—the stallion would fight the intruder to the last drop of his blood. But mostly he merely tolerated the colts, and that only as long as they were small. As they approached the age of yearlings, the stallion would begin to persecute them, the males because of jealousy,—their hides would be scarred and bleeding from his bites—and the females because they took up too much of their mothers' attention and created a division of loyalty. His mares must follow him only, think of him only, look to him only.

It was really a right and proper system, thought Nell, well planned for the good of the herd, which must never get too large, which must have one competent leader, which must never be divided by disloyalties.

On the Goose Bar Ranch, for the better development of the colts and the easier wintering of the mares, Rob separated them in December when, depending on just when the colts had been born, they would be from five to seven months old. He would bring the whole band into the corrals, pen the colts, and drive the mares out. It was always a long, arduous, exasperating day. As fast as the mares were driven off, they would circle around and come back. The colts would climb over fences and gates of impossible height in the effort to get back to their dams. And both mares and colts kept up a continuous crying, whinnying and squealing. Banner thoroughly approved of this weaning. He had his part of the work to do and did it well, taking his post between the corrals and the mares, driving them away again if they attempted to get back to their colts. He received his orders from Rob's word or gesture or merely from the glance of his eye. Their understanding and teamwork were perfect.

Nell topped the crest of the Saddle Back, gasped for breath and snatched at her hat. Even a gentle wind up here, with that two hundred mile sweep from the west, sang in the ears with a sound that was like the taste of metal in the mouth.

This particular view always gave her the feeling of being suddenly made empty. She pulled up her horse.

The plateau, at an altitude of eight thousand feet, had the wideness of the sea. And it had the waves and the rounded billows, here and there a long crested ridge or a monster comber whipped to a peak. It was a seascape painted in shades of ochre and olive. The immensity of the sea filled her eyes, and where it ended the immensity of the sky began. Thirty miles or so to the south, the

Colorado border was marked by the rough crags and rocky headlands of the Buckhorn Hills, and far in the distance, west of the rich orchards and farmlands of the southern state which she knew of but could not see, the Neversummer Mountains, snow-capped the year around, hung among the clouds, belonging to the sky rather than the earth.

In Nell all thought was stilled and she sat motionless, letting the vastness beat upon her.

Flicka stood alert, her ears pricked sharply, her head turned. The foal was quiet too, his head up, his nostrils spread, his eyes staring.

The wind, the smell of the snow, or perhaps some other scent that reached him, excited him, and he left Flicka's side and trotted forth to meet—what? Something. It was as if he quested for it. His head was higher than usual. His action was assured and peremptory. Nell watched him, amused at his change of bearing. She wondered if his sharp scent caught the smell of the herd. He stopped, searched the wind with his small quivering nose, circled slowly, stopped and again examined all that his eyes and nose could sense. It was as if he were taking possession of the Saddle Back.

Nell turned Flicka along the ridge and proceeded on her way, trying to pierce every hollow, every little ravine, every far hillside with her eyes. Somewhere there, Banner and his mares were hidden.

She had forgotten to bring the whistle with her. At intervals she gave a long-drawn cry, "Ba-a-a-anner— Oh, Ba-a-a-nner!" And the wind snatched the sound from her mouth.

Goblin turned to look at her, astonished.

Banner came with the wind behind him, mane blowing over his eyes. Nell slipped off the mare, removed the bridle, hung it on her arm, and stood waiting. The foal was out in front, staring at the great horse bearing down on them.

Banner came to a halt and stood looking them over.

Goblin squealed and trotted out to meet him. Banner seemed not to notice him but began to circle, trotting slowly, coming up-wind behind them. Nell and Flicka turned to meet him. The foal, with an air of taking command of the situation, circled within Banner's circle, and, just as the stallion reached Flicka, presented his small rear and kicked. His heels rang on the stallion's belly. Banner paid no attention. He had the scent of Flicka now, and they both whinnied shrilly. Nell stepped aside.

"Go on, Flicka," she said. "Go with Banner."

The stallion was in magnificent action, trotting here and there around the group, rearing lightly, or sinking his head and forequarters to nip at the mare's heels, then sweeping over the crest of the ridge, taking the lead so that she might follow.

Flicka went slowly and Nell stood watching. The mare stopped, looked back and whinnied for her foal. Goblin squealed and made a circle around Nell.

Banner curved behind Flicka and hurried her pace with a nip at her heels.

Goblin began to "scrabble" between Flicka and Nell.

Flicka was getting quite far away. There was a little rise in front of her. Banner had already disappeared over it. Goblin stood near Nell with head hanging and four legs braced out—his favorite position for deep thought. Another whinny came from Flicka. The foal squealed in answer, put his head down, kicked first one leg and then the other, and galloped with small thunder of hoofs after his mother.

Nell stood watching until Flicka and the colt disappeared over the rise.

She stood a moment longer, head tilted and turned sideways. Not a sound but the singing wind. Not a movement now, in all the billowy world, but clouds and blowing grass.

She looped the bridle more securely over her left arm and began to walk quickly back down the Saddle Back.

8

Fortunately for the little white foal with his thin silky coat, winter came late that year. Nature did her best for him. Daily his coat grew thicker. And up on the range there was the long sweep of the wind against him to strengthen him and the far distances of the plains inviting him to run and to smell and to adventure.

There were many things to excite his interest. There was the Water Hole down between two hills, with the Antelope Trail—a bare, threadlike path—leading to it.

Near the County Road there was a big chunk of yellow salt with holes and caverns worn in it by the tongues of the horses. He took a lick at this himself, then stepped away, mouthing the strange taste, at first unpleasant, then delicious.

There were also other horses on the Saddle Back besides Banner's band. A few miles away were the yearlings who had been foaled and weaned and raised together. Born in the spring, as most colts are, technically they had become *yearlings* the following New Year, since, for convenience, horsemen have decreed one birthday for all horses, namely, January first.

These were not "long" yearlings, being actually seventeen or eighteen months old. They were never permitted by the stallion to approach the brood mares—their dams of two springs before. The presence of these other horses, glimpsed only occasionally and at a distance, tickled the Goblin's nose with exciting scents. Sometimes he trotted away from the brood mares to a hill top and stood there, his ears pricked, his little black muzzle lifted and quivering, his eyes learning to focus at great distances.

But by far the most interesting phenomenon in Goblin's world was the stallion, the leader of the band. This great creature was obviously a horse like the rest of the herd, but yet different. God-like. Unpredictable. So commanding and terrifying that he was something to be watched and puzzled about like a great ball of fire that slid up over the eastern horizon every morning.

Goblin followed Banner around. Often there is one colt who attaches itself to the stallion, and the stallion, in turn, seems to adopt it, or at least to be contented to have it near by. Banner and his small white stepson were often near each other, and now and then would stop grazing to look at each other, motionless for a few moments, exchanging thoughts.

Sometimes Banner and Goblin stood on top of the Saddle Back looking down at the ranch. The red roofs of the houses and barns huddled close to each other. A sort of quivering went through Banner whenever he looked at the ranch. Goblin could not understand that. He watched Banner and he watched the ranch. There was a mystery here—

As winter approached all the heat went out of the ground. It lost its shades of gold and olive and became a sere brown. The curves of the soft-bosomed hills were velvety taupe and fawn. And the last of the wild-flowers, goldenrod and purple asters and the tiny, brave, forget-me-not of the plains, faded and shriveled and blew away in dust.

The dazzling white thunderheads and clouds shaped like ships or castles disappeared and the sky was pale and empty.

Along the streams shone the November yellow of the cottonwood trees, and under them, thickets of wild gooseberry and currant and chokecherry turning amber and gold, studded with the scarlet haws of the wild rose. The quakin'-asp in the little ravines and gullies and in the

66

big grove behind the stables were a bright ochre spattered with crimson. The young cottonwoods on the Green were globes of yellow, and dropped their heart-shaped leaves softly and ceaselessly to form little running streams and whorls on the ground.

All the animals altered in appearance and habits. Chipmunks, gophers and whistling pigs disappeared entirely, buried in the earth and rocks to wait for the sun to draw them out again. Rabbits and ermine turned from brown to white, and the cows, as well as the horses, grew heavy coats of fur.

Because of the open hunting season the deer sought refuge on the ranch in greater number, and in the early mornings stood by twos and threes near the house. They watched it with never-ending curiosity and wonderment, well aware that here was the hub of the wheel of their safety. Does and half-grown fawns flashed through the open aisles of the pine woods. Now and then an antlered stag stood out of the trees on an eminence and looked at the world down his lifted nose.

It became bitterly cold but still there was no snow. The last of the leaves fell. The skies faded to a leaden gray and sank low. The air was full of stillness and menace and there was a moaning around the chimneys of the house even when there was no wind.

Nell leaned at the window, staring out, her eyes blank and her thin pink lips curving down at the corners. The world looked desolate to her, and there was desolation in her heart. It was always so in the fall. She got in the habit of tramping out to the railroad every evening to watch number Twenty-Seven go by. It was the de luxe passenger train. The windows of the dining car were brightly lit; late diners sat at the little white damask tables with obsequious Negro waiters hovering.

Nell, in woolen trousers and lumberjack with scarf around her neck and a visored cap protecting her eyes, would put one foot on a rail of the fence, fold her arms on the top, and lean against them. She would hear the sound of the train coming, she would hear the whistle as it approached the crossing—that mournful, hollow, echoing sound which, to human ears, is the enticement and promise of something other-worldly—and then she would see it flash by, a series of blinding bright squares alternating with blocks of darkness.

She tried, with intense alertness, to grasp the picture of some one person or group of persons on the train. Sometimes, trudging back to the ranch, her feet, in spite of fleece-lined shoes, getting so cold that she curled and twisted her toes, she could remember one scene. Once there was a woman seated, a man bending over her, the waiter helping two children into the chairs opposite. And Nell wondered about them, momentarily freed from the narrow constrictions of her own life. Who were they? What was their life? What was taking them from the Atlantic to the Pacific coast? It was civilization sweeping past her eyes, leaving her on the side lines. It was the life she might have had.

Sometimes there was such an ache of loneliness in her heart that it was almost panic. She felt she could no longer endure—she hadn't the strength one needed for the life here— She flung back her head and her eyes swept the heavens. It was all gray, moving cloud, with here and there a star blazing out between the rifts. Its vastness blotted out the little human lives. And the endless procession of the winds—all this coming and going —from where? To what? Suddenly there would come to her an unearthly deep breath rushing through every cell of her body.

And soon appeared the little pricks of the ranch lights through the darkness.

Rob and Nell made the usual changes inside the house. They closed off part of it by heavy wooden doors to keep the heat in those rooms that were to be used, the ones grouped around the big central chimney between dining room and kitchen. The dining room became their living room, made cosy with davenport facing the open coal grate and big chairs on either side, and they cooked and ate in the kitchen.

Rob put in the storm windows and Nell hung the red hangings, thickly lined, a warm, cherry red. On the end of the table behind the davenport was a low glass bowl which she filled with the button-like yellow flowers of the rosinweed. They were very gay and lasted almost as long as immortelles. On the table in the corner by the window she put a wide-mouthed vase with a mass of scarlet autumn leaves. The frame on which she made her hooked rugs was pushed back at one side of the fireplace, the other side was filled with the brass coal hod and the wicker basket full of kindling and logs. A black iron kettle hung on a crane over the fire, easy to swing out. In the evenings, while Nell hooked and Rob mended harness or waxed the four pair of skis, ready for the winter snows, or worked at his books, Kim, the collie, and Chaps and Pauly lay on the rug before the fire. Like many children, Matilda found it difficult to keep still indoors and preferred to prowl outside.

Rats invaded the house and Pauly and Matilda did plentiful murder.

"Did it ever occur to you," said Nell one day, as she watched Matilda with a rat in mortal combat on the terrace, thrashing up and down the length of it, emitting tiger-like growls and snarls, "that Matilda couldn't possibly be a girl? Look at her! She wrestles like a hairy ape! She's thrown that rat over her head five times!"

"If she turns out a boy we can call her Matt," said Rob.

"I read a book once," said Nell, "called *Rats, Lice and History* which said that the human population of the world and the rat population is about the same. That would be about two billion, wouldn't it? Two billion rats —one for each person. But here on the ranch we'd have to count the horses as persons for we've killed dozens of rats already."

They kept the Marlin twenty-two handy and shot those that got past the cats. One evening, sitting at the kitchen table after dinner they saw a big rat run across the floor and through the open door into the dining room.

Nell held the gasoline lantern for Rob to see by. They

located the rat crouched against the wall under the sideboard. Rob stretched at full length on the floor and shot the rat. The bullet clipped the edge of the narrow apron of the sideboard.

"Mind," said Rob, "when you're shooting in the house, you daren't miss—or our house will be shot full of holes."

Above the kitchen was their bedroom, a square, bright-windowed room, warmed all day long from the kitchen stove below, as well as its own open fire. They went up to bed early. Nell had put heavy blankets under the sheet on the mattress of the big walnut bed. For a spread she covered it with the down puff of crimson silk. She had changed her summer slippers of bright blue satin for fleece-lined ankle shoes, loose and warm. She had a knitted wool bathrobe, two layers, blue outside, white inside; and for a housecoat, a dark blue silk robe thickly quilted with lambsdown and lined with red. She had pale pink pajamas of very thin wool made like ski suits, close at the ankle, and warm bed socks to draw over them. She had spread the white polar bear skin before the fireplace. It was her habit to sit on it when ready for sleep, close to the fire, warming herself thoroughly before getting into bed. Rob's big chair was close by. There he would sit, wrapped in his old blue flannel robe, weary from the day's work, smoking a last pipe, staring down at her.

There was a suspense about waiting for the snow. Always, for a month or so after the boys had gone back to school, Rob and Nell felt empty and aimless and talked to each other with excessive cheerfulness. Gradually that would pass and they would draw closer together, more intimate because more alone.

If it weren't for that, thought Nell, *no—I couldn't stand it—*

She was nervous and sleepless, lying there in the big walnut bed beside Rob. Quietly she drew herself up and looked at him. His back was to her, his head resting on his arm. The room was flooded with moonlight and she could see his hard, chiseled profile, the mouth sagging a little. He looked younger in sleep, but tired.

She clasped her arms around her knees and laid her head upon them, her tawny hair falling over her forehead. Her hands were gripped so tight the knuckles showed white.

Winter again. Blizzards. Wild storms. Days of terrible loneliness and fear with Rob out in weather when a man should be safe beside his own fire—perhaps on the highways hauling feed in the truck, and the day passing—hours crawling past with no sign of him returning. Then night coming on. She'd be standing by the north window at the far end of the house looking out into the darkness, watching. For what? What could you see in the inky blackness? Or even if it was daylight what could you see but snow falling and falling, white as a winding sheet? You could see the lights. The two big headlights of Rob's truck coming, way off on the ranch road. You could catch them soon after the truck left the Lincoln Highway, lose them when they curved in near the woods, then catch them again before they came down the hill. Lights boring through the darkness coming slowly down the hill with a load of oats or baled hay.

Wind—and wind—and wind—knocking you down when you tried to walk or stand against it. Making a noise that was first like a whine, and then a howl that hit a high note and stayed there—piercing you, getting into your head and making you crazy— And the snow. Days, weeks of being shut in by deep snow that sometimes drifted over windows and doors so that even to get out and see the sun you had to make a tunnel— Oh, all of it hard! Hard!

Suddenly she was in a state of frenzy and despair. They hadn't wanted it to be like this. The horses were to have made money enough so that she and Rob could have had plenty of help—a furnace in the house—a vacation to a warmer climate every winter when the boys were at school and there was little to do on the ranch except try to keep warm and alive.

71

Money, money, money—it all came back to that! Her mind dashed this way and that, doubling on itself, trying to find a way out.

Horses. Nothing but horses. The Goblin—suddenly she seized that impossible dream of Ken's—*was* it so impossible? Think of the ancestry of that colt! It was Rob who had first admitted he wanted one horse of the Albino's line who should be tractable—*"and I'll have a race horse!"* It was she herself who had planned and suggested breeding Flicka so they might get a colt with both her sweetness of disposition and her speed.

But the Goblin had neither. Nell tightened her hands into a harder fist. That inner fury which comes over high-spirited people when they are too often defeated filled her. She couldn't and wouldn't take it. *Something* had to succeed. Goblin—his short thick legs could grow long and swift. His bumpy shape, his big head, his bad balance, could somehow smooth out into magnificent proportions. His mean temper, that ugly readiness to bite and kick and stand at bay in enmity to all, could change to the intelligent docility of Flicka. And *speed!* Flicka's very same speed. Rocket's speed. The Albino's speed—*speed—SPEED!*

Suddenly Nell was riding a racing dream, running away to victory. Goblin! No, not Goblin any more, but THUNDERHEAD! *The racing stallion of the Goose Bar Ranch!* The big white brute leading the field on every track in the country! What colors would their jockey wear? Cherry red and white. Who would be the champion he would displace? *Seabiscuit,* of course—and would himself become then, not only great racer but great sire of racers, begetting hundreds of winners after him, every stud fee bringing thousands of dollars. Goblin must never be gelded—

The bubble of her dream burst.

Suddenly she was exhausted. She had lived through the winter; half a dozen blizzards; the winning of scores of races by Goblin; an altercation with Rob as to the gelding of him; had made thousands of dollars and spent them. She was sick of it all. Besides—none of it was true.

One does not come back immediately or easily from those swift journeys of the imagination. She drew a deep sigh, lifted her head and shook back her hair. She looked around the room. She was emptied and spent. The realities of her life, the familiar square room, the biting cold, Rob's big shoulder hunched beside her, stared her in the face. She felt a sick ennui. Dismounted from her dream, she could not find footing again on solid ground. Her realities repelled her.

To Nell, who, underneath her quiet exterior, lived every moment of her life with passion, this was an agony, and for a moment she was lost, struggling to get back—to get home—to get into herself again—

She had been through all this many times before and she knew the technique. You must embrace the very thing that repels you. Do not look away—never try to escape—clasp it close—press your lips ardently to the cold face of reality—bore deeper—to the very core— and there, at last, you will find the fire—

She forced herself. She studied the room. *That* was real. There was moonlight flooding through the window. Look at it. That hump was Rob sleeping beside her. This was the ranch. It was going to be winter—just like all the other winters—just like all the storms and dangers— they were poor and going to be poorer—nothing had ever succeeded and it was quite possible, even likely, that nothing ever would. She had read something clever about that one day, telling you that if you wanted to know what the future would be—look at the past and merely extend it!

Laying the whip to herself in this fashion, she began to come to life, and again her anger rose. There wasn't a day or a moment that you were really safe here. The elements could kill you as easily as a fly-swatter kills a fly. And at any season of the year, a bad storm, or flood, or drought, or plague of grasshoppers, or an epidemic, or a fire, or merely the wrong sort of weather at the wrong time could

73

sweep away all the work of a year and all hope with it. *That*, she thought sarcastically, is probably the fascination of it for men like Rob. Adventurers. It's such a big gamble, with all the odds against you. It's the most exciting, dramatic life in the world.

Feeling the life stirring in her again, even though it was the liveliness of anger, she tried to penetrate the truth still more deeply. Was her indignation true? Did she actually hate her realities?

Peering down, almost mischievously, into this secret corner of her heart, she saw the deepest truth and accepted it. She was as ready as Rob to take all the chances, share all the dangers, endure the privations. She too had been born "facing the wind."

There stole into her the hint of ecstasy. She pressed her face on her knees. The very terribleness of the winters—the very fear and dread seduced her and filled her veins with strong wine. And the beauty—the fierce, dreadful beauty of winter! The summers—Oh, the summers! The unbelievable deep blue of the mountain skies —the huge sculptured clouds, the green grass—the young animals, wild and free with startled eyes, the swift running, heels kicking, the perfume, smell of mint and sage and pine and grass and clover and snow, clean from a sweep of hundreds of miles of emptiness— And the loneliness— Ah, not loneliness, but serene, deep, tranquil solitude—just herself and Rob and the boys—

All her fevered thought became still. She crouched quietly there, full of a mysterious happiness.

She turned to look at Rob. The violent adventures she had just been having had not disturbed his sleep. She leaned closer and laid her cheek on his shoulder. She had never got over feeling like a girl—*that man in the bed beside her!* And yet it was very sweet.

A low song wavered up from the Green. It climbed three plaintive notes of the scale and sank again in a hesitant and wistful cadence.

Nell raised her head and turned it toward the window. So strange a sound there in the solitude—so pure and musical the tone— Was it real? Was she imagining it? Was it the voice of the singer of songs, the dreamer—wanderer—within her own heart? But it seemed to come from the window—

She slipped out of bed and ran to the window and searched the scene of enchantment below her, the diaper of brilliant silver spread before the terrace, the inky shadows thrown upon it by the spikes of the pines on the cliff opposite, the bulk of the stone fountain. One shadow seemed to move—a shadow shaped like a tiny bear walking on hind legs. It was a porcupine. It came slowly from the lower edge of the Green to the upper, moving parallel to the terrace, and from it came the soft moaning song, the rare song of the porcupine, a sound as innocent and unconscious as the voice of a very young child, murmuring itself into sleep. It walked along upright, very slowly, singing to the moon.

Nell clasped her hands in artless joy. She had never heard it before.

And now between her face and the dark cliff opposite, there was something in the air, glittering. Under the clear starry sky this had drifted in, filling the space above the Green. It was falling out of a blue nothingness. The moonlight shining through it made it a rain of diamonds. The first snow!

In the morning the ground was white, the flakes falling as silently as something in a dream.

Rob and Gus harnessed up Patsy and Topsy to go for a load of firewood.

They passed Nell dressed in her ski suit of green cloth. On the back of her head was a white knitted cap that left her tawny bang soft and straight down to her eyebrows.

"She don't never grow old," marveled Gus. "She luk lak a little gurl. A little Swedish gurl in de snow."

Rob said proudly, "When it snows you can't keep her in. She has to be out in it."

Nell walked through the snow, now and then turning up her face to catch the flakes in her mouth. All her life when fresh snow was falling she must be out in it, even as a child, careering around, sticking out her little chest, crying *I'm a hero! I'm a hero!* It made her want to throw away weakness and pining and do brave things.

She went up through the Gorge and kept walking until she was so far from the house that she seemed to be lost and alone in a wilderness of falling flakes. She stopped walking and stood listening to the silence, as deep as if the world were hollow.

Her dark blue eyes, that lay flat and full on her face, were protected from the snow by the thick hedges of her dark lashes. She blinked off the powdering of flakes. Looking up at the long white slopes of the Saddle Back she saw a small dark shape crawl out of the pile of rocks near the base. She speculated as to what it might be. It went slowly up the white mountainside, dragging a long brush on the snow. It was the size of a dog. It could only be a black fox—silver-tip—worth its weight in gold. Before it had reached the summit, another one emerged from the rocks and followed the same trail. If there had not been snow on the ground she would never have seen them.

She felt exultant. She would have liked to follow the foxes, to go farther and farther into the snowy wilderness. If I had a sleigh, she thought, and paused, while in her mind's eye, an old-fashioned swan sleigh took form, drawn by the little black mares, Patsy and Topsy, that Rob had broken for a light work team a couple of years before.

The vision of the horses sweeping up the Saddle Back with the light swan sleigh careening behind them, filled with bearskins, one figure leaning forward waving the whip over the plunging blacks—it was almost as distinct as the foxes.

Why shouldn't she have a sleigh? She had seen one in the back yard of a junk shop in Denver. It was in pieces, the runners off and the body broken, but it might be repaired and probably could be bought for a song. And the black mares—they were saddle stock, really, and shouldn't be used for work, but such a perfect match you couldn't tell them apart—and Rob had needed an extra team, a light team, and "Anyway," he had said, "what luck do I have getting prices for my saddle horses? This way they'll at least earn their keep."

The mares had hated the wagon at first and Rob had the dickens of a time breaking them, but here they were now, all harness-broke, trotting off with the wagon today for a load of wood. They'd like the sleigh better—they'd be wonderful with a sleigh!

All the time she had been watching the swan sleigh and the black mares go zooming up the hill.

When they disappeared over the top she turned and started back down the snowy path, thinking about the bitterness that flared out in Rob now and then. Always talking about his bad luck. Suddenly her heart swelled with deepest longing for some good fortune to come to him. She remembered her dream about the Goblin and she came to a stop and stood thinking. It had deposited a seed of hope. Who could say what might happen? The colt had extraordinary ancestry. Colts changed as they grew. If only nothing happened to him! Nothing *must* happen to him—

She walked slowly home. The snow had brought peace into her heart. The winter no longer frightened her. She loved the look of the world this way—who would know that it was the same world? All so changed! The earth that had been brown and tan was now an undulating expanse of oyster and pearl. The pines that had been dark green towers were etchings in black and white. The ranch house and bunkhouse and spring house—they weren't houses any more, they were neat little winter Christmas cards with white roofs that had their edges turned and wadded with cotton wool.

9

Goblin knew the storm first as intense cold and a prolongation of the night.

Though he had been born in a storm and had been aware of the world as floods of icy rain sluicing upon him before he had been aware of it as anything else, yet then his consciousness had been only faintly awakened and he had received the experience as if through a veil. Now it was different. His awareness had quickened rapidly, sharpened by every hour of living; and his natural independence and tendency to solitary investigation had given him an ability to take life straight without filtration through his dam.

He was nearly three months old.

Intense cold at dawn was a usual thing in late November but in an hour or so would come the sunrise, and mares and colts would turn themselves broadside and stand basking with heads hanging in complete relaxation. Even with zero temperatures and snow on the ground the rays gave warmth and life and penetrated to the vitals.

Today there was the dawn and the falling temperature and a great stillness. It continued. When there should have come the sunrise there came instead a dim twilight. It showed an ocean of cloud hanging low, solid and deep, without shading and without a break. It showed the world crouching beneath it, colorless and withdrawn.

There was something else abroad that could be sensed rather than seen, and Goblin trotted away from the herd to the edge of the rise as if he could find this strange new thing by pursuing it. His muzzle lifted and his nostrils flared till they showed the crimson lining. He was trying to catch the scent of fear.

Now came the snow, moving against them from the east, quiet and hardly noticeable at first, little flakes like tiny cool feathers falling softly on their rough fur coats and melting immediately. As it grew colder the flakes were smaller and harder. The sky sank lower—a fog of snow, surrounding them. The world vanished and the colts looked around in terror and clung close to their dams.

There came a pressure into the storm and a sound, and the mares and colts turned their backs to it and began to move slowly with patient heads and tails blown forward between their legs. The colts whinnied nervously. If it had not been for the stolid resignation of their dams they would have been frantic.

The sound was a wind rising. It came from those caves of disaster far in the northeast, the winds that bring shipwreck on the Atlantic, cyclones in the mid-continent states and blizzards in the Rockies. Called an "easterner" in the mountain states, it lasts without letup for at least three days, sometimes a week.

As the hours passed, the mares tried to graze, pawing up the snow, and the colts imitated them. They moved in a south-westerly direction, backs to the storm. Banner occasionally climbed a rise and stood there entirely hidden in the white smother. But the mares were oblivious of him, whether he came or went; they had eyes only for their colts.

As the wind rose the sound of it rose too and a whining note came into it. The snow flakes were needle points of pain. When the colts, whirling about in confusion and fear, felt them for a second on their eyeballs they whinnied with agony and turned again to their mothers and thrust their heads under their bellies for shelter and a taste of warm milk. For whether or not the mares had food for themselves they never ceased to make milk for their colts. In twenty-four hours of such a storm tens of pounds of weight would be stripped from the mares.

The bodies of all the horses felt different. The snow burrowed into the long fur with which they were prepared for the winter, and the blood-heat melted and froze it and they became strange white phantoms moving silently through the white storm. Only their manes and tails, rippling constantly in the wind, were dark.

To themselves, they were heavy and unnatural and the colts asked their mothers, *Are you afraid?* And the dams answered them, *No, it is simply something to endure. All will be well in the end.* And the colts told themselves, *It is nothing to fear. All will be well.* And though they were nervous and panicky yet their faith was complete.

All the fear, all the courage, all the doubt, all the calculation, all the responsibility, all decisions to be made, were Banner's.

An outstanding horse personality is born with one ambition—to be the leader of a great herd. To have the finest mares—a sickling will be driven out or isolated until she regains her health. To raise the finest colts—handsome, strong, swift. To achieve this the stallion will fight and suffer, risk his life, starve, wander in strange lands, steal and plunder, take what punishment comes. Once he has achieved it he is tireless in the care of it. He finds his mares the most luscious pastures—north, south, all over the state; finds them shelter during storms; protection from all enemies. He fights any who would challenge him or steal or hurt his charges, investigates every danger with intrepid bravery and disregard of himself. A stallion always carries scars and fresh wounds, got because of his fearlessness in discharge of duties toward his herd. And because the aim of his master, if he has one, is the same as his own, there is partnership and teamwork between the two.

In this storm Banner was not still a moment. He circled the herd quietly, watchful lest one mare or colt wander away. He climbed every rise. He opened his eyelids against the flaming ice of the storm. His great neck was arched, his mane and tail whipped behind him on the horizontal stream of wind-driven snow. His eyelashes were fringes of tiny icicles. A long one hung from his chin—it was his frozen breath.

How long would it last? Standing on a rise, he peered into the blind smother as if he could find an answer there. Was it just a flurry which would pass with a change of wind?

There was other life around in the storm. The jack rabbits were the most at home, warmly hooded in white fur, invisible until they leaped. Then they shot through the air as if propelled by the kick of a mule.

Banner's ears came forward suddenly and he turned his head, straining to hear. The faint yammer of the hunting pack drifted to him through the snow—coyotes, lurking in the neighborhood of his band, of anything living, on the lookout for strays or casualties.

He gave a sudden start. Three coyotes, galloping soundlessly with red tongues lolling out, appeared close before him, passed him, vanished.

Banner turned, picked his way down the hill, and joined his mares. He took them to the water-hole. It was in an exposed place and when they had made the turn of the hill they had to face the storm. They balked and turned away. The stallion forced them. They obeyed reluctantly, then scented the water and it drew them and they drank their fill. While they drank, suddenly there were antelope on the other side of the pool, staring at them, bending their slim necks to the water.

Banner guided the mares to a draw between two hills where they had shelter from the wind but no feed. As between days of hunger or days of scourging by the wind he knew they would suffer less from hunger. But still he was questioning. Was it really going to be days? Or only hours?

There was increase in the force of the wind rather than diminution. The craggy peaks of the hills where the rock jutted through the soil were bare; the snow swirled around them and packed the lee side deep.

Drifts were curling down the centers of the draws, piling smoothly up, shaped like waves. The temperature was falling fast. If the wind did not change it would be thirty below that night. Now, in the daytime, the storm was white. That night it would be a black fury with a bedlam of sustained, screaming sound.

The wind did not change. Night came early. The herd bunched for warmth, and on the outskirts of it the coyotes circled, terrifying the colts with their long trembling howls.

A few of the mares slept flat on their sides and all of the colts lay under or close to their mothers. The blizzard screamed over them.

When morning came and Banner again forced them out of the draw to keep them moving and grazing, two of the colts were unwilling to rise. At the sight of their dams moving away from them, they struggled and fell back, tried again, got weakly to their feet, shook themselves and followed slowly.

One colt stood, whimpering, over the prostrate body of the old mare which was its dam. Banner and the other mares passed them as if they did not exist. Doom was already written upon them. Before the heat had gone out of the mare's body the coyotes were at it. The colt screamed and fled, three coyotes racing after. They crowded it and leaped for its throat. The colt reared and struck at the fanged faces but the teeth of a big gray coyote closed on its jugular vein and the colt went down —its last agonized scream cut sharply in half— The coyotes ripped at the belly of the dead mare. They ripped the walls of the uterus and found the foetus and snarled and fought over this tidbit.

Banner found shelter for the herd where it was neither swept by the wind nor too deep in drifts. A little grove of aspen in a draw caught the snow. It skipped over the trees, touched earth again and curled in great combers. Beyond it was a space protected from the worst of the wind and the worst of the drifts. Here the dry snow blew fetlock deep like a flat, boiling tide.

The colts had the best of it. Hot milk at any moment they wanted it, and the warm bulk of the dam standing between them and the storm. It was the cold that bit into them; and when they slept on the ground the blood in their veins ran thick and slow and they woke shivering.

Many times that second day Banner climbed the peak again. One of his questions was answered. It was not a storm of hours or a single day that any band of healthy mares and colts could weather, it was a blizzard from the east. There was another question—and for this answer he faced the ranch, tail whipped between his legs, mane blown over his eyes. He stood watching, protecting his eyes with his ice-fringed lids, listening for some sound that was not the whine and roar of the storm.

A small figure stood near him, just beneath the peak, looking up at him. Pure white in the storm even without the powdering of snow, he was hardly visible. Banner bent his great head and looked down at him. The Goblin looked back. Neither moved. Then Banner lifted his head again and without taking notice of the colt gazed in the direction of the ranch.

Goblin had not been one of the two colts who nearly succumbed during the night. He was filled with interest and curiosity. He was curious about the storm, about the sudden mysterious disappearance of the grass under a deep white blanket. Curious about the white stuff which buffeted his head and blinded his eyes and whined in his ears. He opened his mouth and felt the icy flakes melt on his tongue and mouthed them with astonishment. He did not suffer. He was filled with vigor. In his veins was a hot, swift-running blood, strong to cope with storms. He was at home on the range in any weather.

From the first he had been curious when Banner left the herd. He strained his eyes and his nostrils after him as if it was necessary he should know just what the stallion was doing and why he did it; and at last he followed him to find out. He sniffed, leaned a little closer, then turned his own head here and there in imitation seeking, listening, noticing, wondering.

At last he moved away. Banner took no notice of him. The white colt vanished in the snow.

Banner was waiting, not for an audible sound nor visible sign, but for the sudden sure knowledge within himself.

It came at about four o'clock in the afternoon.

Rob and Gus had piled the mangers full of hay and fought their way out to the County Road and opened the gates. Rob had raised his face toward the Saddle Back and had given the long cry into the teeth of the wind, useless because it was snatched from his lips even as he gave it so that it seemed like no cry at all.

"Ba-a-anner! Bring 'em in!"

He did it because giving voice to his command brought it to a sharp point within himself. It was the close communion between the two—man and stallion—that would acquaint Banner with the fact that the gates were open, the corrals and mangers ready, and that Rob had called him to come.

The white-shrouded stallion, standing on the crest, felt his own sudden decision. The time had come. He plunged down the slope toward his mares and roused them from their lethargy. They moved out of the shelter into deep snow, sluggish and stiff with the intense cold. Banner nipped and lashed. He drove at Gypsy, who was dry this year, and Banner's favorite and lead mare. She floundered out of the drifts that barred the way and plunged around the shoulder of the hill. The rest followed, gaining speed as they felt the stallion's driving power. They caught his determination. Besides—they knew where they were going. The colts clung close.

Banner took the lead, once they were under way, and the mares followed. They were three miles east of the Goose Bar gates. They ran with the storm behind them. Now and then Banner turned and circled the band, driving them from the rear, his head low, snaking along the snow, his muzzle ruffling it. The hairs of his tail and mane were erect, springing out with a separate life of their own.

The mares began to warm up as their blood ran faster. Excitement spread through the herd and they found strength to squeal and toss their heels and leap the ravines which opened suddenly under their feet.

What Goblin lacked was the long slim legs and the speed of the other colts. But when the command came to go, he galloped at Flicka's side with a fierce eagerness and zest. It was his first run with the herd. The icy air burned in his lungs. His chest expanded. Short-legged as he was, he had to labor to keep up. He did more than scrabble now—he stretched his legs and galloped mightily. A mare side-swiped him and he went down and the herd thundered over him, one big body after the other lifting in the air to clear him. He fought to his feet and stood. They were gone. He could neither see nor hear them, only the wind screaming about his head. He stood trembling and cried for his mother. He saw a white shape coming at him. Down wind from him as she was, he couldn't smell her and hardly recognized her. Close to, he heard her voice and whinnied ecstatically in answer. They plunged forward again, following the herd. Once more he galloped as hard as he could. Suddenly a ravine opened beneath his feet. He leaped bravely—his feet went deep into soft snow—his head went after them. He hit ground and turned a complete somersault and lay stunned, half buried.

Flicka stood over him nickering. She tried to paw the snow off him. The colt struggled, his feet kicking wildly —but he had no purchase. There was a swirling movement behind them. It was the stallion, coming at a gallop, his eyes shining like fire-opals through the snow.

He thrust his head into the drift, caught Goblin by the neck as a cat takes a kitten in its mouth, lifted him out, shook him, set him down, and was away again, thundering after the herd—other business to attend to.

Flicka and Goblin galloped on alone. They passed a mare standing motionless in the storm. One foreleg was lifted, the foot dangling loose, broken by a step into a badger hole. Her fine bay colt stood in the lee side of her, still finding his shelter from her crippled body. She tried to follow Flicka and Goblin, hopping on three legs. Then she stopped. They never saw her again.

They passed through the open gates, raced down the Stable Pasture, and reached the corrals.

The whole herd was feeding at the mangers in the barn and out at the feed racks, those in the east corral under the lee of the cliff. Other horses had come in too. Yearlings. Two-year-olds. Some older horses.

Banner would not go into the stables. He never had. Rob held a bucket of oats to him in the lee of the wall and the stallion stood before him, his sides heaving, the snow melting off him from the heat of his body and freezing again in icicles here and there. He dipped his mouth in, taking great mouthfuls of the heat-giving grain, lifted his head to chew and looked around, to look into Rob's eyes.

Did I do well?

Good work, old boy.

Rob talked to him. The stallion's full dark eyes looked at the man with intelligence and understanding. There was this about humans—this peace and confidence they could give. More than that, the deep friendly murmuring voice of his master lifted his load. The stallion laid down his responsibility, his fear, his never-ceasing vigilance, and rested.

His sides expanded and collapsed in a huge sigh.

Before dark, a fine bay colt came whimpering and neighing down the Stable Pasture, without its dam. It shoved in amongst the other mares. It fed greedily at the feed boxes. Rob, looking at it, saw long, bleeding gouges on haunch and shoulder. Coyotes! Or perhaps timber wolves! Where was its mother? Rob moved around looking for the mare—no sign of it. He left the shelter of the feed racks and went to the fence facing out toward the Saddle Back, trying to pierce the white smother—the mare might be anywhere out there—dead or alive. No— not alive. Else the colt wouldn't have left her. Wolves.

It was a fine bay colt, well grown and strong, five

months old. Kept in, and sheltered and fed, it would survive. Write off another mare lost.

The band could stay in as long as the storm lasted. There would be a day, perhaps even before it had stopped snowing, when Rob would go to the stables and find them empty, and he would know the stallion had begun to fret for the wind and the wideness of the upland and that as soon as it was safe, he had taken the mares away.

Following the blizzard there was a ground blizzard. Though it had stopped snowing, for forty or fifty feet over the earth the fine powdery snow was lifted and whirled and driven by the wind. Easy for life to be lost in a ground blizzard.

At last the wind stopped and the air was calm and crystal clear, perfumed with so intense a freshness and clearness that it stung the lungs with tiny needles.

Glorious was the sun blazing on the whiteness. Glorious, the deep blue cup of the sky. The whole world glittered and shone. And on the upland the mares moved contentedly on familiar grazing ground and told the colts, *Did we not say so? It is over.*

Goblin kept this knowledge in his heart. And more knowledge of his own finding. *When the cold burns too deep, when there is death in the wind, take the way down the mountain. Gates are open. Mangers are full of hay. There is shelter and food and kindness for all. And the screaming whiteness cannot follow you in.*

10

As Goblin developed there were changes in his appearance and behavior. Certain habits left him, certain coltish accomplishments were acquired.

The "scrabble" was gone, and in its place came the long springing trot characteristic of young colts, this owing, perhaps, to an inch or two of added length on each leg.

He learned the art of wrestling. His usual antagonist was Pepper, a tall black colt. On an expanse of level ground where the wind had blown off most of the snow, they galloped in opposite directions, circling in figure eights. When they passed each other at the center point they would pause, rear and strike at each other. Here began the beautiful play, bending to one side or the other, intertwining heads, then sliding down, almost kneeling to bite at the foreleg, rising high on hind legs again to exchange a flurry of boxing blows, their manes and tails—the black and the white—lifted and stiffened by burning vigor until they flared like open fans. Suddenly the young stallions would plunge past each other and, as if in a pre-arranged dance routine, rush away in the figure eights again, their hoofs thundering on the ground.

Goblin also became an accomplished bucker. On icy mornings when the sun blazed down and the air was a fierce intoxication, all the colts broke away from their dams and banded together for play. They raced up and over the brow of a gentle rise and came down the other side bucking. A few playful bucks sufficed for most of the colts, but not for the Goblin. His bounds became higher, his legs stiffer, the twist of his solid, powerful little body more acute. It seemed to go to his head. At last he would be alone there, when the game was all over, bucking solo in a mad, intemperate ecstasy.

When, in December, the spring colts were weaned and kept at the ranch for handling and graining, Goblin was left on the range. No more wrestling or boxing now, for he had no playmate, and when he tried it with Banner, rearing before him and putting up his fists, the big stud went on grazing, oblivious of his existence.

Goblin played alone. He raced on the curving hills, thundered in figure eights, reared and shadow-boxed, put down his head and bucked—sunfished—jack-knifed—cork-screwed— He knew them all.

Three times more before his six months of nursing were completed, Banner swept the whole band down to the ranch, for not a month passed without a blizzard. Goblin came to know the way so well that he tried to shoulder to the front, and only his lack of speed kept him from being there.

One day, after a heavy blizzard, he was not allowed to return to the Saddle Back. He was to be weaned.

The fury of the wind was dying away and only occasionally sent up a cone of whirling snow. Ken McLaughlin, warmly dressed in a blue ski suit and cap, stood in the Stable Corral, holding Flicka's halter. He had been summoned home for one of his winter week-ends, to witness the weaning of Goblin.

The corral was mid-leg deep in snow, churned to slush by the milling of the brood mares. For two days they had been in and out the stable doors, in and out the corral gates, free to leave when they wished, free to stay and fill themselves with hay and oats.

Ken's face, pale from the winter confinement and the cold, was full of peaceful love as he looked into Flicka's eyes and stroked her forelock. His thin, sensitive lips were slightly parted.

Flicka's golden coat had darkened with the cold. Running his hand down her neck under her thick blond mane, Ken felt the hair deep as fur. Her chest was broad and strong. Her wide nostrils flared as she breathed. And her legs— Oh, why couldn't Goblin have had those long slim legs of a runner?

Flicka was with foal again.

Standing there with her young master, she was paying no attention to him. She was looking over his head toward the Green, her ears strained forward. Now and then her whole body shook in an anguished whinny. It was in that direction that they had led her, a few minutes before, with Goblin following. Then they had brought her back without him. He was down there, with all the other colts, shut into the corral which adjoined the big cow barn below the Green. She whinnied violently again, ending in a series of short groans.

Ken patted her face and talked to her. "Don't you care, Flicka—pretty soon you won't mind so much—you'll have a new baby—and it's better for you not to be nursing him—you've been getting thin. I can feel your ribs under your fur coat."

Ken was torn between the desire to stay with his mare and comfort her, and go down to the Goblin. He stayed with the mare.

Banner had wandered out toward the Country Road gate. Evidently he had had enough of domesticity. He began to call his mares and round them up. The afternoon light was failing and the full moon, that had been nothing but a transparent globule of mist, was turning to bright silver.

When the last of the band had followed Banner out, Ken led his mare into the stable, filled her feed box with oats and left, closing the door behind him.

Then he exploded into a swift run, tore down the Gorge, across the Green, the color flaring into his face, his blue eyes darkening with excitement. *Now the Goblin! Now his race horse!* Now—at last—

As he opened the gate into the colt corral his father

held up a hand and Ken moved quietly. The last fifteen minutes had been full of shocks for the Goblin.

In the excitement of meeting his old friends and investigating this new place, Goblin had not at first realized that he had been separated from his mother. Then he heard her anguished neighing. That whirled him around and started him toward her. The five-foot fence stopped him. The gate was closed. He was completely penned in.

He raced around the enclosure seeking an exit. A confusion of feelings stirred him. There were the colts crowding around him, Pepper, the tall black, rearing and begging for a game. A strange intriguing smell came from the long center trough; he wanted to investigate that. But he was still angry. He didn't know what to do.

At sight of Goblin, Ken's heart began to pound. What a change! The colt had grown all over, so that he was still shaped like a mature horse—most odd-looking. But there was no mistaking the power in him. Measuring him quickly against the others Ken saw that he was as big as the biggest and oldest of them. In six months he had caught up.

Ken advanced slowly into the middle of the corral and held out his hand, calling the colt by name. Goblin stopped running around and looked at Ken. The colt's big head reached forward, his legs were planted stubbornly, his teeth showed between his black lips and there was the white ring around his eye. Ken called him again.

Impelled by insatiable curiosity, Goblin approached the boy cautiously, obliged to satisfy himself as to this small human being, not much taller than himself, and why memory rang a bell at sight of him. His muzzle strained forward. His body held back. He got one sniff— and at the same time Ken's hand moved to pat his nose. The colt's ears flew back—he whirled and lashed with his heels. Ken ducked.

"Pretty close!" laughed Rob. "You've got to be fast with that fellow!"

"Gosh! How he's grown," marveled Ken. "Bigger than any of the others, isn't he, Dad?"

"He's a husky."

Goblin was tearing around the fence. It made a wild fury in him that there was no way out. In the other corral, when they came down from the range in a storm, the gates were always left open. They were there of their own free will. Even when they crowded into the barn there was a different feeling.

He began to buck. This wasn't bucking in fun. This was protest, this was pure fight. He went through his repertoire. The other colts got out of the way and Rob and Gus retreated to the fence.

"Yiminy Crickets!" exclaimed Gus. "Luk at dot colt buck!"

The Goblin tied himself in a knot, his nose and four hoofs bunched; twisted and bounced stiff-legged three feet off the ground.

"It's the bronc in him," said Rob disgustedly, "he'll never make a race horse unless he gets over that."

Race horse! The word went through Ken like a flame. Did his father really believe, then, as he himself believed?

Gus walked along the trough pouring oats from a bucket. The other colts jammed around him, scrimmaging with each other, burying their noses in the trough.

Rob's harsh voice rose, reprimanding them. He liked good manners in his horses. "Here, you fellows! Cut that out!"

At his voice Goblin stopped bucking, looked around, shook himself, then, realizing that he was missing something, rushed to the trough. He forced himself through the crowd, biting and kicking, stuck his nose in and took a mouthful of the oats. Then he whirled away to the fence and stood there, mouthing the oats, thinking it all over.

That night, across the vast expanse of the snows, flattened under the bright moonlight, Ken rode Flicka bareback up the Saddle Back and down the length of it, looking for the brood mares.

He went very slowly, to make it last longer. He had played a trick on his father. He had kept Flicka in the

92

stable instead of sending her with Banner just so that he could ride her out alone that night and ski back. It hadn't fooled Rob. He had looked at his son hard until Ken had to drop his eyes, but after all he had said he could go.

Far down the ridge Ken found the mares, inky black shadows against the whiteness.

Banner came sweeping out to get Flicka. Ken dropped his skis to the ground, dismounted and removed the bridle.

Some knowledge of further and more permanent separation from her colt came to Flicka and she neighed wildly and tried to run away from the stallion. Ken watched the chase. The circling, the dodging, the racing side by side. It ended as such chases always ended. Banner drove the mare ruthlessly where he willed, and the two dark figures merged in the band of brood mares. One last whinny of despair came ringing down the ridge to Ken.

The boy stood, powerless to move, looking around. It was all too much for him—the snowy world too vast. the silence too eternal, the solitude too awful. For a moment his abnormally sharpened consciousness detached itself, making him see himself standing there, a small, lonely, dark figure, in the midst of the endless whiteness.

He felt the impact of all that was beyond him—the larger things. His future manhood. Women and love. Death. It hit him so sharply that he could have cried out in pain, and he looked up at the moon trying to blink the hot tears from his eyes. Such swift maturing fused him to adult life before he was able to bear it. There is always a first moment of realization—

In his fear and helplessness the image of his mother rose before him. Her smile, the serene violet eyes, the feel of her hand on his hair, the way she would look at him, understanding, reading his heart. It needed only the sudden faraway howl of a timber wolf—the hunting howl, endlessly long-drawn and melancholy—to make his heart burst into a flurry of pounding.

His skis—he fastened them to his feet. A few strokes

started him. Angling along the slope it was downhill all the way. He gathered speed. The icy air burned his cheeks and eyes and roared in his ears and shattered his thoughts to bits. Death and terror—Nell—the wolf-howl— They spun in his brain like a Roman wheel! *Oh, gosh what fun*— Speed and more speed! Watch out for that rock there—*Hi-i-igh!*

In a wild ecstasy he opened his mouth and a long exultant yell trailed behind him with two high curls of moon-silvered spray.

Far back on the ridge Flicka stood motionless among the dark shapes, her head turned as if watching a white colt that was no longer there.

11

It took Goblin only one night to learn that something of the utmost importance had come into his life.

Oats.

Here was an experience that touched his very soul. What independence! No need to go following and begging behind his mother! No need to paw and scrape at the snow for a few mouthfuls of dried grass! Here was belly-filling heat and strength and deliciousness spread down the long center trough in the corral; once last night, and now again in the morning. What a strange, foreign, altogether seductive taste! He mouthed and crunched it in delight, and if any other colt jostled him he was quick and vicious with his teeth.

A loop of rope fell softly and surprisingly over his head,

drew taut, and pulled at him. He reacted like a bomb exploding.

The boys had halter-broken him in the fall, but since then the pride and kingliness of the mountains and the freedom of the wind, and the rhythm of the plains, and the strength of the storms had poured into him. His spirit was enlarged and annealed. Not for him to be tamely tied and led about! The fight was on.

Two hours later, sweating, hatless, and nursing one hand which had been bruised by a twist of the rope, Rob said. "I guess he's licked. We'll leave him to think it over. Lucky to have got through that without killing him. God! What power!"

They were all in the corral, Rob and Nell, Gus and Ken. The Goblin, worn out at last, successfully haltered but now freed from the snubbing post and the tie rope, was panting, shaking his head to free it of the halter and the trailing rope.

Suddenly he reared, pawing at the side of his face.

"Ah!" It was a short, explosive cry from Rob.

The colt had thrust his foreleg through the cheek strap of the halter and it was caught so that he could not withdraw it. Ken started to run to him.

"Stand still," ordered Rob. "If he blows up now and falls over he'll break that leg."

Ken groaned.

The colt, standing on three legs, shuddered and grunted.

"But I've got to get it out, Dad!"

"If any of us takes a step toward him he'll blow up and go over."

Rob spoke to the colt. The deep compelling voice, the outstretched hand, had no effect. Goblin's eyes rolled from one to the other of his tormentors. Nell and Ken called him too, coaxing and reassuring, their hands held out.

"Plenty of sense," muttered Rob. "Look at him. He's thinking. He knows he's got to be helped."

The terror of the colt showed only in his eyes. He

95

looked at Rob, at Gus, at Nell and at Ken. Then, carefully, on three legs, he began to cross the corral, going toward Nell. Each plunge of his body jerked his head down. His foreleg flapped helplessly close to his eye.

"Come boy—come Goblin—I'll fix it for you—" Nell's voice was encouraging. Rob and Ken held their breath.

Reaching her, the colt halted, bent his head and endured it, trembling, while Nell took his foreleg in her hand. She was obliged to unstrap the halter. When the colt felt the sudden release and his leg touched solid ground, he stood heaving, froth dripping from his mouth. Nell put her hands on both sides of his head. As once before, he leaned against her, his face hidden, resting and comforted.

"We'll go," said Rob to Ken. "She'll do the rest. He's accepted her."

For an hour Nell played with the colt. She put his halter on and off. She rubbed him dry with a sack. All that he had learned before came back to him now. He gave her his trust, he ate from her hands, he looked into her eyes. She was Goodness. Like the oats. Like shelter. Like warmth. She was for him. She was his mother.

At supper, before they drove Ken back to school, Ken asked his father, "Do you think he'll ever be tall?"

"I fancy so. That Albino must have been over sixteen hands—a whale of a horse. And Goblin throws back to him. He'll probably develop in the same way. Albino might have started with short legs too."

"Well then—if he grows tall, maybe he can be a racer after all."

Rob bent his stern blue gaze on his small son. "Don't count your chickens before they are hatched."

Ken dropped his eyes. "No, sir."

Nell looked at her husband with an oblique glance. If he knew what *she* had been dreaming about the Goblin! But he puffed at his pipe thoughtfully without seeing her. "I've been thinking—those three stallions in Goblin's immediate ancestry. Appalachian. Banner. Albino. There's blood for you. Personality. Thinking power. *Will*—! And back of those three what other outstanding individuals that we know nothing about! The Goblin derives from all of them. He showed it today. The prepotency seems to have been the Albino's. He outweighs all the others, in color and type at least. Heredity is a fascinating mystery. In no other way, but by just those certain inherited characteristics that went to the making of Goblin, could he have become just what he is."

Nell began to suspect that Rob too had been counting unhatched chickens. He got to his feet and moved restlessly around.

"By God!" he suddenly exploded. "That Albino interests me! I wish I knew where he was!"

Ken stopped eating and looked at his father.

Rob sat down again, his eyes on the floor, his pipe in his hand. "Horses, you know, are the most intelligent of all domestic animals, and this has been proven by research. They think and they reason. Add instinct to intelligence and you get a faculty that seems almost supernatural. They act, sometimes with miraculous wisdom, as if having miraculous powers. It is often apparent that they know things that we cannot know—for instance, what goes on at a distance from them. This being the case, and the Albino being the outstanding individual he was, what could we expect of him? I don't think he would take his defeat and the humiliating loss of his mares lying down. He's probably still around." Rob gestured with his pipe in a southerly direction. "Maybe down there in the Buckhorn Hills. There are miles of open country between our ranch and the Colorado border, you know."

"But wouldn't someone have seen him, Dad? And talked about him?"

"A thousand horses could be hidden in those mountains and never be seen by man. They go up to fourteen thousand feet—some of those plateaus. And hell! How can anyone get up there? A few miners—prospectors. There are no roads. They might get part way in when the rivers are frozen up, but when the thaw comes in the

97

spring and the ice goes out, the torrents come down those gorges, swollen, impassable."

"But aren't there any ranches up there?"

"No. It's all government land. Nearly half of Colorado and of the other Rocky Mountain states has never been taken up. The government holds the land—doesn't even let any timber concessions out any more, because that would denude the mountains of timber and destroy the watershed. Besides, there's nothing to be done with the land. Most of it has never been penetrated even by the rangers. There are mountains there, and valleys and peaks and rivers that have never been seen."

"What would the Albino be doing up there?" asked Ken, his eyes wide with wonder.

"What any stallion does," said Rob dryly. "And you ought to know what that is by this time."

Ken returned to school and the Goblin settled down to his new way of life.

There was much to submit to. Though he was rid of his dam and his sire, yet, even as with young human animals, authority had been delegated to a nursemaid. This was a big, piebald gelding named Calico, a natural-born "Granny."

Calico led the colts to water morning and evening. Calico taught them that when the whistle sounded they must run to Rob and that good things would follow. Calico taught them manners. Taught them not to be wild—not to run away. Not to fight the barbed wire. Taught them that the ranch house and the corrals and stables were their real home—taught them to stand quietly while they were being brushed and groomed, while their tails and manes were combed and pulled, while their legs, one by one, were lifted and handled.

Much of this went hard with the Goblin, but there was always Nell, his comfort. Goblin would walk toward her very slowly, his eyes directly on her, ears pricked forward and steady. Reaching her, within touching distance of her hand, he would come to a halt and stand regarding her.

It was as if a shy young man placed himself before the one of his choice like an offering—no word spoken—his presence there, his humble, direct gaze, saying all that was to be said.

But in spite of the oats and the shelter and the care and companionship, all of which put pounds on his body and strength into his muscles and inches on to his height, Goblin felt a gnawing desire for freedom. He would stand at the southern fence of the pasture, his high-held head reaching over, his ears pricked toward the Saddle Back. Suddenly, with a quivering of his whole body, he would whirl away from the fence, trot off, then circle back, stand again, and give a cry of desperate longing.

In the late winter, not only animals and human beings, but the earth itself was sick with longing for the spring and the greengrass.

It was pronounced by ranchers in Wyoming as if spelt all in one word.

"You got enough feed till greengrass?" "Stock's mighty poor—seems like they'll hardly hold out till greengrass." "Cain't hardly wait for greengrass. I'm plumb homesick fer it."

Early in May came the last big snowstorm, falling on the barren brown earth. In that wrapping of snow there must have been a magical, mothering heat, for when the sun peeled it off, the world was green. An emerald lawn as far as the eye could see.

Nell found a whole migration of bluebirds lying frozen on the floor of the barn. She gathered them up and carried them in baskets to the kitchen. As the warmth thawed them out they began to flutter their wings and sit up and, finally, took flight out the open door and windows. The last one seemed unable to find its way and dashed itself about in terror, followed by Rob crying "Whoa, baby! Whoa, baby!" It found the door at last and dove out in a beautiful sickle thrust of blue steel. A moment later the birds gathered themselves above the Green and disappeared over the cliff opposite.

The noisy mountain plover, with white and black

barred head and breast, ran swiftly down the paths on twinkling yellow legs, or tilted in the breeze above the meadows, crying *Killdeer! Killdeer!*

The big white summer clouds came sailing up from the horizon, throwing dark floating shadows on the plains.

Antelope walked single file to the water-hole, or stood in little groups on the prairie, their exquisite heads turned and lifted inquisitively. They looked like small porcelain figurines that a lady would put on a green stand on the table in her drawing-room.

And Pauly presented herself before Nell, who was seated in her arm chair darning socks, and earnestly requested permission to have her litter in Nell's lap, and when she was refused, crawled into the scrap basket beside the chair and had it there.

As for the colts, the greengrass meant that school was over. They were freed of their nursemaid and curry combs and halters and tie ropes and were put out on the Saddle Back again, and now *they* were the yearlings, and the band of yearlings of the summer before were the two-year-olds.

Banner and his brood mares were no longer on the upland. On April first Rob had put them in the fenced meadow below Castle Rock. Here was less exposure for the heavy mares and any early foals that might be dropped. Late spring storms were dangerous to the newborn. Besides, with breeding season approaching, Banner would have his eye out for new mares, and up on Saddle Back there were young mares, his daughters, who, with the spring, would be coming in heat. The stallion, even from five miles away—if he was not under fence—would seek them out and force them into his band. He might fight with and kill some of the young stallions. In the meadow-bottom was fine shelter from a grove of aspen at the far end. A stream of water ran through it, and there was still plenty of last season's grass, grown after the cutting. Castle Rock, a huge pile of stone as big as a hotel, stood leaning over the lower end of the meadow like a guardian.

Goblin tasted his first greengrass. Babyhood was over.

He had no mother, needed none. He needed not even a trough of oats and the care of men. The whole world under his feet was delicious to eat and his for the taking. And for the first time in his life he was really and completely free—not even a piebald Granny to demand obedience of him.

There is no such speed on the range as the speed of the yearlings running like deer on the crests and ridges; no such wild irresponsible, prankish fun, such flinging of small bodies across ravines, such races on the straightaways, such tossing of heads, such frisking of heels. A yearling has little weight to carry. He is all long, piston-like legs, ragged hair, and wide, nervous eyes. He learns to jump all natural obstacles, he learns the free gallop down the steep mountainside; learns to pick his way at top speed over stony ground studded with shrubs and badger holes. He is always outdoing himself, surmounting difficulties he never met before. And so begins the development of chest and haunch muscles, and of staying power, and of heart.

For Goblin there was more than fun and freedom galloping over the greengrass on the Saddle Back. With the first breath he drew, standing alone on a rise of ground looking south, a new personality entered into him, and it was so keen an excitement that his body tingled. It filled him to bursting with heat and power and fierceness. It drove him. He began investigating the range. The Goblin no longer scrabbled. His legs stretched out with a long powerful clutch. The pasterns bounced him a little at each step, so that he went as if on springs. He trotted tirelessly the length of the Saddle Back.

Movement came into the grass. It rippled like watered silk as the blades became long enough to bend and spring with the wind. Rabbits were thick in it, browny-gray now, having shed their white fur. They hid in their burrows or in the rocks, invisible against the stone, and at the slightest alarm, shot away, their great leaps carrying them over the tall grasses like small kangaroos.

Goblin climbed the peaks to stand as Banner had so

often stood, his nostrils tremulous for every scent that came, his ears so alertly pricked that they caught sounds from miles away.

Goblin faced the ranch, as Banner was wont to do, and the same quivering ran through him at the sight and the scent of it. It was Nell. The remembrance of her hands touching him, gently untangling the strap from his fore-leg, quieting him with her voice—then, when it was all over, the way he had rested, his face hidden against her, shutting out the confusion and fear; the way her being there, holding him, had, for the moment, ended all his striving and violence.

Nell and the oats. Nell and the oats and the ranch and the hay mangers where he had found shelter and food in the winter storms.

His heart had been won—*half* his heart. The other half—!

His quivering ceased. He turned away and searched the plains and the high mountains to the south. His nostrils flared, tremulous for wind-messages from Colorado, from the jagged peaks of the Buckhorn Hills, from the high plateaus that lay beyond them.

He dropped his head and pawed the earth. He began to circle with his nose low, snaking along the ground. He broke out of the circle and climbed again—to the highest peak upon which Banner used to stand with a little white foal standing below him looking up.

He faced the ranch and immediately the trembling began. A long cry reached him, faint with the distance. Just Rob shouting to Gus—then a dog barking— But the sounds went shuddering through him, making him plunge and prance as if about to rush down the hill.

Then with a grunt and sudden twist of his body he turned again. The air today was so crystal clear that the Buckhorn Hills, etching their fantastic outlines against the deep blue of the sky, displayed a variety of rugged detail. The soft breeze came, sweet and wild and per-fumed, and *strange*—

It was all strange and incomprehensible—the fierce

desire within him to leave the ranch that he loved and seek out those far and unknown places. But it happens sometimes, even to human beings, that they are propelled in the direction of their destiny without conscious understanding of what is happening.

Something called to the Goblin. He answered with a loud neigh, and flung himself down the slope. Leveling off, he fell into his long springing trot, his head high, his nose pointing up, taking the way toward the open country and the Buckhorn Hills.

12

Once the yearlings were out on grass, there was no regular inspection of them during the summer. If anyone chanced to be riding on the Saddle Back a report would be brought home as to their condition and growth, any changes of coloring or appearance, whether the band was split, or whether it had disappeared altogether—which would mean that they were feasting in one of the little ravines of the mountainside and that the next day would see them out in the open again.

But it happened that the very day after Goblin's departure, the boys came home from school. The first thing they did was to fling themselves on horseback and ride out to see the yearlings—the Goblin in particular—and after a thorough afternoon's search, returned and reported him missing.

Everyone hunted for him. Rob drove the car to the neighboring ranches and made inquiries. He posted a notice at the Post Office. The ranch itself was combed from end to end, for it was possible that the Goblin, with a precocious and unseemly interest in mares, might have joined one of the older bands. But at the end of a week, Rob gave up, and the work of the ranch went on as usual. He said, shortly, that the colt would turn up again. He had run away—he would come back. Horses always did. Once oriented, they returned to the place of their birth.

Ken was stupefied with grief. All winter long he had been thinking of the Goblin, of being with him, of beginning his training. With the money he had been able to save from his allowance, he had bought a stop watch before he left Laramie. His fingers found it almost unconsciously—smooth and round and cool there in the little pocket of his pants beneath his belt. To touch it even had been exciting—as full of promise as a dinner bell. Now it was like a dead thing—cold and heavy.

When he went to bed at night he invented fantasies of what might have happened to the colt. The earth might have given way beneath his feet as he leaped a ravine— and then a fall, a broken leg—lying there dying—dead by now, and the coyotes and crawling things eating him. A clump of shrubs could have hidden the corpse so easily —and how many thousands of such shrubs there were on the ranch! That had happened to Dixie, a year ago. They had found the skeleton six months later.

Another thing that had happened—a band of horses was grazing near the highway. A car passed, filled with noisy, ugly-looking men. Going up the hill by the overpass, one of them had shouted, "See that old mare? Bet I can hit her!"

He had taken his gun, stood up in the car, and pulled the trigger.

The section gang working on the railroad that ran alongside the highway saw the whole thing. They saw the man shoot, saw the mare leap spasmodically, then go down with a crash, heard the burst of raucous laughter from the men, saw the car speed up and vanish over the hill.

Ken began to shake in bed. A white colt in a band of

dark horses—how easy to mark and single out! However, there would have been the body—they hadn't found any body. There was some comfort in that.

Goblin, meanwhile, was feeding in lush pastures south of the border. Though in a single afternoon's play on the Saddle Back he or any one of the yearlings could run twenty miles and not know it, he had taken a full week to work his way to the foot of the Buckhorn Range. There was so much to see on the way. So many dells and ravines to explore. So many hillocks to stand upon, gazing and studying and sniffing—so wide a country—so many bands of antelope and elk. The grass in every meadow tasted different.

There were, also, those many hours when he stood facing north—the ranch. And his body would become taut, and that tingling and quivering would go all through him.

Horses often appear to move as if propelled by their unconscious, rather than their conscious minds. Call them, and they will pay no attention but will go on grazing as if they had not heard. Walk in the direction of the stable and finally disappear out of their sight—they will continue to graze. But slowly they will be working toward the stable. At length, as if entirely by accident, they will be here at the corral gate, saying, "Well, here we are."

It was in this fashion that the Goblin moved. After his first start southward he had just drifted. Now—here he was.

It was the river that interested him. He had smelled it for miles before he reached it. He had never seen anything like it. It took him a long time to decide that there was nothing dangerous about it, though it moved. It plunged and leaped. It hurled itself over rocks. It tossed chunks of itself into the air. It was alive therefore. It had a voice too. A loud voice that never ceased its burble of sound. Incessantly, it talked, whispered, gurgled, chuckled.

Having power in himself, he knew that there was power in the river. Facing it, standing there on the brink,

105

he felt that it challenged him, and he gathered himself to fight back.

In an hour he had accepted the fact that the river would not attack him. It ignored him. Nothing he did altered its course or its behavior. He drank from it, at last, and the river did not even mind that.

He followed it upward. It was leading him further into those hills which got steeper as they got closer until they sheered up, leaning over him. And the river was narrower, between higher walls. Its voice was a deep roar now. Occasionally, looking ahead, he would see it coming down over a wall of rock—blue on the slide, a smother of white below.

The going was more difficult and the feed more scarce. He had to leave the river to find pockets of grass and clover, but how lush and rich they were!

All this time he had a satisfied feeling that he was going where he wanted to go. But in the mornings he would find a high point and climb it and look north toward the ranch. Sometimes he would give an eager whinny. But when he got going again, it was on up the gorge.

It must surely have been from the observation of horses that the proverb was drawn, "The farthest fields always look the greenest." The path on the opposite side of the river always looked better to Goblin. He crossed many times. A leap from one rock to another, from there a scuffling plunge and a few swimming strokes would get him across. Presently it would look better on the side he had left, and he must go back.

So it happened that he was standing on a flat rock, just gathering himself to leap to another rock in midstream when *the thing* was flung against his legs, so terrifying him that he made his leap badly, and was swept into the channel, and from then on knew nothing but the struggle to keep his nose above water and claw himself out.

When he accomplished this he was some yards downstream. Even while he was shaking himself, his head turned to look back. What was it that had hit him? He must know. It was still there on the rock on which he had been standing, and it didn't move.

With his ears alert and his eyes fastened on it, Goblin went back and investigated.

A foal! Not so unlike himself, except that instead of being all white, it had brown markings on it. It was, in fact, like Calico, his piebald Granny.

Goblin was shuddering all over. The foal had no eyes —they had been picked out. In half a dozen places there were bloody gashes—

It was at this moment that he leaped to meet the flapping black cloud that dropped down upon him from the sky. Huge pinions beat about his head. The creature was as big as he was himself. Goblin emitted the first real scream of his life when, for a moment, the terrible face looked closely into his own, and the great hooked beak drove for his eyes.

Goblin reared and went over backward, the eagle flailing him with wings, beak, and talons. Rolling on the narrow rocky beach half in and half out of water Goblin struggled to get from under the creature. When he gained his feet, with the instinct of the fighting stallion, he darted his head down to bite the foreleg of his enemy. He got it between his teeth and crunched.

He was clawed by the other leg, his shoulder was raked and gouged. The beating wings buffeted his head like clubs. He held on. The beak struck him again and again. Blood spurted from his neck and belly.

Suddenly it was gone, shooting straight upward, then sliding into the shelter of the pines. Goblin stood alone, the thin shank, partly covered with fine, closely set feathers, and the curled, cold, fist-like claw dangling from his teeth. There was a thin, bad-smelling blood oozing from the end of it.

He dropped it and stood shuddering. It terrified him. Then, with his insatiable curiosity, he must stoop to smell it again.

Never would he forget that smell. It sent him up on his hind legs, snorting. His ears were filled with the sound the eagle was making—a furious screaming. *"Kark! Kark! Kark!"* He leaped away from that fatal spot and went scrambling over the rocks downstream, working away from the river bank toward easier going.

The eagle peered from his pine tree. He sat on a bare bough, balancing himself on one claw and one stump and his spread wings. At his repeated cry of rage the woods around became alive with small, frightened, scurrying animals. His eyes, terrible in their far vision and their predatory determination, were fastened on the colt galloping northward, a white streak down the dark brink of the canyon and at last a moving dot on the plains, five miles away.

The Goblin used the speed that he had never used before; that had reached him, coiled like invisible, microscopic snakes, in the chromosomes passed down to him by his forebears.

It was a great run.

Next morning when the sun rose, the Goblin stood comfortably among the yearlings of the Goose Bar Ranch, turned broadside to the delicious penetrating rays, snoring softly in peace and blissful ease.

13

It lasted for a week—the peace and the bliss. A week in which, as it happened, no one of the McLaughlin family discovered that the prodigal had returned.

It was during that week that young Ken McLaughlin, in a fury of despair over the loss of his colt, stood on the top of Castle Rock and hurled down the cherished stop watch which was to have timed the future racer.

At the end of the week Goblin left the herd of yearlings and drifted south again. His terror had changed, as all terror should, into knowledge and acceptance of a danger; a lesson learned. And those mountains down there exerted an irresistible fascination over him. He went more slowly than before. He spent a week grazing with a little band of antelope in a dell-like valley on the way. And he explored extensively on both sides of the lower reaches of the river.

When at last he reached the rock where he had been attacked by the eagle it was near the end of July. This time there was no piebald foal lying across the rock in mid-stream, no monster bird in the air.

Goblin spent a half-hour by that rock, smelling and snorting, going over every inch of the little beach where he and the eagle had fought. Something like a dried curled branch lay upon it with a darkish clot on the end. He circled it, then reared and came down pawing at it. He cut it to bits and ground it into the earth.

He followed the torrent upward until he could follow it no longer. It filled the gorge. Streams ran over the sides of the cliff to join it. In the crevices of rock were pockets of snow. The stream was choked with the spring floods. It pounded and churned. A dead tree drifting down was hurled tens of feet into the air.

Goblin looked at the river a long time. He raised his head. What was beyond? Up there? His nostrils flared. The river and the rock walls were so steep and so high that he could no longer see the sky, only craggy peaks, and ever more of them. But up beyond all that was where he must go.

Cows and horses are by instinct expert engineers and will always find the easiest way through a mountainous country. Goblin detoured from the river on the eastern side. He had stiff climbing to do but there were breaks in the river-walls and running with the brood mares on the Saddle Back had made him as sure-footed as a goat.

Hours of hard going brought him at length to the last grassy terrace before the rocks shot up in an almost sheer cliff. The place was like a park with clumps of pine and rock, little dells and groves; and, scattered at the base of the cliff and on its summit, numbers of the huge smooth-surfaced stones like the one balanced on the top of Castle Rock on the Goose Bar Ranch.

Some of them as large as houses and perfectly smooth and spherical, these boulders are to be found all through the country of the Continental Divide, creating a wonder in the mind of any beholder as to what great glaciers in what bygone age could have ground and polished them and left them at last hanging by a hair on narrow shelves of rock, or balanced on peaks, or suspended above crevices where one inch more of space on either side would have freed them to go crashing down.

Goblin was hungry. He took his bearings first, then began to gaze. Rounding a clump of trees he halted and lifted his head sharply. There, not a hundred yards away, close to the base of the cliff wall, were two handsome bay colts grazing.

Goblin was quiet for a moment, savoring the interest and delight of a meeting with some of his own kind. Then he whinnied and stamped his foot. The colts looked up. With innocent friendliness they trotted toward him. Being a stranger Goblin had to discover certain things immediately. Were these mares or stallions? Where did they come from? Would they be friends or enemies? So, just as children, meeting, always ask each other, What's your name? How old are you? Where do you live?— these colts exchanged information, squealing and snorting and jumping about.

This was interrupted by a ringing neigh that came, it seemed, right out of the wall of rock. The colts responded immediately. They whinnied in answer and galloped toward the wall, angling off to a place at some distance where a ridge ran jaggedly up the cliff. And then, to Goblin's amazement, they galloped right into the wall and disappeared.

Goblin galloped after. Turning the shoulder of the ridge, he found himself in a narrow chasm which split the rampart of rock and led some distance into the heart of it. There was no sign of the colts, but the passageway was full of the smell of horses. Goblin trotted confidently on.

Suddenly there was a harsh scream from above, and the shadow of wide wings drifted across the chasm.

As long as he lived a moving shadow falling upon him from above would galvanize Goblin into terrified action. He crouched, backing, and his up-flung head and straining eyes tried to spy out his enemy. But not by looking could the colt see and apprehend the eagles' eyrie, clinging to a ledge far up on the peak, with one eagle sitting on the edge of the nest, and the other—the one-legged eagle—drifting down over the chasm.

Colts and eagles live on different planes. Only by the cold shadow falling on him, only by the scream, with its strange mingling of ferocity and sadness, only by the horror and shuddering within himself could he know his danger.

He plunged forward, driving straight toward the rock which apparently closed the path. But arriving there, the passageway turned. He went on, zigzagging. He saw and heard nothing more of the eagle.

At last the sides of the chasm sloped away, exposing a wider wedge of sky. And in front of him was a mass of the great boulders which seemed to have been rolled down the sides, choking the chasm completely.

But there was still the smell of horses—Goblin went on. And a turn showed him an open way through—a sort of keyhole, roofed with a single great boulder which hung on slight unevennesses on the side walls. Beyond, Goblin glimpsed blue sky and green grass. Galloping through, he came out into brilliant sunlight and a far vista of valley and mountains.

Goblin had found his way into the crater of an extinct volcano. Two miles or more across and of an irregular oblong shape, the valley was belly-deep in the finest mountain grass. Here and there, rocky or tree-covered

111

hills rose from the valley floor, reaching as high as the jagged and perpendicular cliff which ringed it and shut it in. Outside of the crater walls rose still higher mountains, timbered with pole-pine and juniper and aspen. On the lower slopes of the stone rampart were narrow ravines in which were close thickets of quakin'-asp, their roots deep under the rivulets that gathered from a thousand crevices to pour into the valley and join the broad river that wound across it. Reaching the rampart, the river burst through, changed to a foaming torrent by the compression of the narrow cliff walls.

Here, at an altitude of fourteen thousand feet, was a valley of incomparable richness, unknown to man. Vacationers and climbers are familiar with those ranges which are close to civilization but not the inaccessible mountain fastnesses which stretch for hundreds of miles through the Rockies, lifting their lonely peaks to the clouds and the sun and the drifting eagles.

Goblin stood motionless, his eyes scanning the valley, his muzzle lifted to suck in and savor and read all the messages it flung at him. He knew much about it already. This was the country that had called him and he had answered the call. Those horses over there, the big, loosely-flung herd, grazing quietly, were the horses he had been hunting.

Mares! His nostrils quivered. He neighed loudly. The mares raised their heads, the foals faced around. What magnificent animals—big, smooth, glossy—the very smell of them was sweet and strong with health and power. The mares were blacks and bays and sorrels, and the colts were the same, except for a few piebalds.

Nickering, they lifted their heads and trotted toward the newcomer. Goblin rushed happily to meet them. He was at home with mares. Most of his life had been spent with them.

They milled around him, thrilled and excited by the advent of a stranger. He lost all thought of fear or caution in the happiness of having arrived. He met and smelled and talked to them one by one. The squeals and whin-

112

nies, the jumps and snorts and playful kickings were all delightful fun. Some of them tried to drive the intruder out, but their bites and kicks were half-hearted.

On the summit of a near-by hill stood a great white stallion.

He was upwind from his mares, which was fortunate for the Goblin. As it was, the Albino noticed the commotion in his harem and lifted his head to observe it.

This animal stood sixteen and a half hands high. He was pure white. His body had power and strength rather than gracefulness. He was not smooth. He was gnarled like an old oak tree. His coat was marred by many scars. His great age showed in the hollows of his flanks and shoulders and face. Behind the dark glare of his eye, a blazing fire burned and on this flame was projected an irresistible will-power, and a personality that was like the core of a hurricane.

He looked over his kingdom. He had stood there for years, looking over his kingdom. And—if horses think—wondering who would take over when his end came. He had no heir. How could he have? He permitted no colt older than a year to remain in the band of mares, nor any stallion older than a two-year-old to be in the valley. Here and there, in the deep grass, were the polished bones of those who had challenged him. And if any attempted to return after he had driven them forth—they did not try a second time.

When Goblin caught the unmistakable strong scent of the stallion he trotted out from the herd to find him. He saw him up there on a hill—just where Banner would have been—and with a joyful nicker, started toward him.

The Albino came down to meet him.

Goblin, a creature of fire and magnetism himself, felt the oncoming stallion in terms of voltage, and it was almost too much to be borne. Goblin came to a stop. It occurred to him that he was going in the wrong direction. But he held his ground.

He watched. He had never seen or felt anything like that before. The stallion was so contained, his power was

113

so gathered and held within him that he was all curves. His great neck was so arched that his chin was drawn in and under, the crest of his head was high and rounded with long ears cocked like spear-points. His face was terrifying—that ferocious expression! Those fiery eyes! And his huge, heavily-muscled legs curving high, flung forward so that the great body floated through the air—then the massive hoofs striking and bounding up from the earth with sledge-hammer blows that made the hills tremble and echoed like thunder in the valley!

The Goblin still held his ground. The Albino slowed his pace, came closer—stopped. Their noses were about two feet apart.

For as long as a minute they faced and eyed each other.

They were the same. Trunk and branch of the same tree. And from that confusing identity—each seeing himself as in a distorted mirror—there flamed terror and fury.

No self-respecting stallion would deign to attack a mere yearling, or even to take him seriously enough to administer heavy punishment. But suddenly the Albino raised his right hoof and gave one terrible pawing stroke accompanied by a short grunting screech of unearthly fury. And in so doing, he both acknowledged and attempted to destroy his heir.

The stroke was delivered with lightning speed. From his great height, if the blow had come down on Goblin's head, as was intended, it would have killed him instantly.

But Goblin was endowed with the same speed, and reflexes that acted quicker than thought. He swerved. The great hoof glanced down his neck, ripping the flesh at the shoulder, and sent him rolling.

To complete the attack, the stallion dropped nose to earth, turned and lashed with hind feet to catch the body of the colt as he fell from the blow and finish him off.

But the Goblin rolled too far and too fast, landed on his feet, and whirled to face his antagonist.

The stallion plunged toward him—head stretched out like a lethal missile, the twisted mouth open and reaching

114

to bite—the great teeth, like slabs of yellow stone—bared—and in the wild and terrible face, two eyes blazing like fire-opals.

The Goblin whirled and streaked toward the band of mares. They were bunched, watching, fascinated. They opened their ranks and let him in.

They scattered at the impact of the Albino's head-on rush. Goblin dodged. He felt the rake of the Albino's teeth down his haunch—a chunk bitten out—he squealed and doubled behind another mare. The Albino's charge knocked her off her feet and Goblin went down under her. He felt a burning pain in his ear and tore it loose. He was up again, shouldering into a group of mares and foals. When he came out the other side, the Albino had lost him for the moment. It was his chance. He fled toward the keyhole in the rampart, Albino in thundering pursuit. Entering the passageway, the Goblin followed the zigzag path which led through it, and here his smaller size gave him an advantage. Emerging on the other side, the Albino was some distance behind, but still coming fast.

It was a long chase.

Goblin's youth and his quickness at dodging and doubling—and the cover given to him by the rocks and clumps of trees—saved him. Six miles down the river, he was alone at last, as the afternoon light began to fade. He was limping from the painful wound in his shoulder. He carried his head on one side, favoring the torn ear, now and then giving it a little shake to shake the pain away, scattering drops of blood. He ached all over. To move, now that he had stopped running, was an agony. He stood under a tree, twisted and quivering. He ate nothing all night.

In the morning he went to the river and drank deeply.

The memory of all that had happened was graven in him. He faced the rampart, cocked his one good ear, turned his head until he caught the wind, and stood straining, listening, smelling, bringing to his consciousness—almost as strongly as if he could see him—the ter-

115

rible monster that had terrified and bested him. He had the impulse to neigh and challenge him—but not the strength nor the courage. Never mind—there would be another day. Wait. He had wounds to heal.

Goblin grazed until he had filled his belly and renewed his strength, then took the way home.

14

Ken walked slowly along the dry irrigation ditch with his gun on his shoulder. His mien was sullen. He knew he was going to be late for supper and didn't care.

Dragging his feet, his eyes on the gravel he was kicking up, his mouth down at the corners, his cap hanging out of one pocket and his shock of brown hair untidy over his forehead, his appearance announced to anyone within a quarter mile of him, Here is an unhappy boy—in trouble and likely to be in more.

Presently he sat down on a rock and laid his gun across his knees. For weeks he had been nursing his grief. In fact, he had done nothing else. Every morning he woke in a dull misery, feeling that something was wrong, but for a few moments not knowing what it was and not quite believing that it was anything real. Then with a shock he would remember. The Goblin was gone. It was hard to believe. To have lost the Goblin was just something that couldn't have happened—*not to him*—

That was what really got him. Awful things happened to other people, he knew that. You read about them in the newspaper, you heard about them, but to him him-self—to his family— He felt bewildered and his eyes

roved the meadow. If that was the way life really was—
that no one was safe, not even you yourself—

He raised his gun and shot at a hawk that was sailing
low. It veered up sharply. That had been pretty close. He
felt like killing something.

In his mind, he had cut a groove of ugly thinking.
Blame of his father who kept saying that the colt would
come back of its own accord—that he was oriented to the
ranch—that animals always returned sooner or later to
the places where they were born. That was all very well.
Here it was the end of July, and Goblin had been gone
when he and Howard had got home from school on June
15th. Besides, with such a valuable animal, destined to
make all their fortunes, no chances should have been
taken with him. He shouldn't have been put out on the
range with the other yearlings.

That wasn't all. There was his stop watch. The watch
he had spent all that money on.

Ken's fingers slipped into the little watch pocket below
his belt. That was where he had been accustomed to feel
it—empty now—his fingers explored it futilely.

Howard—he might have known Howard would do a
thing like that. And so smug! Not at all as if he had played
a nasty trick, but was just interested in getting information—asking his father last night at supper—

"Say, Dad, I want to ask you something."

"Well, Howard?"

"You know Ken bought himself a stop watch before he
left Laramie."

"Oh, he did!"

"Yeah—to measure Goblin's speed, you know—and
see if he could be a racehorse—" (Howard's calm, imper-
sonal tone—*hypocrite—snake-in-the-grass*)

There was a moment's silence, and a funny sharp look
on their father's face.

"Well?" he asked.

"Well now, what I want to know is—if Ken got mad at
the watch, and threw it away—stood right up on top of
Castle Rock and pitched it down as hard as he could—"

(so informing his father that Ken had had a tantrum) "and if I found it, would it be mine or his?"

And the helpless misery that had made him choke furiously as his father turned to him and asked, "Did that happen?"

"Sure," Ken had sneered, "he can have it. I don't want it."

"But what I want to know," insisted Howard, "is—is it really mine or his?"

Their mother had looked very straight at Howard, her eyes narrow and blue.

But Howard had insisted, "Whose is it?"

And their father had answered harshly, "It's yours, Howard."

And so Howard had got not only the watch but even a sort of title to it.

The sun was sinking low. Grudgingly, Ken got to his feet and trudged the rest of the way to the house.

He got his chance to kill something just as he arrived. That skunk—his mother had been complaining for days of the smell around the house.

Aiming at the skunk as it ambled along the terrace, Ken forgot until the last moment that, behind the skunk, was the house. It made him jerk his arm a little. The bullet missed, hit one of the flat rocks that edged the terrace, ricochetted, and went right through the kitchen window where the family had just sat down to supper.

"What the hell do you think you're doing!" shouted Rob McLaughlin, rushing out on the terrace and seizing Ken by the shoulder.

"Cripes! Look at that neat little hole right through the glass—" this from Howard, gloating.

"Kennie!" An outraged cry from Nell.

And a terrible smell all over the front terrace from the skunk.

"This is just the last straw," roared his father, taking the gun. "I've had all I can stand of this! You beat it upstairs to your room and stay there. Forget about supper. You won't have any."

118

It had all happened so quickly that he found himself seated on the edge of his little chair, alone in his bedroom, before he had time to think. He didn't care about missing his supper. Didn't want any. What was the use of eating, anyway?

As always, when he was shut up or sent to his room, he strained his ears to hear what the other members of the family were doing. They had finished supper. His mother was washing dishes. Howard was helping her—he could hear their voices. What would they do when they had finished supper? Would anyone be thinking of him shut up there in his room? His lip quivered. His mother perhaps. She might come up. How would he act if she did? Should he be sad and show her how awful everything was this summer with the Goblin gone and no fun? Or should he frown and sulk and stamp his feet around and refuse to say anything? Or should he be reading a book—not caring about anything—and if she seemed sorry for him, just sneer?

He heard them all going out of the house and ran to the window. They were going off somewhere in the car! Not thinking about him at all!

He counted his miseries. First and worst, he had lost the Goblin. Second, his father was mad at him. Third, if he wasn't to have a race horse, he would never be able to give his mother any presents, or take down the barbed wire and put up wooden fences for his father.

He stopped struggling with his problems and sat in a stupor.

When things had gone wrong, there was usually certain comfort that he could find. Indoors, from his room, and the pictures on the wall, because he could get into the world of the picture and have fun there, and forget his own trouble. Outdoors, there were lots of things. Things he called "kernels"— That meant the very center point of things. Like the last, tiny egg you find in a Chinese egg when you have peeled off all the outer eggs. You go hunting for that littlest center thing. When you find it you stop hunting because *This is It*.

Birds were kernels. You couldn't look away from them. Whatever you were looking at, if a bird came close and stayed there, you would have to look away from the other thing and look at the bird. Birds were IT.

He thought of Sappho and Sapphire, the pair of bluebirds who had got the name of being regular summer dudes on the Goose Bar Ranch. Last spring, they had come again to build in the familiar place where some plaster had fallen out between two stones near the front door. His father had mended the hole with cement during the winter. And the birds perched on the Pergola, chattering and not knowing what to do because they had lost the home they built in every year. Seeing the family going in and out the door, they had decided to do the same. So one morning his mother discovered their nest well started on top of Aunt Emily's framed picture over the davenport, and Sappho and Sapphire busy flying in and out over the Dutch door, carrying sticks and straws. And there they had raised their family—because just to humor them, his father had postponed putting up the screen door, and left the top half of the Dutch door open, day and night. Ken could still feel a faint reminiscent thrill—remembering how he had looked up from a book he was reading to see the bluebirds flashing in and out the room. That was a kernel!

There were other kernels. You could find kernels anywhere. A place could be a kernel. You wouldn't want to live in a place that *wasn't* a kernel. Here at the ranch it was a kernel of a place—a place *to be*—right in the center point of everything.

Thinking about kernels did not make him any happier. He mused dully about this. Usually it did. You can only feel the kernels when *things are right*—when they're wrong, nothing matters. He looked around his room forlornly. Where had it all gone?

As grown people return after many years to the scene of their childhood and wander about in dismay—missing the spell, the enveloping arms, the certainty that here, right here, and not by any possibility anywhere else, is the very core of life—so Ken searched his room and his world. And found a sick emptiness. He sat in silence a long time.

Presently he noticed the sound of his alarm clock ticking. That made him think of the stop watch. He wondered if Howard carried it with him everywhere, or left it in his room? This would be a good time to find out.

Ken went into Howard's room and began to look for the watch. He searched bureau and desk drawers; all the pockets of the coats and pants that hung in the closet. He sat down and let his eyes rove around the room, looking for catchy little places, like the inkwell, only it wasn't big enough. Or, hung on the back of the alarm clock—only it wasn't there. That was a good place though—sometime he might use it himself.

He wandered aimlessly around, looking at the pictures on the wall. His liked his own pictures better, and best of all, the picture of the big duck—the Audubon print, his mother called it—on the stair landing. Only, right now he couldn't like anything. It was like eating food that was all the same, with no taste.

He stood before a page of framed text on Howard's wall and read it through. He knew what it was. Howard had it there because it was an heirloom, and Howard was the eldest son and had a right to heirlooms.

The words said,

STOP PASSENGER!

And here view whatever is amiable
Summed up in the character of
    Mrs. Elizabeth Salton, wife of
    Peter Salton!
Her person was delicate, full of grace and dignity,
Kindled by beauty and enlivened by sense!
    She was loveliness itself!
Yet the beauties of her person were exceeded by
    those of her mind.
Adorned and dignified by a happy elegance of thought

Refined by virtue.
Her manners were easy and engaging,
Her temper was gentle, serene and sweet.
Her heart was meek, benevolent and virtuous.
   She walked in the path of religion
   And lived for eternity.
   Oh, best of wives!
   And worthy of longest days,
She lived esteemed and died lamented
On the first day of May, 1806 in the
   thirty-first year of her age.

GO PASSENGER!

Reflect upon thine own mortality

AND LEARN TO DIE!

The last words fitted nicely into the way Ken was feeling. The whole put him in a sad and religious mood. He examined the text, an elaborate old English script that was hard to read. He examined the parchment upon which it was written and the crest at the top of it. He was familiar with the crest which his mother had on the back of her silver brushes and a lot of other things. The crest was a tiny dove with an infinitesimal leaf in its beak and below it a scroll of ribbon upon which were the Latin words, *Sine Deo Quid?*

Returning to his own room, Ken drew his chair to the window and sat down to await the return of the family. He would hear the car drive up.

Sine Deo Quid, he said to himself. I know what that means. It means *without God what?* He mulled it over. It wasn't really true—not most of the time anyway, because without God there was plenty. (Most of the time.) There was fun and riding and horses and plans and dreams and the other kids and playing with them and sitting at the table with his family and eating and talking and teasing and laughing (the dinner table was a kernel!) and the good food, and the way his mother smiled at him and—

sometimes—his father. So who would say *without God what?* when there were all those good things in the world? He felt a sort of jar inside him because—now—none of those good things made him happy. He didn't want anything but the Goblin. That was it—*without Goblin what?*— Nothing!

He turned in his chair, folded his arms on the back of it and laid his touseled head on them, sitting silently so while the room grew dark and one star shone out over the pines across the Green.

Later, when Ken had gone to bed, his father came in and stood at the foot of the bed and talked to him.

"With Howard, if he can't have what he wants he just grits his teeth and holds on to himself and pretty soon he can be philosophical about it. But you—all your life long, if you can't have what you want, you howl!"

Ken was shocked. "I don't howl, Dad!"

"Your way of howling. All this moping. Going around as if you were about to die. Looking like a corpse. Not eating. Breaking your heart. Worrying your mother and me. None of us in this life get what we want all the time, Ken—it just doesn't happen."

The boy's face quivered. "But—Goblin, Dad—"

"I know, Goblin. But before that it was Flicka. In a year or two it'll be something else. People go through their lives wanting—but what if they don't get what they want? What then?"

Ken's absorbed face stared back at his father, the dark blue eyes full of feeling and thought. The light of the candle on the bedside table flickered across his pale cheeks. Here it was again—just what he had been thinking about—suppose the bad things happened to you yourself instead of the people in the newspaper—like the Goblin really being lost and never coming back—and if Flicka had died instead of getting well—and if all the things you dreamed about and looked forward to would never happen at all, and instead, other things

123

happen—awful things—*to you*—*to himself, Kenneth McLaughlin*—

"What then?" repeated McLaughlin peremptorily. He took the brush from the bureau, leaned over the bed and began to restore order to Ken's hair.

"Well—well—" stammered Ken, trying to think hard. It was a big question to answer, because—because—if you didn't get what you wanted, what was the use of living?

"Well, answer me!" demanded his father, putting the brush back on the bureau. "Can you take it, or can't you?"

The boy stared at him. His face was streaked with tears and dirt. His father stamped from the room and came back with a wet wash cloth and a towel. "I said, *take it*. You've heard that before, haven't you?"

"Yes."

"Well, what do you think it means? There's many a day you've seen me walking through this house when I've not had what I wanted—perhaps I've just lost something I had hoped for and counted on. And you don't see me neglecting my duties or forgetting everything I ought to do or making a general nuisance of myself."

Here was the real blow. That not even when you were grown up—your own master, stamping around, giving orders to everyone—did you get what you wanted. Within himself he writhed—that thing he had always thought, that he had only to arrive at his twenty-first birthday and any possibility of misery was over.

His father was giving his face a vigorous going over with the wash cloth. Ken screwed his eyes shut but held up his face helpfully. Then McLaughlin dried it and flung cloth and towel on the chair. "Well?" he asked.

"Neglecting duties—?" muttered Ken questioningly.

"You've made a mess of training those two-year-olds and you know it. You don't put your mind on it at all. You left the oat bin open and barn door too, while one of them was in the corral and he got at the oats and almost foundered. He isn't over it yet. You're never on time for

124

meals. You aren't clean or tidy. When it's supposed to be your time for work, you're off somewhere moping and I can't find you."

He paused for breath. His hard handsome face, bronzed and clean-cut, lit by the intense cobalt eyes, held the boy's gaze. It slid through his mind that his father's face was a kernel—

Ken's self-pity died. He longed for his father's regard. Longed to understand—really understand *all* about life and what happened to people—and to be able to "take it."

"*Take it*, Dad? What does that really mean? Right now? About Goblin?"

Rob's face became gentler. He sat down on the edge of the bed, with one arm propped on the far side of Ken. A sweetness went through the boy—it was as if he was within his father's arms.

"Ken, you can't always win. Much more of life is failure than success. And if you can adjust yourself only to success—"

"Adjust myself?"

Rob explained impatiently. "That means, if you can only be your right self, well-behaved, cheerful, up-and-coming—when you are successful, then you're not safe. You're weak. You can't take it."

He stood up, but Ken held him, clutching his hand. Rob stayed a moment longer, his mind seeking some way to clinch the idea for the boy.

"There was a book I read once, called *Fortitude*. I've forgotten what was in it, but I've always remembered the quotation it began with. '*It's not life that matters—it's the courage you bring to it.*' That means, the things that happen to you, good or bad, don't matter. The thing that matters is the fortitude with which you meet them."

Ken's face was shining up at his father's. He still clutched his hand.

"Dad—haven't I got—*fortitude?*"

There was a long silence, before Rob suddenly stopped, pressed his full hard lips quickly on the boy's

125

forehead and answered, "That's what I'm waiting for you to prove to me."

He loosened his hand and strode to the door. Ken sat up and called excitedly, "Dad, I've decided to *take it*."

Rob turned to say, "Deciding to do a thing is very different from doing it."

Ken was disconcerted. "Why?"

"You can decide until hell freezes over and still, maybe, it won't be done. But if you *do it*, it's done, isn't it?"

"Ye-e-es, but why? If you *decide*, you can go ahead and do it, can't you?"

"Sometimes. Sometimes not. Things happen. It doesn't come off. You can try and break your heart trying and still you can fail."

With this incomprehensible statement the door slammed and the boy was alone. It was meant, he decided, as a warning, not to forget, not to let anything get in the way tomorrow, when, with the help of his new fortitude, he would begin to *take it*.

Growing pains were beginning already. No such seed as fortitude can be planted in a young heart without pain.

In the next room Nell put her arms on Rob's shoulders and looked into his eyes. "What did you tell him?"

Rob sank into the big chair, drew her to his knee, and told her. She sat perched sideways, the brush with which she had been brushing her loose hair still in her hand.

"It's all true," she said thoughtfully. "I've often worried. If he hadn't got what he wanted the other time—his first colt—Flicka—and if she hadn't lived and recovered, I wonder how it would have been with him?"

Rob nodded. "That's what I told him. That you can't go through life setting your heart on things with such violence that if you don't get them, you go all to pieces and won't play any more."

Nell nodded, "About Flicka, he was just sad and crushed. But this summer about Goblin, he's been ugly."

"Yes," said Rob, "because he's older. That's natural."

Nell slowly drew the brush through her tawny hair, so

fine and silky that it caught light from anything and followed the brush in a spray of gold.

Rob's eyes often devoured her with a sort of hunger—hunger for peace, for respite. Now he put his arms around her and drew her against him and laid his big bullet head on her breast.

"He's the *wantinest* little son-of-a-gun," he said against the blue silk of her robe. "Can you beat it?"

He felt her hand against his cheek. "Like who else?"

After a while he said slowly, "I—guess—so—"

In his own room Ken was lying on his side, looking at the one bright star that shone through his window and thinking about FORTITUDE. Fortitude would be a good thing for a horse to have too. Now, if the Goblin came back, and proved to be very fast, and had FORTITUDE—

15

Fortitude was demanded of Ken next day when Flicka went unexpectedly into labor and Rob said she was going to have a bad time and they would need the vet.

Driving over to the telegraph station with his mother, Ken's face was white and furious. "God made the world, didn't He?" he asked suddenly. "Well, I don't think much of the way He made it. I could have done it better. I can think up awful nice worlds."

Nell glanced down at him. What could she say? Goblin —now Flicka—it was a pretty big dose of trouble for him.

127

"Why do all the horrible things have to happen?" he asked passionately.

Why indeed? She was silent. How to explain. *What* to explain. The problem of human suffering and evil—over against God's love and power, the problem that begins and ends every theological discussion and disconcerts the ignorant and wise alike. She had been pondering it in church last Sunday, coming to a conclusion of a sort, a faltering, doubtful explanation; that, in the final act of creation by which a human being must be endowed with God-like free will, there can so easily be a time when he seizes his power and uses it wrongly; sows evil and reaps it, before he grows mature enough, wise enough, good enough, to know that free will must always be good will—else disaster follows.

"Why, Mother?"

She *must* answer him. "We can't understand entirely, Ken—"

"Why not?"

"You can't understand something that's so much bigger than you are. Not wholly understand. You can't even wholly understand your father or me—only one side of us. And even less, your Heavenly Father, the Father of all of us. It would be as if a small circle, like a nut, could get outside a big circle, like an orange."

Ken was silent.

"And so before you even begin to ask questions you must know that they can't be answered in a way that will satisfy you—the rest you have to take on faith."

"Faith."

"You know what that is. That's *believing* when you can't understand. You believe in God; you know He's there and He made us, and He is wise. And in the end will bring everything out right if we don't spoil things."

Ken thought about this for a while, then asked in a quieter voice, "Did your mother tell you about God when you were a little girl?"

"It was my uncle," said Nell, casting about in her mind for something that would interest him. "My great-uncle,

128

rather. He was the brother of my grandmother with whom we lived for many years, and he was a Jesuit priest."

"Gosh!" said Ken, having read about Jesuits and heretics in historical novels. The Jesuits were always the villains.

"They wear long black robes, you know, instead of a man's suit."

"Gee! What was he like?"

"He was the sweetest human being I have ever known in my life. I've never forgotten him. One day I was standing at the head of the stairs with him. He was just going down. And our cook, who was a Catholic, had heard that Father Salton was in the house, and she came hurrying upstairs to see him and she fell on her knees right there on the stairs so that he could bless her."

"Bless her! How did he do that?"

"He made the sign of the Cross in the air above her head."

"The Cross!" Ken had no comment to make on this. He was submerged by all the mysterious connotations of the word—church, Sunday school, hymns, ritual, symbolism—

"Tell me something more about when you were a little girl. Tell me about Father Salton."

Nell's thoughts wandered back. She remembered the many times her grandmother had clergy at the table. Clergy of different denominations. When they were there, life was strung to a higher pitch. Talk was more interesting because philosophy and understanding and scholarship were behind it. She kindled at the memory of the vigorous current of living force that played about the table. No dullness—no ennui—no self-pity— After all, such men—they met life in the raw every day. They were men with their backs to the wall for humanity's sake, and they were still praying, still hoping, still striving, still promising. A touch of the hero or saint about them and therefore (it almost always followed) men of great good humor and lovers of fun of all kinds.

"Go on—" insisted Ken. "Don't think—talk—"

"Well—one year I was sick in bed. And my Uncle Jerome—that was Father Salton—came to visit us. And my grandmother brought him up to see me. He sat down on the edge of the bed and talked to me and had my hand in his and presently I saw that he was looking at my fingernails and I knew they weren't clean! And I was so ashamed I screwed my fist up tight so that he couldn't see them."

Ken laughed. "What did he do?"

"It wasn't any use. He opened my fingers one by one, looked at the nails—looked at me with a kind of a shocked look and still a twinkle in his blue eyes—"

"Did he have blue eyes?"

"Yes."

"Like yours?"

"No—more like Gus's."

"Just about everybody's got blue eyes. Dad's are the fiercest."

"Uncle Jerome's were like pale blue marbles, very light and clear, the merriest eyes I have ever seen."

"Go on. What did you do about your nails?"

"I tried to make an excuse. I hardly had any breath to speak with I was so ashamed, but I gasped out, 'But I've been sick!'"

"Oh, Mother!" said Ken, shocked.

"Yes—wasn't it sickening of me. He didn't say a thing, but he pulled up his gown, put his hand in his trousers pocket, and that was the first time I knew he had on real man's trousers under that black gown—and he took a small nail-file out and cleaned my nails—one by one!"

"Gosh! Didn't you hate it?"

"I could have cried every moment he was doing it. And for a long while, when I would remember the awful things that happened to me, I would remember having my tonsils taken out without an anesthetic and Uncle Jerome's cleaning my nails."

They rode for a while without speaking. His mother, then, too, spent some time thinking about awful things happening to her—

Awful things—the world was full of them. On the land between the highway and the railroad track, some dead cattle were lying, their bellies bloated and swollen until the legs stuck straight up like stiff sticks. And Ken was reminded of the misfortune of their neighbor, who had leased this land for the good grazing there was on it, only to have his cattle begin to die—one on the third day, two the fourth; and on the fifth, his fine young registered bull. This loss crushed and enraged him. And the McLaughlin boys had been sent by their father to help drive the cattle off the tainted land. The reason for the death of the cattle, McLaughlin had ascertained at the University in Laramie, was that on that land grew, besides the grass, a small flower, quite common on the plains, and harmless. The cattle were accustomed to eat it. But its root was poisonous. On this strip of land near the railroad, the soil was made lose by the cinders from the locomotives, so that the cattle, tugging at the grass, got the root of the flower from the stalk, and so were poisoned.

The *treachery* of it! How could anyone have known? Ken turned his head away from the sight of the dead cattle. But they weren't the worst—the worst was that such things could happen to him too—suppose one of those was the Goblin—

"I wish God wouldn't ever let us spoil things!" he said violently.

"So do I," was Nell's heartfelt reply. "Perhaps He won't—in the long run." After a pause, she added, "I'm sure He won't. But we must do our part."

Ken's face was impassive. Nell knew that every word she spoke was important. Children meet religion head on. Violently. Sincerely. They recognize instantly the importance of it and their need of God, and the need of their parents.

She wished she could help him more.

131

They went under the overpass and Ken's eyes, wandering over the plains to the right of the road, had the look of one who sees only his thoughts.

"Mother, you know there are plenty of people who don't believe in God at all. A lot of the boys at school don't."

"Maybe they think they don't," said Nell, "but just wait till they get in a fix! Colonel Harris was talking about that once when he was here, telling me of some of his experiences in the last war. He was drowning in a shell hole, in the mud. Too weak to cry out, just scratching at the banks and wondering if they were going to let him drown there before their eyes—and he said he prayed! How he prayed! He said all the men did. No atheists when they were about to die! And once, in a trench, half the wall had fallen on him and pinned him down, and all the men had left without seeing him, and he couldn't move. And some rats came and began to scurry around him, and his feet were sticking out, and they ate the leather off and began to chew at his toes! And did he pray!"

"What did God do?" demanded Ken.

Nell was brought up short. "Oh, Ken," she exclaimed, "I don't know. It isn't like that. But Colonel Harris was here, wasn't he? Eating dinner and riding on Taggert the day after your foal was born? I suppose he got rescued somehow." She fell into silence, pondering how to give Ken the faith she wanted him to have. "But it isn't that way, Ken—that if we pray and ask for help we'll always get what we want, because very often we won't and aren't supposed to. This world isn't heaven or anything like it. We won't always be here—we just go through it. And there's death at the end of it—that's the door we go out by. I don't mind that. I can take it. I think there's a lot of silly fuss about dying. The animals know better—they know death is natural. No one with any sense can fail to see that this life is a gymnasium. A place of testing and training and trial and development. And we ought to take it that way. Not everyone can win what they want—but they make spiritual muscle trying for it, and giving it up, too. Everyone loses at the end—if you call dying losing. So the battle of life is a losing battle, but what you don't have to lose is your heart and courage—your grip—your—"

"Fortitude," prompted Ken.

Nell laughed. "Where did you get that?"

"From Dad, last night."

"Oh. Yes—well, if you pray for *those things*—God will give them to you."

"Always?"

"Always has with me."

"Do you always kneel down to say your prayers?"

Nell twinkled down at him. "Not if it's awfully cold—or I'm awfully tired! Then I say them in bed."

"Mother!" reproached Ken. "Isn't that being a sissy?"

"I found something in the Bible that sort of gives me an alibi," Nell defended herself, "several things, in fact. To begin with, it tells you to pray all the time. And you can't be on your knees all the time, so that means you have to be praying while you're dressing, or cooking, or riding— And the other thing is—it says King David prayed sitting on the ground, with his arms around his knees, and his head down upon them. So you see!"

Ken was silent, composing an important prayer. "Please God, make me have fortitude. And don't let me lose my grip. But if you could manage it to have the Goblin come back, and Flicka get through this foaling all right, that would be *just keen*. For Jesus Christ's sake, Amen."

There was a flash of radiance on his face as he looked up at his mother.

Arrived at the railroad station, Nell entered the telegraph office, and Ken stood listening to the mysterious dots and dashes which asked the telegraph agent at Laramie if he would be so kind as to do Captain McLaughlin of the Goose Bar Ranch a favor, and telephone the veterinarian, Dr. Hicks, and find out if he could start to the ranch immediately to deliver a foal?

Within five minutes the message came back that Dr. Hicks would come.

16

On the Goose Bar Ranch the weather was hot—really hot—for only two or three weeks in midsummer. On this day the thermometer stood at a hundred and one with a burning dry heat which lay on the land in shimmering waves, reminder that it was not far removed from the desert.

Inside the barn, in spite of wide open doors and windows, everyone was soaked with perspiration and Dr. Hicks had constantly to turn aside and shake the water from his forehead. Rob and the boys were naked from the waist up.

Flicka, exhausted by hours of unavailing labor, lay on her side. It was a dry birth. For a long time before the veterinarian's arrival one of the foal's forelegs had been protruding.

"Which means," said Dr. Hicks when he arrived, "that the other leg is curled back and makes birth impossible. The foal is in the wrong position, it will have to be straightened out." He asked for a gunny sack, cut holes in the corners for his arms and one in the middle for his head, removed shirt and undershirt, donned the gunny sack, greased his arm and went to work.

Ken watched him, vowing to himself that never again should Flicka be allowed to have another foal.

The doctor puffed as, holding the tiny yellow foreleg, he slowly forced it back into the mare. Ken saw it vanish with a strange sensation. Could the foal still be alive after being handled like that? At length the doctor's hand and wrist disappeared too, and Ken, watching his heavy brown face with its humorous expression, as if at any moment he was going to crack a joke, tried to read on it just what was going on inside there. Lucky, thought he, that Doc was so big and husky. To be able to straighten out a foal inside of its mother took strength!

While Doc worked he talked in short grunts. "This mare'll never foal again—that infection she had when she was a yearling injured her—scar tissue—it's a wonder she's as good as she is. All right for saddle—ah, there, I've got it now—"

"Got what?" breathed Ken.

"The other hoof. Both of them. This isn't going to be so bad, after all."

Nell was kneeling at Flicka's head, sponging her face and mouth with cold water. Now and then the mare gave a spasmodic heave.

Presently Doc was pulling on something. Flicka groaned and labored mightily. Ken groaned and strained too, but Howard watched every move the doctor made, keenly interested. Two tiny hoofs and a muzzle appeared and the doctor got to his feet and mopped the sweat from his face.

"She may be able to manage the rest herself now I've got it in the right position," he said.

But Flicka couldn't. Most of her strength was gone and it seemed that something still impeded the delivery.

McLaughlin looked at his watch. "It's been going on three hours now." He and Doc talked together in low voices. It frightened Ken to hear them—so casual and fatalistic. Ken touched the protruding hoofs. They were not hard yet and were covered with rubber-like pads. He

135

tried to pull on them and was dumbfounded to find that it was like trying to pull a bough from a tree.

McLaughlin sent Gus for ropes. They tied a rope to the foal's legs and Doc and his assistant put all their weight on it. The foal moved a little, the head was nearly out. Then it stuck, and when they continued to pull the only result was that Flicka's whole body slid across the floor. They tied her forelegs to a post and pulled again. Flicka's body stretched out straight and taut, ropes at each end of her, but the foal did not budge.

"Sacrifice the foal," said McLaughlin, "the mare won't stand much more."

"May not have to," said Doc. "I'm not stumped yet."

They fastened a block and tackle to the wall and ran the rope through it. Then Doc fetched an instrument like a pair of ice tongs, and to Ken's horror, thrust the points into the foal's eye sockets. Then they all pulled together.

It moved a little. Flicka heaved and struggled convulsively. The men hauled until they were red in the face. And suddenly the whole little body slid out.

Instantly the men undid the ropes and Gus went to prepare a hot mash for Flicka.

The doctor kneeled over the foal, which was barely alive.

"Is it premature?" asked Nell.

"It might be a little. The teeth are just through. When was the mare bred?"

"We don't know exactly."

"Will it live?" asked Ken.

The doctor did not answer. He wiped the foal dry and clean, massaged it and gave it a hypodermic injection. It was a very small but neatly made filly. It had a short back, long spidery legs close together and a small fine head with a dish face. It was a pinkish yellow with blond tail and mane.

"Just like Flicka!" exclaimed Nell.

"Will it live?" insisted Ken.

"Can't say for sure, it's pretty weak. But sometimes these little fellows surprise you. It's just touch and go."

They were all astonished to see that the terrible hooks had not injured the foal's eyes at all.

Nell noticed Ken's face. It was white and drawn. When Flicka suffered *he* suffered. She wondered if, after all the suffering, there would ever be any good thing come from the Albino's blood. Would it be, perhaps, this tiny filly?

Soon Flicka was able to get to her feet and eat her mash. The filly showed signs of life and struggled to rise. Doc and McLaughlin lifted it and held it up underneath its dam to nurse. When the teat touched its lips it opened its mouth and began to suck, and everyone watching smiled and relaxed.

When it had had enough, it was put down on the hay again and the veterinarian prepared to leave.

At this moment, a shadow at the door blocked out the sunlight. They turned to look and saw the Goblin standing there.

If Ken had seen someone returned from the dead he could hardly have felt a more violent shock. Over his whole body there poured a wave of heat, followed by such bliss that he could not see clearly.

Then Gus's voice exclaimed, "Yiminy Crickets! Luk at him! He's torn to pieces!" And Ken's eyes cleared and he saw the wounds and scabs on Goblin's white coat and rushed to him.

Goblin was startled and fled around the corral. He did not, however, go out of the open gate, but circled and came hesitatingly back.

McLaughlin reprimanded Ken sharply, then, himself, went quietly toward the colt, his eye running over him. "Steady, old boy! God! Look at that ear! That's a nice fellow—what a rip in the shoulder—"

"And there's a piece chewed out of his fanny!" said Howard.

"That colt's sure been in a fight," said the vet, eyeing the swollen shoulder wound. "That was done by a hoof, and a mighty big one. I'd better take a look at it while I'm here."

"Get a bucket of oats, Howard," said McLaughlin, "and Ken, bring the halter."

The Goblin was ravenous for the oats. They haltered him and McLaughlin and the vet examined his wounds.

"Look here," said Doc, "here are some other wounds that are nearly healed. He's been in two fights. Look at the mark of claws here on the other shoulder—might have been a wildcat—"

"And," said Howard excitedly, "look at the little scars all over the underside of his neck and belly—what did that?"

They were scattered snags, nearly healed. Doc was puzzled. He shook his head. "Might be wire snags," he said doubtfully.

Every time the Goblin lifted his nose out of the bucket he turned his head toward Nell. She smoothed his face, wondering if this ended all their future hopes. That shoulder wound looked deep. If it had reached the bones or tendons—

Rob voiced her thought. "This shoulder wound, Doc—will it hurt his speed?"

"I don't think so," said Doc. "It was a glancing blow."

"What gets me," said McLaughlin, "is how did he get in here? There's a four-strand barbed-wire fence between his pasture and the County Road."

Doc laughed as he pulled on his shirt. "My guess is, you've got a jumper."

"I've seen plenty of wooden fences in the east jumped." Rob shook his head. "But horses don't jump these wire fences. No—there must be some gates open somewhere up the line."

"Train him for a hunter," said Doc, "and send him east to a hunt club. You'd get a big price for him. He's a husky—how old is he? A long yearling?"

"A short yearling," said Ken proudly. "He was foaled last September."

"By Jinks!" said the vet. "He's a baby elephant."

"He's made a good beginning as a stallion," said McLaughlin dryly. "He'll carry these scars all his life."

"Gee! It must have been some fight!" exclaimed Howard excitedly. "Do you think he mixed it up with Banner, Dad? Banner's the only stallion around here."

"It might have been one of the other yearlings," said Nell. "They might have been fighting—"

"Not a hoof of that size," said Rob, indicating the shoulder wound. "It could only be Banner. If Goblin has started fighting Banner—but I can't understand Banner's giving him such punishment—the colt must have done something to deserve it."

It seemed to Ken that when the answers to prayers come they are apt to come overwhelmingly. For after supper that night Howard made a mysterious face, asked him to come upstairs to his room, and, up there, opened his top drawer and took a little box from it and gave it to Ken.

"Open it," he beamed.

Ken opened it. There lay his stop watch with a new crystal replacing the broken one.

"And it's got a new mainspring," said Howard, capering around the room in delight. "It's as good as new. You'll want it now, because you've got the Goblin back and we can run him and time him!"

Ken was speechless. "Gee, Howard! Thanks ever so much. But Dad said it was yours—"

Howard danced at him with his fists up. Now that he was getting muscles like Hercules' he was always flexing his arms and wanting to fight. "That's all right—I'm giving it to you—" He punctuated his words with little jabs at Ken's chest. "I'm the oldest, you know, and older brothers give things to their younger brothers"—*Ping*— Ken put up his fists. "We'll have it—kind of, together— we'll have a lot of fun with it—"

They exchanged a flurry of punches, the boxing changed to wrestling, and the boys rolled on the floor.

But Ken didn't have the colt for long. He had been put into the Home Pasture, to be close at hand in case his wounds needed tending. Flicka and her filly were put there too as soon as the little foal could run at her mother's side. There sprang up between Goblin and his little sister one of those strange attachments that exist between horses. When he was near, she must leave her dam's side and wander to him. He would stand, his high head curved and bent to her. She would reach up her little muzzle to touch his face and neck.

The boys carried oats to them morning and evening. One morning the Goblin was not there. Rob examined all the fences. "I'm beginning to think Doc must have been right, and that he can jump these fences," he said frowning. "Unless he rolled under that place on the south side where there's a little hollow."

The boys saddled up and rode out to hunt for him. He was not with the yearlings, nor brood mares, nor the two-year-olds. He was nowhere to be seen.

This time Ken was not so unhappy. The colt had come back once—he probably would again. The new fortitude was sufficient for this strain upon it, although when he was ready to say his prayers that night, it did cross his mind to ask the Almighty if He thought it was quite fair to be an Indian giver? He suppressed this impulse as being not entirely respectful and, possibly, prejudicial to future favors.

The little filly grew and thrived. Her hoofs and bones hardened. She came to know the family, the dogs, the cats, and to be interested in all their comings and goings. In the early mornings she would stand sunning herself. At sunset, when foals love to play, she raced on the Green and flung her little body about and frisked her heels. Before long, she could make a little thunder on the ground as she ran.

Nell named her Touch And Go.

Rob McLaughlin was crazy about her. She meant something to him—the justification of his theory of line-breeding. His eyes were very keen and blue and narrow as he looked at her.

"Now there's a little filly that's got points!" he said. "Look at those perfect legs!"

He began to feed her oats almost from the start. He

would let her mouth a few grains at a time. With plentiful feeding she would overcome the handicap of her premature birth—she had it in her. What she had in her would come out. They halter-broke and handled her early without any trouble at all.

"I always had a hunch that if Flicka was bred back to Banner I'd get something out of the ordinary."

They were sitting on the terrace after supper, Flicka and the filly near the fountain in the center of the Green. Suddenly they heard the thunder of hoofs from below in the Calf Pasture and saw, rounding the shoulder of the hill, the Goblin coming at a canter. Rob rose to his feet, astonished—how could the colt have got into the Calf Pasture?

In a moment they all knew. There was a four-strand barbed wire fence between the Green and the Calf Pasture. Goblin cantered easily up to it—swerved to aim at the gate post, and cleared it easily. He came cantering to Flicka and the filly, neighing a greeting.

"Well I'm damned," said Rob, then put his pipe back slowly into his mouth. "If he's started fighting Banner and jumping all the fences, there's going to be hell to pay from now on. This means he can come and go as he pleases."

The boys rushed down to the Green chattering excitedly.

Nell followed them with Rob.

Goblin and his little sister were in an ecstasy of reunion.

"He's kissing her!" shouted Ken. "Look Mother! Look at Goblin!"

"It's simply ridiculous to call him Goblin," said Nell. "That's not a Goblin. That's Thunderhead."

There was a moment's silence. Ken felt his mother's words go right through him. It had come at last— The white foal seemed inches taller. He had grown in all his parts so that he had still that appearance of maturity and strange precocity—like a boy carrying a man's responsibility.

Nell looked up at her husband. "Don't you see, Rob? He's completely changed. He's been changed ever since he was lost the first time, when he got those awful cuts."

"How do you mean—changed?" demanded Howard.

"Well—sort of grown-up. More dignified. Something has come into him that was never there before, and it's ironed out a lot of his awkwardness and meanness. We must call him by his right name from now on—he deserves it."

"The Goblin is dead—long live Thunderhead," shouted Howard.

Ken got a bucket of oats and fed the wanderer. Then Flicka. Then offered the bucket to the tiny filly. She jabbed her inquisitive little nose into it, took it out with a few grains sticking to it and jumped away, mouthing them, tossing her head up and down.

"Dad," said Ken, "where does he go when he goes off —Thunderhead, I mean?" Ken almost blushed with embarrassment when he gave his colt the great title.

"I wish I knew," said Rob slowly. "And that jumping of wire fences—he's had no training—he's inherited that— straight from the Albino. He's an absolute throwback. That fellow was a great jumper. No fence could hold him."

When it drew darker they put the three horses down into the Calf Pasture.

"Not that it will do much good," said Rob dryly. "That bronc'll come and go as he pleases."

They sat on the terrace again for a while in the dark. Across the Green two hoot owls were calling to each other.

Rob said at last thoughtfully, "Well—Thunderhead can jump. Thunderhead can buck. Thunderhead can fight. But none of these accomplishments are important to a racer. It remains to be seen if Thunderhead can run."

17

Thunderhead could run, but another year passed before they knew it for certain. The boys had come home from school for their summer vacation again, and the colt, being now a two-year-old, was started on a course of intensive training.

He had had his freedom all winter. There had been times when, Rob and Nell knew, he was nowhere on the Goose Bar Ranch. He went south—that much had been discovered. He stayed away awhile. He came back. But now that Ken was home and had begun training him in earnest, he was to be kept in all summer. No more gallivanting.

Ken worked with the colt for a fortnight. He went through the drill with halter, grooming, blanketing all over again. He rode him bareback, then with saddle. He rode him in the corral, neck-reining him, doing figure eights, making him back and advance, stand. Seldom was a day that he was not bucked off. He finally took him out of the corral and struggled with him in the open. The colt wheeled, lunged, balked—galloped a little, then fought and backed and refused—refused—then bucked. Ken remounted him and the fight began again.

Thunderhead didn't like his master. Often he seemed animated by a definite spirit of hatred. He galloped at a big tree and tried to scrape the boy off. Ken yanked his head around just in time. Then Thunderhead learned how to take the bit in his teeth and run away. It was a rough, fighting gallop, with the weight of the horse's head so heavy in Ken's hands that he was racked to pieces.

Late one afternoon, after an hour of such struggling, a fury came into Ken and he began to lash Thunderhead with his crop. He lashed him until he was exhausted. With his other hand he held the reins and forced the horse this way and that. With his heels he spurred him. Tears of weakness and rage stood in his eyes.

Suddenly Thunderhead had the impulse to obey. Generations of breeding had put a knowledge into him of the horse's part of horsemanship, a realization that obedience to a skilled rider makes one out of the two, makes teamwork out of the ride, something almost like a dance, a performance that a horse cannot achieve alone. He leaned his mouth against the feather lightness of Ken's hands, and, obedient to them, exercised skills that he had never exercised before. There was grace to his movement now, grace and control and technique. There was joy in it. He stopped fighting the bit. As if he had learned all that Ken had been trying to teach him, or had known it all along, he swung right or left at the least touch of the rein on his neck or the lean of his rider's body. His steps were pliant, prancing. He delighted in the quick, easy turns, in responding to the hands that lifted him into a longer and longer stride.

When Thunderhead achieved obedience, he enlarged himself. The skill and the will of another being were added to his own skill and will. He was having a new experience and it ran through his body like quicksilver. He loved Nell, but nobody had fought him and warred with him and lashed him and taught him obedience but Ken.

At last Ken let him out fully and urged him with voice and hands and heels.

Thunderhead began to run. His hoofs reached forward and seized the ground with a slashing cut that barely touched and rebounded.

A feeling of extraordinary ease went through Ken. No effort was needed, there was no more struggling, he and

the colt were one at last. The fight was over and now—
this!

Mastery! Underneath him was something of such strength and power as he had never dreamed of. It surged into him. It was his own. A clump of rocks was ahead of them. Ken did not swerve—the least tightening of his knees, lift of his hands—and the stallion sailed over, hardly altering his stride. The fence over there by the road! *Take it, Thunderhead,* and the long soaring leap—the light landing—

Everything seemed different to Ken. He looked around. He saw, felt, apprehended as he never had before, as if he had been let into a secret world that no one else knew anything about. The wind whipped his cheeks and filled his mouth and beat upon his eyeballs and whistled in his ears. The pace! The incredible speed! The strange floating gait! Those long reaching strides seemed almost slow, like the overhand strokes of a swimmer. Then the lightning-quick slash at the ground, and again the rush through the air. No obstacles could stop him. There were none. They floated over them.

The world rolled out from under the stallion's hoofs. They were covering ground Ken had never seen before. He made no effort to guide him. They were on the mountains—they were in the sky— Clouds, trees, earth, streamed past. A group of antelopes! He saw their frightened leaps—their startled faces—they were gone! Ken's consciousness was fused with all that there was in the world. He had gathered it in. He was the pulse-beat. He was the kernel. *This is it*.

He sat at the supper table that night in a dream, unable to speak or eat.

He wondered if Thunderhead would ever do it again. When he had dismounted and unsaddled the colt and had stood looking into his face—looking into the future, his hands trembling because he knew, now, beyond all doubt, what the horse could do—he saw that Thunderhead still hated him. The dark, white-ringed eye looked at him sideways, viciously.

"How did the colt go today, Ken?"

"He went—better, Dad."

"Did you get him to go forward under the saddle?"

"Yes, sir."

"Did you get him running?"

"Sort of—"

Rob McLaughlin looked searchingly at his son. He asked no more.

18

It was a warm August evening. Rob was driving to a ranch southwest of his own to inspect a mare. He had been told she was a registered thoroughbred, had been a racer, and was for sale cheap. The number of his own brood mares was down to sixteen. They were getting old. He had lost four in the last two years, and two more must be sold before fall because they would not live through another winter on the range. Colorado farmers who kept a few horses stabled through the winter might buy them for the sake of the foals they would drop in the spring. They would bring very little at auction but anything would be better than feeding them to the coyotes on the Saddle Back.

Nell was driving with him. They were on one of the back roads, not much more than wheel tracks on the prairie grass. It was at just that moment of the evening when headlights are of no use and daylight is not enough. The car swept ahead so swiftly, and at times so roughly, that Nell was about to protest, but one look at Rob's face stopped her. He had his angry driving look.

Nell withdrew a little into her own corner and sighed. It might have been a pleasant evening. She always enjoyed a drive at the end of the day when her work was done, but if he was going to be like this—

"Gypsy hasn't long to go either," said Rob abruptly. "At this rate, my band of brood mares will soon be cut in half."

"Couldn't you put some of the younger mares in the brood mare bunch?" asked Nell. "There are those three five-year-olds—the sorrels—they're wonderful mares."

"To be bred back to their own sire?"

"That's line-breeding, isn't it? You're always talking about it."

"But you can't do it indiscriminately. They have to be picked individuals. There isn't one of those mares good enough."

"What'll you do for brood mares then, Rob?"

"Buy some more, I suppose, the way I bought all the others. Travel around to the race tracks—pick up mares of good blood that can't race any more."

Nell had a sinking sensation. Those buying trips that he took every three or four years cost upwards of a thousand dollars.

"Or else buy a new stallion," said Rob, "so that I can use my own young mares. That might be the best way."

"A new purebred stallion!" exclaimed Nell. "Oh, Rob! Why couldn't we just keep one of our own young stallions—not geld him?"

"That's the way to start your horses on the downgrade," said Rob coldly.

What difference does it make! The words were on the tip of Nell's tongue, but, for the hundredth time, she held them back, Rob must be thinking the same thing— he must know that *she* was thinking it, but to say it would be like giving the little tap which would bring down the house of cards.

147

"Or," she suggested, "you could get a Government stallion. That wouldn't cost anything."

"Do you suppose I could turn a Government stud loose on the range to take care of the band the way Banner does? You can't get a stallion from the Government unless you guarantee to keep him in. His mares must be corral bred. He must be fed oats the year around. That's what they are used to and they can't live any other way."

Nell made no answer. Rob wanted to fight. He didn't want to see a way out or to make any compromise. She changed the subject.

"Rob—this horse I'm riding this summer, Cheyenne, I'm tired of him. He doesn't really give me a good ride. He's dull. And as far as his training goes, I've finished him. I don't want to ride him any more."

"That's *fine*," said Rob.

Now, what does he mean by that? thought Nell. Aloud she said, "I'd like another horse."

"Who would you like?" asked Rob with elaborate politeness.

"I was thinking I might take one of those you've been training for the Army sale. How about Injun? Do you think he'd do anything to me?"

"If you're going to ride Injun you'd better get wings," said Rob, with a charge of his best sarcasm. "But go on and ride him if you want to. Suit yourself."

"Well, *that's* nice!" Nell muttered.

A few moments later Rob leaned toward her. "What did you say?"

"Nothing." She withdrew farther into her corner and again the heavy silence wrapped them about. Strange, she thought, that two people could be so near each other, physically, and yet so divided that they could hardly exchange a thought.

The car plunged down a slope, ran through a creek, curved up the other side and came out on the level again.

The day was nearly done. Nell saw a flight of wild ducks against the evening sky. Sitting at Rob's right, she had the sunset at her window. The wind was from the

148

southwest, the prevailing fair-weather wind that blows steadily over the United States.

"Is the wind getting stronger?"

"No. It's just that we're coming out to where there's nothing to interrupt it. No shelter of any sort. It's got a two hundred mile sweep here. Ungodly place to live."

Presently, on a sudden impulse, Nell put her hand on Rob's thigh. She gave it two or three little affectionate pats. Often they rode for hours so. Often he would say, Where's your little hand? And she would put it there. But tonight that muscular leg under the whipcord breeches felt like a stone. She withdrew her hand.

"Rob, I've been thinking about Thunderhead. Ken is so awfully happy about him now—the speed he's developed. Do you think it's absolutely necessary to geld him?"

"He's a two-year-old," said Rob harshly. "All the other twos are to be gelded, why shouldn't he be?"

"Ken is simply having a fit about it," said Nell.

"Ken is a pain in the neck."

"Besides," said Nell, "he's not really two yet—just twenty-two months."

Rob explained, with weary patience as if to a child of subnormal intelligence, "We wait until they are two to geld them in order to give their necks time to develop. But Thunderhead's neck is already developed like a three-year-old's. He could have been gelded six months ago."

Nell's cheeks burned. When Rob talked to her like that she turned completely from him and fled away in spirit. She laid her arm along the open window and rested her head against it. She floated out on that westerly wind— she drifted on the shadowy plains.

It was getting darker, Rob put on the headlights. A half-hour passed during which a panorama of heavenly beauty composed itself as softly as a dream before Nell's rapt eyes. It was a sunset of blue and silver. The light had gone away from the earth, leaving a sea of darkness beneath a sky as blue as turquoise. The eyes, straining to discover at what far-distant point that dark earth met the jeweled light of the sky, were lost in mystery. That was not all. There was a mile-long, torpedo-shaped lake of quicksilver some distance above the horizon, its edges as finely turned as if blown in glass, and below it, thrusting up from behind the earth, the tops of thunderheads, burning white, like great alabaster lamps lit from within.

Must it wane, that scene of impossible beauty? Must it disappear? From moment to moment it was changeless before her eyes as if it had been created for her alone and her gaze sustained it. Perhaps no one else in the world was looking at it. The whole breadth and depth of creative power manifesting itself in flawless artistry for her delight— But yes. It was changing. The imperceptible altering and fading and flaring up and waning was incessant, like the movement of the earth rolling in space, all the stars rolling, the universe rolling, turning one face, then the other . . . it is . . . it is not . . . The sunset dawned, burned, died at the slow swing of a gigantic, omnipotent arm. What were those lines from St. Augustine's *Confessions*—something about the beauty of the elements proclaiming God. . . .

"In another week or so you can ride Injun if you want. I'll give him a good work-out every day."

Nell did not answer. Rob glanced at her. On her face, lying against the window frame, was the silver of the sunset. Her bang was ruffled and blown back; her eyes, pools of shadow.

"Did you hear me?" he asked harshly.

"Yes. About Injun. It doesn't matter."

Rob's voice rose. "You said you wanted him, didn't you? What's the matter now? Have you changed your mind?"

Nell sat up suddenly. She was quivering all over. "Don't shout at me!" But her face was still turned away and the wind took her words.

"What?"

"Nothing."

"What did you say?"

Burning words rose to her lips. She could shout as well as he. But if she did, then in a moment they would both be at it, and there would be one of those unspeakable interchanges resembling the snarling of cats and dogs. The quarrel would blow over, but those words would send their echoes down the years and never be forgotten. *I hate you. You're a brute. I wish I'd never seen you.*

Nell shivered in her thin dress of poppy-printed silk. "I'm cold," she said.

Rob brought the car to a jarring stop. "Where's your coat?"

"In the back."

Every elaborate, leisurely motion he made as he got her gray reefer, invited her out and held it for her, made her feel she was holding up the procession.

They got in the car again and went on. All evening a moon had been sailing high in the heavens. Now, with the darkness, it began to glow.

Presently, off to the right, they saw something suggesting a house. A little branch road led toward it. "This must be it," said Rob doubtfully. He brought the car to a stop in front of a huddle of walls, fences, corrals.

"It must be," muttered Rob again, staring. Nell stared too. The moonlight made of the place a crazy silhouette.

Rob got out, and went toward the house.

Nell continued to stare. Here it was. The decrepit buildings, one shed tacked like an afterthought on to the side of another. Fences made of wire, palings, ties, or poles, pieced together, fallen in places, begun, abandoned, begun again somewhere else. The house, with a single dim eye looking out, was a haphazard collection of boards, shakes, boxes, building paper, sheets of tin, not one line on the square. Here it was. The horror of her childhood seen from the Pullman car windows, the carefully built and stubbornly cherished house of human despair, ceaselessly pounded by the wind that kept every fence corner filled with tumbleweeds, broken shingles, newspapers and rubbish. Here it was.

A thoroughbred mare!

151

Nell saw the figures of her husband and a tall bent man coming from the house. The man carried a lantern. They went to the pile of sheds off across the yard and disappeared from view.

Nell sat there in the car in so deep a depression that when she heard a voice by her window it startled her. It was a cultured voice, the grammar perfect, the accent almost English. "Wouldn't you like to come in and wait until our husbands have finished their business?"

An old woman was standing beside the car, her thin gray hair, which had pulled loose from the little knob at the back, whipped by the wind. It was a face often seen on marginal farms and ranches deep in the country. A face of character and refinement—the beak of a nose just a bladelike bone covered with skin, the long hanging jaw, the small shiny false teeth, the walnut-colored skin quilted with deep lines, and in the sunken colorless eyes, the look of endurance that had begun ages ago—and would never end.

The patient voice repeated its question.

"Oh, thanks very much!" exclaimed Nell. "I think I'll just wait here—or—could I go to the stables? I'd like to see the mare too."

"I'll show you the way," said the old woman courteously.

They picked their way between weeds, clods of dirt, upturned kerosene cans, farm tools, rolls of wire, to the yard before the barn and went in.

There was the mare. The man had led her by a rope halter into the foreground and Rob was looking her over.

Oh, why! Why! Why does he even look at her? The poor thing! Why does he give them any hope at all?

The fine long legs of the mare seemed barely able to support her. There was a sway in her back. The aristocratic head hung lifelessly, she did not even turn it to look at them. There was a deep collar groove at the base of her neck.

"You use her for ploughing?" asked Rob.

152

"Yes. She can do as good a day's work as any horse you could find."

Nell looked at the man, trying to decide who it was he reminded her of. It was Uncle Sam. There was even something of the same cocky jauntiness. He *would* be like that, Nell thought, to have got himself and his old wife into such a place as this to end their days in.

She held out her hand to him. "I'm Mrs. McLaughlin."

"How-do, Mrs. McLaughlin." Nell noticed that his voice too was educated.

"I—er—I—er—" stammered Rob, who was bad at names, "I beg your pardon, but I've forgotten your name—"

"My name's Kittridge," said the man, grasping Nell's hand and shaking it warmly. "Thomas Jefferson Kittridge."

Rob looked up and his teeth flashed in a smile. His dark face was startlingly handsome lit by the soft glow of the lantern. Nell noticed that the old woman was staring at him with her mouth open.

"Any relation?" asked Rob.

"Yes indeed. I'm on the female side. My grandfather came from Virginia to Oklahoma, and my father—he had a big family—moved on out here. I had a big ranch once, but things went against us a bit."

"And the boys grew up and went away," interpolated the deep uncomplaining voice of the woman.

"Boys!" exclaimed Nell. "How many?"

"Two. One died. The other works in the city. Pittsburgh."

"So I got a smaller place and tried my hand at dry-farming," said the man. "This mare—she's done all my work for years."

"I don't need a work horse," said Rob. "I was interested in a brood mare."

"Well she's a registered thoroughbred," said the man with an attempt at boastfulness. "She'd have a fine colt. I can show you her papers."

153

"I'm sorry—she'd be too old for me. I'm afraid she wouldn't get through a single winter out on my ranch."

As they walked back to the car the old man was still leading the mare.

Nell said gently, "Besides, you must need her for your work, don't you?"

"No. We're turkey-raising now."

"Do you find it profitable?"

"Oh, pretty good, pretty good, when the coyotes don't get them. It's work we can do. Ma, here, herds them for a spell, then I herd them. I could do without the mare."

Rob and Nell got into the car. The woman still stood at the window, her hands clutching the edge of it, her eyes peering at Nell. At last she smiled. "You're awful pretty —too pretty to be living out here. Have you got any children?"

"Yes, I have two boys."

"How old?"

"Sixteen and fourteen."

"You don't look old enough to have such big boys." The woman smiled again—a strangely sweet, childlike smile.

Nell smiled back at her with a choke in her throat.

Mrs. Kittridge stood away from the car. "Well—it's a pretty night, isn't it?" She looked around vaguely. "There was a beautiful sunset."

"Did you see that sunset?"

"Yes. I went out and sat on the back porch and watched it for a long time."

Nell reached her hand out of the window and they clasped hands. "I was watching it too."

Rob started the engine.

"Then you don't think you could use the mare?" asked Kittridge.

"I'm afraid not." The car was moving. "Thanks very much for giving me a look at her."

Nell leaned out, calling a last good-by. The three of them were standing in a row, the old woman's hand clasping her husband's, the mare at his shoulder. In the moonlight they made an odd silhouette. As the car drew away the wind and the plains and the night closed over them.

The ruthless joy one feels when one contrasts one's lot with others and realizes one is better off, the shame that one should be so crudely exultant, and the compassionate wish that there might be a cornucopia pouring out plenty for all—these three strong emotions surged within Nell on the drive home.

There was one other. It was fear. Because, after all, it could happen to anyone—it could happen to them—At this thought she experienced one of those inner tremors that left her physically weak. A sort of spiritual sinking spell. Panic always followed, and the terrible details of destitution, like grimacing pictures, flashed before her eyes. Her slim brown hands clenched in her lap and she leaned back stiffly.

She heard Rob say, "That really was a thoroughbred. I hated to leave her there."

"Rob," said Nell, opening her eyes, "wasn't that awful?"

"Terrible."

"Oh, Rob, let's *us* never—"

He turned on her in sharp anger. "Now there you go! Putting yourself in other people's shoes! Are you imagining that *we* could ever come to that? Forget it! Not people of intelligence, and some—some *sense*—some start in life—some advantages—"

"But *they* had all that! It's no use having sense if you don't *use* it. There might have been a turning point for them—way back—they didn't use good judgment."

"They didn't have any—or they wouldn't be there."

Rob's flat, violent tone of voice served notice on her that he didn't want to hear any more of *that*. She closed her lips tight but the seething thoughts went on behind them. They themselves were heading into financial disaster just as fast as they could gallop. It was this fall that Howard was to go east to Bostwick's Preparatory School, and the tuition was twelve hundred dollars and half of it had to be paid in advance. Where was that money going to come from? And the money for his outfit and traveling expenses? She hadn't dared ask Rob. There would have to be eight hundred dollars by September the tenth. Perhaps there wouldn't be. At the thought of abandoning their plans for the boys' education her hand began to tap nervously on her knee. No. Anything but that. It would only be two years at Bostwick's and then into West Point and no more expense. A way *must* be found. But that wasn't all. What about their own expenses for the coming year? They would need two thousand dollars to live on, and there was a thousand dollars of unpaid bills—hardware, veterinary, elevator, machine repair shop—and that five thousand dollar note to be paid in October—it *had* to be paid. Last year the man had extended it for a year and said that was the last time.

She sat nervously upright. "Rob—is Bellamy going to take the lease for the sheep again this fall?"

"I don't know. Haven't asked him yet. But I suppose he will. Why?" The last word was shot at her belligerently.

"Well—I was just wondering. The lease money—that fifteen hundred dollars—it means a good deal to us."

Rob playfully grabbed her by the head with his free hand and shook her. "Now you're worrying about money. Don't bother your little head about that. I'll attend to it."

"Ouch!" said Nell, catching at her head. "You hurt." She rearranged her hair, and returned to her thoughts. Rob, of course, would never see or think what he didn't want to. But suppose he were different? Suppose he were openminded and reasonable—what ought they to do? What did people do when they had spent half their lives doing something that was, apparently, going to bring them to the poorhouse if continued? They did not fling good years after bad. They changed. They took another road. But Rob? It was as if he were hypnotized—as if he *could* not turn or change. He wouldn't even discuss it. Suddenly she felt angry. Here they were partners in the greatest possible enterprise—family life—and she must suffer the consequences of failure as well as he, yet he would never allow discussions on unpleasant themes. He would shout at her, browbeat her, create such friction and unpleasantness that she could not bear it— It wasn't fair.

Rob took the road out onto the highway and pulled up at the Tie Siding Post Office. He went in for the mail and came out carrying a small box, about the size that holds a dozen eggs.

"Will you hold this?" he said to Nell, putting it gently on her lap.

"What is it?" she asked. "Oh, it's chicks! I hear them cheeping."

"Yes. I ordered them for that old hen that's going to kill herself setting if we don't break her up."

As the car started off again, Nell held the box to her ear and listened to the tiny, eager cheeps. How would they take to their new mother? She was an old hen who laid no eggs—no right to have a family, really—fit only for the stew-pot, but Rob had said, No, see if she will take some chicks.

The car was turning in at the ranch road. As Nell felt the warm comfort of home-coming, again came the fear. "Rob," she said with desperate courage, "don't you ever think of giving up the horses and doing something else?"

"What?"

"Well—you graduated from West Point as an engineer."

"You mean—give up everything? Sell the ranch?"

"Yes."

There was a long silence before he said slowly, "I've often wondered if you weren't sick of the life out here—if it wasn't too hard for you."

"It isn't that." She clasped her hands together. "It's not that at all. This is my home. I love it. I'd like it to be easier, with more help, and a furnace, and money enough for us to go away for two or three months in the middle of the winter, but it would break my heart to lose it."

"Are you sure of that?"

"Yes."

He looked into her eyes and saw there the bleak dread

of the woman who contemplates the loss of her home. "Then why did you say what you did?"

"Just the money. The situation we're in. A Government loan on the ranch—this other note besides—we're so at their mercy—they could close us out any time. And then there's the education of the boys—Howard and Ken both. We can't be sure they'll make West Point. And ourselves—our future—we're not getting any younger."

"The money," repeated Rob slowly. "What do you think I would get if I sold out my horses at present prices? Not a third of what I put into them. Not a quarter. And it would be the same with the ranch. I'd just have to *give* it away."

"What would it matter? You'd get enough to keep us all until you got doing something else—engineering—or some business—"

Rob began to shout. "What would it matter? It would matter like hell! I'm not an engineer any more—or a business man. I came west—and you came with me—*just to raise horses!*"

"What if you did! That was long ago. The thing you want to do now is not raise horses or any other special thing! Just to make a living and pay our bills!"

Rob continued as if she had not spoken "—raise horses because I was sure that up here in this high altitude, in a section of lime country, the finest horses could be raised, with strong lungs and hearts and endurance—as sure-footed as goats—that's what you need for polo—and I was right. I've proved—" the tirade continued, battering down all Nell's attempts to answer. At last she made no more, but sat silently waiting to get home.

Rob calmed down and spoke more quietly. "Nell—you can't give up your business just because you have some bad years. It's all a question of markets. Markets are bad for some years, then they change around and they're good. I would look like a fine fool, wouldn't I, if I sold everything I've got for a song, and then polo picked up—as it's bound to sooner or later—and horses began to sell for good prices. How would we feel then?"

Nell was disheartened and confused. It hadn't been for just a few years. It had been since the very beginning.

Approaching the house she glanced at the windows. The lights were on downstairs. Upstairs, no light in the boys' rooms—asleep. Rob parked the car and they got out, Nell still carrying the chicks.

"Come up with me to the stable, will you?" asked Rob, "and help me with the hen."

"Suppose she doesn't want to take them?" asked Nell anxiously, and could have bitten her tongue out the next moment.

Rob shouted, "I'll eat them! One by one! Feathers and all! Twenty-five of them!" Scalding tears burned in Nell's eyes as quickly as a welt is raised by a lash. Rob got his electric lantern out of the car, turned it on, and threw a beam of light on the ground before Nell's feet as they went up to the stable.

He had put the yellow hen in the tackroom. She sat there in her open-topped box, an enormous, stubborn, broody hen, burning with the fever of her longing.

Rob held the lantern while Nell opened the box of chicks. Her hands were trembling. Their little cheeps went up in the dark of the tackroom, and the hen lifted her head, which had been buried sulkily in her feathers, and turned it, cocking an eye this way and that—listening.

The chicks were huddled in one corner of their little box.

"Did you say twenty-five, Rob? There can't be twenty-five here."

"There are. You'll see." Rob's big hand came into the box, took a handful of the chicks and put them down before the hen. They balanced themselves unsteadily, teetering on their tiny yellow feet. The hen's head darted suddenly at one then at another.

"She's pecking them, Rob."

He hastily placed more of the chicks in the hen's box and then more, until they were all there. They looked like a fluffy yellow ruffle around the bulk of the old hen.

She had pulled her head back into her feathers again. Rob turned the light away from her so that she could be alone in the darkness for her stupendous decision. When they looked again they saw the hen making suave, graceful, expert motions with her head and neck, curling it this way and that, under one wing, under the other, underneath her body. A soft murmurous clucking accompanied her motions.

"She's taking them and tucking them in," said Rob in a low voice. They turned the light away again and waited. When next they looked there were no chickens to be seen, just the hen very large and full, head motionless in profound contemplation. One tiny chick's head stuck out like a button at the joint of a wing.

Rob was talking in a quiet, wondering voice. "Isn't it the strangest thing? There she was, no eggs. No right to a family. But she sat and brooded and burned and suffered for a month—and if that isn't praying I don't know what is—and suddenly, without her doing anything at all, she gets her family. Big hands come down from above, she can't see where—they just come down with handfuls of chicks for her and set them down in the box all around her. Twenty-five of them. More than she could ever have got of her own."

A Bible verse sprang into Nell's mind. "Try me now . . . and I shall open the windows of Heaven and pour you out such a blessing that there shall not be room to hold it." Twenty-five chicks. Hardly had there been room for her to hold them. One tiny head out up on the top of her back like a button. Hardly room for that last little Benjamin.

Walking down to the house Nell kept thinking about the hen. How did she feel now with her feathers full of life? Did the little ones sometimes struggle and quarrel there, kick and scratch with their tiny yellow legs? Peck each other and flutter their wingfluffs all inside of the feathers of the old yellow hen—a world of hidden life there—

160

Half way down to the house Rob suddenly stopped walking. "I can see that I've been awfully dumb," he said.

"What do you mean?"

"I've always thought that you were *with me*."

"With you?"

"In everything I did. The ranch, my work, the horses, my plans—everything."

"But Rob—of course I—"

"You *used* to be," he interrupted. "I don't know when you changed. I've just been going along like a fool taking it for granted."

"Taking what for granted?"

"That you had confidence in me."

"You oughtn't to put it that way. Married people ought to talk things over with each other and you never will. It isn't that I haven't confidence in you—"

"But you haven't. That is, you have no confidence in my ever making a go of the horses. *I* know I will if I hang on. I'll force it to succeed. You used to know it too. You were with me. But you don't know it any longer."

Nell was silent.

"Just exactly what would you like me to do?" he asked grimly.

"I—I—don't know—"

"That's just it. You don't know. You don't know anything about it. But while I'm doing all I can to make a go of it—lying awake nights planning how I can keep up or improve my horses and find the best markets, you're just sitting back waiting for the crash so that you can pick up the pieces."

"Oh, no, Rob—I—"

"Don't deny it, Nell. Don't lie. I know it." They were standing on the Green before the house, the moon so bright that now he switched off the flashlight and they were bathed in radiance. Two horses moved along the corral fence. It was Thunderhead and his little sister Touch And Go. She follows him everywhere, thought Nell, even as she was aware of the feeling of burning weakness flowing through her body. *I've done it now. I*

161

shouldn't have. It's his work—his responsibility—I should just back him up—always and always back him up—no, that wouldn't be sincere—wouldn't be fair—because then if a crash came, he'd have a right to say I should have warned him.

"I know it," continued Rob doggedly, "because for a long time now, everything you say and do and think is on the supposition that we will continue going down—poorer and poorer—"

"Well," she suddenly whispered, "we *are* on the downgrade, have been for years. You've said it yourself. You're the one who told me. You're the one who's worrying yourself sick about it. And we're not making any sort of change in our lives, in our plans, so why expect a change in the results?"

Rob stood facing her, feet apart, his dark head, so significant and arresting, dropped on his chest. The moonlight changed his ruddiness of skin to a greenish pallor.

Suddenly Nell held out her arms—nothing mattered—she went to him. He pushed her away. "Don't, Nell, I can't stand it."

She backed away, feeling humiliated. She might have known he didn't want comfort or coddling, he wanted his head up again—before her. But what could she do about that? While she stood, clasping her hands frantically together and fighting the tears that in a moment could be a flood, Rob walked away from her and disappeared.

In such moments of unendurable hurt, lovers run away from each other.

Nell walked down toward the corrals and stood against the fence. Presently she saw the horses approaching, Thunderhead and Touch And Go. He came to the fence, she spoke his name and held out her hand. He came close, she laid her hand on his face.

"Thunderhead—Thunderhead—" He felt her grief as horses always do, and shoved his nose against her. Touch And Go must do as her big brother did and pushed her nose up for petting too.

When Nell went in, half an hour later, she found Rob

162

sitting in his den, reading the paper, knees comfortably crossed and pipe in his mouth.

As she approached him, everything forgotten but the longing for closeness and understanding, he looked up at her. Her iris-colored eyes were dark with emotion. They were shadowed underneath, but they were full of gentleness and affection and her smile pleaded for reconciliation. Rob held out his hand to her. She leaned over to kiss him and he kissed her in return. Their eyes did not quite meet.

"Are you going up?" he asked.

"Yes."

"Don't wait for me. I'm going to read awhile."

She walked slowly upstairs. Eyes have to be honest, she thought. When you give a direct glance to a person you give something of yourself. When you cannot give, when you are hiding something, eyes cannot meet. They look past each other—unless you are hardened in deceit. She lit the lamps in their room and began to undress.

It was not finished yet, because he would come up, they would sleep in the same bed. It ought to be finished. They were both spent. Well—she would be asleep when he came up—she was exhausted—and he would not wake her. In the morning it would be easier.

As she undressed, her thoughts slipped back over the evening, the Kittridge ranch, the ghastly house, the mare, the quality of that old woman. Farther back—to the blue and silver sunset. At the thought of it, a deep breath filled her and her face relaxed in a smile of happiness. Where had she read that, against life's hurts, there are four panaceas—nature, religion, work, human fellowship—these helpers all around you ready to prop you up when you falter. No one need actually go down. But for her, human fellowship meant Rob and the boys, and it was just those three that she worried about. The thought of them was not calming—it was nature that helped her most. She had almost made a religion of that. You could find healing for your soul in that— She wondered why, as she brushed her hair until it lay in a soft mass on her

163

shoulders. Perhaps because you loved it. It was so beautiful, and alive, and it spoke to you. And whenever you have a feeling of love it makes you draw that long breath of peace. Even the old woman had been sitting on the back steps watching the blue and silver sunset. After all, nature—it was the classic mother.

Slipping into bed Nell picked up the small leather book on her bedside table and thumbed the pages through, looking for those words of St. Augustine's she had not been able to remember. Ah—here it was:

The Heavens, sun, moon, stars did answer, "We are not the God whom thou seekest." And I said, "Tell me of Him." And they cried out with a loud voice, "He made us!"

My love of them was my question. Their beauty was the answer.

With her knees drawn up and the book open upon them, Nell read it over and over, then laid it back on the table and blew out the lamp.

19

Next day Rob walked briskly up the Gorge toward the stables. The fact that he was in boots and whipcord breeches rather than bluejeans meant that there was riding ahead of him.

He had never lost the military carriage acquired as a cadet, nor the habit of meticulous grooming. His black hair was carefully trimmed, his head carried chin-up. His step had none of the drag of the farmer, nor the roll of the cowboy. It was the long, reaching tramp that covers the ground and takes possession of it—the typical West Point walk. And if, behind the keen, incessantly roving blue eyes was ever a thought or reverie detached from the process of observing the smallest detail of the physical universe around him and making quick deductions therefrom, it was well concealed.

Arriving at the corrals he was instantly aware of every animal that was within sight or earshot, how much the chickens had grown, what doors were open, what hinges or locks were hanging and in need of repair, whether or not any tools had been left lying on the ground.

Gypsy was in her stall and gave a little grunting whinny as her master emptied a can of oats into her feed box. While she ate, he currycombed and brushed her. "How do you like it, eh? Living the life of Riley like this —no more roughing it out on the range—no more runs with the herd—well, you deserve it, old girl—" He lifted her forelock and wiped her face carefully with a soft cloth. He looked at her teeth, worn down to smooth stubs. "Getting on, baby, aren't you? You and me both. Ain't what we used to be—" He began to hum "The Old Grey Mare" standing back to look at her.

The thoroughbred's head was turned to him, her fine ears sharply pricked, her neck curved. "Gypsy, my hat's off to you. You're still a fine-looking gal if you *are* a quarter of a century old—let's see, is that right?"

He slowly took pipe and tobacco from his pocket and filled it as he counted back to his last year at West Point. Gypsy had been five years old when he rode her in the polo game between Army and Willowbrook. That was three years before his marriage—four years before Howard was born. And Howard was sixteen now.

The facts smote him as if he had not known them. *Howard sixteen!* The boy had suddenly begun to shoot up, ankles and wrists out of all his shirts and pants. And just this morning at breakfast they had been in gales of laughter at the way his voice had slipped down now and then to a deep bass.

Sixteen. Howard was nearly grown-up. Almost a gen-

165

eration had passed since he had bought the ranch and brought Nell there, both of them so full of hope and confidence—and what had he accomplished? Those were the sixteen years which were to have established his success and made the future safe for all of them. But they were behind him now—not ahead, and neither success nor safety achieved.

That can happen—that a person comes to the end of a chapter and it does not contain those things it ought to. A whole generation—a large section of life gone by—just that section in which big things were to have been done —and they were not done. But he had never expected to have it happen *to him*.

He led the mare out, mounted her and rode into the Stable Pasture, thinking again of Howard. The boy was very bright, a good student, always got high marks. If he got the proper schooling—and at Bostwick's he would— he ought to make West Point in two years.

Bostwick's—and that reminded him of the eight hundred dollars he must somehow find before September tenth, and Bellamy, the sheep man.

What ever would he have done without the rent from the sheep? It hadn't seemed anything of importance, three years ago, when he leased grazing rights to Jim Bellamy for his band of fifteen hundred ewes—they hadn't interfered with the horses. They ate different grass. There had been enough for both. And the twenty-five tons of hay he sold Bellamy left plenty for the horses and cows—well, if not plenty, at least enough, though he had to be a bit tight with it. So, really, it hadn't put him out any or cost him anything to have the sheep on the place, and here he had come to count on the yearly rental of fifteen hundred dollars, paid promptly twice a year, as the easiest and surest revenue of the ranch. Just suppose he didn't have it—what about sending Howard to school then? What about—

His mind gathered up the various items of indebtedness that he and Nell had discussed the evening before. It wasn't pleasant figuring. It never was. He tried to guess at what his summer sales of horses would amount to but this gave him internal jitters. He had figured so often and been fooled. His sales never amounted to half—not to a third—of what he expected. His mind pursued a familiar groove. Should he sell off all his geldings that were over four years old at the Army sale in the fall? If he did, it would be quite some money, but still not half what the animals were worth for polo or hunting. Army paid one hundred eighty-five dollars a head, tops. It really wouldn't pay him back what they had cost him, counting everything. If he kept them, he might make a good sale here or there; but the horses were getting older all the time; their feed cost money; worst of all, they needed daily care and riding, otherwise they went half-wild again, and he hadn't men enough to do it.

The mare carried him easily. Taggert had a colt this year so he was riding Gypsy instead. Besides, he wanted Gypsy in the stable, sheltered and cared for and well fed. She must never have another foal—she was getting too old. He hated the thought of losing her, she had been part of him for so long. Even before Nell and the boys, Gypsy and he had been together. She was the link to those carefree cadet days. He and Gypsy had their beginnings together in the east. Perhaps, if it had not been for Gypsy and for the fact that he had been so crazy about her, he would not have abandoned his Army career and come west to raise horses. Gypsy was the first foundation mare of his band. And here she was, a quarter of a century old, and still stepping out with that long springing trot, still quick to answer his least word or movement, still eager to take him for a ride whenever he wanted to go.

Cantering along the ridge above Castle Rock meadow, he drew rein to overlook the meadow and calculate the hay crop. It had another month to grow, but it was thick and deep already. If it weren't for the many large flat rocks in that meadow, it would produce a hundred tons of hay. He got out his notebook and pencil and did a bit of figuring on the amount of surface those rocks stole from the hay—how much dynamite it would take to blast them out—how many days' work to drill holes for the dynamite and cart away the broken rock. There were also several little draws that ran down into the meadow where he never cut any hay. He fed it out. If he developed those draws, grubbed out the shrubs, blasted out the rocks, drained them, ran irrigation ditches along their sides and put dams up above, there would be many more tons of hay.

He put away his notebook and rode on. The hay was a sure income. The hay and the rent money for the sheep. The horses not sure at all. He ought to be doing everything to develop income from the ranch apart from the horses—dynamite those rocks. Develop those new meadows. But where was the time? The horses took it all.

Crossing Section Number Nineteen, he became aware that the sky was darkening. Looking up, he saw a mass of purple clouds rushing up from the horizon. There seemed several layers of them, moving in different directions. Some queer twisting of winds there, he thought, blowing in several directions at once. He cantered on. If it rained, what matter? He must see Bellamy and ask him if he could pay the first half of the lease money a month before it was due—on September the first instead of in October. That would take care of Howard's tuition.

The storm gathered. Rob cast a glance at the dark heavens and touched spur to his mare. They galloped faster. If he could reach Bellamy and his camp before the storm burst he would save himself a wetting. But suddenly he pulled rein. He felt as if he were in the very core of an electrical storm.

Above the ranch hung a canopy of royal purple. The great cloud seemed to be made of plush—as if one could thrust arms into it and feel the fabric. At its far edges tatters of it hung down in points. Lightning was playing through it.

Rob sat still on Gypsy, spellbound at the sight. As often as he had seen such spectacles on the ranch they still were awe-inspiring. A spear of lightning stabbed down to earth not far from him. Then another and another. The fence, some distance away, caught one of those spears and it ran along the wire in liquid flame. All around him the bolts of fire were falling.

Appalled at the danger he was in—he and the mare—and thinking of the pieces of metal in bridle and saddle, he dismounted quickly, stripped the mare, laid the stuff on the earth at a distance, and mounted Gypsy again with just a rope twisted around her nose.

He rode on toward Bellamy's camp. The cloud changed from purple to blue-black. There was first the rumble of thunder, then a crash, then, following the lightning bolts, ear-splitting cracks and explosions. They shattered the cloud. It opened and poured forth floods and there was no more lightning. All the electricity was carried off in the rain, and Rob remembered that he had read somewhere that lightning, when it strikes the earth, plants nitrogen there. That meadow he had been riding across must be rich with nitrogen then.

The storm ended as suddenly as it had begun. The sun came out and Rob's drenched shirt began to steam.

Presently he heard the sound of the sheep; the deep, stuttering ba-a-as of the ewes, and the bleating of the lambs, like children crying. Coming to the crest of the ridge, he saw the band spread out in the valley below him and drew rein a moment to look at them.

With one of those sudden impulses which animate all the lambs of a band at the same moment, the desire to nurse came upon them. They abandoned their pasture on the slopes of the valley and one and all, bleating like sick children, rushed for their mothers. The mothers appeared to share in this unreasonable sense of crisis. They looked up from their grazing and ba-a-aed frantically, running to meet the lambs. It was bedlam. When mother and child met—and it seemed miraculous that they could recognize each other—the lambs fell on their knees, thrust up their heads and nursed violently, butting, making gluttonous gurgling sounds.

Continuing on his way, Rob rounded a bend and saw

Bellamy at a distance. He was sitting on a rock, watching his sheep. Near him were two black shepherd dogs which set up a barking at sight of Rob, then ran to meet him.

Bellamy was a small man with a shy, bearded face. As he came to greet Rob, still wearing his loose white slicker, Rob thought, as he often had before, that he looked like an Arab.

Rob dismounted and sat down for a chat. Bellamy, starved for companionship and talk, rattled away at such a pace that Rob could hardly follow him.

Puffing contentedly at his pipe, Rob listened and watched the movements of the sheep below in the valley, estimating the value of the band—fifteen hundred ewes —at present prices, worth seventy-five hundred dollars. Quite a property.

Bellamy had acquired the foundation ewes of his herd in the days of the depression when sheep were being sold for a dollar or fifty cents a head, or were even being given away or turned loose on the prairies. No one had money to pay herders or taxes or to buy feed. For some years following that he had made a good salary herding, and had put it all into sheep.

The sheep were in fine condition. Rob ran his eye over the grass—plenty of sage on the hillside.

Pointing at it, he said, "Good grazing for sheep, isn't it?"

"Couldn't be nuthin' better," said Bellamy. "This ranch has got everythin'—shelter, feed, water—and that crik down there—" he pointed with his dirty hand in a northerly direction, "there's sompin in that water they likes. They goes nuts about it. Wen they gits a sniff of it they starts running—wen they gits to the water they piles on top'n each other to drink it."

"That's curious," said Rob. "Must be some mineral in it that they need. I'll have it analyzed some time."

Bellamy gave a sharp exclamation. He was staring across the valley. Suddenly, with a stream of profanity, he leaped up, grabbed his rifle and took careful aim.

Rob saw a disturbance among the sheep. There was the

crack of the rifle—then a slinking gray form ran out. Bellamy shot again. The coyote leaped in the air and fell dead.

The two men walked down to look at it, Bellamy talking excitedly of the number of coyotes he had shot that summer—of the half-dozen or so lambs he had lost.

He shoved at the gray corpse with his foot and pointed proudly to a round bleeding hole in the head. "Got 'im right in the noodle!"

The dead lamb lay near by. They carried both corpses up to the sheep wagon. Bellamy took out a sharp skinning knife.

"I'll help you if you've got another knife," said Rob.

They removed the pelts. Bellamy tossed the coyote to the dogs. "And this'll make stew for me," he said, pointing to the lamb. "I'll sell the pelts."

"By the way, Jim," said Rob, "I suppose you'll want another lease this fall?"

A light sprang into Bellamy's eyes. "No sirree!" he said proudly. "I'm a-gittin' a ranch of my own."

Rob pulled at his pipe in silence. It was amazing that he should experience such a sinking sensation just because he wasn't going to have this lease again.

"Have your own ranch, Jim—that's pretty nice. Have you bought already?" He laughed in a loud, kidding manner, "and if so—what did you use for money? When you came here, three years ago, you told me the ewes were the only thing you owned in the world."

He turned his head around to look at the man with eyes that were narrow blue slits in his dark face. His heavy jaw was thrust forward pugnaciously and his white teeth bit hard on the stem of his pipe.

Bellamy was eager to tell. "It's the sheep! I bin gittin' good prices these three years and, herdin' 'em myself, I got no overhead but what I pays to you, and the cotton-cake and corn I buys fer the sheep, an' a leetle extry help at lambin' time, and the shearin'—"

Rob figured slowly. "Well—you pay me fifteen hundred, and two hundred more for the twenty-five tons of hay I sell you—and how many tons of feed for the sheep? Three—about forty dollars a ton?"

Bellamy had it all figured out. "The corn an' cotton-cake last year costs me two hundred. An' oats fer my wagon team another fifty—"

"That's nearly two thousand already," said Rob.

"That's right. An' then some extry salt fer the sheep; my own grub; two extry men at lambin' time—call it another five hundred—and all the rest's profit!"

"*All the rest!*" Rob took a long pull at his pipe and blew the smoke out slowly while he figured. Bellamy's yearly expenses had come to a good twenty-five hundred dollars. "All the rest was profit, you say—"

Bellamy had a soiled piece of paper in his hand and a pencil and was excitedly jotting down figures. And what Rob got now was the other side of the account, the income. First the price of the wool—at twenty-three cents a pound minus the two and a half cents a pound to the shearers—the ewes averaging ten pounds of wool apiece —fifteen hundred ewes—that came to a little over three thousand dollars. And the lamb crop, at the end of the summer, even with deductions for losses and shipping and commissions—over four times that!

Rob rode away from the sheep camp so shaken with conflicting emotions that rational thought was an impossibility.

An income of over ten thousand dollars yearly! *That illiterate Bedouin! He can go out and make ten thousand dollars! I can work like a dog over my horses—and breed good ones—and not make enough to buy their oats! Oh, hell! What's the use! I suppose it's because I'm producing a luxury and he's producing a necessity. I might as well cut my throat. I must get my one-track mind from Ken. But sheep! Gha—ah! I'd rather raise rabbits!*

His legs tightened convulsively and Gypsy leaped forward. He rode furiously.

The sight of his saddle reposing on the turf pulled him up. He dismounted, saddled and bridled his mare and continued on his way.

172

His thoughts kept pace with him. "But it's luck too," he muttered. "That fellow has had the luck of the very devil. A lot of sheep men have gone bust. Here's Gaynor, up on the hill, scab got in his herd. He threw good money after bad—thirty thousand dollars he told me—until everything he had was gone. He wouldn't touch the sheep business again."

Gypsy felt the spur. "God damn it! There *is* such a thing as luck—some fellows have it—I haven't—never did. And—God! What shall I tell Nell?"

He rode into the corral, unsaddled and fed his mare, turned her out, and strode down to the house. He saw no one. As he entered the front door the emptiness of the house hit him. He was glad of it.

His clothes were still wet. He went upstairs, took a shower and put on flannels and a blue shirt. Looking at himself in the mirror as he brushed his hair he saw reddish spots on his face, almost like bruises. He was glad Nell wasn't there to see them.

He went downstairs, took a bottle and glass from the sideboard and carried it to his desk. Seated comfortably there, drinking his highball, he began to feel better. He poured himself another. Looking around, he saw a white envelope on the floor near the screen door and went to get it. An open safety pin was stuck in it—Nell's handwriting on it and his name. It had fallen from the screen door, no doubt. He opened and read it.

Hello darling!

Charley Sargent came over and, as you weren't here, the boys got him to go down to their track and see Thunderhead run. I'm going too. It's because Charley is racing some two-year-olds at the Saginaw Falls race tracks in Idaho this fall. If Thunderhead's good enough he might go too! If you get this note in time, come on down to the track and see the fun. Anyway, I'll bring Charley home to supper. Please put some coal in the

173

kitchen stove. I might be late. Here's hoping. Rah for Thunderhead!

Nell

Rob read this note several times and for some reason or other, found himself getting angrier. Ken and Thunderhead. Ken always creating a commotion. Nell and Charley down there, watching the colt run. They'd be sympathizing with Ken too in his grief about the fact that Thunderhead would have to be gelded with the other two-year-olds. *Well, that's one thing I won't give in on— not by a damned sight!*

He poured himself another drink and was surprised, when he looked at the bottle, to see how little whiskey was left.

He leaned comfortably back in his chair and tilted the glass to his lips.

Over the rim of it he saw Gus, through the window, driving the two black mares in the light wagon up to the stables.

While he finished the drink a little pattern was forming in his mind. Those two black mares—a fine, fast team. The race track. An audience. Some competition for Thunderhead. And suddenly all his depression vanished. He finished his drink at a gulp and jumped up—the chair went over as he did so—he went striding through the house, up to the stables, calling for Tim and Gus.

"No, don't turn the mares out, Gus! Give them some more oats and the best grooming they ever had in their lives! I want them to shine! Tim—gimme a hand with this trailer—I want to drag it down to the tool shop— bring that old wagon tongue—"

Working furiously, Rob and Tim attached the wagon tongue with a couple of bolts to the trailer hitch. Then Rob took the spring seat out of the wagon and set it across the trailer. Gus brought the mares and harnessed them in. Rob climbed into the seat, took the long whip from Tim, and said, "Giddap!"

The mares started forward. Startled at the lightness of the trailer, when they were accustomed to the wagon, they halted and turned their heads around questioningly. No weight to pull! No rattling and banging of the wagon! What was this anyhow?

Rob gave a yell and waved the whip. "Whoopee! Atta girls! Go to it!" His outstretched arms flapped the reins.

Patsy and Topsy leaped. The little trailer on its rubber wheels bounded after them.

Tim and Gus stood watching, with broad grins on their faces, while the odd-looking contraption whirled down the road and disappeared around the bend.

20

The "track" was a half-mile oval on the level range north of Lone Tree Creek, about two miles from the ranch house.

This had been selected by the boys immediately upon their arrival home from school this summer as Thunderhead's practice and trial ground. There was a natural grandstand to one side, a peak of craggy rock spearing up. They had outlined the oval track by setting posts at the curves. These posts—Thunderhead must understand— he was to run outside of, not in. Sometimes he did, sometimes he did not. Not that he did not understand! They had painted a broad band of white across the course at the finish, just in front of the grandstand and here Thunderhead had run many a mile, wondering, no doubt, where was the sense in it. Running to shelter in a storm —running away from enemies and dangerous places—

just even running with his own band for fun and exercise on the Saddle Back—this could be understood. But running on the flat range, often at top speed, around and around those posts, with a small demon yelling on top of him and another jumping up and down on the rock—this was incomprehensible.

The air was fresh after the storms, the range green and dustless. Nell was in white linen jodhpurs and white silk shirt with the sleeves rolled up on her slender brown arms. Her face was without care or worry, like a child's when a picnic is ahead. She sat beside Sargent in his car, pointing out to him the way to the track, for it could not be reached by any of the roads on the ranch.

In the back of the car was Howard with the bucket of oats. Just before they had started they had heard a yell, and Ken came running with a bucket half full of oats and a halter rope. His face showed embarrassment as he apologized for Thunderhead and stuck the bucket in the car. "Just in case—in case he got away or something—and I had trouble in getting him back."

"So," said Sargent, as they drove along, "he gets away, does he? And is hard to get back?"

"Aw—" said Howard, "he's pretty good. We haven't been training him very long, you know, just this summer."

"Sometimes," said Nell, "he runs clear off and doesn't come back for a long time. Look, Charley—you go down this slope here and through Lone Tree—that shallow place there." Charley slowed down to put the car through the creek.

"Where does the colt go?" he asked.

"That's what we'd all like to know," said Nell.

"He came back once with cuts and scratches," said Howard, leaning over the back of their seat. "And a terrible big wound in the chest. Dad said a stallion had pawed him."

"That's what I was just going to suggest," said Charlie grinning. "If he's leading a double life, you can depend on it, there's another band of horses somewhere around, and he's mixed it up with the stallion."

"But there isn't," said Howard, shaking his head. "There isn't any stallion except Doggie."

"Who's Doggie?" inquired Charley.

"He belongs to Barney—a rancher up west. We named him Doggie. He's nothing of a stallion—just an old work horse."

"Is he a Percheron?"

"He's not anything. Just a mixture—kind of buckskin. Dad says he thinks he must have some mule in him. He's not big or strong, and he's so old he's just about falling apart. Why, when Thunderhead was a baby, he could have licked Doggie with one hand tied behind him. We rode Thunderhead up there once to see if they would act like enemies, but Thunderhead just went up to him and smelled him all over, and Doggie stood there, kind of cringing and turning his head to watch him, and they didn't even squeal or rear."

Arrived at the track they got out of the car and showed Sargent the way it had been laid out.

After some time Ken arrived on Thunderhead, with Touch And Go running free behind him.

"Two of them," exclaimed Charley. "Did he bring a pace-maker? But that's just a yearling!"

Ken cantered up and dismounted, his face shining with excitement and the fierce scrubbing he had given it. His hair was slicked under the small jockey cap. His pink shirt was clean. The cowboy boots into which his blue-jeans were tucked were shapely and polished. Obviously, he had done some dressing up for the occasion. And Thunderhead too. His pure white coat shone like satin. Mane and tail were brushed until they were light and floating.

"Ken!" exclaimed his mother, "how ever did you make his hoofs shine like that?"

"That's *Furness' Marble Hoof Lustre*," explained Ken with some embarrassment. "It was one of the ads in my last month's *Racing Form*. I sent for it, because you see, if he's to be a racer, he ought to look like something swell. It's a kind of enamel."

"What's that blue streak on his neck?" asked Nell.

Ken tried to rub it off. "Oh, maybe I got it a little bit too blue—"

"Too blue!"

Howard explained joyously. "He puts blueing in the water when he washes him!"

"Well, Mother puts blueing in the water to make the clothes white, so I use a little now and then—"

"A little!" said Howard. "He darn near empties the bottle."

"So that's where all my blueing has gone!"

Charley Sargent seemed to have been struck dumb. He stood looking at the horses, first Thunderhead, then the filly. She had moved away a little and was grazing quietly. Finally he reached for the makings, rolled himself a cigarette and took a long puff.

"Ken," he said quietly, *"I'll be damned."*

Ken, at the colt's head, looked at him anxiously, the color coming and going in his face.

"So *that!*" said Sargent in his drawling voice, "is Thunderhead out of Flicka by Appalachian!"

"Yes, sir, he's by Appalachian all right."

"How old is he?"

"Just a short two. Do you—do you think he looks pretty good, Mr. Sargent?"

"He's nothing of a racer—"

"He isn't!"

"Nothing like any horse I ever saw before. He's like a statue of a horse that sculptors think up—all big curves and muscles—that head—"

Thunderhead's face, eyes, head—these were, indeed, the outstanding things about him. Such a face would make a person suddenly stop in passing, look again— then stand hypnotized. The intensity of the black eye with the thin thread of white around it—the wildness, the implacable determination—the bigness of the head —the way the heavy neck curved and drew the chin in to the chest—then suddenly flung the head high—with the black muzzle reaching up—the nostrils flaring—

"I'll be damned," said Sargent weakly again.

"Isn't he a racer at all, Mr. Sargent?"

"He's not a racing type. Not a runner. Not that he might not, perhaps—beat a racer—! With that power, no telling what he could do! Is he fast?"

"Well—sometimes, if he wants to be. He really *can* run, but he doesn't always do it."

Sargent couldn't take his eyes off the stallion. There was a slight flush on his long brown face. "I'm beginning to think I may be proud of him yet," he said, and suddenly, with excitement. "What did I tell you, Ken? About all the winners Appalachian had sired?"

"Sure, I remember, Mr. Sargent. Coquette, and Spinnaker Boom, and Mohawk and a lot of others. That's why, you know—that's why—well, that's why I wanted him for Thunderhead's sire. Do you really think he looks good, sir?"

"He's the biggest bunch of muscle I ever saw!—and no training to speak of—how in hell did he get that development?"

Thunderhead lifted a big hoof, shiny with enamel, and pawed impatiently. In proportion to the weight of his body and neck his legs were still short. Or, thought Nell, studying him, was it just that they looked short in comparison to the size of the rest of him? He stood fifteen and a half hands high. His neck was heavy, strongly muscled and arched. He was not yet fully grown. He had always been shaped like a mature horse, even when he was born. If he continued growing all over, as he had so far, his legs would grow more too. Perhaps—fully grown— they would be long enough.

"You don't think he's too heavy, Charley?" she asked. "Not like a work horse?"

"My God, no! Those legs—they're strong but they're trim and clean. He's a heavy hunter type. All the power in the world there."

At every word waves of hot and cold went through

Ken. Praise of Thunderhead! Power? Ken knew his power. Would he ever forget the first ride he had had on him this summer? It was not just the ride. It was an experience of power and will that had been communicated from the horse's body to his own and had left a mark in his consciousness that would never be erased.

He smoothed Thunderhead's nose softly. "He's strong all right."

The stallion's eyes turned a little, fastened on Ken. Ken stared back. Suddenly Thunderhead's teeth bared and reached for Ken's arm. Ken snatched it away and cuffed him. Thunderhead reared, came down prancing. Ken hauled on the reins and shouted at him. Charley stepped back quickly.

"Nasty-tempered, eh?"

"It isn't that. He doesn't like me."

"Doesn't like you! That's pretty tough, when he's yours and you have to train him."

"I keep thinking maybe he'll get to like me. Mother's the only one he likes. He's never mean to her."

"Look at the saddle, Charley," said Nell.

As Thunderhead heard her voice he turned his head to look at her and she laid her arm on his thick arched neck where the ridges of muscle stood out, and leaned against him.

"What is it? Horsehair?" asked Charley.

"Yes," said Ken proudly. "I made it. Dad showed me how."

Sargent fingered the saddle. "How do you make them?"

Howard told him. "First you fill a sack with a lot of horsehair—tails and manes—then you use it for a saddle blanket for about a year. And that grinds and weaves it all in together so that it makes a thick mat. At last you can't see the sack at all—just a thick pad of hair all woven in together."

"And then," Nell added, "you cut it out the shape of the saddle—you can see the outline on it where the saddle has pressed it—and there you have a tiny, light little saddle—soft and fitting perfectly."

Charley lifted the small stirrups that were fastened to the surcingle under the saddle. "Like a jockey saddle—pretty neat." He put his hand on Ken's head, laughing. "You aren't missing anything, are you, Ken? If a horsehair saddle and Furness' Marble Hoof Lustre and blueing in the water can make a colt win races, why then Thunderhead will win, won't he? Now let's look at the filly. Why did you bring her along?"

"He's very fond of her. She's his little sister. She's kind of a mascot for him."

"Oh, she's out of Flicka too?"

"Yes. And they always stay together. It kind of quiets him, if he should get excited, to have her around."

"He gets excited, does he? And mean?"

Ken was shocked. "Oh, never mean! But he bucks and fights. Sometimes he runs away with me."

"But never mean!" laughed Sargent. "I see. But can't you hold him in?"

"He takes the bit. He's better when Touch And Go's around. He's happier. You see he isn't a very happy horse most of the time. He's got something eating him, Dad says."

Sargent was studying the filly. "That's a nifty little filly."

"She's exactly like Flicka was when she was a yearling. When I first got Flicka, she was just about that age and a bright golden sorrel like that, and the light mane and tail."

"She's like her sire," said Sargent. "She's by Banner, isn't she?"

"Yes, and she's very light and fast."

"You don't say." Sargent was not going to be enthusiastic about a colt of Banner's when one of Appalachian's was around.

"Yes, she can go like the wind! But of course nobody has ever ridden her. She just runs along with Thunderhead when we train him, or by herself."

"How much do you weigh, Ken?"

181

"Ninety-five pounds."

"It doesn't seem to me you've grown any in the last few years."

"Well, I haven't. Dad says I haven't started yet. He says boys shoot up all of a sudden. Howard's just done it."

Sargent glanced at Howard. He had, indeed, just done it. There was a long piece of sunburned hairy leg showing between the top of his sneakers and the bottom of his pants.

"What's your weight on a horse?" asked Sargent.

Ken was stumped. "How do you mean?"

"Well you know, don't you, that some people are heavy on a horse and some people are light?"

"Dad always says I'm light on a horse, but that doesn't mean my real weight, does it?"

"Sure. Didn't you know that? Weigh horse and rider. Add the weights together. Sometimes it comes to more than the sum of both. That means a heavy rider. Sometimes, less. That means a light rider. If you're light, perhaps you don't weigh more than fifty pounds on a horse—if that."

"No kiddin'?" asked Howard. This seemed very strange to both boys.

"Come over to my place some time where I've got scales. And I'll prove it to you."

"Mr. Sargent," said Howard, "our two-year-olds are going to be gelded right away and Dad says Thunderhead's got to be gelded too. Do you think he ought to be?"

At this unpleasant reminder of the one thing that was preying on his mind, the happiness went out of the day for Ken.

Nell's cheeks colored with anger and she turned away and walked over to the "grandstand." "Come along, Howard, give me a hand up here! We'd better get started!"

Sargent looked at Ken's white, sullen face.

"What's the matter, son?"

Ken gave a little jerk of his head toward Howard.

"What he was saying there. Dad's going to have all the two-year-olds gelded."

"When?"

"Some time this week. He's sent word to Doc Hicks to come and do it whenever he's in this neighborhood. Then Dad won't have to pay for his driving out and back just for our horses."

"Is he going to geld Thunderhead too?"

"Yep."

"Well, what if he does? He won't be the only one. They all have to be gelded, you know."

"But he's going to be a race horse!"

"What's that got to do with it? Race horses get gelded too—most of them. It won't hurt him. And it may improve his appearance. I wouldn't like to see that neck of his get any thicker."

"But he might die!"

"Oh, nonsense!"

"But we had one that died when he was gelded. His name was Jingo. He was a risling."

"Risling!" Charley laughed and looked at Thunderhead. "Well—what's that got to do with Thunderhead? Don't insult him!"

Ken dropped his chin into his neck and chuckled.

"It won't hurt him. But maybe, if he runs well enough, we could get your father to change his mind."

Ken shook his head. "He never changes his mind."

"Never does?"

"No."

"Well, anyway, let's see what the colt can do now. Up with you." He clutched the seat of Ken's pants, and the boy went lightly up into the saddle. He hitched his feet into the little short stirrups and grinned down at Sargent. "I don't usually ride with these short stirrups. I ride bareback a lot. It's kind of hard to get used to. But I can do it."

He squeezed his knees together, and bent over the horse's withers like a jockey.

Sargent's long brown face was twinkling with enjoyment. "Give him a bit of a workout first to warm him up. Remember, I've an interest in this colt too!"

This was very cheering to Ken as he gave the signal to Thunderhead and the colt started forward. Perhaps, if Mr. Sargent had an interest in him too, he might say something to his father about the gelding. Sargent stood looking at him as he cantered down the course, noticing his action. Then he climbed up on the grandstand beside Nell and Howard. There was a ledge quite high up from which they could overlook the whole track.

Howard held the stop watch in his hand.

Touch And Go left her grazing and cantered playfully beside her big brother, down to the end, around the curve, and back again. The white colt moved slowly and easily.

After ten minutes or so, Sargent shouted to Ken, "Get him going now, son— Let him out."

Ken swung around to the starting line and flung the horse over it in a gallop.

For a half-hour then, Ken struggled to make the colt give a good account of himself. He had very little success. Thunderhead cut a corner once, Ken pulled him up, made him go back and outside the post. Suddenly the colt got ugly—fought for the bit—Ken spurred him and reined him back, then lifted him forward into a run. Touch And Go ran with him.

By turns Howard and Charley Sargent held the stop watch. Finally they climbed down and Ken rode up to them. His face was flaming, his eyes wild, the horse nervous and prancing.

"*Can he run, Ken?*" said Sargent. "What have you been giving me?"

"Oh, yes, he can—*if he wants!*" answered Ken passionately.

"I'm beginning to think he's too much horse for you," said Sargent.

"You know," said Nell thoughtfully, "he *really can run*. It's quite different from this hard galloping. It's a different

184

gait. Do you remember that black mare—Rocket—his grandmother?"

"I sure do—she was almost *my* mare."

"Yes. That one. You remember the time we ran her in front of the automobile and clocked her—and she just floated along without trying—no effort at all?"

"I do. Never saw such a gait in my life."

"He's got the same gait. He does it sometimes. I wish you could see it. Ken, let's try again. I'll tie up Touch And Go. I think she distracts him."

Nell got the tie-rope, snapped it to the filly's halter and fastened her to the bumper of the automobile so that Thunderhead could not see her. Once more they took their places on the ledge and Charley gave Ken the signal.

Ken brought his horse over the line as he had done before—the same, hard gallop, with the colt fighting his head and unwilling to obey. It made Ken mad that just now when he wanted performance Thunderhead would do nothing but fight.

All right then—let it be war. This battling with the stallion was bringing out something in the boy that had never been there before. He raised the light crop he held and brought it down on the colt's haunches as hard as he could. Thunderhead leaped in the air and tried to shake Ken off. Ken could feel the power and anger surge into his own body. He raised his arm and brought the crop down again. When the horse lit this time he was going.

It was the long floating effortless pace that had been Rocket's. Ken sat motionless on the tiny saddle. Down to the turn, around the posts, up the other side—

Nell glanced at Charley. "See that?" she said "That's what I mean."

"And he's not even trying," said Charley in a daze.

"He's coming! He's coming!" screamed Howard, "Look at the watch—"

Sargent gave a start. He hadn't had his eyes off the

colt, he hadn't timed him. He waved his arm and yelled at Ken, "Keep going! Go around again!"

Ken's eyes flickered up to him as he passed, but he didn't turn his head. There was a rapt look on his face.

"God! He runs in the air!" howled Sargent. "He doesn't touch the ground!"

Howard was jumping up and down. "Keep it up! Keep it up! Thunderhead! Thunderhead!"

Nell felt hysterical. She suddenly put her face into her hands. The beauty of it. The super-performance—and Ken sitting so still—the victory at last—the two-year-old battle—the faith—the exhaustion—the cuts and bruises and strains she had had to bind up—and now, Victory— She raised her head and looked again. Coming back up the home stretch!— Coming! One long sustained yell from Sargent—and the horse over the line, Ken trying to pull him up—swinging around in circles—Howard's voice squawking—"What did he make, Mr. Sargent? What did he make?"—while Sargent was trying to scramble down the rock.

Thunderhead had made the half-mile in forty-seven seconds.

"Oh, Kennie—Kennie—"

"Gee, Ken—he did it— Gee!"

"That horse! He's one of the seven wonders of the world!"

Thunderhead was fighting. He wanted to keep going. Ken had hardly come back yet from the ecstasy in which he had ridden. His glowing face with the slightly parted lips was half unconscious.

"Could he do it again? Has he ever done it before? We'll let him rest a little, then give him another spin."

"Rest?" said Howard. "He's not tired. He never gets tired. He hates to be stopped when he gets going. That's why he's mad now."

They decided to try the colt again; and again they climbed to the ledge and timed his start, and again Ken fought with him to control him, forced him over the line,

186

and was shaken by the angry, rough, gallop—by his breaking through the posts. The struggle went on—the lashing of the crop—the scarlet face of the boy, while Charley grew grave and the little group on the ledge no longer chattered with excitement, but stood silent.

At last Sargent was hopeless. "It was a fluke," he said. "He's uncontrollable."

"Look, look, Mr. Sargent! He's doing it again!"

The colt had broken through his temperamental impediments. He burst into his swift, floating pace, and went streaming around the track. As he crossed the line Sargent punched the watch. They held their breath. Sargent's mouth was wide open in a crazy grin. His eyes popped.

Suddenly there was the noise of a man shouting, horses galloping, a strange rattling. And down onto the track a few yards behind Thunderhead tore the team of black mares carrying a light, bouncing rig, a man half sitting in it, half on his feet, leaning forward over the haunches of the horses, waving whip and reins and roaring, "Hi-i-i! Whoopee! Keep-a-goin', girlies! Yah-h-h! Atta girl! Yippee!"

The black mares were stretched at a gallop, straining to overtake the colt ahead of them. The whip was cracking above them. "Come on, Patsy! Keep it up, Topsy!"

This was too much for Thunderhead. He bolted between the posts and began to buck. Rob swept past him in a whirl of flying hooves and tails, completed the circle of the track and crossed the finish line with a yell of triumph.

Ken sat the bucking horse valiantly. He had his feet out of the short stirrups, his knees gripped hard. He leaned back until he was nearly on the colt's haunches. His body whipped this way and that, his head snapped, his cap went flying. Thunderhead worked himself up into one of his mad bucking jags. Ken still sat him.

Nell was so buffeted by shocks that she could only clutch Charley's arm, screaming, "Oh—Oh—" Rob cir-

187

cled back to the grandstand and pulled up to watch. Charley and Howard scrambled down the rock.

Thunderhead still bucked. Rob muttered, "It's the bronc in him—but Ken can ride anything that has hair—"

Suddenly, completely exhausted, Ken let go. He rose in the air, described a wide parabola, and lit, tackling a small shrub in a long sliding dive.

Thunderhead kept on bucking. Ken sat up dazedly, brushed the hair out of his eyes and watched. They all watched. At last Ken got to his feet, shook himself, picked up his cap and walked over to his father. Thunderhead bucked out between the posts, bucked across the track, past the automobile to which Touch And Go was tied, then burst into a run and went tearing away over the plains. Touch And Go, whinnying desperately, tugged at her rope. The loosely tied knot came free, the filly leaped away and galloped after her brother.

21

The gelding.

For days and nights Ken had been thinking of it. The better the colt behaved, the more speed he showed, the more despair Ken felt. They told him, and they argued with him, and they proved it to him. The colt would lose no iota of his speed—might even have more, because his energies would not be wasted in fighting, in running after mares, in breeding them. It made no difference to Ken. He had seen the colts before gelding, the power that flowed through them like hot lava, making them rear and play and fight and wrestle; making their tails and manes lift like flying banners; giving a look of individuality and passion to their faces—and he had seen them after. Seen the change in the carriage of the head, the look of the eye, the appearance of the colt, the general behavior.

Nothing would reconcile him. But his father had decided. What could one do in such a jam? Fortitude. When you couldn't have what you wanted, you accepted defeat with fortitude. His mother said you could pray— but you needn't think you'd get what you wanted, you'd just get the strength to bear the disappointment. He felt as if two sides of a vise were closing in on him.

Those days made a change in Ken's face and character. He said little about it. The more you argued and pled the less likely his father was to yield. His mother was really on his side, but she left such things to his father. She felt that he really knew best.

It happened that on the morning of the day of Ken's trial race down on the track a call came into the office of the veterinarian at Laramie. It was from Barney, the rancher west of the Goose Bar, stating that he had a sick cow who needed to be cleaned out after a premature calving. Could Dr. Hicks come out and take care of her?

Dr. Hicks and Bill, his assistant, arrived at the Barney ranch about one o'clock. They worked over the cow for a couple of hours. When they were leaving, Dr. Hicks said, "It's only a few miles down the back road to the Goose Bar. We'll stop in there and geld those two-year-olds of Captain McLaughlin."

They arrived at the stables soon after Rob had driven off with the blacks. Gus went out with a bucket of oats and called in the colts, and the men got to work.

"Is that all?" asked Doc, when he had gelded seven. "I thought the Captain said eight."

"Dere's one more," said Gus, "Ken's colt. De white one."

"Oh, the throwback!" said Doc. "The one Ken thinks is going to be a racer. How's he comin' on?"

"He runs right gude now," said Gus.

"Maybe they don't want him gelded."

"De Captin wants him gelded all right. Mebbe you cud wait a little, while I go down and help Tim wid de milkin'? Ken tuk de colt out a while back—he might be home any minnit."

Doc and Bill took seats on the corral fence and rolled cigarettes and waited.

The shadows grew longer. They heard the cowbells as the cows, after being milked, wandered out into the pasture; then the sound of the separator whirring in the milk house as it cut the milk in half, pouring a rich, foaming, white fluid into one jar, a thick yellow cream into the other.

At last Doc told Bill to pack up the stuff. They got in the car and drove away.

Ken felt almost awed when he arrived at the stables with Howard, having driven the blacks home in the "jouncing cart," and heard from Gus what had happened. There stood the seven gelded colts in the east corral, their heads hanging lifelessly, their hind legs covered with blood. Thunderhead, said Gus, had come galloping in with Touch And Go some ten minutes after Doc had left. He had unsaddled him and turned them both out into the Home Pasture.

Ken stared at the geldings while the blood rushed through his body and sank again. This meant—this meant—Doc had made his trip to the ranch! His father would never order him up again to geld one colt!

Ken leaped in the air with a whoop of triumph.

"Gosh!" said Howard. "You're shot in the head with luck!"

Ken walked away, clasped both arms around the snubbing post and laid his head down upon it. This seemed the direct answer to prayer. The snubbing post was not exactly reverential, but he remembered King David's undignified take-off.

190

22

"The blacks?" shouted Rob, waving the steel with which he was sharpening the knife to carve the roast. "Thereby hangs a tail. A coupla tails. And if you'd like to hear it, Charley, I'll tell it to you. You never saw a better match, did you? The off one, Patsy, is a bit heavier because she's with foal. Of course she ought not to have foals, but that's her price. Only on condition that she is allowed to have a foal every year will she agree to have a harness put on her and pull a wagon. And a very special sort of foal, too! Not Banner's, mind you! His colts are not good enough for her! Oh, no. *Her* colts—well, when I try to describe them words fail me. But that's a woman for you! When she appeared one spring, smug and cocky, with the first of them, you could have knocked me over with a feather. How had she got out of Banner's band? Where had she found the sire for such a museum piece? *That* almost turned my hair gray. Here I had been worrying all these years about the Albino's blood getting mixed with my stock. Now I had some other blood to worry about.

"Anyway, that was the spring I decided to break the two blacks for harness and put them to work. So we began. You may have noticed the peculiar look in Patsy's eye. She sort of winks. That's the only way I can tell 'em apart. Patsy winks and Topsy doesn't. She winks because she got the best of me. Topsy gave me a heck of a lot of trouble breaking her, but just reasonable trouble. Regular horse trouble. But Patsy! Well, we went through the usual procedure and all went well until I had her harnessed to the wagon—that old wagon I use for breaking horses. I had old Tommy harnessed in with her. She looked like a kitten beside that hulk. The colt stood off aways, its head on one side, watching. When I gave the signal and Tommy moved forward and Patsy felt the pull of the wagon behind her, she started to back up. We did the usual things—yelled at her and whipped her up— one minute of that is usually enough for any horse—but she kept on backing. Tommy leaned into the collar and pulled like a good one. She felt herself going along like she ought to, and *lay down*. We whipped them both. Tommy dragged her along the ground. Any horse hates that and they soon scramble to their feet. Not Patsy. She relaxed completely and lay there like a swooning woman, dragged behind old Tommy wherever he went. But the moment we unharnessed her she came to life, jumped up, looked out the corner of her eye at me and winked. The colt galloped up, stuck his head underneath her, took a few sucks and galloped away again. We tried again. Patsy lay down again. She would go down by inches— just slowly collapse, the way the air goes out of a balloon. Lean a little, sag, lean a little more, and Davy Barker, the kid that was working for me that week, would nearly split his throat yelling at her, and I'd whip them both and Tommy would pull like a good one—but nothing worked. She'd sag a little more and at last, *sproush!* Then we'd try to get her up again. We exploded enough human T.N.T. under that mare to send a truck twenty feet in the air. Nothing doing. We unharnessed her, she stood up, turned her head and winked at me. This went on for hours. I bet she lay down twenty times. I dislocated my shoulder beating her. I hitched her to the snubbing post in the corral. She deliberately began to wind the rope around that post, plodding around and around it, until she was snubbed up so short her nose was pinched. Then she got her head under the last hitch, let her legs go out from under her and hung there. She did it on purpose. she groaned and gasped. She would have choked to death in five minutes if we had not cut the rope to save her. But that time I didn't want to save her.

"I went away and sat down and tried to think calmly. I figured it might be the colt. It was about three weeks old. Sometimes a young colt seems to deprive its dam of all common sense. Davy Barker was leaving that night. He was crazy for a colt of his own, so I gave him Patsy's colt. We tied its feet and put it in the back of Davy's little old ramshackle sedan. He drove the car up to the front of the house to say good-by to Nell and there was that damned colt sitting up looking out of the window.

"Then I gave Patsy time to recover. *She* wasn't the one that needed to recover. It was I. God! I was a wreck! I waited a week, then we hitched her up and tried her again. This time she didn't merely lie down, she gave a kind of leap—spread all four legs and landed on her belly and lay there. We lambasted her. Tommy dragged her. Nothing doing. We worked with her all afternoon. She repeated the belly-flop every time. Then when we would unharness her, she would stand right up, look around at me, and wink.

"Well, I gave up at last. And did that gripe me. It was a humiliating defeat. Even to remember it makes my gorge rise. I just turned her out into the Stable Pasture and made up my mind I'd give up all idea of getting a light work team out of those blacks, and forget her. But something about the way she pricked her ears and started off caught my attention. She went as if she had a definite plan. So I slipped a bridle on old Shorty and went after her at a distance. She headed west. She didn't trot—just walked along swishing her tail like a woman in a hurry, knowing just what she was going to do. She went five miles without stopping till she came to the fence between my ranch and Barney's.

"Barney's got an old stallion—the boys call him Doggie—you've heard about Doggie. There he stood the other side of the fence waiting for her. She crawled under the fence—just lay down and edged herself under the loose bottom wire, while he grunted and squealed and

193

made all sorts of empty boasts and promises. She spent an hour with him in playful dalliance, then crawled back under the fence again and swished primly back to the stables. It just occurred to me, a few days later, to try her again. You should have seen her! She presented her rear to the wagon and begged to be hitched up! She didn't have anything to learn, she knew it all. Had known it all the time. She purred. She went along beside old Tommy, pulling the wagon behind them, as if she'd done it all her life. As well as she went today. You saw her!

"Next spring we had another of those colts to give away. Of course it couldn't be done. It was against nature. Doggie's as old as Methusaleh. But she did it. Young Davy's got three of those colts now—but I've got a team!"

Rob got a big hand for his story, then Charley had one to tell. But most of the talk was about Thunderhead—his marvelous performance on the race-track that afternoon, and his future.

Nell had hardly recovered from the emotion she had felt when she saw Ken's triumph. And the fact that the colt had escaped gelding (for Rob had said that since Doc had come and gone he could wait another year) gave her an even stranger feeling of unreality. When obstacles vanished, they just floated away—as if they never had been—

She mixed her salad at the table while the roast beef and corn on the cob were being demolished, sprinkled the chopped egg and parsley on top of the loose lettuce leaves in the big yellow kitchen bowl.

She glanced at Howard. "Heat the crackers in the oven, Howard—with grated cheese on top—"

She mixed the French dressing in a small bowl, fished out the mashed bud of garlic, poured the dressing on the lettuce and turned and turned it with the long wooden spoon and fork. She was flushed. Her skin had a glow in it, lit from her inner excitement, and her eyes, with the dark unseeing look of one half in a dream, yet had an extraordinary blue brilliance. It *was* a dream—the dream

194

she had dreamed one night two winters ago—Thunder-head triumphant. Thunderhead winning races. Money for all they needed. No more worry—no more fear.

"He *is* going to be a racer after all, isn't he, Dad?"

"Looks like it, son."

"And all our troubles will be over."

"What are you going to do with all the money, Ken?"

"He's going to pay back a lot that he owes me!"

"And he can pay for his own education!"

"And pay off the note on the ranch."

"And put wooden fences around it—he's promised me that!"

"Mother, you've got to tell me what you want! I've asked you and asked you and you never have."

"Can I have three wishes?"

"Yes—three things. Make them big things, Mother!"

"I want a Swan Sleigh all covered with bells! I want a Monkey Tree! And I want a Little Girl!"

"Oh-Oh-h—that isn't fair!"

"What in hell is a Monkey Tree?"

Nell recited,

> *"Twisted old pine tree, I can plainly see*
> *That you are just making a face at me.*
> *You wink one eye and you bend one knee*
> *And that's why I call you the Monkey Tree."*

"I still don't know what a Monkey Tree is—" said Charley, passing his plate for more salad, "and why Nell should want one—and what she'll do with it if she gets it—"

"Plant it on the Green," explained Howard. "It's a kind of big old pine tree here on the ranch—there are only a couple of dozen of them. We were looking at one one day long ago— They are a queer shape with branches all twisting every which way, and Mother said it had a face like an old man's, and she made up the rhyme, and Dad went around with one knee bent and one eye closed—"

"Mother," insisted Ken, "tell me some other wishes—*real* wishes that I could get you."

"He wants to buy her *joo-oo-ools!*" clowned Howard. "And velvet dresses—and—"

"Better cross your fingers, Ken," said Charley. "Many a slip betwixt the cup and the lip, you know—"

In the interchange of talk and flashing glances that played around the table, Nell's look crossed Rob's. They stared a moment. She felt the impact of his animosity. He hadn't forgiven her for what she had said last night. When they were alone together, he was smooth and easy —as if it were forgotten—but with people around, he lowered his guard and let her see the truth.

While they argued as to whether it would be better for Thunderhead to be raced this coming fall or wait until he was a three-year-old, and decided on the latter, she sat at the end of the table, feeling all her elation dying down. Thunderhead's success began to seem very remote—indeed, unlikely. No. The odds were, nothing would come of it. The colt had, apparently, run a half-mile faster than it had ever been run before. Could that be true? According to recorded runs, yes. But there were many colts in the world besides those who ran in races—many colts who had been clocked on makeshift tracks like this one might have—must have, broken records, and yet, for one reason or another, never were heard of. Why? Things happened. They got hurt, or stale, or proved a flash in the pan, or unmanageable—

"For you see," said Charley, "we know now he's got it in him. It's *there*. But he's an unmanageable brute. He can't be depended on. He needs a lot of training and discipline. Besides, he hasn't got his growth yet. In another year, when he's settled down, he'll be unbeatable!"

He gave Ken's back a resounding whack! "Young fellah, me lad, you'll have a winner! How'll it feel to be the famous owner of a famous horse?"

But Ken had a thought. "Suppose," he said lugubriously, "we get him all trained for a race, and then he runs away and we can't find him?"

Rob glanced at Ken, then at Nell. His expression was sardonic. "Ken, you take after your mother more than any boy has a right to."

Nell's eyes met Rob's—and clashed again. She looked down and finished her sliced peaches. What was the matter with him? It wasn't only the quarrel of last night—that had left him hard and cold toward her, but he was *in a state*—had been all evening—ever since—ever since —yes, ever since he arrived at the race track in that ridiculous cart—what had he been doing before— Oh, yes, he went out on Gypsy—went out on Gypsy to see Bellamy and ask if he was going to take the lease again this fall— Ah!

She put down her spoon and sat motionless, staring a hole through the table—her mind rushed forward.

Charley was shouting that with a horse of such potential value as Thunderhead, they would never dream of putting him out on the range that winter.

Rob conceded that Thunderhead had been promoted. Since the speed he had shown that afternoon, he would be guarded, cherished, watched over like the Crown Prince.

Ken could hardly believe it. "Do you mean you'll keep him in this winter, Dad? And—and—feed him *oats*— and *hay*?"

"With my own fair hands! What's more I'll ride him and continue his training whenever I have time. That's the least I can do if he's going to put wooden fences on the ranch and buy a furnace for us! What do you think, Nell?"

He had seen her sitting there, silent and white, after the hard look he had given her.

She looked up as he spoke to her. His face was genial and smiling. First the blow—then the smile—

But she didn't answer for a moment and Ken was impatient. "Mother!" he exclaimed.

"Yes," she said. "By all means! Keep him in."

197

When Nell asked Rob, she made it very casual. She was brushing her hair for the night. "By the way, Rob— did you see Bellamy?"

"Yes."

"What about the sheep?"

"It's O.K."

"Thank Heaven! Will he be able to pay us the first half before Howard leaves?"

"No, he can't do that. He has to wait until he sells his lambs."

"What'll we do? We have to have that eight hundred by September tenth."

Rob had his back to her, standing before his chiffonier. There was something very rigid about his body—the legs braced apart a little, head back.

"I'll take some horses down to the Denver auction this next week."

Nell made no comment. She calculated rapidly. Every summer he had half a dozen or so "scrubs" to sell at any price he could get—horses who were too small, or poorly developed, or with some defect. Sometimes he sold them to Williams, a horse buyer who went around to ranches with his own truck; or at one of the near-by auctions. Wherever he sold them, he would be lucky to get fifty dollars apiece for them. There were also the two old brood mares to be sold. All together, that would make, perhaps, four hundred dollars. What else would he sell to make up the difference?

There had been many arguments between herself and Rob on the subject of providing for their current needs by sales of horses—no matter at what sacrifice. He always refused to do it. "What? Sell a horse that's worth fifteen hundred dollars for fifty? Not if Y was starving."

"But Rob—how many sales of that sort do you get?"

"I've had *some*— We've lived, haven't we?"

"Yes—four horses four years ago at seven hundred dollars apiece. Then, none the next year. Then one for two thousand—I admit that was a good sale— But you must have thirty or forty horses just waiting for one of those sales—and they only come once in a blue moon— When we need the money, you might as well sell half a dozen for *anything*—you would still have enough fine horses for any sort of deal that came along."

"I'd rather sell one for two thousand than twenty horses at a hundred dollars a head, or forty horses at fifty."

Such remarks as these were unanswerable.

But he wasn't talking like that now. Nell glanced at him. Did he mean that he *would* take some of his fine stuff down to the Denver auction and let it go cheap?

As he turned she saw his face, weary and harassed. He went into the small adjoining bedroom where he kept his boots and clothes.

They talked back and forth through the open door while she washed her face in oil and carefully dried it.

"Wasn't it exciting about Thunderhead?" she asked.

"Yep."

"You didn't see the best of it," she said. "I wish you had."

She could hear him polishing his shoes before he put them away.

"Oh, he can run!" he said. "He's fast, if he ever gets the kinks ironed out of him— Don't wait for me— I'm going to smoke a pipe before I turn in."

"You don't seem to take much stock in him, Rob."

"No, I don't."

After a short silence, Nell said, "Neither do I. It just seems unlikely, somehow, that he'll pan out." She put on a thin white silk night gown—it was too hot tonight for pajamas.

"It's been the best thing that ever happened to Ken," said Rob after a pause. "The struggle with this colt. Thunderhead really fights him. It's making a man of him."

"Yes. But I hate to think that, after all, he'll lose out with him. It would break his heart."

"Do him good," mumbled Rob. "He *ought* to lose out on something. He's got the luck of the devil—look at this about the gelding now! He gets his way again! I hope I'm around to see it when Ken gets his at last."

"Heavens! Aren't you bloodthirsty tonight! What's put you in such a temper?"

Rob made no answer. She heard him walking down the hall to the bathroom.

She went to the open window and stood looking out. There was no moon, but the milky way was so brilliant, so crowded with stars, that the earth was bathed in a soft translucence. Across the Green, under the shadow of the pine trees, she saw a white shape moving. It emerged slowly, followed by a small dark shadow. They moved to the fountain in the center of the Green. Thunderhead dipped his head and drank. Touch And Go followed suit. They raised their dripping muzzles and stood quietly there, mouthing the cool spring water.

"Come here," called Nell, when she heard Rob returning. He obeyed her and looked out over her shoulder.

"I'm glad he's got that filly," said he. "It'll keep him home more—and it'll keep him from bothering the other mares."

"You'll never see him with any other horse."

"Horses have those attachments. Well—good night—" She turned her face and he kissed her lightly. "Don't wait for me."

"No."

Nell still stood at the window. It wasn't the sheep then —something else. How long was this going on? There was a dragging at her heart as she breathed. It had been only two days, but they seemed like weeks. She wasn't practiced in quarreling. She was miserably unhappy.

Why had she said that tonight— *I want a Swan Sleigh all covered with bells. I want a Monkey Tree. I want a Little Girl.* Because it was true. The old nagging desire— Wasn't it ever going to happen? Suddenly she felt that if she was never again to put out her arms and gather into them that small fragrant bundle—an infant daughter, an infant son—never again know that supreme and glorious sense of achievement—never feel the enhanced importance of life, never know the excitement and wonder and humility of looking into the tiny infant face and knowing that here was an individuality—a soul—a stranger to her, come to live with them, be one with them, grow with them—

She walked restlessly around the room. It would renew life for them all. The boys would soon be gone. Never would they come back in the real mother-and-boy relationship. Oh, how could she live alone at the ranch with Rob? Another child would begin lifm over for herself and Rob— It would soften him. How sweet and tender he was with all helpless things! But it must be a girl—it must, it must— Even more would a little daughter get her fingers around his heart—a Flicka—just what she had said to Ken when he was sick—that she wanted a "little girl," a "Flicka" just as passionately as *he* had wanted her—!

She could see Rob's face—the brightness, the laughter, the big teeth beaming down, and the little creature no bigger than a cat in his arms—an infinitesimal fist waving out of the knitted afghan—the movement below the blanket of a foot kicking—about as big as a mouse. . . .

She heard the connecting door close softly.

After a while she blew out the lamp and slipped into bed.

When she woke in the morning Rob was there in the bed beside her. He said he felt sick. Thought he would stay in bed. Nell looked him over anxiously. She was accustomed to dealing with colds, digestional upsets, fevers, and was a good nurse.

"I think I have a fever," he said. He didn't seem at all like himself. He was in a lassitude, said he felt weak.

She took his temperature, and shook it down, puzzled. He looked up at her hopefully. "How much have I got?"

"Normal," she said. He looked disappointed. "Do you feel as if you have a cold?" she asked.

201

He thought a while, struggling with the unaccustomed effort of throwing his thoughts inward. "Maybe," he said doubtfully.

"Where?"

He thought some more. "I don't know. But I feel very bad. I feel awful."

Nell was beginning to be suspicious. Rob only got sick when he had given in on something or taken a beating. Within her began an irrepressible tide of laughter, but she kept her face grave. Yes! When he *gives in* he feels *queer—so unlike himself*—so he thinks he's sick! But what had defeated him? What had he given in on? She couldn't think of anything. Certainly he had showed no sense of defeat last night—

"What do you think it could be?" he asked anxiously.

"Rb—did you ever have—RICKETS?" Her voice was almost sepulchral.

"*Rickets!* God, no! What's that?"

"Get up a minute."

As obediently as a little boy he got out of bed, and stood there in his pajamas. She unbuttoned his jacket and began to feel his ribs, drawing a finger down the line of his breastbone.

"Are there any on me?" He shuddered a little.

She didn't answer, proceeded gravely with her examination.

"God, Nell, don't drag it out so! Have I got 'em?"

She would not be hurried, but finally dropped her hands and looked up with an air of relief. "No. You haven't. I'm so glad, Rob."

But his anxiety did not leave so quickly. "Are you sure?" He fingered his own chest, and went to the mirror to look. "What are they, anyway? What do they look like?"

"You haven't got it," she said with decision. "It makes bumps on the bones—little knobs. They call it 'the rosary.'"

Satisfied that there was no rosary on his chest, he got back into bed. "Gosh, Nell, you gave me a scare!"

"How do you feel now?"

"Seems to me I feel better."

"Hadn't you better change your mind and have some breakfast?"

"Perhaps I *could* eat a little."

"What would you like?"

"Well—ham and eggs, I guess, fruit and coffee—and toast—"

"Any oatmeal?" she asked at the door.

"Oh, sure—"

Ken always got sick, too, when he'd told his mother a· whopping lie.

But in this case, Nell knew of no lie. She felt certain Rob had a guilty conscience about something, but remained puzzled as to the cause.

23

"Shall we take Skippy to the auction with us?" yelled Howard, busily brushing and grooming Sultan, the big blood-bay who, his father said, was worth a good five hundred dollars to anyone that wanted a well-trained heavy hunter.

"I should say not!" yelled Rob from the other corral where he was giving Injun the work-out he had promised Nell the horse should have every day. "Do you want to disgrace me? What sort of horse-breeder would raise an animal like that?"

Howard began to laugh as he scraped the brush against the curry comb and the dust flew in a cloud. His voice suddenly slid down from a childish treble to a deep bass, and he stopped laughing and looked around as if wondering who had made that noise. It was embarrassing. But no one had heard. His father's head was bent with violent determination over Injun, who was misbehaving, and Gus was backing the truck up against the open chute for the loading.

"No luck, Skippy," said Howard to the strange-looking little buckskin who was standing on the other side of the corral fence, her long, donkey-like ears pointed at Sultan.

Skippy knew something was going on and she didn't like to miss anything. In spite of her tiny size and ungainly shape—the barrel-body, big hammer head—she had an uncanny intelligence. She had never needed breaking, deciding in advance that she would attach herself to those who commanded the bins and buckets of oats. Nothing disconcerted her, she could be ridden by anyone (though if they were tall, she would walk out from under them) but she was a troublemaker. If a group of horses was clustered around a feed box, taking their turns at the oats in a well-mannered fashion as they had been taught, Skippy would wedge herself in, shouldering and kicking until she had the best place. On account of her dwarf-like appearance, the result of some chance mismating on the range, the other horses despised and ostracized her and the stallion would not have her in his band. In return she missed no chance to steal their food, aim a kick at them, or nip and bite. At the mere sight of her the other horses laid back their ears, and, if there was a kicking rumpus, it was always a certainty that Skippy was the cause and center of it.

Sometimes the other horses ganged up on her, crowded her close to a fence and kicked her over. Skippy was always covered with bites and bruises. She made capital of her wounds. She would come up to the men or the family begging pathetically for extra rations, like a beggar showing its sores, and would always win comfort and tidbits.

There was a box of oats on the ground near Sultan's

nose. Skippy, on the other side of the fence, reached her head through the palings, opened her mouth, and her loose tremulous upper lip and long tongue waved anxiously toward the oats.

"Hi there, Sultan!" The horse had made a sudden lunge at Skippy's head, but she had overturned the oatbox, and jerked her head out of harm's way. She stood sideways to the fence, munching and smiling and rolling her eyes slyly.

"Gosh darn you," muttered Howard, righting the box under Sultan's nose and trying to scoop up the oats, mindful that he did not get any sand with it. Sultan sniffed at his back, and snorted.

"Don't blow your nose on me, old Snorty!"

"What's the matter?" yelled Rob.

"Just Skippy. She upset the oats. I wish you'd take her to the auction, Dad. Even if you didn't raise her on purpose, she happened somehow and here she is. And she's just a pest around here. Someone might buy her—" He resumed his polishing of Sultan. "Get your fat fanny over there—"

Rob made no answer. He forced his horse parallel to the fence, down to the corner, a sharp turn, and back again.

There was the sound of galloping. Three beautiful sorrel mares, Taffy, A-Honey, and Russet came cantering down the pasture toward the corral with Ken, mounted on Thunderhead, behind them.

Howard hastened to open the gates, the mares trotted in, and Ken slid off his horse.

"That's all, Dad," he yelled. "They're all here. Thirteen of 'em."

"All right. Unsaddle your horse. You can wipe him off, but don't take all day. I want you to help Howard groom those others."

The gate of the corral where Rob was exercising Injun was carefully opened. Nell entered and stood watching. She was dressed in a summer suit of light blue linen and a tan straw hat with a round brim that curved off her face.

It was nearly the color of the tawny bang that gleamed on her forehead. With her hands thrust into the pockets of her jacket and her small feet in their sturdy flat shoes planted in the loose soil, she had her little girl look.

Rob, coming up toward her, made as if to ride her down. She stood her ground, grinning, he swerved at the last minute, and the horse, a dark powerful chestnut, with heavy arched neck drawn down, and nervously gathered body, pranced past her.

"He's getting mad," said Rob.

Nell watched uneasily. He was such a big brute. There was something about the way he swung his haunches and lifted his feet that showed rage.

"I can see he is," said Nell. "Hadn't you better get off?" It wasn't so long ago that Injun had bucked and tossed Rob four times running.

Rob's eyes blazed at her. "Get off! I should say not! Who in hell is he?" His knees squeezed the horse's ribs harder, his body forced him forward.

His words struck Nell as funny and she began to laugh. A personal combat! Either the horse would get the better of him or he would get the better of it! That was the way Rob felt about everything—even business. His rage flamed against anything that would not accept his domination.

Rob again rode Injun up to Nell and reined him in. "Stand!" he commanded. The horse, shuddering, champing at the bit and tossing flecks of foam, obeyed.

"Do you think he's about ready for you?" asked Rob with a solemn, gibing face.

Nell patted Injun's nose. The horse reared, came down plunging. She had not moved—put out her hand again.

"Stand there, sir!" shouted Rob, and the horse stood, quivering, drawing his head down against the reins and showing a white ring around his widening eyes as he felt Nell's light hand on his muzzle.

"He probably would act like an old plug with me," said Nell smiling. "I'm not so exciting to horses as you are."

"Besides," said Rob, "you don't really discipline them.

Any horse objects to its trainer." His eyes ran over her costume. "Are you going to Denver with us?"

She shook her head. It gave her the horrors to think of it. It always made Rob wild to see his horses sold for "nothing."

"You're taking Sultan?" she asked.

"Yes."

"And Smoky and Blue." She noticed them in the string that Howard and Ken were grooming. They were blue roans—a pair of beauties, with sweeping tails and gentle eyes, just too small for Army or polo, but well broken and beautifully matched. Nell had always thought of them as belonging to two little girls, sisters, who would love them and saddle and groom them themselves.

"And Taffy, and A-Honey and Russet," said Rob, turning Injun and riding him down along the fence again.

Nell's question was answered. Rob was going to do the thing he had always vowed he would never do—throw away some of his best stuff to meet an urgent need of the moment.

Injun turned and came back. Rob's face was hard as nails. Nell hated to look at it. She could see the real suffering underneath.

"I'd have saved Sultan for the Army sale—he'd have been certain for a hundred and eighty-five dollars—except for that scar on his chest. Damn the barbed wire!"

As if Injun felt the passion and violence of his master he began to crouch and lunge. Rob turned him sharply away from Nell and forced him to resume his measured pacing up and down the corral fence. When he reached Nell again he paused and said more calmly, "You don't often see such horses as these in this country."

"I know you don't," said Nell sadly.

"There won't be anything at the auction to touch them!"

"I don't doubt it."

"Mother!" yelled Howard from the other corral. "Don't you think we ought to take Skippy to the auction and sell her?"

"Sell her!" scoffed Rob, "*sell Skippy!* The boy must be out of his mind!"

Nell laughed. "Someone might buy her. A child could ride her."

"I think this fellow has had enough," said Rob, dismounting.

"Would you like me to unsaddle him?" asked Nell.

"If you don't mind." He handed her the reins. "Better change your mind and come along."

Nell shook her head. His eyes hardened. "You'll learn something—"

She looked at him, wondering just what he meant. It was a shock to meet the hard, glinting animosity of his eyes. He was doing it on purpose—to pay her back for the other night—the look was like a blow across her face —then he walked away and into the other corral.

The blood rushed up and down her body and her hands closed into fists.

"You coward!" she said to herself. "If he shouts, you begin to cry. He gives you a dirty look and you nearly faint—haven't you any guts!"

The horse eyed her with his flaring, frightened eyes. He tossed his head up and down. Nell looked at him, hardly seeing him for the mist of rage that veiled her eyes. It cleared slowly, and suddenly Rob's own words came to her lips— "*Who in the hell is he?*"

With the laughter that these words brought, both her anger and her tremors left her. Injun seemed to agree. She patted his nose again, looking him over thoughtfully.

"Am I a coward, Injun?" she asked. "What do *you* think?"

When she led him into the stable, she fastened him to the manger. "You wait," she said, "you're not going to be unsaddled just yet."

The thirteen horses were ready for loading, crowded into the small corral which opened into the chute. It was always a difficult business. Nell stood near by, watching. It depressed her. She didn't mind the ancient brood

208

mares and the scrubs, but Sultan! And the three sorrel mares! And the two blues!

"Skippy might help," said Nell, "and you could squeeze her in—she's so small they wouldn't know she was there."

"Ken, come here!" yelled his father.

He put Ken on Skippy, placed her in advance of all the others and told the boy to ride her through the chute and up the ramp. As Ken did so, Rob and Howard forced the other horses after them.

Skippy led the procession triumphantly but laid her ears back when she found herself penned into a corner of the truck with no room to kick and no oats.

"Just promise not to bring Skippy back, even if you have to give her away," called Nell as they closed the truck.

She walked up onto the hill to see the last of them. Kim and Chaps sat down beside her and watched too. She thought she saw a hand waving just before the truck went around the curve. Then it was gone and she hurried indoors, changed into riding pants and shirt, pulled a cap on her head and went back to the stables.

Injun cocked his ears and turned his head at the sound of her voice.

Rob says you must never let them know when you're scared, she reminded herself as she tightened the cinch and shortened the stirrups. Well, I *am* scared, but it isn't going to make any difference. I'm not going to go on being simply a *rabbit*.

She mounted the horse without difficulty—the first thing Rob always taught them was to stand until they received the signal to go—

"I know all about you, Injun, what a hellion you are, and that I ought to have wings if I'm going to ride you. But I'm going to all the same. And if you want to buck, why just go ahead and do it. You won't get any opposition from me. I'll go off at the first bounce. I ride by balance, not by knee-grip. You won't feel me squeezing your ribs

209

until you grunt. But if you want to be decent and take me for a nice ride—you'll have fun too."

Whether it was the extreme lightness of her body after Rob's, or escape from the master who permitted him to make no single move of his own volition but forced him every moment to go forward, stand, turn, swing to right or left at command, Injun took her riding.

Confidence came to her as she began to feel a coordination with the horse. He was nervous—there were some plunges and starts at the touch of her hands or heels, but they understood one another. And it was a day of sun, wind, cloud—the air was dry and piercingly sweet—Nell forgot her troubles. She took Injun far away.

Seeing something like a small fox, she turned her horse to investigate it. It was not a fox, it was a badger bumbling along awkwardly, humping its fat rear and waggling its thick pointed tail.

With something of the instinct of the small boy Nell gave chase, and headed it off. The Injun was interested too. The badger stopped, turned to face them for a moment, drawing back its lips and hissing at them, then bumbled away again. Nell followed. She suddenly realized that without guidance from her Injun was trailing him. His turns were lightning quick. He followed the badger, dodging this way and that, until the little creature took refuge in a pile or rocks. Injun stood before it, pawing impatiently. Heavens! What a polo horse! thought Nell. Full of the instinct to play a game, to spot and pursue, to wheel and run and overtake. She thought of Injun's being sold for a song at some country auction ring —perhaps put to the plough, or ridden to death in a cow outfit, and the same misery filled her that had showed on Rob's face that morning.

The badger suddenly charged out at them. Injun leaped, Nell almost went off. She regained her seat, circled around and came up to look at the badger again. It had backed into the rocks. She had never seen one at such close range before. It had a really beautiful animal face with three bars of black and white running down the head to meet at the sharp nose. Its teeth were bared. Alternately it made a long snoring noise, then a sharp hiss. It charged again.

Nell marveled at it. "There's courage for you! The size of it! And the size of us! My hat's off to you, little boy!"

She cantered home, gave Injun a good feed of oats and turned him out with Thunderhead and Touch And Go. He had lifted her spirits. She changed her clothes and drove into Laramie to lunch with an acquaintance and see a show.

24

The old brood mares sold immediately for forty dollars apiece after it was ascertained that each one carried a foal.

"Better that than the coyotes," muttered Rob.

There was more bidding for the scrubs. They were ridden around and around the ring by the ring boys, while whips cracked and the raucous voice of the auctioneer rattled as fast as the tobacco sellers on the radio.

"See this fine four-year-old sorrel gelding! Sound as a nut! Who wants him? Who'll bid fifty? Fifty? Fifty? Am I bid fifty? What's that, you over in the corner? *Fifteen* did you say? I'm bid fifteen! Fifteen! Fifteen! Who'll bid twenty? Twenty! The gentleman in the top row bids twenty! Twenty! Twenty! Who'll bid twenty-five? Come right down and look at him, gentlemen! Look at his mouth! Twenty! Twenty! Who'll bid twenty-five? Twenty I'm bid—who'll bid twenty-five?"

The auctioneer's assistant kept his eye roving over the

audience, watching for bids. When he got them he pointed them out to the auctioneer. The din was terrific. The horses thundered around the track, the ring boys slid on and off, running beside the horses, leaping up on them, shouting, men standing on the ground made their whips crack like pistol shots.

Interested buyers went down into the ring, examined one horse while the auctioneer ran up another.

"Forty-five I'm bid! Forty-five for this fine black. Who'll bid fifty? Is he registered? Someone's asking if he's registered."

"He is!" shouted Rob, slightly purple in the face. "He's a registered pure-bred. His papers go with him. He's only four years old. Never had a sick day in his life. He's well broken."

"There you are, gentlemen! He's a registered pure-bred from Captain McLaughlin's stud. Everyone knows the Goose Bar horses. You're getting a bargain! Forty-five! Forty-five! Am I bid fifty?"

He permitted a silence to fall while his eye roved pleadingly over the audience. "Oh, come now! Forty-five for a horse of this sort! Trained for saddle—for polo—for jumping— Jumping, Captain? Yes—for jumping— Come down here yourself, Captain, and show them what he can do! Forty-five! Forty-five! Am I bid fifty?"

Rob shouldered his way through the crowd, mounted the horse, put him through his paces.

"See that action, gentlemen? Forty-five! Forty-five! Am I bid fifty? Who'll bid fifty? You up there in the bowler hat? Fifty? Fifty? No? I'm bid forty-five—forty-five—going—going—gone—for forty-five dollars—"

The hammer clanged and Howard and Ken, leaning against the ringside fence, drew long breaths and wiped their perspiring hands on their pants.

The ring boy leaped on the next horse in line, the whips cracked, the horse plunged forward in a gallop, the auctioneer began again.

The scrubs were auctioned off for an average of forty-five dollars each.

A big bay horse pounded into the ring, ridden by a plump woman with tightly frizzed black hair, and startling pancakes of rouge around her painted black eyes. She had low, highly ornamented white leather cowboy boots on the tight legs of her black riding breeches; her sombrero, pushed well back on her head, was wide and black, her shirt bright red satin. Her hands were encased in white leather gauntlets with cuffs that reached nearly to her elbows. As she galloped around in the bedlam of cracking whips, ribald yells, and "Forty-five—forty-five, who'll give me fifty? Fifty, fifty, fifty, who'll give me fifty-five?" she threw her arm up at dramatic moments, yelled, "Hi!," made the horse rear, took off her sombrero and waved it, bowing right and left, manhandled the horse with a show of violence, screaming, "Hey, you brute!"

"Sixty-eight, sixty-eight, sixty-eight, who'll give me seventy? Seventy? Seventy? Gentlemen! Gentlemen! Have you got eyes?"

"Does the rider go with the horse?"

"Whoopee! Looky them black eyes!"

"I'll give seventy—"

"Seventy! seventy! seventy!—I'm bid seventy, who'll bid seventy-five?"

The horse brought eighty dollars and was ridden out of the ring by its buxom rider in a storm of cheers.

Ken and Howard faced around and were embarrassed at the sight of the sea of faces that went up in tiers to the roof— Red faces—faces busy chewing—grinning faces —dull, clod-like faces. The place steamed with smells, heat, perspiration and lung-exhaust.

Sultan was led in.

"My God! Look at that horse!" exclaimed the auctioneer. The hammer crashed. "Who'll bid a hundred for him? A hundred! A hundred! Who'll bid a hundred!"

As he poured out his line, the ring boy made a leap for Sultan's back. Sultan reared and plunged away, tore loose from the rope, and went galloping around the ring. Three boys pursued him, cornered him, got his rope; he still fought them, the whips cracked, he lashed with his heels, and the auctioneer, not looking at him, was crying, "Who'll bid a hundred? Am I bid a hundred? Fifty! Who'll start it with fifty?"

"Who can ride him!" yelled a sharp voice from the top row. "Is he broke or ain't he?"

Howard yelled as loud as he could. "He's broke! Anybody can ride him!"

"Yah—ah—ah—" There was a roar from the audience.

The auctioneer howled, "The young gentleman says anyone can ride him, and these are Captain McLaughlin's boys—they ought to know! Who'll bid fifty? Forty? Thirty? Who'll start it with thirty?"

"Let the kid ride him if he's broke!" shouted the man in the top row.

Ken felt his father's hand on his shoulder. He was thrust toward the ring. "Show them," said Rob between his teeth. "The sons-of-bitches."

Ken squirmed under the fence.

"Come on, Sonny, and ride him for us! Who'll bid thirty? Thirty? Am I bid thirty?"

He was not. He was bid nothing. The hall was suddenly silent as Ken went to the horse.

"Sultan, old boy—" The horse dropped to all fours, and stood trembling.

"If you'd just stop cracking those whips," said Ken. "He doesn't need those to make him go! And he's not used to it. He's a *horse!* He's spirited! He's not an ole plug!"

There was a roar as the auctioneer took up his words, "Hear that, gentlemen! He's a spirited purebred! He's not an old plug! And Captain McLaughlin's little boy—how old are you, Sonny?"

Ken's short answer, "Fourteen," reached only the auctioneer.

"He's just eleven—just a little fellow of eleven will put the horse through his paces! Who'll bid forty? Am I bid forty? Look at that action! Sixteen hands high and just five years old! Ah—that's more like it—fifty-five—am I bid sixty? Fifty-five! fifty-five! Am I bid sixty? Sixty? Sixty? Look at those legs! Look at his manners—am I bid sixty?" Suddenly he paused and mopped his head wearily. "Gentlemen! Gentlemen!" His voice was slow and persuasive. "Do you know what you're looking at? Did you come here to buy *horses?* Do you know a bargain when you see one? He's a bargain at a hundred—at a hundred and fifty—"

Sultan circled, stood at command, backed, went into a canter from a dead stop—

"Sixty!" screamed a voice.

"Sixty I'm bid—"

"Sixty-five!" screamed another. The roar rose again. The auctioneer pointed swiftly at one bidder, then another, his own voice went up an octave as he poured out his line, "Sixty-five! Sixty-five! I'm bid sixty-five! Who'll bid seventy? Seventy? You there in the bowler hat, you know horse flesh when you see it. Seventy, sir? Seventy! Seventy! I'm bid seventy! Who'll bid seventy-five?"

"Seventy-five," bid the heavy-set farmer in the sweaty shirt and galluses.

"Seventy-six!" bid the man in the bowler hat.

The farmer bid "Eighty." The man in the bowler hat bid "Eighty-one."

Sultan was sold to the farmer for ninety dollars.

The farmer was at Sultan's side as Ken slid off him. He was pleased with his buy.

"That's what I call a real horse. He'll do me as well as a Farmall would, and without gasoline too." He chuckled and ran his hand over the horse's withers.

"Are you going to use him to plough?"

The farmer looked at him in astonishment. "I sure am. What do you s'pse I'm payin' ninety dollars for?"

"He's a hunter," exclaimed Ken desperately. "A heavy hunter."

"Hunter," repeated the farmer. "Hunt what?"

"Foxes."

"Foxes! You mean coyotes? I hunt plenty of coyotes—but I hunt them with a Ford and a couple of greyhounds. I won't need a plug for that. What do you call him?"

"Sultan."

The ring boy led the horse away and the farmer followed. Ken stood, looking after them miserably.

"That's a good horse, Sonny."

Ken looked up. The tall man with the bowler hat stood beside him. He had a red face and a sharp nose.

"Any more where he came from?" he asked.

"Yes," said Ken sullenly. "A lot more."

"Whose horses are they?"

"My father's. Captain McLaughlin." Ken walked back to Howard.

Taffy was brought in, and suddenly there was a roar of laughter. Trotting at her side was Skippy. The ring boys tried to chase her back, but she evaded them.

"Is it for sale?" yelled someone. "Put it up!"

"Hold the sorrel," shouted the auctioneer. "Anyone interested in this pony?"

"Pony? That's a burro!"

"Is that one of Captain McLaughlin's purebreds?"

The audience rocked with laughter. A man was coming down one of the aisles, shouting, "Sure! A purebred nuisance! Guaranteed to drive anyone nuts!" Rob vaulted over the ringside barrier and went toward Skippy who was backed against the rail, eyeing the crowd distrustfully. One long ear came forward as she saw her master.

"Skippy! Come here, Skippy!"

"Come here, Skippy!" yelled the crowd. "Mind Papa, Skippy!"

Rob gave her a whack and she rocked over to the other side of the ring. "Doesn't know a thing," he yelled, "hasn't any sense—hasn't been broke—"

"What am I bid? What am I bid?" roared the auctioneer. "Twenty-five? I'm bid twenty-five! Twenty-five! Twenty-five! Who'll give thirty? Who wants a pet for a little girl? Thirty! Thirty! I'm bid thirty! Who'll give thirty-five?"

Rob whacked her again and chased her back. "The meanest little bitch in Wyoming!"

"Thirty-five! Thirty-five! Who'll give forty? Gentle as a

kitten. Forty? Am I bid forty? Forty! Forty! Forty! Who'll bid fifty? Make your little sweetheart happy with a pet!"

"I'll pay anyone to take her," yelled Rob whacking her again. Skippy whirled and flirted her heels in his face. He dodged and the crowd roared.

"Fifty! Fifty! I'm bid fifty! Who'll bid fifty-five? I'm bid fifty! Who'll bid fifty-five? Fifty! Fifty! Who'll make it fifty-five?"

"Not worth a dollar," howled Rob, "not a dime—not a nickel—not a damn!"

Skippy ambled back to him, stretched out her head, parted her lips and waved at him— "No oats anywhere?" she seemed to say. "What *is* this!"

Two farmers, seated beside each other, were bidding for her, convulsed with laughter.

"Fifty-five! Fifty-five! Who'll bid sixty?"

"Sixty!"

"Sixty-one!"

"Sixty-one! Sixty-one!" Who'll bid sixty-two? Sixty-one! Sixty-one! Sixty-one! Going—going—gone at sixty-one to the gentleman with the red tie."

Howard felt his father's hand on his shoulder. "You boys stay here. I'm going out for a drink. I'll be back."

When the auction was over the man in the bowler hat had bought Smoky, Blue, Taffy, A-Honey and Russet for prices ranging from sixty-five to ninety-five dollars.

Rob stood with his boys out in the road, while the jam of cars, trailers and trucks edged out of the parking places and started on their way home. The man in the bowler hat was with him.

Rob said, "This is Mr. Gilroy. My two boys, Mr. Gilroy, Howard and Ken." The boys shook hands.

"I want you to go home in the bus with Gus—" he stuck his hand in his pocket, brought out some bills, and gave them to Howard. You'll get home by nine o'clock. Buy some sandwiches and eat them on the bus—you can get them where you take the bus. Over there—" He pointed, giving Howard precise instructions. "Mr. Gilroy

217

and I are going to have dinner together. I'll bring the truck. Tell your mother not to wait up, I'll be late."

At dinner Rob asked, "Would you tell me what you bought all my horses for? Are they for your own use?"

"No. I bought them for resale."

"Where will you send them?"

"I'll sell them at Doc Horner's auction, in Setonville, Pennsylvania."

"When?"

"He has two sales a year, one in the third week of September, one in May."

"Do you expect to make a profit on them?"

The man grinned. "I sure will. Those are fine horses."

"Do fine horses bring prices at Horner's sales?"

"I go around buying up horses at country auctions. I collect a carload of them a couple of times a year and sell them there." The man reached into his pocket and brought out a bunch of cards. He shuffled them through, picked out one and gave it to Rob. "And they do bring prices. That's a hunting community. And polo. Horsey, you know—people of wealth. Horner collects really good stuff and they bring good prices."

"What will you get for those horses you bought—the two blues, for instance?"

The man shrugged. "It's pretty hard to say. There's always an element of gamble in horse-trading you know —but that's a nice little pair—they'd be nice for a couple of little girls—so gentle and pretty—"

"Yes. How much?"

"I'd be surprised if I got less than four hundred for the pair—if just the right buyer is there, six hundred."

"And big geldings? Polo ponies?"

"Ah—those are the ones you really get prices for. I've seen a polo pony—experienced, you understand—bring two thousand dollars. But that's not every day."

"You must know, in round figures, about what it costs to ship horses from this district to Pennsylvania—say two carloads—about twenty-four horses to a car."

They did some figuring. It would cost in the neighborhood of five or six hundred dollars.

When they had said good night and parted, Rob started a search through the junk shops of Denver. Fortunately, such shops kept open at night.

He found it at last, in pieces, as Nell had said, the runners in a pile of metal oddments, the graceful swan body, headless and broken in several places, reposing at an angle against the yard fence.

"It's got no head," said Rob to the junk dealer.

They found the head in the other corner of the yard. Rob held it in his hands, looking into its eyes, wondering if even Gus' skill would be sufficient to unite the pieces and put life into them.

"You *want* it?" asked the junk dealer in amazement. "What for? The neck and head for a stair post, maybe? The body for a flower-box on the lawn? You could grow strawberries in it."

"How much?"

He shrugged his shoulders and his face was agonized. "How much will you give me for it?"

"Five dollars."

"Take it."

Rob collected the pieces carefully and carried them out to his truck. He arrived home at about two o'clock, drove up to the stables and deposited his trophy in one of the lofts.

25

Howard had two new suits.

Rob McLaughlin always said, "Get them clothes that will show every spot—that'll learn 'em!"

One of the suits was a dark blue serge guaranteed to show every spot. It was double-breasted. When it was on Howard, buttoned around him, he was hardly bigger than a young tree, but Ken felt his dignity and was awed.

The other suit was a silvery gray tweed, very becoming to Howard's slick black hair and good color. Both boys had fine skins; smooth, honey-tan and rosy. Both had blue eyes, but here was the difference—the changing shadows of Ken's, the bright, unwavering stare of Howard's.

There was new interest in Howard's room for both the boys. The new suits hanging in the closet. The new suitcase upon the floor in the corner. The duffel bag leaning against the wall, already half full of sweaters, lumberjacks, sheepskins, caps and boots. They packed and unpacked them.

Ken stared at Howard's new tan oxfords. They looked like his father's. How could they be so big! How could Howard be so tall! Ken stood in the middle of the room on one leg, breathing heavily. How could there have come, suddenly, this great difference between himself and Howard, so that he felt respectful? He looked down at himself. He was too small to count. Well, Howard had only done this shooting up in the last year—there was still time.

The most impressive moment was when Howard put on the Fedora hat. The nearly six feet of his slender height had done nothing to his head and face. The head was so small you wondered at it up there, and the face was the face of a little boy. Topped by the Fedora hat—! Nell had to turn away to hide her laughter.

Ken began to feel very close to LIFE with Howard going away like this. The Fedora—the long blue suit—the huge oxfords—LIFE was an enormous hollow to the right side of him. It was as big as the world. It was gray and filled with darker gray clouds, swirling about. Often he turned his head and looked into it.

Howard going away to West Point! Well, almost West Point. He'd learn how to walk the West Point walk. All their lives it had been fun—it had been an exciting stunt to get their father to walk the West Point walk for them. When they begged him to do it and at first he paid no attention and then suddenly stood up and then stepped out, it always struck them dumb. You could feel something at the roots of your hair. At times he had tried to teach it to them—right foot and left arm and shoulder-forward—left foot and right arm and shoulder forward—the knees lifted high (just for practice) feet going in a circle like the curving trot of a horse. But it was like trying to command the wobbling legs of young colts.

When they went to the movies and, in the newsreel, saw the shot of the West Pointers marching, they strained to catch the details of the walk before it was flashed off.

Howard had an odd walk. He slouched. When he tried to stiffen up and do it correctly he had a little jerk. It wasn't smooth.

"What'll they say about that?" asked Ken anxiously.

Rob roared, startlingly, *"There goes McLaughlin bouncing in line!"*

This was the last straw for Ken. It removed Howard utterly. At intervals during the day, the words rang in his ears, *there goes McLaughlin bouncing in line*. He wasn't even Howard any more. He was McLaughlin. And HE WAS IN THE LINE!

To save expense, Howard was to go east with the shipment of horses his father was taking to Dr. Horner's sale. The railroad allowed one man to each carload of horses, free of charge. There were to be two carloads. Every horse on the ranch, three years old and up, was to go, and a few of the twos who had had enough training. In all, forty-eight horses.

Howard sat talking to his father in the den, one ankle hanging across the other knee just as his father did it. "Dad, how about selling Highboy to help out with my tuition?"

"Good idea, son."

Taggert was to go. She was a good polo player. Gypsy, Flicka, Thunderhead and Touch And Go, would be enough to keep for the family. In the spring there would be a new crop of two-year-olds.

The days went by for Nell in misery and confusion. Rob had not forgiven her. Indeed, since the auction, when he had sacrificed some of his best stock for a few hundred dollars, he had been, she said to herself, fit to be tied.

She tried to think it out. Had she done anything so terrible that she must be punished like this? The thing she had done—her criticism of him—had shattered the illusion that he was perfect in her eyes, and a man of his pride and self-confidence simply could not take it. Most of the time, when he looked at her, his face had an expression of sardonic animosity. Occasionally it was worse than that—it was like a blow. And all the love and tenderness was gone.

One night, before going to bed, she went into Ken's room for a moment. He lay on his back in the moon-flooded room, the sheet thrown off, the pillow on the floor. He was spread-eagled—arms and legs thrown wide. His breath came evenly. The top button of his pajama jacket was fastened. From there it was drawn away by the twist of his body exposing the thin, bare, frail-looking torso of a child. The legs of his pajamas had slid up, one foot hung limp over the edge of the bed.

His face was blissful, his lips parted in an ecstatic smile! Dreaming of Thunderhead, thought Nell, as she gently turned, straightened him, replaced the pillow and drew up the sheet. It did not wake him, he had felt these hands since his birth. He made a murmurous sound, rolled on his side, drew up his knees, gave a deep sigh and was instantly quiet again—breathing deeply and regularly.

Nell went on down the hall to Howard's room. There was a line of light under his door. Howard was standing half naked, examining his physique in the small mirror over his chiffonier.

"Howard! Why aren't you in bed?"

"Gee, Mother! I was just standing here a minute—" His voice slipped down to bass and they both laughed and it slipped again.

"How's your muscle?" asked Nell.

He flexed his arm. "Feel it, Mother! What do you think? I was wondering if I was getting a little bit muscle-bound."

She squeezed the small egg of his muscle and looked solemnly at him. His shoulders were narrow, his smooth chest very childish, his ribs stood out bravely over a little waist she could almost have clasped with her hands. But she had to reach up to slip her arm around his neck. He gave her a shy, naked hug and she laid her cheek against his.

"What do you think?" he insisted.

"No—I wouldn't call you muscle-bound. Howard—go to bed. You must get your sleep."

He slung on his pajama jacket and kneeled to say his prayers, then leaped into bed. His clear blue eyes begged her for something he would not put into words.

"Want me to tuck you in?"

He nodded. If that was a smile on his face, she thought, it must be the way the angels smile. As she leaned over him, fussing with the sheet, smoothing the pillow, fastening the buttons of his blue and white striped jacket, his eyes did not leave hers. The little ceremony

223

had never lost the quality it had in his infancy. It never would. To both of them it was a nugget of pure gold.

"Don't go yet, Mother," he begged, "sit down a minute."

She sat on the edge of the bed. Over her nightgown she wore a little silk wrapper printed with nosegays. Her hair was on her shoulders. Her hands smelled of sweet-scented soap.

"You're so pretty, Mother," he blarneyed, "your face is tan and pink and blue."

She laughed. "You want me to stay."

He took her hand and smelled it.

"Howard, do you mind at all that Ken's got this colt and that maybe he's going to be a racer?"

Howard shook his head. "Nope."

"Don't you ever wish it was you?"

"Nope. I get just as much fun out of it as he does. And besides, I'm going away."

She smoothed his hair. "Yes . . . you're going away. . . ."

He smelled her hand. She smoothed his hair.

"Who will fry my egg for me in the morning—*over and easy*—when you're gone away?"

He laughed and his voice slipped down.

One hand on his black hair . . . over and over . . . the other hand held in both of his against his face . . .

"Mother. . . ."

"Well?"

"Don't you think—now that I'm going away—that you ought to give me kind of a little lecture?"

She put her head on one side and considered. "Tell you how to behave and things like that?"

He nodded.

"Well, perhaps I ought." She thought deeply. "Always say your prayers. That's very important. The life of a person who prays is very different from the life of a person who doesn't pray."

"Better?"

"A thousand times better."

Outside, a night bird gave a sudden passionate cry.

Nell looked at her watch.

"Oh, Mother! Don't you think you ought to tell me about—about the *principles* a man ought to have?"

Nell had to laugh at this, then gave it serious thought. "Well—about honesty, Howard." Her eyes wandered. "If I could just find words to tell you how wonderful it is—it's something you have to *learn*. It's hard to learn. Mostly, there has to be someone to teach you. But if you could get it, it's better than a million dollars in the bank."

"Did someone teach you, Mother?"

"Yes. You know my old Uncle Jerome that I've told you about?"

"The priest?"

"Yes. He taught me. It requires a great deal of study to be a really honest person—deeply honest. When I was talking, he used to stop me over and over again—compare two of my statements, show me how one contradicted the other, and abolish my protests until at last I would keep still, go deep down into myself, see what the truth was and admit it."

Howard moved uneasily.

Nell looked mischievous. "You asked for it!" she said. "But it's worth all the pains it takes to get it! When you've got it, you know so much more! See so much more! Have so much more power!"

"Why?"

"Well—truth is power."

"Why?"

Nell cast about for an illustration. "Suppose you had an automobile, but you had always wanted a sailboat, and some way or other you got yourself thinking this was a sailboat. (That's called wishful thinking.) Or perhaps, in this case, you were just ignorant and didn't know any better. Anyway—you try to sail the automobile."

Howard began to laugh. "It would sink!"

"Then you decide it's a horse and you try to ride it. But spurs don't make it go—"

Howard was roaring.

"You don't have any success. You don't have any fun.

225

Everybody laughs at you, and you begin to think you've got a jinx. Then you find out the *truth*—it's an automobile you've got—the more truth you find out about it the better you can drive it, take care of it—and all that. That's power. You get power as you learn the truth."

The boy's eyes were reflective, trying to find some practical application.

"The thing we're all riding—as you might say—is life. This earthly existence. And the more truth you learn about it, know about it, the better you'll get along with it."

"What kind of a machine is it?"

There was a sudden snarling scuffle on the roof and heavy thuds galloping across. They both jumped.

"It's just Matilda!" exclaimed Howard. "Go on, Mother—"

"Well, I've decided that life is a gymnasium. If you take it that way—a training school, not just a vacation or a pleasure trip, then you're not too upset when you find yourself up against things you can't handle—you just know it's the apparatus—you're making muscle—spiritual muscle—" Her head suddenly turned aside, her eyes became absent and fixed, and the animation of her face vanished.

Howard watched her. "What are you thinking about, Mother?"

Presently she came back, sat silently, smoothing his hand. The night bird cried again and again.

Howard turned to look out his window. The waning moon had rolled over on its back.

"I never can see," said Nell, "how people get the idea that this life is going to be heaven or that it's a place where they'll get their own way, because from the very start we have nothing to say about what happens to us! From birth to death we're shoved around. When we're babies do we eat what and when we want? No. A bottle is poked in our mouths—take it or leave it. We are set upon little pots and told to perform whether we feel like it or not, and when we're through we can't get up until

226

someone comes and attends to us. And getting older means just learning all the different people and conditions we have to obey. Parents, teachers, policemen, signs, the opinions of our friends, conventions, working hours, styles, and health rules and hygiene. Oh! All our lives, a pistol at our heads—DO THIS—OR ELSE! Even my mind compels me. I can't say that two and two make five, can I?

"But if it's a *gymnasium*, Howard—if it's all *training*, making us bigger and better souls—for a bigger and better life after this one—then there's sense in it, isn't there?"

Howard looked at her wistfully. "It seems—awfully big, Mother."

"It's never *too* big for us, dear—"

"Isn't it?"

"No. There's always—lots of—help around."

The night bird began to cry again.

"What *is* that?" asked Howard.

"I don't know. I often hear it."

"Mother—in church it's all about sin. Is there really such a lot of it?"

Nell laughed. Howard laughed a little too. "Well—*is* there?"

Nell sighed. "Howard! You certainly are asking me to stand and deliver tonight!"

"It's the last time, Mother," he said solemnly. "I think you ought to, don't you?"

"Well—*SIN*. Yes, it's all around us—like dirt. Did you ever see anything like the way people have to scrub and wash all the time? Just try, for a moment, to visualize all the brooms flying! Dusters whisking! Cleaning establishments steaming and renovating! Hands soaping clothes! Hair brushes switching! Rags polishing!" Howard was laughing. "The whole world is in an orgy of purification all the time! I've often thought, if it weren't for our sins, the world and the human race and everything it touches wouldn't be dirty. Maybe that's a silly idea."

"Have I got any sins, Mother?"

227

"You've got one that is especially vile and I hope you'll get over it." As the blood crept up under his skin, she leaned to kiss him. "You like to be cruel, Howard. Teasing comes very close to cruelty you know. You have always teased Ken unmercifully. And I think, if your father hadn't been so strict about it, you might have been cruel to animals. Perhaps you have been anyway."

Howard's face was a picture of guilt and shame.

"But that can be finished for good and all right this minute, darling—people don't have to go on being the same if they don't want to. Now and then people ought to overhaul themselves the way you would an engine. Overhaul your habits. Take inventory. See if you've got any traits on your shelves that are no use to you! Stock up with different goods."

Howard was crushed. He couldn't get feeling right again.

Nell sat a long time looking out the window, his hand in hers, listening to the night bird. At last she said as if thinking out loud, "But when you overhaul yourself, be sure you don't throw away any of the wonderful qualities you've got. . . ."

The long pause was electric.

"What, Mother?"

"That nice unselfishness about you—and the way you never hold grudges—. There is your sense of responsibility too. You're going to be a man who can do things—who can be trusted. Now Howard, I really must go—"

As she rose Howard sat up hurriedly. "Do all mothers talk this way to their sons when they go away from home?"

"They do, dear."

"I'm very glad you told me all about life. Thank you ever so much."

Laughter seemed close to Nell's lips that night. It bubbled up again. "Howard! I'll tell you and tell you and tell you—and probably all the same things over again. Maybe you'll remember some of it."

She kissed him again and blew out the lamp. She

228

paused in the moonlight, looking at his pictures, at his clothes, the things on his dresser. At the door she turned for one last look at him sitting up there in bed, his dark head—so like the head on a coin—a sharp silhouette against the white wall.

She went out and closed the door behind her. *Like the head on a coin—*

As she walked down the hall she pressed both hands to her eyes and brushed away the tears. "This is awful," she muttered. She hoped Rob was not in their room. He wasn't. "I might have known," she said. "He's never here when I am if he can help it."

She laid her arms on the top of his chiffonier, put her head down on them and cried uncontrollably. *Where do I get all these tears?* she thought. *It never used to be this way. Now I cry every day.*

There seemed an endless fount of them. The sobs convulsed her clear down to her waist. "Oh, God! Oh, God!" she cried softly.

She opened the top drawer of the chiffonier, took out one of Rob's big handkerchiefs, mopped her eyes and blew her nose and thought maybe she could stop crying. She started walking around the room, but the tears were pouring as abundantly as ever. She drew aside the curtains and stood right in the window. If there was any air moving it would be cool. Cool air blowing on a tear-drenched face helps to stop the weeping, helps to wipe away the marks of it. But she could not yet stop. She leaned against the window-jamb, put both hands over her face and sobbed, "Oh, God! Oh, God!" The tears streamed over her hands. She mopped her face, shook back her hair, made cool judgment on the flood—*I think it's letting up a little bit*— She leaned her head back, felt the soothing comfort of the air on her face. *Who can cry like I can?* She gibed at herself with a little wry smile.

Exhaustion was helping her. When physical energy was completely exhausted then emotion would be too. She'd be able to think soon—to figure it out. Those words of her own to Howard— "You're not too upset

when something comes along too big for you to handle—"
With a rush the tears came again and she held the big
handkerchief up to her face. *Oh, are you not indeed?*
Fine words! Oh, God help me—

The night bird suddenly began again. It was a surpris-
ing, abrupt cry, bold and hard but musical. Even while
she was weeping Nell listened to it, wondering what it
was, what it looked like, and her tears diminished. She
thought of God helping her and wondered how He would
do it. *Somebody's got to help me.* "There's a lot of help
around." "Is there, Mother?" "Yes, nothing's ever too big
for us." What was the matter with her anyway? Loneliness. Bitter—bitter—loneliness. Rob had drawn away
and closed himself against her. She had wounded his
pride *(but not his self-confidence—I might have known
he'd never give up the horses, he'd sooner give up me)* so
he had put her outside. She was the enemy for him. And
he was all she had.

The tears rushed again. This flood was like the freshets
of spring. She sat in the arm chair, cradling her head on
her lap. She felt something against her leg. "Oh, Pauly—
Pauly—" She took the little cat up into her arms and held
her tight, sobbing distractedly. Pauly was unconcerned.
She moved, purring, in Nell's arms, on her shoulder,
around her neck. When she could get at her face she
licked the salt tears. The long topaz eyes blinked softly.

It occurred to Nell that she was spoiled. She had lived
in, by, and for love so long, it had come to be the very air
she breathed, and without it she would asphyxiate. But
there must be people who lived without it—at the
thought she was filled with panic and collapse.

In those quicksands of loneliness one flings out, clutching emotionally at anyone. For a moment she clung to the
thought of Ken and Howard, then drew back. Not on
those young hearts should the touch of her pain and need
rest—not even for a moment. Oh, no—never cling to
your children—they're too young—never let them feel
their mother a weight—let them go free, completely free
and young, looking away from you, looking out at the

path they must travel—no, there was only Rob for her—
and now not Rob.

Nell was still sitting there, holding Pauly in her arms,
breathing deep, sobbing breaths, but without tears, when
Rob appeared at the door. She had no time for the usual
covering up and she did not move or look at him. He
stood staring at her a moment, then went to his chiffonier, opened a drawer, got out whatever it was he wanted,
and went into the adjoining room.

26

When she waked in the night, half-conscious, her
thoughts drifted out to the accustomed place. Rob and his
love. But as when a person walking through a swamp
steps on an apparently solid hummock and feels it sink
beneath the foot, so did her mind fall away without support, and terror swept her. Rob! Did *he* feel nothing?
Didn't he care at all? Didn't he miss her as she missed
him? Suffer for the loss of her? No. People who get angry
save themselves, at least for the time being, from suffering. You throw up the barrage of anger—you escape the
hurt. Rob got angry. He was always angry.

She slept again, and forgot. And again woke, and
reached for him in spirit, but he was not there. After
sleeping and forgetting, for a few moments you couldn't
believe it. It was like a wholly new blow a dozen times a
day. Each time the reaching, each time the sinking and
nothingness. And she would press her hands against her
eyes and say, "Oh, God—don't let me cry—don't let me
start crying again—"

Nell dreamed of a pine tree, as big as a mountain. It was round. And between the great branches, and surrounding it, there was the deep cobalt of the sky. It was as big as the world, and there was nothing else in the dream.

She awoke and lay thinking of the beauty of the single things. "Fair as a star when only one is shining in the sky." A single snow-peak on the horizon. One line of melody, played by one violin, rising out of the roar and bustle of the orchestra, soaring like a bird. Just one friend. Just one love. . . .

His physical body was in the bed beside her. She wished he would sleep in the other room. Did she? She thought she did. She could not lay her head on the pillow beside his, turn or sleep against him, fling her arm across his shoulders, feel the touch of her limbs against his warm length in peace and rightness. This was like sleeping with a stranger.

She went to the window and looked at the eastern horizon. Between herself and the mother-of-pearl sunrise, every blade of grass was silvered with dew. And the shapes of the grazing horses in the pasture were dark silhouettes.

She saw a flock of tiny birds sitting on the branches of the biggest cottonwood tree. They were all facing the east, their eyes fixed, their beaks open. At first she thought they were silent. Suddenly she was aware of a fine, high, sustained thread of sound. They were singing to the rising sun.

It is in the country, she thought, that human beings are wrapped around with poetry and with emotion. Life is filled with it. Emotion is the wind of the soul. You can no more do away with it than with the wind. . . .

In the afternoon she rode up the green hill into the sky, slipped off her horse and threw the reins over his head. She flung herself down on her back and tried to leave the earth behind.

Clouds seemed on a level with her, as if she could

reach hands out to right or left and touch them. It was far below, on the plains, that you saw their shadows. Dark, floating shapes, mysterious and beautiful. If one were there below, she thought, and had not the ability to look up, and stood staring at those shadows, where would one think they came from? Like the hen—down below, broody and feverish in the box, and all her destiny arranged by the big hands in the upper air. In another dimension—always—is the answer to the mysteries amongst which we move.

Over and over again, she suddenly did not believe it. Nothing real, nothing serious, could ever come between her and Rob. And what was it all about? Money. How could money—having it or not having it—do such a thing as this to a human relationship? If they had to be poor, could they not be poor loving each other? Happy with each other? Striving and working together whether success or failure came? No—not Rob. If Rob brought himself and her to destitution, there would be no living with him. He would simply cease to love her—perhaps he had already. Bitterness would warp his nature, put a blight on him and everything he touched.

Some way out *must* be found then. Again she felt that she had done right in sounding the alarm, even if it had turned him against her. But oh, could she endure it?

She sat up and hugged her knees. Kim, who had followed her, came pushing into her chest, and she buried her hands in his thick electric fur. He sprang away after a rabbit, and again she lay back on the warm tangy grass. There was always comfort in it for her. Nature—religion—work—companionship—but no longer Rob's companionship. He was the very woe itself.

The sky was a procession of clouds today, but all different. Clouds like ships. Like caverns which you could enter and walk around in. And over there was a fleet of small square-bottomed boats, all on one level.

She turned on her elbow and thought as calmly as she could. When you're in trouble, *do* something to help. Don't just weep and moan. What could she do? She stalled on that thought, for the only help would have been—not to do—but to undo. Go back behind that night when she had shown Rob that she was, in his own words, just "waiting for him to crash so that she could pick up the pieces." Faced with the realization that there was no going back, could never be any undoing of what she had done, that the only emergence would be by fighting through it and coming out the other side, that it was one of those formidable passages of life through which one struggles as if through a morass, she felt again the racking constrictions in her chest and throat which presaged another burst of weeping. There was nothing for her to do but hang on—sit tight—and try to put a good face on things. After all, it takes two to make a quarrel. Oh, does it? Not by a long shot. Rob could fight like a good one—all alone. Besides, it was really all in *his* hands—not hers.

She sat up and ran her hands through her hair and pressed them to her forehead. There was a tight band around her head and her eyes burned. She called to Injun. Anything to break her train of thought and head off the tears. Injun lifted his head from his grazing, looked at her, then continued to feed.

The worst of it was that, knowing Rob as she did, she knew he had it in him to encase himself in a shell and live in it forever. *He* could stand that—*she* could not. She could not even stand a waning of the love and companionship she had had all her life. Not and live on the ranch with Rob—Rob and the horses and the storms and the hills and occasionally—for vacations—the boys.

She thought about the sale at Dr. Horner's auction. If Rob got the prices he expected, it would give him the victory. It would be a lot of money. No reason, then, to give up raising horses. She could put her hands in his and look at him and say, "I was wrong, Rob—they did pay after all—and I'm glad." Would he forgive her then? Perhaps. The sharp edge of this discord would wear off. But if the horses went cheap—if he did not get enough to buy more brood mares or a stallion, perhaps not even enough to pay their debts—there would be no living with him.

The big clouds had gone. There was only one left, shaped like a question mark, sailing all alone across the middle of the sky. She watched it a long time till a weary quietness filled her. And at last she got to her feet and went to Injun. He lifted his head and stood quietly while she picked up his reins and mounted him.

On the day before the departure, Rob, with Howard and Ken as flank riders, took the horses over to Tie Siding and penned them in the loading corrals there. Not a horse on the Goose Bar Ranch but knew what was happening.

Next day the horses were loaded. Rob led them up the ramp one by one, reassured them with his voice, put them in their places. They were sardined in—head to tail, alternately, tightly enough to support them and hold them steady when the train was moving. At certain stations there would be long enough stops for the horses to be taken out, fed, watered, walked around.

Nell watched them go up the gangway. Taggert, Highboy, Pepper, Hidalgo, Cheyenne, Tango, Injun, and a lot of others. If things had been different between her and Rob—perhaps she wouldn't have felt so terrible. It seemed like an end of things.

Rob and Howard were dressed in bluejeans for the trip. When the horses were loaded and the big doors closed, Rob came to stand beside her near the car. He was very quiet, almost distrait. There had been no shouting. His thoughts were all for the horses—he hardly seemed aware of her there beside him.

"I often wonder," he said meditatively, "if we should ever have anything to do with animals or ever do anything *for* them. We make them helpless. Without us, they take care of themselves so well, but when we have once taken charge of them they depend more and more on us, and what do we do but harm to them? And yet they look at us so trustingly."

235

Nell found no words to answer. She was wondering if in the moment of good-bye his hard shell would crack. Would there be, when he put his arm around her and held her against him while he kissed her, any reassurance, any promise, any warmth?

Rob and Howard were to ride in the day coach next to the freight cars in which were the horses. While they waited they all stood near the steps of this car. The brakemen were attending to the last business they had in the station. Up front, the engineer was hanging out of his cab window. He waved his arm, and at the call "All a-bo-oard!" good-bye kisses were exchanged and Rob and Howard went into the car.

As Rob bent his head for the kiss his eyelids had covered his eyes. The kiss was as cold as a knife. But when he had taken his place in the car with Howard, while Howard and Ken grinned and waved at each other, through the window, mouthing words, he did look at Nell and meet her eyes. And it was one of those hard looks by which he served notice on her that she had offended him and was not forgiven.

27

There were only five days remaining before Ken too must leave the ranch for school. Five days which ordinarily would have been occupied with shopping and going over clothes with his mother, a hurried perusal of books assigned for summer reading and a melancholy wandering about on farewell tours. But the time was spent in a quite different and much more exciting manner because when

Ken and his mother returned from seeing Rob and Howard off, Thunderhead had disappeared.

If his father had been home perhaps Ken would not have got permission to go in pursuit of the colt so easily.

His mother said doubtfully, "But Ken—he may be far away. It might take you several days to find him. You might not find him at all."

"Well, I can try—I know he goes south. Howard and I have seen him coming back a couple of times. And suppose I do have to camp out for a night? I've done that often. Dad always lets us."

It was true. To take food and a small camping kit and go off on horseback was something their father had taught and encouraged the boys to do.

"But all you know is that he goes *south*. South is a big place, Kennie."

Ken grinned. "I'll trail him. I've marked his right front hoof. I'd know his track from any other horse's."

"How did you mark it?"

"I cut a little V in the outside edge."

"What horse will you ride?"

"Flicka. And I'll take enough oats for Thunderhead too. When we find him, it's a cinch he'll come along with us. And then will that old boy get a surprise! Dad said he should be kept *in* this winter, and that doesn't mean just in the Home Pasture, that means in the corrals or in the Six Foot Pasture so he can't jump fences and run away!" (The Six Foot Pasture was so called because of its high barbed wire fences.)

As Ken groomed Flicka and fed her in preparation for the trip he told her all about it. It excited her when he filled her nose-bag with oats and rolled it up and tied it. She knew that meant an expedition, and there hadn't been many of them lately—Ken had been riding Thunderhead so much. Ken had a cap on, that meant something too, and he was more than ordinarily generous with the oats.

She plunged her nose into the feed box, munched vigorously, then raised her head and turned it with sharply

237

pricked ears to watch Ken as he curried and groomed her haunches, running the brush slickly down her hind legs, then straightening up to rasp it against the curry comb and free it of dust.

He smacked her haunches. "Get your fanny over!" and Flicka hastily pranced over and Ken did her other side. She was in magnificent condition. She had had no foal this year and had been kept in and grained so much that her coat was glossy and shining, a bright red-gold, like Banner's. At five years of age she had attained her full growth and stood at fifteen and a half hands high.

Ken dragged the curry comb through her thick blond mane. "Maybe you can help me, Flicka. We're going to trail that son-of-a-gun of yours. Think you could smell his tracks? You oughta—you're his mother." But all Flicka was thinking of was getting out to the upland where she had spent her days of wildness and freedom running along the crests of the Saddle Back like a crazy thing with the other yearlings; and of the wind blowing strong from the snowclad mountains of Colorado; and of the enticing smells that came from so far way. She snorted and trembled as Ken pushed her this way and that, brushed her blond forelock, arranging it neatly between her eyes, and wiped her pretty Arab face.

When she was groomed and shining as a prima donna he threw the saddle and bridle on her and with the nose-bag under his arm, ran down to the house, Flicka trotting at his heels.

His mother was packing provisions into the saddle bags. From long practice she knew exactly what the boys would need on an overnight trip. They always liked to build a fire and cook, so there was a little frying pan and bacon and a couple of big mutton chops. Ken saw that she was putting up enough for himself and Howard both— that was keen. There was a loaf of her own salt-rising bread, nutty and rich and filling. There was a small jar each of fresh butter, raspberry jam, and potato salad; a dozen hard-boiled eggs and a pint thermos of hot chocolate.

238

"Dot'll keep you fur a week, Ken," said Gus, as he strapped the saddle bags on to the saddle.

"I might need my gun!" Ken ran indoors for his twenty-two and fastened the gun-boot under the stirrup leather.

Flicka watched every motion. She knew that the more they put on her the farther she was going, and oh, how she longed for the pastures that were the greenest—because they were the farthest! Her feet danced.

"Keep still there! How can we load you properly with you sidestepping like that?"

Ken brought his blanket roll, covered with canvas, and strapped it across the cantle, then his slicker in front on the pommel where it would be easy to get at in case of rain or snow.

Nell glanced at the sky. It was full of big clouds, sailing along before a boisterous wind. "What do you think of the weather, Gus?"

The Swede looked about slowly. "All right today, Missus, und tomorrow too if de wind hold."

Nell looked at Ken critically. He had a light sweater on over his cotton shirt, bluejeans and low shoes. "If you're going into the mountains, Ken, you don't know what you'll run into. Better take your sheepskin and a pair of heavy socks to pull on at night."

While Gus and Ken added these to Flicka's load Nell went into the house and came out carrying Rob's field glasses. She put the strap over Ken's shoulder. "With those, you ought to be able to see Thunderhead ten miles away."

"Gee! That's keen, Mother! Thanks ever so much!"

The boy kissed his mother and mounted Flicka.

"Have you got your compass?" she called. He slapped his pocket, smiled at her and was off.

Up on the Saddle Back Ken took his bearings. The ranch behind him was due north. The Buckhorn Hills ahead of him, due south. And he knew exactly the way Thunderhead came and went. Once, when he had seen him coming he had lined him up with the mountain behind him, that highest peak of the Neversummer Range called the Thunderer. Ken had never forgotten it because the mountain had a name so like the colt's, and the colt's satiny hide was as white as the snow on the flanks of the mountain—they were obviously closely related. It wasn't often that you could really see the Thunderer—not clear to the top—because there were always clouds hanging around it, but you could see where it was. And he was now following that line. And even without dismounting to look he could occasionally see the print of a V-jagged front hoof on a spot of bare earth. He was on the trail all right.

Up here Flicka was wild to go. She drank in the wind and the sky and a thousand exciting scents and stretched out in a gallop whenever Ken would let her.

When they had gone five miles Ken dismounted, loosened Flicka's girth and stretched his legs. The mare stood alert with pricked ears examining all that was to be seen. Now and then she gave a snort and a sudden toss of the head and pawed impatiently.

Ken focused the field glasses on the land south. As this was Government land there were no cows or horses or sheep on it but there was other life. Wherever there was a clump of rocks little creatures moved, rock chunks or chipmunks. He saw a gray coyote seated near her den with three young ones playing around her. On the level plain he saw a small herd of animals and at first thought they were sheep—no, antelope. Something startled them and they scattered and slid over the grassy dunes as if they were on wheels. Only antelope moved like that. But no sign of Thunderhead. The mountains, brought close by the glasses, presented a face of mystery and enchantment. What was in them? What was beyond them? They seemed higher than he had thought. And as he swept the glasses slowly across them an endless variety of detail was disclosed. Gorges, forests, parks, rocky headlands, great soaring peaks with glaciers in their flanks, and beyond them other peaks and glaciers—and beyond and beyond all the way up to the Thunderer hidden in his castle of clouds in the sky.

There was a queer tight feeling in Ken's stomach. Those mountains seemed awfully big! To find his colt there—he began to feel as if it wouldn't be possible. He lowered the glasses and then quickly put them back to his eyes. Something white had entered the field of vision coming up from one of the undulations of the plains. It was still there. Ken watched it until his eyes burned from strain. Yes—it was Thunderhead—could be nothing else. Too big for a sheep or antelope, too white also. Blazing white. No animal was as white as Thunderhead. He was moving slowly forward over the low saddle which connected Twin Peaks—a familiar landmark—and presently disappeared from view.

Ken mounted quickly and went on, and presently it seemed to him that he was following a course that was almost a trail. Antelope trail, perhaps. And of course, when once the faintest path has been laid on the prairie, other animals follow it. Flicka was following it. Either Thunderhead had made the path, or he had instinctively followed a path made by other animals. At any rate it was leading straight to that little Pass between Twin Peaks.

When Ken reached the Pass he expected to be able to catch sight of Thunderhead again, but from here on the ground rose rapidly and it was more broken. The only sign of Thunderhead was a pile of dung a hundred yards or so ahead.

Ken cantered on, lifting his head now and then to see the mountains that were leaning more and more steeply over him. The Thunderer had slid down behind the other ranges as he came closer to them. Five or ten miles ahead of him were the lower slopes of the Buckhorns, thick with pines. Above was open ground, very wild and broken, going up to rounded summits. And beyond and still higher was a towering, jagged rampart of rock. This did not look like the other ranges. Ken wondered if it might not be the wall of an extinct volcano.

At sundown, when Ken had ridden about twenty

miles, the trail led him around a hill and he found himself on the brink of a river. It was a turbulent mountain torrent, and Ken drew rein and sat for a while watching it, held by that fascination which whitewater always exerts. It was, he knew, the Silver Plume River, the river which runs north out of the Buckhorn Hills then swings around to the west and finally joins the Rio Grande.

He dismounted, and while Flicka drank, examined the ground. Here Thunderhead had stopped to drink too. The tracks led to the river brink and then on upwards!

Debating as to whether he should go further or camp there for the night, Ken heard a sound that made him turn to the mountains and listen. His face became pale as he heard the deep, hollow roar. It was the river, but nothing like the chuckling and gurgling of the wide spread of whitewater here below. It was like the thunder of bass kettle drums that never ceased. Before Ken's eyes there rose imaginary pictures of waterfalls leaping a thousand feet; great gorges with the river hurtling through; trees and boulders pounded and tossed as if they were pebbles. No—not darkness and night up there in that forest by that terrible river! He would adventure the river in the morning when there was plenty of light and the good courageous feeling of daytime. Meanwhile he would camp here in the open for the night.

Making camp was good fun, since he knew how to do it and had everything he needed for his own comfort and Flicka's. He took off her saddle and bridle and fastened the end of his lariat to her halter. He cut a stout stake from the willows beside the river, drove it deep into the ground, using a rock as hammer, and tied the end of the lariat to that, giving her a grazing radius of twenty feet.

When he went to her, carrying her nose-bag of oats out of which he had taken half for tomorrow, she gave a grunting whinny and nosed into the bag even before he had the straps fastened over her head.

With Flicka attended to he ate his supper, then spent an hour wandering around, examining the river up and down stream. As the sun set he saw trout leaping, and took a stick wound with line from his pocket, climbed a big boulder which jutted out into the stream, dropped the line over and caught half a dozen nice trout on his *Captain* fly for breakfast.

At last he piled brushwood on the fire, spread the canvas on a flat piece of ground, and with his rifle beside him, laid himself down and drew the blankets over him.

Shadows covered the world, but a rosy pink filled the western sky and tinted all the clouds which floated above him.

He could hear Flicka breathing, cropping the grass, now and then giving a little snort. He could hear, from far away, that deep roar of the river, and close at hand the occasional flop of a trout. Before he fell asleep, just when he had begun to count the stars, he heard the yammer of a coyote pack, off on the plains. It hardly roused him. It seemed like home.

28

Soon after daybreak Ken was on the trail again. It was very different going from yesterday's, there was no unreeling of the miles at a gallop on this sort of ground. But there was still a trail and here it was more distinct, traveled more, he figured, because it ran beside the river on the left side of it, and more animals used it. Deer had been here, and Thunderhead had been here. Where they could go he and Flicka could go. There were many places he had to dismount and lead her, many times that he stood blocked, steep rocks or the river all around him, until, leaving Flicka, he did some scouting and found that by a series of rabbit-like leaps a way could be found through the rocks and there was open going again beyond.

Always, hour by hour, they climbed. There was one waterfall after the other. Dense forest edged the gorge; and now and then, walking a ledge in the rocky wall, covered with spray and half deafened by the thunderous echoes of the canyon, Ken's heart failed him. When he walked, Flicka followed at his shoulder.

Ken rounded the cliff wall and came to a great pool into which tons of whitewater fell over a hundred-foot slide. He stood motionless in awe. It was the thunder of this fall he had been hearing for the last half-mile. The pool was churned to a boiling white at the base of the fall, shading off through tints of aquamarine to the dark holes at the edges. The walls rose up topped with rich and fragrant loam in which an endless variety of ferns and mosses and small forest flowers were embedded, making a lush and fragrant carpet around the boles of the tree-trunks.

Slowly the boy's eyes moved from spot to spot, taking in every detail of the scene. Across the stream, in the deep water under the cliff, the sun threw a patch of amber and there was a dark shape of a monster trout lurking. Below the pool, that clutter of short logs and saplings was surely the remains of a beaver dam. He saw two sleek heads swimming—they dove under the dam— beaver or muskrat? Dozens of brilliantly barred rainbow trout leaped in the foam at the base of the fall as if attempting to scale that mighty mountain of water. Birds and squirrels flitted through the trees of the river bank, and far off Ken saw five deer moving silently. They turned and looked at him, then leaped away and vanished.

Almost oppressed by such grandeur, Ken threw his head back and looked upward. Far above was a strip of blue sky and a speck floating in it—a great bird on motionless spread wings. He felt as if he were in the bowels of the earth.

That excitement felt by all adventurers, compounded of fear and curiosity and intrepid daring, upheld him. He must go on. Even if he didn't find Thunderhead, he must see what was to be seen from the top of that great rampart, and he must find the source of this river. Silver Plume? More like Hell's Cauldron.

As he went on he came to other such falls and pools. Once there seemed no outlet whatsoever. Going behind Flicka he whacked her and shouted, "Go on, Flicka! Get out of here!" She scrambled unhesitatingly between two great boulders and disappeared.

Following her, he found the path again. The going was easier. And before noon he came to a little beach where again he saw the print of the V-jagged hoof. It excited him. What he would have to tell his father about all this! And Howard! That he had trailed his colt thirty miles into the impassable Buckhorn Hills and found him!

The path was still on the left or eastern bank of the river.

These tracks of Thunderhead's seemed very fresh. Ken and Flicka had been traveling faster than the colt and had nearly overtaken him.

From here on, they left the river and reached rolling ground. The forest ended, they came out upon the last grassy terrace before the rocks shot up in that almost sheer wall which Ken had thought might be the rampart of an extinct volcano. Here below the rampart it was like a park. He had seen terrain like this near home with clumps of trees, rocks, little dells and ravines, but that rampart! He had never seen anything like that before. Its level summit was here and there interrupted by a jagged peak, or a depression; it stretched to right and left, barring his way.

Ken was tired and his heart was pounding. His body felt very light. He remembered what his father had said —that some of these mountain valleys had an altitude of fourteen thousand feet. He had been climbing steadily since daybreak—ten miles at least, and the river had gone over one waterfall after another.

"Flicka, let's have our lunch," he said, and Flicka seemed very willing. He removed her saddle and bridle, haltered her and gave her some oats.

While he lay on the grass, munching his sandwich, he stared at that rocky rampart and wondered if it could be climbed. Certainly not on horseback. Beyond it there seemed to be a space. It might be a lake. There were often lakes in the craters of extinct volcanoes. Or a valley. At any rate, only very high mountains could be seen behind it and they were far away. The Thunderer was in sight again. Ken's father had said that when suddenly all the clouds lifted and you could see that great peak clear to the tip it meant that a storm was coming. You couldn't see the peak now. The clouds gathered from all over the sky, making a shape just like the Thunderer's, only upside down, and came down over it like an inverted cone. You could hardly tell where the mountain ended and the clouds began.

Ken saw some big birds soaring very high up. He counted them. One, two, three. A moment later he saw another. Four. Could they be hawks? There were many hawks on the ranch but hawks had bent wing-tips. The wing feathers of these birds were straight clear to the tip, and their wing-spread was greater. They must be eagles. Ken had read of the Bald Headed Eagle—a dark bird with white head and tail. These birds were dark all over. If they were eagles, they must be Rocky Mountain Golden Eagles. They mounted into the sky until they were the tiniest dots. Two of them kept over to the west, two to the east, as if they had separate precincts.

Just about to take a big bite of his sandwich he paused and sat up. He had heard a dull boom. It had come suddenly—a startling interruption of the silence of the mountains. It sounded more like an explosion of dynamite heard from far away than anything else.

There is was again—a hollow, crashing *BOOM!* He

could tell the general direction from which it came, over beyond the river to the west where there was a steep and craggy peak. Flicka was looking in that direction too.

There seemed to be nothing there which could explain the noise—no dark hole in the mountain side with smoke pouring out, proving that someone was mining there and using dynamite. Ken trained the glasses on it. The sound came again and at the same moment he saw what caused it. Two rams on a high narrow ledge overhanging the sheer wall of the mountain backed off from each other with lowered heads, stood motionless for a moment, then charged. Their heads met and the sound of the impact was like an explosion of dynamite at a distance. The rams backed away again, paused, charged and crashed again.

Through the glasses Ken could see every detail of the fight. He could see the large symmetrical horns curling back, see the shock of the impact, could calculate which one would win. Incoherent exclamations burst from him—"Gee! Golly!—Gosh! Look at him!"

Once the heads had joined the two rams strained against each other, each struggling to push his opponent back. Then they backed off and charged again.

One of them was weakening. As another great *BOOM* floated through the air, one of the rams fell. Once down, the other pursued him mercilessly. There was a desperate struggle on the narrow ledge—he was over! His body hurtled through the air and as Ken lowered the glasses he saw a shape coming down from the sky. The eagle dove with wings folded. The sheep had hardly disappeared from view before the eagle also vanished into the tree-tops.

With his skin going goose-flesh, Ken sat listening. There was no sound. Up on the ledge of the mountain the victorious ram stood alone, his head lifted.

Ken had to gulp a few times. Not from fear exactly, but from the solitude and the awfulness of this place. The ram up there, standing like a king on the mountain ledge with his head up. The mile-long dive of the eagle.

Suddenly he saw the eagle rising from the trees holding a mass of white stuff in his talons. It flew swiftly to a peak of the rampart somewhat to the left and east of where Ken was. Ken trained the glasses on him and now saw the most extraordinary spectacle. On a wide ledge of the peak was the eagle's eyrie, an enormous nest about ten feet across. In this nest two eaglets—nearly as large as their parent—were dancing up and down, flapping their wings, anticipating the arrival of the parent bird with food. The big eagle lit on the edge of the nest, dropped the provender inside and flew away again. One of the eaglets seized the mutton and spread himself over it, attacking it as if it were prey, treading it with his feet. The other danced angrily in front of him, flapping his wings and chattering. Before two minutes had passed the parent bird arrived with another installment of mountain sheep, dropped it into the nest and flew away again. Ken could imagine the expert dismemberment of the corpse among the trees. Presently there were two eagles bringing the food in turns. All four birds satisfied themselves, then the parents flew away, leaving a quantity of the meat pushed to one side in the nest. The two eaglets stood side by side, gorged to repletion. They leaned against each other. Ken had heard that eagles always roost facing the wind—even baby eaglets. He licked a finger and held it up. The eaglets were facing the wind.

All was silence again. The ram had disappeared from the ledge. The eagles were lost in the sky. The baby eaglets had gone to sleep.

Ken dropped the glasses and heaved a deep sigh. He felt very queer. He had lost the thread of his thoughts and it took him some minutes to shake off the spell that was on him and remember what he was there for. Thunderhead. He was after his colt. And he felt now as if the climax of his expedition was past. He wanted to find the colt and find him quick and get to the bottom of the mountains before night, then home in the morning. But there was one thing to do first—and that was, to clamber up that rampart and see what was on the other side of it. He couldn't go home without doing that.

He picketed Flicka and started to climb. Part of it was nearly perpendicular, in other places it was an incline, and here the rock was soft so that he could dig his fingers and toes into it. At intervals he stopped to rest and get his breath and turn and look about him. It was much higher than it had seemed from below. Above him, the summit appeared to be fairly flat, but off to the left was a series of small peaks on the highest of which the eagles had their eyrie, and to the right, as it approached the river, the rampart seemed as jagged as a broken bowl.

For most of the climb, when Ken looked up, he saw nothing but sky. At last he saw an inverted cone of clouds, and then, below them the wide snowfields of the Thunderer. Going on, other mountain peaks came into view and at last the whole of the Neversummer Range.

He scrambled up the last few feet, pulled himself over and sat down on a rock. For ten minutes after that it felt as if the blood were draining away from his body. A numbness spread through him. He lost the feeling of being himself. It was all too big.

A wide green valley lay at his feet, winding away southward. All around it were mountains towering tier upon tier, ever higher and farther, their sides glistening with glaciers. These mountains he had seen at a distance and his father had pointed out and named to him the individual peaks—Kyrie and the Thunderer, Excelsior and Epsilon and Lindbergh and Torry Peak and all the others. But they had been like dreams, floating in the distant sky—not real at all. Now they were close and real. He was in the very world of them, hemmed in. And he shrank to nothingness before the vastness of that world—the unending progression of lofty snow peaks from which, now and then, a white plume arose like smoke from a chimney; from which, now and then, there came a sound—a deep jarring mutter which vibrated the drums of his ears.

Ken drew his knees up, clasped them with his arms and laid his head upon them to shut out the awful sight. A terrible fear and loneliness entered into him. Oh, to be safe and at home! *Mother! Howard!* It seemed to him that if he could only be standing at the door of his mother's room watching her do her hair, sitting over there before her dressing table, her arms up, her soft wrapper falling to the floor, her face smiling at him in the mirror, he would never want to leave again.

It was some time before he raised his head and then it was because, as happens when one is in a high place with one's eyes closed, he began to feel as if he was falling over the edge.

They were still there. Opposite him the Thunderer seemed to float in the sky and its escort of clouds floated around and above it.

He looked down at the valley. It made him feel better. How wonderful a place! The deep mountain grass! The broad river winding through! And all sorts of little hills and dells and trees and creeks. The rampart on which he sat dropped down sheer for a hundred yards or so, as if it had been cut with a knife. From there down to the floor of the valley, it sloped, cracking into fissures and ravines in which were streams and clumps of aspen and wild berry bushes. A few hundred yards to the right of him the river escaped from the valley through a cut in the rampart. Surely, as he had thought, this valley was the crater of an extinct volcano and this wall he was sitting on had once been boiling lava. And down there in the valley had been a cauldron of hell—where now he saw animals peacefully grazing—antelope—elk—horses—

Suddenly he stood up and looked closely at the horses. There were a lot of them. They looked like mares and colts, and off to one side there was a white horse grazing. And when Ken saw him, all his tension was shattered. And first the tears sprang to his eyes, and then a burst of laughter came. Thunderhead! Just the sight of him down there made the mountains lift their weight off of him! He and Thunderhead together would be a match for all of them!

He snatched off his cap and waved it and yelled, "Thunderhead! You son-of-a-gun! How'd you get in there?"

They were upwind from him and too far away to notice him. He took the glasses that hung over his shoulder and trained them on the horse. A puzzled look came over his face. He lowered the glasses, stared across the valley for a moment, then adjusted them to his eyes more carefully.

That was not Thunderhead's body! Those gnarled and knotted muscles! Those heavy limbs! Those big twisted veins! Leaning over until he was in danger of falling Ken examined the stallion from his ears to his hoofs.

At last he dropped the glasses and looked around crazily. He rushed to the edge and back again to the other side. "Dad! Oh, Dad! Mother! Here he is! Here he is! Flicka, here's your grandfather! Oh, gosh! Oh, gosh!" He leaped about on the crest of the rampart waving his arms and giving war whoops of triumph. "Flicka! Flicka! It's him! I've found him! It's the Albino!" He started to go back down the rampart to Flicka, then changed his mind and rushed to the other edge. If there had only been someone there to yell and dance with him!

It took him a long time to quiet down. His heart was going like a triphammer and his cheeks were crimson. Restlessly he moved about on the crest of the rampart, hardly able to think clearly, feeling that something should be done about this immediately but not knowing what.

At last he got himself in hand and stood quietly, watching the Albino, every step he took, every lift of his head. He would glance at his mares and around the valley, then peacefully continue grazing.

Ken compared him to Thunderhead. He was taller and looked as if he weighed much more. Thunderhead! Where was *he*? He had almost forgotten him.

Ken was puzzled. What had Thunderhead to do with those mares and that stallion? Something, surely. It must be for them that he made these runaway trips every so

251

often; it was to this valley that he came. But he was no-where in sight—

Taking the glasses again, Ken carefully explored every foot of the valley. Could Thunderhead be hiding anywhere there? If he was in the valley would he not be with the mares? And how did he get in? Where was the entrance? And why did the Albino ever permit a strange stallion to come near his band?

Suddenly the Albino raised his head and began to search the wind. Almost instantly he showed excitement, dropped his nose and galloped at his mares with his head snaking along the ground and began to round them up. Ken, wondering what had given him the alarm, watched him, thrilled at the fury and speed with which he whipped every mare into position. In a trice he had them in a solid bunch. Then he whirled, trotted out before them like a gladiator, raised his head to the rampart and neighed a brassy, whinnying challenge.

Ken followed the direction of the Albino's gaze and saw Thunderhead standing on the rampart some hundreds of yards to the left of him, looking down into the valley. He was standing very quietly, without excitement or surprise, as if he had been in that spot, seen that valley and the mares, many times before.

The Albino went closer to the rampart. He neighed again and again. He trotted up and down beneath it. Thunderhead continued to look down at him for all the world as if he were saying, "Don't get excited. I'm biding my time."

Suddenly the colt heard a sound which did arouse his interest. It was a long impatient neigh from Flicka who had had enough of being tied to a twenty-foot picket rope. Ken heard it too.

Thunderhead whirled around, looked, listened, lifted his nose with nostrils flaring. The whinny came again; he whinnied loudly in answer, plunged down the slope and disappeared among the trees.

29

The wind was uncoiling the clouds from the Thunderer. They blew about like spume. Billows of snow mingled with them, all of it rolling away and up until the sun struck underneath and lit the vast snow fields to the blazing whiteness of diamonds.

The Thunderer hung in the sky clear and naked, looking down at the lower peaks and ranges, at glaciers and forests, across the patch of emerald valley to the volcanic wall on which stood the small figure of a boy, looking boldly back at them.

Ken could not bring himself to leave. For a long time he had watched the Albino and the mares. When Thunderhead had disappeared, the Albino continued to observe the rampart for a while, trotting up and down nervously, his ears sharply pricked, an occasional neigh proclaiming the fact that he was still ready to fight if his opponent would show up. There was no answer and no movement on the summit of the rampart. At last the stallion returned to his closely bunched mares and gave them permission to relax and resume grazing. He did this by plunging straight through them and scattering them. As they broke away he stood watching until they were once more grazing, then he too quieted down and began to graze. Peace descended on the valley.

Ken continued to stand there. The pain and loneliness he had felt under the weight of the mountains had changed to a bold ecstasy. He stood drawing in their icy breathing, with his feet braced apart. He wanted the mountains to make their mark on him before he left, so that he could take them away with him and never lose them.

He saw the clouds leaving the Thunderer and remembered what his father had said—that when the clouds left the Thunderer a storm was in the making. This did not worry him. He studied each peak, impressing upon himself that here were the highest mountains in the United States, the Rocky Mountains; that they were full of gold, silver, copper, tin, lead; had been mined since time immemorial, and still were mined. He remembered all his father had told him about the old mining towns—spreading a map on the table to pick out the funny names of them. Slumgullion. Sour Dough. Pancake. Frying Pan. Piping Hot.

But there was still business to attend to. He had to find out how Thunderhead had got into that valley, for of one thing he was convinced, it was the Albino who had given him that terrible blow when he was a yearling. And that meant either the Albino had got out, or Thunderhead had got in.

Ken thought of the river. There, where it cut through the volcanic rampart, might be a gap wide enough for a path as well as the stream itself. This gap was a few hundred yards to the west of where he was standing. He went along the summit of the rampart till he reached that great hole and lay down on his stomach and looked over. He need not give a second thought to the possibility of anything living entering the valley by that door. The broad river fell into a narrow chasm with sheer walls that went up hundreds of feet. It was a churning white cauldron fearful to look at, and there, as it made the plunge, the quiet river opened its deep throat and began that terrible roar which he had heard miles below.

After Ken had spit into the torrent, to show his utter superiority, he returned along the rampart and noticed that there was a whirlwind of clouds gathering high above

254

the bare slopes of the Thunderer. From over the valley, from other mountain peaks and ranges, clouds were rushing to help form that rotating mass. In all the upper air there was a growing excitement and movement, and even as Ken watched, the clouds spread out, descended upon the mountains, and joined each other. In a moment the Thunderer, and Kyrie and Epsilon and Lindbergh and Excelsior were blotted out. Only the valley left, and glimpses, now and then, of a precipitous mountain side, or a peak, as the clouds parted and swirled and closed again.

Ken began to have a feeling of haste.

It was unthinkable, however, that he should go home having been as near to an eagle's eyrie as he was at this moment without a feather in his cap. Before climbing the peak he carefully examined the sky and the tops of the trees. No parent birds were to be seen.

When his head came up over the edge of the great mass of sticks and clods and branches that formed the eyrie he saw the eaglets as he had last seen them, standing leaning against each other. But he saw something else that had been out of his line of vision until this moment. The parent bird sitting on the nest perch, which was a steep little jut of rock around the other side of the nest and somewhat above it.

The eagle attacked instantly. Ken turned and leaped—scrambled—slid, protecting himself with his upflung arms against the eagle's fury. If he had been motionless for one moment he might have been severely injured, but as he continued bounding as if with seven league boots, occasionally falling and rolling, he was not still long enough to offer the eagle a real opportunity. That came only when he hit bottom, and, on his back, fought the eagle off with fists and feet. He realized for the first time that it had only one leg. The bird drove his beak at Ken's eyes. Ken bashed its head to one side. The eagle recovered quickly and drove again, catching Ken's underlip in its mandibles and cutting it deep. At the same moment Ken felt a searing pain in his middle where the bird had thrust in his talon, driving for his vitals—four terrible hooks of steel, each one two inches in diameter.

The buckle of Ken's leather belt saved him, for the eagle's talon encircled it and the steel gimlets went only half as deep into Ken's flesh as they otherwise would have.

Suddenly the eagle, having had enough of the kicking and hammering, loosed his hold and rose vertically in the air.

Ken's shirt was soaked with blood across the middle. Blood was running down his chin from his cut lip. All down the right side of his hip he was minus pants and the flesh was raw. His clothes were in ribbons and his right wrist lamed. The heel of the hand was covered with tiny cuts and abrasions into which gravel and dirt was ground.

But what boy knows when he has had enough? Before Ken washed and bound up his wounds, plastering them with adhesive carried in his small first-aid kit, he did a little more investigating, determined to find out where the entrance to the valley was. And he found the fissure in the cliff, close under the eagle's eyrie, with the keyhole at the valley end. And he found—a little farther east— the path by which Thunderhead climbed the rampart, and saw there evidence to prove that Thunderhead had been there many times. The path was well worn. There were hoof marks everywhere. The surface had been trampled. There was manure both old and fresh. It was easy to reconstruct the whole story now. After his first encounter with the Albino, Thunderhead had come to this spot to look down at his enemy—at the mares—at the lush valley, but never again had he ventured through the pass.

Thunderhead, of course, had joined Flicka at the camp when he heard her nickering; and as Ken threw the saddle on him, bridled him and packed his kit, the air was filled with dancing snowflakes. There was no sky, no tree nor mountain tops to be seen. But the light was still good

256

and Thunderhead knew the way. How well he knew it! As well as he knew his way from the Goose Bar stable to the pasture. And Ken had to laugh at the mad eagerness of both horses to be gone from this place and get home!

Ken let the reins loose on Thunderhead's neck and Flicka followed close behind.

What a ride! Untroubled by the snow storm, or the clouds of spray that drenched them on the river paths, or the waterfalls leaping over their heads or the many obstacles on the nearly invisible trail, Thunderhead took his young master down the mountains and safely home without a misstep or a pause.

It was a very sore and aching boy who lay in the walnut bed at the ranch next afternoon while Rodney Scott, the doctor who had cared for him when he had pneumonia and who was a good friend besides, extracted dirt and pieces of shale from his hip and hand and took stitches in the underlip and stomach. "And all that done by a one-legged eagle!" he joked. "Just suppose he had had two?"

Ken laughed.

"And now, Mamma" (the doctor called all women *Mamma*, testifying to a small town practice in which maternity cases preponderated), "put hot salt water compresses on those abraded surfaces—ten minutes on and ten minutes off."

"What about his going to school in three days?"

"In three days he won't know anything happened to him—unless infection sets in. Send him to school and I'll look in on him there."

That night as Nell was brushing her hair in Ken's room (by special request) he said, "Mother, discoverers can name the places they discover, can't they? So I can name that valley. I've named it the Valley of the Eagles. How do you like the name?"

"I think it's just right and perfectly stunning!"

Ken sighed happily. Then, looking out the window, he added, "Only thing is—I didn't get a feather—*darn it!*"

30

Eat something, said Nell to herself, as if she were speaking to a child. You'll feel better if you do. You must.

But she continued to stare out the window, sitting in the arm chair in her bedroom wrapped in her dark blue robe, her feet drawn under her because of the chill that filled the house. There was no fire on the hearth and the bed was not made and her hair was not brushed.

It was one of those raw October days that should be shut out by fires and curtains and cheerful voices. On some such days Nell worked furiously from dawn till dark, cleaned and mended and made new curtains and counted and took out and packed away and potted geranium slips and cleared the flower borders. And there were other days when, if she moved at all, it was to wander listlessly, pausing at every window, wondering what she had come into this room for, wondering if it was morning or afternoon—what day of the month—

Gus's heavy tread was on the stairs, coming slowly. He rapped on the door.

"Come in!"

"Bring you some wood, Missus."

"Oh, I haven't used up what's here."

"You must have fire."

"It's not very cold."

Gus kneeled down, removed some of the ashes, laid and lit the fire, and carefully brushed the hearth. As he got to his feet he threw a quick glance at Nell. Her gaze was on the fire now, the lips of her soft mouth parted.

There were dark hollows under her eyes and her face looked both old and childish.

Gus started to speak, hesitated, then came out with it. "How de Boss come out mit selling de horses, Missus?"

"I don't know."

"He in de east still?"

"No. In Laramie."

"Laramie! Ven he get back?"

"I don't know exactly. But it was in the paper about a week ago."

Gus leaned to brush up a few more imaginary ashes. "You come down in kitchen, Missus. I'm getting some lunch."

"All right, Gus. Is it lunchtime?"

In the warm kitchen Gus moved about efficiently and set a cup of hot strong tea on the red-checked tablecloth before her, some baked beans, well-flavored, topped with crisp browned salt pork, and some of her own bread, toasted on top of the stove.

Sitting opposite her, stirring his tea, his pale blue eyes studied her thoughtfully. "You sick, Missus?"

"No, Gus."

"You going to ride dis afternoon?"

"I don't know." She looked at the food before her and took her fork in her hand, then felt her stomach shrink and close. Her belts had grown very loose these days; her slacks hung on her hips.

Gus appeared to be giving thought to nothing but the demolishing of the great pile of beans on his plate. "If you cud get a jackrabbit—de chickens needs meat—"

Nell drank a little of her tea and set the cup down. "Well—I might. Later in the afternoon."

"I saddle Gypsy for you, Missus."

Nell stirred her tea, staring a hole through the table-cloth.

"Dot Gypsy—she's wid foal."

"Yes, I know."

"Und de Boss, he don' want she should have no more foals."

259

"She must have been bred before he took her away from Banner last spring—early."

"Ya. Und dot mean she's foal dis winter."

Nell buttered a small piece of toast, made herself eat it.

"You don't like de beans, Missus?"

"I like them, Gus, but I'm not hungry."

She went upstairs again and slowly tidied her room, with many pauses to stand at the window. The bleak skies and the colorless world looked back at her balefully.

Later in the afternoon she put on her black woolen jodhpurs and her warm gray tweed jacket. A few strokes of the comb through her hair drew it back and she fastened it in a little bun, brushed her bang smooth and drew on her small black visored cap. As she picked up her felt-lined gloves and the red scarf for her throat she suddenly wanted to hurry and get out of that house.

The black mare galloped along, and the slim pliant figure sat her with an easy, unconscious swing. Occasionally her head was flung back and the gesture was like a cry for help. Ranging around the horse were the two dogs, Kim and Chaps.

Nell was glad of the small duty to perform, the getting of meat for the chickens, was glad of the gunboot strapped under her leg. She felt as loose and rootless on the ranch as a tumbleweed.

With the passing of her lethargy her mind became painfully active. An excited argument began and she put herself first on one side of it and assured herself that there was nothing serious the matter with Rob nor between himself and her, and then she put herself on the other side and insisted frantically that it was unheard of —the way he was treating her!

Galloping along the County Road, Gypsy pricked her ears and turned her head toward the Saddle Back.

"No, you don't, old girl—we're not going up there."

Gypsy whinnied, getting the wind from the band of brood mares beyond the crest, but Nell pressed her spur against her and held her in the road.

She counted the time since Rob had left on September

tenth. It was nearly a month. Figuring four days for the trip to Pennsylvania, then a week or ten days for the sale, and two days for the trip back—that would have brought it to September twenty-sixth. Where had he been since then? Laramie, apparently, just twenty-five miles away. And hadn't come home. Hadn't even written. And here it was the second week in October.

She turned Gypsy through the gate into Nineteen and they galloped over the uneven ground which led down to Deer Creek. Ahead of her a migration of bluebirds rose like a cloud from the grass, then, as she halted, they descended, and each bird lit on a stalk of grass. It looked like a field of big blue flowers, and when a puff of wind came and made the grasses sway, it seemed as if the bluebirds were swinging on purpose, just for the fun of it.

Nell rode slowly forward, hating to disturb them. They rose to let her through, fluttered and circled above her, then lit again behind her and continued swinging on the grass stems.

Reaching the bank of Deer Creek, Gypsy was belly deep in dried brown grass. She grunted softly and turned her head toward the water. Nell sat relaxed in the saddle while the mare waded into the stream, her feet sinking deep in the soft gravel, and the fresh and delicious smell of water and damp earth and autumn leaves wafted up and made Nell wonder why, now, everything that was sweet sent a sharp pain through her heart.

Long wheezing sucks came from Gypsy. Two magpies were quarreling in a tree overhead. And a little way off there was frantic yipping from Kim as he chased a rabbit. The cocker never yipped nor would he let a rabbit draw him into a hopeless chase. He knew in advance where the rabbit would go and intercepted it.

Nell lifted Gypsy's head, turned her, and the mare scrambled up the bank, scattering water from her hoofs and her mouth. And as she resumed her canter, Nell resumed the argument. Rob had been in Laramie about two weeks and hadn't let her know. Why? Didn't he want to see her?

The dogs had vanished completely. Often they started out on a ride with her, were led off by rabbits or exciting scents and disappeared. She wouldn't see them again until she got home and found them panting on the terrace.

At the thought that Rob did not want to come home her mind spun around to his point of view. How was he thinking and feeling? Was he suffering too? *Oh, I hope so, I hope so, for if he loves me he couldn't help it. But does he? He could come to me, but I couldn't go to him. Or could I?* She thought of herself driving down to Laramie, going about hunting for her husband—No. *No!* She tingled with shame. She had to wait here, but how long? Yes—*how long?* Until he decided to come back. She was entirely helpless.

As these thoughts chased each other through her mind, her body and her nerves were played upon as if by little whips. Alternately hot and cold—weak, or strengthened by a wave of pride. Again and again there went through her heart and stomach a rush of sinking emptiness, and each time she recovered from it as from a shock, slowly, and weakly; a difficult comeback. It was that which prevented her from eating, for it came often just as she had prepared food for herself and sat down and looked at it.

She wondered at those mysterious physical activities, probably governed by the endocrine glands, which are the reactions to violent emotions. What, really, was going on in her body? Was it a sort of shell shock? Was it destroying her health and strength and youth? She could not bear to look at the face that peered back at her from the mirror.

In the timber of Number Sixteen the dogs appeared again, madly chasing a rabbit. Up here the shaded depressions amongst the trees held snow left from a recent storm. The rabbit was in the snow, struggling toward a pile of rocks and Kim was bearing down on it, yipping hysterically.

Nell drew rein and watched the chase, quieted by a feeling of fatalism. What chance did the rabbit have? It was like her mind—doubling and dodging, trying to find a hole in which to hide, or a path of escape, but cornered every time.

The rabbit doubled on its tracks and Kim, who always went too fast, shot past it. The rabbit was struggling to reach the rocks. No doubt he had a safe hideaway underneath them. Would he make it? Kim was almost upon him, and again the rabbit turned and dodged, and again Kim shot past and had to brake and turn and in those few seconds the rabbit reached his haven. But ah—Chaps was there too. The canny black cocker emerged from ambush at the last moment and seized his prey.

And then the kill. The tiny squeals of the rabbit—the sharp nosings of the dog—the sudden jerks of their heads and snappings of their jaws.

No blame to them, thought Nell, as she galloped toward them and called to them to stand back. Wagging their tails proudly they stood off and looked up at her. They were panting, and their long red tongues hung, dripping, out of the sides of their mouths.

Nell picked up the big jack—it must have weighed six pounds—and asked Gypsy's consent to hang it on the saddle. Gypsy pricked her ears and drew in her chin, snorting. Nell offered it to her to smell. Gypsy sniffed the rabbit gingerly, and after that, permitted Nell to fasten it to the saddle.

The dogs watched her, well satisfied. They knew that later, when Gus skinned it, they would get their share.

The hunt and the killing of the rabbit had added to Nell's depression. She could not bear to go home. If she could ride until it was completely dark, and there would be nothing to do but pull off her clothes and fall into bed! If she could ride until she was so tired that she would be sure to sleep!

Occasionally she glanced upward to see if there were any stars, or if the moon was rising, but the sky was a solid gray lid, not low or stormy, but withdrawn and bitterly cold. It made her shiver. If there was beauty and life in Nature, where had it gone? When the skies were like

263

this they put a blight on the world, and on the human soul.

They galloped along in the gathering darkness, the dead rabbit thudding against the mare's side.

Nell reached the stables from the south pasture. She had expected Gus to be watching for her, but no one was there, not even the dogs. She fed Gypsy, unsaddled her and turned her out. She hung the dead rabbit in the meat house and walked slowly and unwillingly down through the Gorge. Physically, she was near collapse, and she walked slowly and unsteadily.

As she approached the house she suddenly stopped walking. Lights shone in all the windows and a row of cars stood behind it.

It was one of those uproarious gatherings which occur when town people descend on their country friends with all the "makings." The house was bursting with food and drink, lights and roaring fires and human noise and movement. Rob had brought T-bone steaks. Potatoes were already baking and Genevieve Scott was just putting the finishing touches to two big pumpkin pies.

When Nell stood in the kitchen door, dazed and almost unbelieving, and exclaimed, "Rob!" she was promptly enveloped in a rowdy bear hug by her husband, and thereafter by Rodney Scott and Charley Sargent. She was told to sit down and rest herself and let her guests do the cooking and set the table. Morton Harris brought her an old-fashioned cocktail. There would be nothing for Nell to do, they assured her, but make her famous dressing for the lettuce.

"And the mustard and coffee sauce for the steaks!" exclaimed Rob.

Gus was concocting the potent Swedish punch called *glögg*.

"And I hope," said Bess Gifford, "that there'll be room in the oven for these biscuits."

"And we'll be ready to eat at about eight-thirty," said

Rob, "and until then there's nothing to do but drink up and enjoy yourself."

Nell ran upstairs to her room. *Rob is home. He kissed me. He is here!* This very night they would be together in this room and all would be explained and forgotten. That dreadful loneliness—that desolation—it was all over. An easy breathing lifted her breast and it was new and pleasant and free and a great change—as if, all these weeks, a painful thong had bound her lungs.

She stood on the threshold of their bedroom, wondering if he had been there already, if there would be some sign, his coat thrown across the pillow, or his boots standing argumentatively in the middle of the floor. Instead, she saw the bed piled high with feminine wraps. Of course. The girls, and their things. Well—it would all wait.

Moving lightly and excitedly, she brushed and groomed and freshened herself and ran downstairs again.

Rob offered her another cocktail. "How's about another?" he asked jovially. "You've got to catch up to the rest of us, you know."

"Have you been here long?" she asked, raising her eyes to his as she took the glass. It was like speaking to a man she hardly knew but was desperately in love with.

His eyes met hers for a split second and then fell to the glass he was handing her. "Oh, a couple of hours!" he said.

"And I'm watching you make your salad dressing!" said Morton Harris. "I've got all the things out on this table for you!"

The radio was roaring. Bess Gifford and Charley Sargent were dancing in the middle of the living room.

It seemed to Nell she was floating on the surface of a river of sound and sensation, that lifted her higher and higher. Her body was warm and quick and pliant, the pupils of her eyes dilated, her laugh rippled. She sat at the head of the table and carved the steaks, putting a lump of butter and mustard in each slice, and a dash of black coffee and then spooning the gravy over the meat until all was blended. When, now and then, the memory of the afternoon—of all the days gone before—came back to her, she put her fork down and leaned her head back and wondered if she was drunk—so unbearably sweet was the pang of the present laid against the desolation of the past. It was over. He was here. He had kissed her. He would kiss her again tonight.

"Maybe *you'll* tell us, Nell!" shrieked Bess Gifford from the other end of the table. "Why is it that Rob and Charley are never so happy as when they can put their heads together and talk about how much money they lose on horses?"

"Lose on horses?" said Nell doubtfully, her eyes going to Rob's.

"Don't believe him," said Rodney Scott. "Come on now, Rob—give us the low-down. You made a mint on this sale, didn't you?"

"You don't have to ask him," shouted Stacy Gifford. "Take a look at him! See that smug grin! He busted the bank!"

Rob was trying to make himself heard. "If you will have it," he said, "I lost my shirt."

"That's what he was saying to Charley," insisted Bess Gifford. "And I can't see what they go on raising horses for—"

"Just for the fun of giving 'em away," said Charley, "or seeing 'em lose on the race track."

"Did you really, Rob?" asked Genevieve Scott.

"I did," said Rob grinning. "Who could have done it but me? I hit that sale with two carloads of horses just when the Argentine polo players were unloading their stuff before they left the States. Their horses sold for fabulous prices. American horses sold for a song."

Nell sat very still. That was the way he had chosen to tell her. Easier on him than to tell it seriously when they were alone together. Easier on her too.

Rodney Scott hit his head with his fist. "And he owes me money!" he exclaimed.

"Owe *you* money!" scoffed Rob, "and how many others! But I'm serving you all notice. No bills going to be paid!"

Nell's eyes widened and flew to Rob's. Was it that bad? It couldn't be— Surely, even if he had had to sacrifice the horses for the lowest prices, with two carloads, there would be enough realized to pay their bills—

Her eyes held a definite question. For the first time Rob met her gaze directly and his hard expression gave her a definite answer. Her eyelids fell. It was true. A disaster. But she didn't care. Money—what did it have to do with them?

While the hilarious and senseless talk crisscrossed the table, Nell listened to the music. An orchestra and Arthur Rubinstein were playing a Rachmaninoff concerto. The broad, impassioned crescendos entered into her blood. So men could feel that way too. It had been composed by a man. It was being played by men. It was the way she felt. Was it the way Rob felt too?

At some time during the evening someone announced that it was snowing, and the men went out and closed the windows of their cars. Gus kept bringing in logs for the fireplaces and bowls of glögg. It was too late and the weather was too bad for anyone to think of driving back to Laramie that night. Nell went into the downstairs bedroom to be sure there was oil in the lamps. Striking a match and shielding the flickering wisp of flame, she suddenly saw another hand resting on the table before her. She could not mistake that hand—the hard power of it— the significance.

The flame went out. The hand closed around hers, completely engulfing it. Her hand was lifted and the palm was kissed twice, then dropped.

Trembling all over she found and struck another match. She was alone in the room.

She lit the lamp and stood trying to pull herself together. She looked at the palm of her hand as if she could see upon it the imprint of that violent caress which had been able to turn all the blood in her body into fire.

267

She would stand there until her trembling stopped and her heart quieted down.

She looked at her hand again and again. She laid it upon her cheek. She wondered if, when she returned to the living room, the mark of it could be seen reflected in her eyes, on her lips, in her smile, in everything she said, for the kiss continued to burn in her. She could not get it out.

She examined the lamps, made sure there were covers enough on the beds, and stood trying to plan the disposal of her guests for the night. Eight people, five beds, two of them double. She couldn't think. It was worse than trying to place guests for a dinner party.

Her guests planned it for her. Two married pairs could sleep in the two double bedrooms, the two bachelors in the boys' rooms, Rob in the bunk house.

Nell slept in Rob's dressing room. If not his own arm around her, then let it be his room.

Not often in a whole lifetime does one lie all night long without sleep even brushing the eyelids, but so it was with Nell that night.

In the morning the men were up early, digging out their cars and putting on chains, while the women got breakfast.

They left immediately after, and Rob paused to kiss her and say—this time without even a glance into her eyes, "I've got to go back to Laramie with them—some business to attend to. I'll be home soon. I'll wire you, and you can drive down and get me."

31

Nell dreamed she was being married again to some man she had never seen. He was about six and a half feet tall and broad-shouldered in proportion. He had straight brown hair, getting a little thin, and a very red face of a shade something like the American Indian. He was punctilious, kindly and attentive.

The marriage ceremony took place in the grounds of an estate, shaded by great trees. It came abruptly, before she had attended to certain important business matters. Indeed she had an uneasy feeling that it was not going to be entirely legal until these things were done. Was it the final papers of a divorce? She could not quite be sure—but certainly the way was not clear for the marriage.

The officiating clergyman, too—there was something a little off-color about him. He had to explain, as he stood before them with a deprecatory smile, that—since he had been told so recently during an adventure (which he recounted to them) that he was now a bonafide priest, he could legally perform marriages.

She and her fiancé were seated before him in two low chairs.

"I know," he said, waving his hands, "that you are anxious and in a hurry—" and she and the huge red man hastily assented and joined their hands as skaters clasp crossed hands in front of them.

The only observers of this marriage were the dozen or two Great Dane dogs who belonged to the estate. She

269

had seen them before in their wire enclosure, hurling themselves against it in an insensate violence. Now, off to one side of the ceremony, they were lying quietly, all in the same position, heads on outstretched paws, the back legs drawn up under. Half of them were dead. These lay in exactly the same position as the living dogs, but they were skeletons only.

Nell felt the feverish dream-misery of having forgotten something important, or lost something, or of being improperly dressed. And while she sat with her fiancé, their hands clasped like skaters, waiting to say *I do,* she felt the eyes of the Great Danes upon her, the living eyes watchful and a little threatening, as if to say, *Be careful now—watch your step.* And the black sockets of the dead ones saying, *It's all no use—it's too late.*

And she awoke with a burst of relief to find it a dream, but haunted by the terrible reality of the big red man with the careful manners, her next husband. He followed her all day, so vivid and unique in appearance, so definite in personality, that when she drove down to Laramie to lunch with Rob and bring him home she found herself nervous, like a woman between two men. And she kept thinking, Let sleeping dogs lie. But they weren't just sleeping.

The past week had been almost as hard on Nell—on appetite and nerves and sleep—as the weeks before, and she was thin and strained. But she dressed very carefully in a six-year-old suit of green tweed and a felt beret of the same shade. The fever that was in her lit her face with color and quickness. Her iris-colored eyes darted in every direction. Her lips were tremulous. She laughed a great deal. When she took off her jacket and sat there in her thin close-fitting yellow sweater she looked like herself again, bright and young. Rob had very little to say. She had to make conversation and did not know how much she dared ask. "Was it true—about the horses— what you told them at dinner the other night?"

"Yes. I couldn't have chosen a worse time."

"I'm sorry, Rob." She hesitated and dropped her eyes

as she said it. "About our debts too? That we can't pay them?"

"We can't pay them."

"And the five-thousand-dollar note?"

"Not that either. That's what I've been doing this week —getting all these things settled. Extensions on the loans and notes, arrangements with our creditors."

This week perhaps, she thought as she cut her lamb chop, but what about last week and the week before? And why couldn't you have been living at home, driving down here in the daytime to attend to banking business as you always have before? But none of this worried her since Rob's visit of a week ago. As long as he loved her— That minute in the dark when he had taken her hand and kissed it! And, too, his absence was explained by the fact that the sale had been a failure and he dreaded to come home and tell her so. *There you are, simply sitting back and waiting for the crash—so that you can pick up the pieces.* She couldn't blame him.

"Tell me about Howard," she said, since he had no intention of talking about the sale. She didn't know yet what the size of the check had been. Wasn't he even going to tell her that?

While he talked about Howard and the school, her mind was divided into several parts, listening, pursuing its own course of reflection and analysis, and observing closely.

It wasn't only the hand that had made her sure again of his love. It was having found Gus mending the sleigh in the loft over the stable. And he confessed that Rob had brought it from Denver in the truck and that it was to be a present for her, and that he was to say nothing about it.

Not only the hand and the sleigh, but the Monkey Tree too. Riding one afternoon, she had come upon a big Monkey Tree around which a trench had been dug. She halted Gypsy and sat looking at it with astonishment. This was the way Rob transplanted grown trees. Dig a deep trench enclosing the roots, then soak the earth thoroughly so that it would freeze when freezing weather came. In dead of winter it could be chopped out without disturbing the roots or the earth enclosing them, and dragged to a new site.

So! He had been doing things for her—thinking of her pleasure—all the time he was neglecting her and nearly killing her with unhappiness and anxiety. She almost burst out laughing. She almost said, How exactly like you, Rob! But Oh, how—*how* could all this misery and unrest be wiped out between them! How could they get really married and at peace together again?

While she was observing his appearance and thinking about that she told him of Ken's trip to the Valley of the Eagles.

Dressed in one of the well cared for tweed business suits which he wore so well no matter how old they were, and sitting opposite her at the table in the Mountain Hotel grill, he seemed merely like someone she knew, hardly as much of a husband as the big red man whose image sprang up so readily before her. Waves of almost delirious impatience went through her every few minutes. What a horrible state of affairs—that you did not feel even as intimate and at peace with your husband as you had when you were engaged to him. Married all these years, a sixteen-year-old son, and again filled with the excitement and passion and frustration and fever of the very first days—only much worse.

It was not only his aloof manner, there was a deeper change in Rob. His face was hard, he kept his own counsel, he held her at arm's length—all that she could understand. But something baffled her. There had been some blow upon his spirit and it had struck him down. Some of his vital flame was quenched. That sale! She had to bend her head over her plate to conceal her face as she vividly imagined the agony it must have been to him as one after the other of his cherished horses went under the hammer for a fraction of their worth. And they were the accumulation of many years of grueling work. The ranch was stripped now of all except the young stuff and the band of brood mares.

"Will you be able to buy more brood mares?" she interrupted herself suddenly.

"No."

"A new stallion?"

"No."

Driving home, with the back of the car filled with provisions, she would have been happy if only he could have been. But how could a man be happy, she reminded herself, when he had just had the hardest sort of a blow and was more heavily encumbered than ever before? Would she, herself, be happy at this moment, unless, as a result of hours of desperate thinking, she had hit upon a plan which, she thought, would point a way out of their financial difficulties?

How soon should she tell him? Should she tell him now, so that they could discuss it while they were driving home? How should she begin it? *Rob—I've been thinking. And I've got an idea—*

She stole a look at his face and decided not to tell it now. He looked so—how exactly did he look? Not bitter today. No—nor as angry as he had been before he left, but hard. And very much on guard. That could only be against her. And determined—what was he determined about now? Perhaps just to keep on punishing her. He always said when he got angry he was angry at himself, not her. But even if that was so, it amounted to the same thing. He simply oozed ugliness and it disturbed everyone around him.

"Rob, I've been thinking. And I've got an idea."

Dinner and a highball had mellowed him a little. He put down the periodical he was reading and looked at his pipe and discovered that it had gone out. "What about?" he asked.

"Well—about our finances."

Rob hunted for a match. "What about 'em?"

"Well—I really think that I've thought of something we could do to make the ranch pay."

"When did you think this up?" asked Rob, pausing in the act of lighting his pipe to look at her.

"This week, since—since you were here the other night and said that—that the sale hadn't—paid—the way you expected it to."

"Oh! So you thought you would step in and save the pieces!"

Nell felt consternation. Was it going to seem like that to him? She was silent.

"Well, let's have it," said he with forced joviality. His blue eyes were staring at her over his pipe, and it made her remember Ken's words, "Dad's eyes are the fiercest of all."

"Shoot!" he prodded her.

"Well—it really began with something you said some years ago."

"Ah! Kind of you to remember that! But don't bother to break it tactfully to me, Nell, let's hear what it is."

"You said that the income tax man said that the only ranchers in Wyoming who made money were dude ranchers. And then you said, *And he knows.*" She glanced up at Rob questioningly, hoping he could not see the fine nervous trembling that shook her body.

"I remember. Go on."

"So that made me think of having dudes."

"On this ranch!"

"Yes. We had talked about it a few times already, years ago, you remember?"

"And you always said it would kill it as a home for you, if we did," reminded Rob.

"I know I did." Nell plodded doggedly ahead. "I always hated the idea. But—if we were in trouble—if you needed money—it seemed to me, Rob, I should not let my personal inclinations stand in the way."

She looked hesitatingly at him, and away again. His

274

face was full of anger—rage really—and it was shocking to have to look at him.

"And so," said he in his best sardonic manner, "you simply decided that I was a complete flop. Had failed beyond recovery. And that you had better give up all hope of retaining the thing you love the best—your home. Give that up, make this place—that I have broken my heart trying to make beautiful for you—the camping ground of any Tom, Dick and Harry that wants to squat here—"

Nell looked at him indignantly. "It's not fair of you to put it that way. It would only be a dude ranch in the summertime. In the winter it would just be our home as it always has been. And what if I did have the notion that I didn't want to have any dudes here? People can change their minds. And if we need the money, and this would make the difference between being able to pay our bills and not being able to I would be a wash-out if I could not adjust myself to a different way of living for a few months every summer." Her indignation rose. "It's disgraceful to be in debt all the time. I'd rather do *anything* than that!"

"And you imagine," said Rob in the same sardonic manner, "that you could make the ranch pay with summer dudes?"

"Yes. And that's what the income tax man said, didn't he?"

"People talk about 'taking' dudes. The real word would be 'getting' dudes. Most ranchers in this state would be glad to 'get' dudes if they could. How would you go about getting them?"

"I've already started!" said Nell, on her mettle now. "I've written Aunt Julia, in Boston. She has a huge circle of friends and acquaintances. And two of my school friends, Adelaide Kinney and Evelyn Sharp."

"You expect them to promote your business for you?"

"Not that way! Oh, Rob! You're being simply horrible!" Nell sprang to her feet and stood by the mantel.

"I simply want to get the idea," said Rob icily. "You

275

wanted to tell it to me, didn't you? Go on—tell the rest. I'm particularly anxious to know, now that I realize you have passed on the fact of my failure to your relatives and friends in the East."

Nell was silent for a while, then drew a long breath and said, "They won't have to promote my business. They'll be glad to give me lists of the right people to write to. And they'll let me use their names as reference. And I've made out a letter, setting out the plan, descriptions of this place and everything, and we'd have to have pictures, and all that can be mimeographed and sent to these lists of people. And we have the complete set-up. Practically no investment needed. Some guest cabins, yes—Gus and Tim and you could build them yourselves. And this is a lovely place, and there's beautiful country to ride in and plenty of horses! And I'm an awfully good cook!"

"God!" burst from Rob's lips.

Nell said nothing more. In a moment Rob asked, "You say you've made out the letter?"

"Yes." Nell picked it up from the table and handed it to him. But Rob put out a protesting hand. "No. I don't want to see it, thank you. And I hope you haven't set your heart on this. Have you?"

"Set my heart on it?" said Nell.

"Because I don't like to deny you any of your wishes."

"I know," said Nell hesitantly. "You're awfully nice about that. I wanted to thank you for—for the sleigh Gus is making—and the Monkey Tree. I do thank you ever so much."

Rob brushed this aside. "It's nothing at all," he said indifferently. "No reason you should not have what you want."

Nell was silent. After a while she said, "Rob, you know this isn't just something I *want*—for the fun of it—"

"Isn't it? I thought maybe you were lonesome here with me alone."

276

"You know it isn't that at all. Rob, you aren't even pretending to tell the truth about anything."

"Just a God-damned liar, am I?"

That struck Nell as funny and helped her recover her poise. "It's because I told you that thing last summer— that the horses would never succeed and it made you mad at me. And you've never got over being mad. And I was thinking afterward that it *was* awful of me, to have knocked everything so—the horses and your work— without having something else to suggest. So I tried to find another plan. That's all."

Rob smoked in silence for a while and Nell sat down again. The fire crackled and a big log fell in two pieces with a shower of sparks.

Rob began to knock the ashes out of his pipe. "I hadn't meant to tell you this, Nell, but I'll have to now. Otherwise you won't be able to understand why I say no to your proposition. I am not going to continue to raise horses as the main production line of the ranch. They can be a side line. I'm going to raise sheep."

"Sheep!" exclaimed Nell. "But that requires an enormous investment! How could we possibly raise the money for that?"

"It's already raised. To begin with, although I did not make the twenty thousand dollars from my polo ponies which I might have made with good luck, I did make nearly ten. That cleans me out of horses. With the exception of the young stuff coming up I'll have nothing more to sell. But I have put every dollar of that, and more too—all I could borrow—into a band of ewes. I investigated the sheep market thoroughly when I was in Laramie. I was lucky in my buy I think. I found these up at the Doughty ranch, near the Red Desert. Fifteen hundred Corriedale ewes."

"When are they coming on the ranch?" asked Nell.

"They're already on," said Rob. "I've got a Mexican as a herder, and we drove them up from Laramie two days ago. We came in the back way."

"But what about Bellamy's sheep? They're out on the back range there. I saw them yesterday."

"If you saw sheep on this ranch yesterday, you saw our own sheep. Bellamy left with his sheep weeks ago."

Nell was about to ask "What about the lease you gave Bellamy for another year?" but thought better of it. She did say, "You just said you hadn't intended telling me this yet. Why not?"

"Because it may fail," said Rob coldly. "It's a gamble, like all stock-raising. It looks good now. The markets have been good for several years. With these sheep I ought to net almost ten thousand in one year. That will make a sizable dent in our debts. And if it continues, in a few years we'll be out from under."

For Nell, the reversal of all she had been thinking and believing and planning was so sudden, she felt flattened out. *Why! then everything's all right! Everything's settled and arranged! Our future provided for—and—and—everything!*

Presently she found breath to say it aloud, and Rob acquiesced.

"Yes, everything's arranged."

"And there's nothing to worry about."

"Nothing."

The words faded into the heavy silence. Nell's eyes flickered to Rob. Everything all right—nothing to worry about—and yet, between them, this cold distance and strangeness. What made it? Was it impossible—once the habits of love had been broken—to mend them again? Even when the cause of the breach had been corrected?

Rob stared at the fire and said slowly, "I would have liked it—if this experiment could have been worked out first, so that, when I told you, I could have told you of a *fait accompli*—money in the bank, debts paid, notes met, a going concern—not just, as it is now, one more hope, one more plan, one more good chunk of wishful thinking."

Nell was leaning back in her armchair and made no answer.

"But," continued Rob, "since you have made it so plain that it was not only the horses you doubted, it was me too—and any ability I might have to care for you and provide a home for you—" he left the sentence unfinished.

The clock struck eleven, and Pauly rose from where she had been lying near the fire and staged an elaborate stretch, then ran meowing to Nell.

Nell lifted her automatically.

"That's true, isn't it, Nell?" asked Rob in a sudden direct manner.

"What?"

"That you *have* lost confidence in me?"

Nell did not answer immediately. Finally she said, "Rob—I didn't think you would succeed with the horses. I told you that. But that's not *you* personally—"

"But it was, *me*, personally," he insisted. "You didn't think I was going to pull us through, did you?"

"You never took me into your confidence," said Nell. "You didn't tell me you were going to try a different line. You kept saying it was to be the horses or nothing."

"I suppose that's as good a way of answering as any," said Rob slowly.

A sudden passionate protest flung Nell to her feet. Pauly hit the floor with a little grunt. "I don't see why *confidence* means so much to you! I've never stopped loving you—not the least bit. Suppose some of the confidence—was gone? That would be only human—wouldn't really matter between us!"

Rob got to his feet and went about blowing the lamps out, and finally answered, "Just that it—sort of—takes the heart out of a man."

It was still possible, thought Nell, as she walked slowly upstairs. When people loved each other as they had, nothing more would be needed than just one look—one word—her name, *Nell*. there would be no forgiving or explaining, just a sudden coming together and all the discord flung behind them.

But Rob stood in a sort of daze in the center of the

279

bedroom, as if he did not feel at home there. One hand
held his pipe as he puffed at it, and he stood watching her
as she moved about, turning the bed down, closing the
window, taking her nightclothes from the closet and
dropping them on the bed.

She went to his chiffonier and took out a set of pajamas
and handed them to him. "Here are some fresh pajamas
for you."

He took them absent-mindedly. Then, as Nell undid
the belt of her skirt and stepped out of it, and peeled off
her sweater, he said to her hesitatingly, "I'm awfully
tired. I think I'll sleep in the other room. Do you mind?"

He looked at his wife.

With just her slip on, she was seated in the low chair,
one ankle crossed over the other knee to untie her shoe,
her slender and beautiful legs shining in their long silk
stockings. Her tawny hair hung loose over the pearl-like
skin on her breasts. Her cheeks were exquisitely flushed.

Without raising her head her dark blue eyes slid up
underneath her brows and she answered easily, "Not at
all. I think it would be a very good idea. I shall probably
sleep better myself."

32

People do not die, thought Nell, they are killed by
inches, because if you're too unhappy you can't eat, and if
you did eat, you couldn't digest, and all through your
body the processes are turned backwards.

Sitting at the desk trying to write a letter to Howard—

"and we have a lot of snow. It will seem strange not to have you home at Christmas, but you'll get lots of skiing there in Massachusetts—"

She raised her eyes to the window and propped her chin on her hand. It was a gray, silent day, with a low sky that seemed full of snow. Yes. Three quarters of life is a slow dying. It's despair that kills us off—slowly or quickly—and I suppose everyone gets a dose of it. Now I know how it works. It works on the glands and they break down, and that ages the body and finally kills it—

She dipped her pen in the ink and wrote again, "We're keeping Gypsy in so that when she has her foal we can take care of her. Your father is rabid because she's going to have a winter foal—"

She finished her letter and sealed it, then hurried to the kitchen, looked into the kettles that were simmering on the stove in preparation for dinner and began to set the table.

Sitting opposite each other three times a day at meals had come to be an ordeal for both of them, worse every week that passed. They braced themselves for it—a sort of horror.

And yet she did not really believe it, and she was waiting, thinking that it would all pass, and that the love, like a stream, had gone underground and was still running there strongly and would some day come up into the sunshine again. Perhaps, she thought, I've had my share of happiness and should not ask for more. But I'm not like that. Nobody is. A little is not enough— always more and more—and we will die if we do not get it—

Rob was explaining that he was going off to the timbered hill on Number Seventeen after dinner to mark certain trees for felling, and she answered, yes, the wood piles needed replenishing.

And to herself she said that she would write an aphorism on the fly leaf of her bedside book that night—"We

are insatiable for happiness. To find an abiding beauty—
this we seek for all our lives long."

Why didn't he go now that dinner was over? Why did
he sit there smoking, looking out of the window? Snow
had begun to fall softly.

She went nervously about the kitchen, gathering up
the dishes, tidying, running the hot water—

This waiting! It was almost as if the air trembled, waiting for the word that would shatter the tension. But
November passed, and December, and nothing was
changed. Rob was dark and hopeless and in a sort of hard
frenzy.

I always knew he could do it, whispered Nell to herself. He likes it. Likes his anger and fury. Likes to harden
himself. *Confidence!* Silly! They don't understand how
women love their children, their men. Confidence has
nothing to do with it. Besides, is it true? Is he really hurt
or is this revenge?

She could not bear to look at him.

And at last she could not bear to be near him. She
planned, all day long, how to avoid him, and drew breath
more easily, and could eat, and could straighten up, when
she saw his back and his big boots tramping up the hill,
disappearing into the woods.

She would run up to the stables and pore over the
work bench where Gus was working on the sleigh. For a
time, she could lose herself in a child's peacefulness as
she watched him lay the bright blue enamel on the wood,
then the red, all the gay Swedish colors. There was to be
gold leaf on the swan's head.

As Gus told her this, his kind blue eyes smiled into
hers and made her forget everything.

"You luk awful bad, Missus."

She knew that—she hated to see her face in the mirror—especially the eyes, so wild-looking—

"You sick, Missus?"

"I don't feel very well, Gus. Nothing special. Just awfully weak."

282

"Mebbe you go see Dr. Scott."

As Nell walked slowly and unwillingly back to the house, she told herself that it could come to be true that she would want never to see Rob again.

33

Nell and Gypsy were both out in the heavy blizzard that hit the ranch near the end of January, Nell because when snow was falling she could not stay in; Gypsy because of that well-known but puzzling natural law which causes animals—if it is any way possible—to give birth to their young in the worst rather than the best of weather.

Nell fought her way across the Stable Pasture hoping to reach a point from which she could see the snow blowing on the crest of the Saddle Back.

Gypsy prepared to drop her foal in the scant shelter of a wooded ridge about a quarter of a mile from the ranch. She had escaped from her warm and comfortable box stall. For years now she had dropped her foals on the wild breasts of the open range and this she was determined to do again.

She had prudence enough to stand in the lee of the ridge, but the blizzard drove through the trees, and drifts began to pile up in long combers. The ground was almost bare between them.

Standing close to a tree in one of these cleared spaces she kept her back to the wind. Her head sank patiently. Her tail streamed between her legs. Her spine humped in cramping pain.

To lie down in the terrible cold was something she didn't want to do. But the pain forced her, and at length she went down in awkward jerks and stretched out on her side. It began again—the gathering of all her strength to a strange, violent straining. She had known it a dozen times before. Through the pain ran hope and love and intense longing. She knew the foal already and wanted it. She knew her motherhood.

Except for her age and the storm, the birth would have been routine, for Gypsy had been a successful brood mare and she had never had a sick day in her life. But the years had taken her strength and her teeth were gone and food did not give her much nourishment. The labor was longer than it should have been.

When at length the foal slid out, Gypsy was unable to rise. She made one or two efforts, then her head sank on the ground.

The little one kicked and struggled free of the enclosing sac, snapping the cord that united him to his mother, and suddenly breathed. He should then have been licked and massaged and warmed by his dam but lacking such assistance he managed, after a little while, to sit up. The freezing wind turned the moisture upon him to a film of ice, and his violent shivering made it crackle.

Gypsy struggled to rise and attend to her foal. She raised her head a few times with weak grunts which caught the foal's ear and drew his attention to her and made him turn his wavering head and his still half-blind eyes in her direction. She wanted him to come closer to her, but she could not hold her head up.

The foal continued to sit there shivering, weaving his head weakly, blinking his ice-edged lids. At last he attempted to get up. Instinct urged him to get to the warmth of his dam's body—the warmth and the milk— and he tried to get his long wobbly legs under him and push himself up. Once up, he went down on his knees, up again, he fell over sideways. Up again, all four legs slid out and he went on his belly. He kept getting up, the blood ran faster in his veins, his eyes cleared a little, he began to move waveringly around the big warm hulk lying on the ground. A strong scent came to his nose and he raised his little muzzle and searched eagerly for the teat where it ought to have been, there above him. There was no teat there.

He dropped his nose disconsolately and stood in a weak shivering curve, his head almost touching the ground. His wet switch of a tail was between his hind legs. He looked like a small naked black greyhound.

He tried again, raising his muzzle and making circles in the air with it. When this got him nothing he began to investigate the prostrate body of his dam. He went slowly and weakly, stretching out his nose. He sniffed, moved on, paused and gave it up. Then he began the tremulous search again.

At last he touched the hot rubbery bag. He knew it instantly and lifted his head into the nursing position. No teat. Only the icy wind and snow. Having lost it, it was some time before he located it again. And again he lifted his head to nurse. Again, no teat.

His head dropped, the bitter disappointment took his strength away, his knees buckled and suddenly collapsed. But the tide of life was on the flow in him, not the ebb. He got up again, searched for the teat and found it quite soon. He was learning. But what good was it unless it was above him where he could seize hold of it and let the hot drink run down his throat? He had to do something about this! He lifted his tiny soft hoof and struck at his mother, pawing her belly. *Get up! Get up! so that I can drink and live and not die!*

Gypsy was drifting toward oblivion, but that demand drew her painfully back. She raised her head. The foal pawed her again. She knew he could not nurse while she was down. Somehow she must get on her four weak legs and hold herself up and give him the teat.

In her, life was on the ebb and there was no strength to respond to her will. And yet she did it. She did it the way a thoroughbred will sometimes win a race without sound legs to run on. She forced herself slowly into a sitting position, waited a moment trying to hold up her heavy swinging head, then made the plunge and was up.

Her legs seemed cut off from the heart and brain that commanded them. As they bent and buckled, she leaned against the tree beside her. She thrust out her feet, bracing herself. The foal made a small bleat and took two sprawling steps toward her and again lifted his little muzzle to where the teat ought to be. It was there! In ecstasy he began to nurse.

Gypsy's head dropped. She jerked it up again. Her knees gave a little, she leaned more heavily on the tree, held up against her outthrust feet.

The driving snow beat upon them both and the pines thrashed and roared.

Upon the mountain a coyote sat on his haunches, pointed his muzzle and gave the long mournful howl that called the pack to him and told them there was going to be good hunting.

Gypsy heard him and knew what it meant for the foal when she had left him. No matter, she could do only this one thing for him—give him the milk which was food and drink, heat, strength, purgative and stimulant all in one.

The foal drank and plucked his head away, making the teat flip and bounce. He seized it again and drank again. He was very much of a prince now, doing as he pleased, commanding this flow of nectar. There was a new miracle of heat and power and arrogance inside him. It was the feeling of bucking. It was beginning now with this first mother-drink. A little more—just a little more food and growth and he would put down his little sea-horse head and kick both heels out to one side!

When his belly was full and tight he stood back. And as if he had told his dam, "That's all—I don't want any more," she released the terrible hold she had over her body and it slowly gave way and slid down.

Nell happened upon the mare and the foal as the whiteness of the storm was changing to darkness.

She fought her way back to the house and told Rob.

"The mare's down and the foal is standing there half dead with cold."

They took flashlights and went out. The mare and foal were just as Nell had left them.

Rob fell on his knees beside Gypsy and felt of her. "She's alive anyway." The mare did not move. "Gypsy! Gypsy girl!" There was no response. Rob looked up at Nell and then wildly around. "God! What a place for her to pick! What a night!" He seized the mare again and tried to rouse her. He shouted in her ear. He lifted her head.

"Her eyelids flickered! She's not gone yet! If I could get her down to the stable she might have a chance!" He thought distractedly of a sledge, a team of horses to drag her—

"Shall I go get Gus?" shouted Nell.

"Yes, and could you take the colt? He might follow you. Or you can shove him along."

Alone with his mare, Rob kept at the task of arousing her and bringing her back to consciousness. He got behind her and forced her head up. He tried to roll her body so that her legs would be under her. He kept shouting at her, calling to her, and at that voice—those peremptory commands— she regained her senses. He cheered her on, he shoved against her back until the veins in his neck felt as if they would burst. At last she sat up waveringly.

"Atta girl! Now come on! Gypsy! Up on your pins! Now we go!"

Standing in front of her, holding the halter with both hands, he hauled on it with all his might and lashed her with shouts and curses.

As she struggled he drew her forward and she was pulled up on her feet and he grabbed and held her. "That's it! Good girl! Hold on now! You're going to be all right!" She kept her feet, swaying.

Gus and Nell arrived with a bucket of hot mash.

"Ah! That's the stuff. Here you are, Gypsy. Get this into your belly!" He lifted the bucket to her nose. "What's the matter? Don't you want it?" The mare's head swung dizzily. Her eyes closed.

Rob handed the bucket to Gus. "She can't eat. Let's get her home. Come on, Gypsy! Come now, girl! Take a step! That's it! Another now!" As if carried by his voice alone, the mare moved automatically forward. Her head rested heavily on Rob's shoulder. They covered a hundred yards or so. Now they had left the shelter of the ridge and the full force of the storm beat against them. Gypsy staggered helplessly.

"Good God! Why did she have to choose a night like this!"

Her head grew heavier, the pauses between steps longer. With a stream of frantic profanity, Rob tried to hide from himself what this meant. He would have carried her if he could have.

When she went down again it was with a crash that pulled him down too.

The thin ray of Nell's flashlight caught his frenzied face as he disentangled himself and stooped for the mare's head again. "Get behind and boot her, Gus, while I pull on her! She can't stay here!"

Under the pelting ice and wind they spent themselves screaming and shoving and hauling at the mare. She quivered a little. She seemed to hear. She groaned. There were a few spasmodic efforts.

"She wants to but she can't," said Rob, at last.

Kneeling, he drew her head against him so that she could still hear his voice and feel his hands. "Nell, you and Gus go on down to the house. No use your freezing here."

"No use nobody freeze, Boss. You can't help her no more. She don' know nuttin."

"She'd pull through if I could get her to the stables. I'll let her rest a few minutes and then I'll try again. You go see to the colt, Gus. I don't want to lose it. Fix a bottle of milk for it. I don't know whether it nursed or not. Put it in with Flicka. I think she'll be good to it but watch she doesn't kick it."

Nell went away with Gus.

Rob knelt there in the bedlam of the storm, holding his

288

mare to life by his voice alone. He did not dare to stop talking to her. Every so often there was a quiver of response—the faint twitch of one ear.

A light appeared again. It was Gus returning. "Dot foal, it got a full belly already. She feed it before she go down."

"Good old girl," muttered Rob, his hand on the mare's head. "You *would* do that. *Thoroughbred.*"

"It don' want no milk now."

"How did Flicka take to it?"

"Vell—she not make up her mind right away. De colt lie down in de hay. Flicka, she snort und she watch it und she smell it. I tink be all right."

"That's good. But you better watch 'em."

"Sure."

He was alone again.

Insanity of wind and snow. Screaming as of something malevolent on the loose. That desperate loneliness of the soul that comes only a few times in life and seems to form a great cavity into which one slides with increasing velocity. And the dark hulk of his mare lying on the bare ground, her closed eyes and her nose encrusted with ice, her breath coming more and more rarely, more and more shallowly.

"If you could only try once more! Come on, old girl! It isn't far—and we'll have many a good ride together yet!"

The ear twitched a little. He rubbed her throat and head. He knew he lied.

It wasn't only a horse dying. It was the end of half his life and all his young manhood, his young willfulness. It was the breaking of the last link with the happy beginnings of things. It was the hell of the last few months pulling himself and Gypsy down into it. He crouched lower over her and still that ear moved when he spoke.

"Gypsy!... Remember all the good times we had... the polo games... remember, Gypsy... remember when we were both young together..."

He crouched still lower. Her breathing had stopped. The ear no longer twitched.

For long he sat there, then bent gently over her. He took that ear into his hand and whispered into it, "A good journey!" then straightened up and put his hand over his eyes, pressing them hard.

He heard Nell's voice calling and felt her hands on his cap, drawing the earflaps lower, wrapping a woolen scarf around his neck. He felt the touch of her bare fingers on his cheek and throat.

He lifted his head hastily, scattering drops that were like ice on Nell's hands. "Nell! Where are your gloves!"

"I took them off just for a second."

"Put your gloves on."

Nell fumbled with them. All her body was weak these days. She had hardly the strength to draw on her fur-lined gloves.

"Yes—they're on." She sank to her knees beside him. "Is she—"

He made no answer. He just kneeled there with the mare's head against him. At last he stripped off his gloves and felt her head, her body, her legs—as if he still could not believe it. The stiffness was beginning.

Nell swayed against him and then straightened up.

"Don't go, Nell!" he cried, loosing one arm and flinging it around her.

"I'm not going," she answered faintly and wondered how, indeed, she would ever be able to make that trip down to the house one more time, or even get to her feet.

"Oh, Nell!"

It was a harsh, anguished cry. He flung the other arm around her too and held her clasped tight against him, his face pressed against hers.

Was he crying? Crying for his mare? Nell couldn't tell for the icy snow that beat upon their faces and melted there. How would they ever get home . . . how would there ever be an end to this . . . Ah . . . There was a change . . . he was not just hiding his face in hers for comfort and assuagement of his grief . . . his hard cold lips were kissing her frantically . . . there was pleading in it

290

...and shame...and love...one of his big bare hands was inside her lumberjacket and it felt as if it clasped all of her narrow back and held her naked body against him ...the hand was warm...how could it be warm...it was warm...and something like electricity streamed from it into her...was it that that made her feel as if she was going to faint...was it cold and exhaustion...was it because Rob—because Rob—

It was ended. The knowledge was absolute and final. And as it turned into pure sensation, searing every cell in her body, the terrible hold she had over herself broke. Rob half carried her as they fought their way down to the house. They passed Gus going up to the mare. He was taking four kerosene flares to put around her body. There was a whole pack of coyotes on Saddle Back now and he had heard them howling.

Nell hurried to the stable in the morning, anxious about the foal. Gypsy's foals were important. Hers had been the two who sold for seven hundred dollars apiece, Romany Chi and Romany Chal. And hers had been Redwing, who sold for two thousand.

She found the foal all alone. He was in the far corner of the stall, his tail-end presented petulantly to her and to all the world, his little sea-horse face turned curiously over his shoulder—not going to miss anything.

Enchanted by the picture he made, Nell bent over laughing, clapped her hands and cried, "Who dat!"

And the foal turned and staggered across the stall to her.

And so was born and named *Who Dat*, out of Sacrifice, by Storm.

34

The wind had stopped and the hills of the ranch lay in quietness beneath their deep swathings of snow.

There was snow everywhere. The boughs of the trees bent with it. The skies were heavy with it. And it still fell softly and slowly, drifting through air that rang with the music of distant sleighbells.

On that far mountain a light sleigh zoomed up the white slope behind two black mares that plunged under a long cracking whip.

The mares were wild with excitement. Their heads scattered flecks of foam and at every pause they reared and pranced, shaking the streamers of bells which hung on their harness.

The little sleigh, as gaudy as a child's paint-box, ran at their heels. The swan was proud with gold leaf and rode with a fixed stare. Every fur that could be found on the ranch had been piled into it, and Nell's face emerged, pink with cold, from a gray mass that had once been Rob's coonskin coat.

"But it's the bells!" she cried. "Oh, Rob! The way they dance and jingle!"

Their talk was not very explicit.

"Patsy! Topsy! You black squaws! Show her what you can do!" He cracked the whip.

The blacks took the rest of the hill at a gallop.

"Like it, honey?"

"Love it!"

He swung the mares in a right angle along the crest. Patsy reared and threw a clamor of bells into the air.

"Oh, hear the bells!"

"Wedding bells!"

"Let them out, Rob!"

They galloped the length of the crest of the Saddle Back. Rob's crazy shouts and the occasional pistol-crack of the whip punctuated the peal and shimmer and riot of the sleighbells.

"This is it, Rob."

"This is it, my darling love. Happy?"

"I've never been so happy."

"Forgiven me?"

"Oh, Rob—"

"I know you have. But I want you to understand too—though I hardly understand myself."

"I know."

"I've been going through an awful hell. Hating myself. Fighting myself."

"I know."

"Something had to—sort of—*die* in me, before I could give in."

"But that's the way it always is. Something dies—so that something better can come to life."

"It was all because I'm so damned bull-headed."

"Well—it seems to me a person has to build themselves around the best that's in them. And let everything else be pared away."

Rob was silent.

"But—the paring away—hurts."

Rob turned the sleigh down the back of the hill and it careened, and Nell screamed and the mares started galloping again.

"Hold on!"

The team whirled through the snow, tossing chunks of it from their hoofs. The motion was so light and swift the sleigh hardly seemed on the ground. It was more like flying. Nell turned her face up and closed her eyes. The falling snow flakes were cool little kisses upon her skin.

And they hung on the fur of the robe, big symmetrical stars, perfect little gauntlets, and then melted away.

"Rob, I never thought I'd be married twice."

"*Twice*, baby! You're going to be married so often you won't know yourself! And always to the same man!"

"Rob, I don't think I'd be willing to change back to my first husband."

"He sure was an egg. Do you mind my kissing you all the time?"

"I'm not at all used to it. I've got out of the habit. I don't know that I can stand it."

"It takes practice. You can sort of work on it."

He took her for a long ride. Off the ranch, down the back road, on plains and past woods that seemed unfamiliar. They swept down near to a wide placid stream that was a dark brown between its snowy banks. The bare boughs of the cottonwood trees that bordered it bent with their weight of snow. A black crow floated through the trees with a wide motionless wing-spread. And then they had flashed past, before the crow had drifted to rest on the white bank. The scene was like an etching, printed on Nell's memory forever.

And lastly Rob whipped the mares up another hill and whirled them around on the crest, and reined them in. They came up on their hind legs and snow flew in every direction.

They were overlooking a little valley in which large patches of gray blotted out the snow. It was the sheep. They stood feeding at long racks packed with hay. From the sheep wagon a little thread of smoke wound upward, telling of the herder's stove and the cosy warmth within.

"There they are," said Rob and there was something sober and humble in his voice.

Nell was silent so long, looking at them, that Rob glanced at her. She met his eyes with a little smiling sigh. "Yes. There they are."

35

Charley Sargent never missed the three weeks' autumn race meet at Saginaw Falls in Idaho, one of the few major or "recognized" tracks in the Rocky Mountain states; and had the same stables for his horses, and hotel accommodations for himself, year after year. Taking his horses down the Continental Divide from a high altitude to one several thousand feet lower gave them an advantage, and he liked the town which lay in the long valley between the Wauchichi and Shinumo ranges and had a season of pleasant autumn weather.

Although the distance from Sargent's ranch to Saginaw Falls was not more than eight hundred miles, he always shipped his horses by rail in charge of his trainer, Perry Gunston, rather than vanning them or taking them in an automobile trailer. This was because the highway made a rather precipitous descent, winding down through several mountain passes; and on the Divide, the unpredictable storms sometimes made the road dangerous or even impassable for trucks. But he himself made the trip by motor.

There were always several events scheduled for two-year-olds, in which Sargent tried out his promising youngsters, and one race, on the last day of the meet, with a ten-thousand-dollar purse, which attracted an impressive entry. It was in this race that Thunderhead was to make his debut, and long before school closed Ken had familiarized himself with the past performances of all winners of this big event. Thunderhead had only to run the two miles on the Saginaw Falls track as fast as he had run it at home to win.

For Ken to hang around his father while the letter containing his report card was being opened, or even to allow the depressing event to catch him in the same room, was so unusual that Rob McLaughlin felt sure something was fishy.

He glanced up at Ken who stood waiting beside his desk with hands driven deep into the pockets of his blue-jeans. "Going to take your medicine and get it over with, are you?" he grinned, then looked at the boy's face again. That wasn't Ken's usual report-card face—the face of one waiting for a death sentence. On the contrary, the sensitive face was now flushed with anticipation, gleams of light played in the depths of his blue eyes and one smile after the other rippled across his lips.

"Read it, Dad. Read it quick!" he exclaimed, and watched closely as his father took the card and studied it, item by item.

Rob simply didn't believe it. He shook his head with bewilderment. "Is this card phony or what? Do you know what's in it, Ken?"

"What?" demanded Ken confidently.

"Ninety-two in Algebra. Ninety-four in Latin. Ninety-seven in Chemistry, and one hundred in English. What's it mean? Has Gibson gone crazy to give you a card like that?"

"Read the letter," chortled Ken. "He told me he was going to write you a letter and—and—congratulate you!"

"Congratulate *me!*" exclaimed Rob. "What in hell about?"

Ken placed his hand theatrically on his chest, bowed, said "Me!" and then threw his head back, burst out laughing, and did a few prancing steps around the room.

Rob read the letter through and abruptly laid it down and turned his head to look out the window. He was remembering a morning just five years ago when Ken was ten, and a report card had come in which there were assorted marks below twenty, climaxing with a zero in English. And in defense, Ken had made the entirely irrelevant plea—*if you would only give me a colt of my own I might do better*. And he had given Ken the filly, Flicka, and Ken had almost killed himself caring for her. He had also managed to write a composition retrieving his disgrace and causing Mr. Gibson to say that he might have another chance with his class instead of being dropped. Gibson had said in his letter that Ken had a brilliant mind, and Rob had asked his wife, "Did you ever think Ken was brilliant? I've always thought he was dumb."

Rob picked up the card and the letter and read both of them through carefully again. Brilliant all right. How in hell had the kid got a hundred in English? That meant no mistakes at all—or superlative performances every now and then.

Rob pointed at the card. "How'd you get this? Was it just one composition?"

"You had to be *excellent* all year, and write a perfect composition to end up with."

"What subject did you choose?"

"I wrote about that time I tried to get the eagle feather —you know—down there in the Valley of the Eagles, and the eagle chased me all the way down the cliff and stuck his claws in my belly and it was only my belt that saved me—but of course I fixed it up a little."

"How'd you fix it up? Seems to me that was hot stuff without any fixing."

Ken waved his hands in a suave and explanatory fashion. "Oh, I put in some romantic dope—you know, the sort of things writers write—I had it that I had a picture of my girl in the buckle of my belt, so she—sort of saved my life, you see."

Rob's big white teeth gleamed in his dark face. He looked very pleased. But continuing to study the boy's expression he suddenly had a recurrence of his first conviction. There was something fishy about this.

"Tell me, Ken," he said, "is this absolutely on the level? You really did it? It's *bona fide?*"

"Sure I did it, Dad," said Ken, his jubilance fading at the realization that a bad reputation is hard to live down. "Don't you believe me?"

Rob thought a moment. "Yes, I believe you. But there's something else. Come on now, out with it! What's behind this?"

Ken's smile vanished and he drew a deep breath, standing there very straight before his father with fists shoved into his pockets. "Well, Dad—I did it—because I wanted—you to say that I needn't go back to school next September fifteenth."

"WHAT!"

"I mean—not go till a month or two later. You see, Dad, the ten thousand dollar race at Saginaw Falls in Idaho comes on October twenty-fourth, and that's the race Thunderhead's going to win!" He pulled a folded paper out of his hind pocket. "Mr. Sargent says it's just made to order for Thunderhead. They don't have to be registered horses or to have any past track records."

The racing sheet fell open at the page all of itself and he laid it on his father's desk and pointed to the picture of an elderly man.

"Beaver Greenway!" exclaimed Rob, picking it up. "And his ten thousand dollar Free-For-All! Sure—I know about it. I bet that old codger has discovered more dark horses than any other racing man in this country. And bought them, too. It's his hobby. If they win, he buys them, you know."

"He won't buy Thunderhead!"

Rob read the paragraph through, then tipped his chair back and ran his hand through his close dark hair. "When did you dope all this out?"

"Last fall, when I went back to school."

"When did you start working for this *phenomenal* report card?"

"Right then. When school started."

"And you kept it up all year?"

Ken nodded.

"Just so you might get permission from me to stay out of school next fall when Thunderhead goes to the post?"

"Yes, sir."

"Put it there, son! I'm proud of you!"

Ken was dazed. His small boneless hand was lost in his father's clasp and shaken hard. He was still trying to explain.

"The thing is, Dad, of course I'll make up all the lessons I lose while I'm out of school. But if I had just asked you, and told you that I'd do that, you wouldn't have believed I could do it."

"And you can say that again, boy!"

"So I had to prove it to you—*before* I asked you."

"You've proved it."

"Dad! Do you mean I can?"

"I mean just that. This brilliant mind of yours seems to work in reverse. Give you horses so that you have no time for lessons and even have to stay out of school and you bust yourself wide open and carry the rag off the bush!"

"Dad—there's something more!"

"Ah! Now it's coming!" Rob's face took on its sardonic expression.

"Two things, Dad."

"Well—shoot!"

"You said last year, when Thunderhead didn't get gelded with the other two-year-olds, that he could go till this year. Does—does he have to be gelded? Wouldn't you just—skip it—Dad? Because he *may* win, you see— And there's a chance that the gelding might hurt him or kill him and anyway if he should be a winner on the race track we'd want to sell his services as a stallion, wouldn't we? And anyway—"

"We won't geld him," said Rob suddenly.

This quick victory was another shock to Ken. Rob raised the report card. "You'll find all your life long, son, that *fine performance* will get things for you that nothing else will."

"Besides, Thunderhead hasn't really made any trouble, has he?" It was hard for Ken to get his mind off his horse. "He hasn't tried to fight Banner or get any mares, or—well, not *anything* like that."

"Thunderhead hasn't had a chance to raise hell yet. It's been a godsend that we could leave Touch And Go with him until early this spring when she came in heat for the first time. That kept him happy. Kept him away from the other mares and delayed the beginning of what you might call his sex life. Besides, he's been trained and worked pretty consistently. You can train an animal, you know, for the kind of life he is to live. We've kept him away from the real life of a stallion. But that won't last forever. The time will come. One day his ears will pop, and he'll suddenly thump himself on the chest and exclaim, *I'm a man!*"

Ken laughed. "I hope it won't be on the race track."

"Sex doesn't enter much into the life of race horses. Stallions and mares race together without any disturbances of that sort."

"I know."

"Well now—what's the other thing? Might as well get it over with."

Ken's face flushed a little. "Remember what you said once, Dad? That I cost you money every time I turn around?"

"I remember!"

"Well—what about the money the race is going to cost? The entrance fee and all that?"

"I see." Rob leaned back quietly and became very thoughtful, rubbing his hand through his hair.

"You're a lot richer now than you used to be, aren't you, Dad?"

"Where'd you get that idea?"

"Well—the sheep—"

300

"The sheep have got me so deep in debt Thunderhead will have to win races to pull me out!"

"Oh, Dad! Are you kind of counting on him?" Ken's face glowed with pride.

"I'm hoping," said Rob grimly. "I've put a lot of work on that horse myself, remember, and I know he's got it in him. But he's an ugly beggar. This summer will tell the tale."

"Of course you know, Dad," said Ken magnanimously, "anything Thunderhead wins will be yours and Mother's."

"Will it? No. I don't think so. We'd want it to be yours. Then you can pay for all your expenses and your schooling and we'll come out ahead anyway!"

"But *some* of it would have to be yours!"

"All right. We'll incorporate. McLaughlin and Son. And I'll take what I need for the present and we can get squared later on."

There was a moment's pause. Rob hadn't yet said anything about that entrance fee.

"You're going to have a wonderful big hay crop, aren't you, Dad? Don't you think you may sell your hay—the part you won't need for the sheep or the horses or the cows, quite early—say, in *September?*"

"Got it all figured out, haven't you?"

Ken nodded.

"I don't know when I'll sell my surplus hay. It may pay better to hold it till later in the season when hay gets scarce."

Ken looked crestfallen.

Rob leaned back in his chair. "We'd better count this up now and know what we're up against."

Ken called on his fortitude and stood waiting.

"You're going with Mr. Sargent so the trip won't cost you anything, but you'll be in Saginaw Falls for three weeks—"

"I'll sleep in the stall with Thunderhead," put in Ken quickly. "Lots of owners do that if they haven't got much dough."

"But I suppose you'll have to eat! Sargent will send the colt with his horses by rail and keep him in his stables in the charge of his trainer, so there'll be no shipping or stable expenses. You're in luck there—but Thunderhead's got to eat too. So there'll be his feed bill and the jockey fee—"

"That's ten dollars if he just rides, and twenty-five if he wins," interpolated Ken, "and Dad, please don't say *jockey*. People that *know* call them *riders*."

Rob ignored this. "And the entrance fee," he finished. "All together quite a bit of money."

He looked out the window again, and in spite of fortitude, Ken began to feel wet in his armpits and around his waist.

"But I'll stake you to the entrance fee for the one big race and all the expenses for yourself and Thunderhead."

"You will, Dad? Gee! Oh, gosh!"

"How'll I be repaid if he doesn't win anything?"

Ken's lips sobered in a line of determination and courage. "I'll work very hard all summer."

"You'll do that anyway," said Rob grimly. "I've never given you the idea you could spend the summer sitting on your fanny, have I? Or just monkeying around your horse either."

"And besides," said Ken, "there's another way I could make money enough to pay you back everything and more too."

"This brilliant mind of yours is getting me dizzy, Ken. How can you make several hundred dollars?"

"Well—you told me once it costs you three hundred dollars to put me through a year of school. See?" He smiled brilliantly at his father.

"I don't see. I haven't got a brilliant mind."

"I—just simply—won't go to school. I could study outside and take the exams—maybe— Anyway, I'd learn just as much and my schooling wouldn't cost you anything."

"And I'd spend the money financing you traveling around with your race horse, I suppose?"

Ken hadn't quite the courage to say yes, but he made a graceful gesture of assent and dashed away.

36

Thunderhead's career was taken seriously by everyone on the ranch that summer, and no one rode him but his trainer, young Ken McLaughlin, who tipped the scale at ninety-six pounds.

During the winter just past when the stallion had been kept in, given a liberal diet ration of oats and hay and exercise and training by Rob McLaughlin, he had achieved a superb development. He was as tall as the Percheron—sixteen hands—and would be even taller when he had his full growth. No longer could it be said of him that he was ungainly or badly proportioned. All his parts had grown together. His legs were long and powerfully muscled, his neck massive and arched, his coat a pure dazzling white and shining with the glossiness of a stallion's skin. Strength, power and willfulness were still his outstanding characteristics.

He was now shod, and Ken was out with him every day before breakfast, running him on the track. He still fought Ken, he still bucked, but when Ken complained of the horse's dislike of him, his father said, "You've got that wrong, son. If that horse really hated you he'd never let you get near him. He doesn't hate you. He fights you because he likes to. He enjoys it. You're his trainer.

You've got to make him do what he doesn't want to do and he's a fighting devil so he fights you back. But I'll bet, when he's waiting up there in the mornings for you to come and give him his work-out, he'd feel pretty bad if you didn't show up."

Touch And Go was still the pace-maker for her big brother, and Rob McLaughlin said, "When I see that filly run, damned if I don't think she's the one that's going to be the racer."

Touch And Go was a regular beauty. Tall and daintily made, with a long reaching neck, straight slim legs, little feet that would fit in a cup, and a playful high spirit that kept her always acting up, always dancing and going sideways. Her ruddy hide was glorious in the sun, and the blond tail and mane gave her a de luxe, made-to-order look.

To Rob McLaughlin her perfect conformation was a justification of his theories of line breeding, and he sometimes studied the racing sheet, making a note of what events were scheduled for two-year-olds. "We might run her too," he said, "put her in the baby class."

The summer passed very slowly for Ken, because it was all a tense waiting for the racing season, and a tense watching of Thunderhead. Besides, it was full of excitement—just one thing after the other. The first excitement was when he got home and found out what was going to happen to his mother. It was hard for Ken to keep his mind from confusion when he thought about that. She had wanted it. Hadn't she said at dinner that night, "I want a Monkey Tree. I want a sleigh all covered with bells, and I want a Little Girl," and of course it was right for his mother to have what she wanted. But it was hard to take. He had argued with her about it.

"But Mother, you've got *us!* Howard and me. Aren't we enough?"

"No. I want a little girl."

"Want her *much*, Mother?"

"Want her lots, dear. Remember how hard you wanted Flicka?"

"It might be a boy," said Ken gloomily, and he added, "Besides, doesn't it hurt awfully?"

Nell was busy putting the laundry away. She counted the piles of sheets she was stacking in the linen closet.

"Doesn't it, Mother?" insisted Ken. "Doc Hicks might have to—"

"Ken! This is going to be a *baby*! And Doc Hicks won't have anything to do with it!"

"Oh, sure—I know that—"

"And as for its hurting—who cares about that?" She had finished stacking and her voice was very gay. "You don't get anything for nothing, dear."

"No." His father had told him plenty about that.

"And didn't you—" her hand was lightly on his head, arranging his soft brown hair so that it did not fall over his forehead, "didn't you sit all night in the cold water holding Flicka—just because you loved her and wanted her so much?"

She was through with the linen and went quickly back to the kitchen. Ken watched her, not answering her out loud but thinking to himself that it was different. How could you love something you hadn't ever seen and be willing, in advance, to suffer for it? With Flicka, he had known and loved her and cared for her for months.

He had to struggle against a feeling of dread when he saw his father watching his mother all the time with such anxiety. It was a wonder he would even let her stack the linen. He wouldn't let her do anything this summer. He himself got up and cooked breakfast every morning, and Tim had to come in and clean the house. Gus churned and attended to butter and cream. Of course, no riding; and there was a new outdoor couch with wheels on the terrace under the Pergola where she lay for many hours, not doing anything, her hands clasped behind her neck, her eyes on the sky or the distant hills. Often the hair of her bang was darkened with sweat, and there were tiny beads on her upper lip, and her hands were not steady.

Their father had called both boys to him soon after they got home and had said with his harshest voice and his fiercest eyes, "Don't do anything this summer that will cause your mother trouble or pain or *the least anxiety!*"

"No, sir," he and Howard had answered instantly. Afterwards, they had looked at each other with a long thoughtful look. This was serious. It mustn't be forgotten. Their father sure meant what he said.

Howard's coming home had been another excitement, because Howard was changed. At least he was changed when Ken saw him getting off the train and riding home in the car telling his mother and father things about the school in a deep voice that never slipped up any more. He was in his gray tweed suit, and the Fedora didn't look funny on his face now.

When he got into a shirt and bluejeans with a bandana hanging out of his hind pocket, Ken began to feel more easy with him. And next day Howard stopped sitting gravely with his mother and father and began to devil Ken and wrestle with him. And on the third day they started to tell each other things. Ken made the acquaintance of Howard's two best friends at school— Jake, who was a football star, and Bugs. And in turn he told Howard all about his trip to the Valley of the Eagles, and promised to take Howard there as soon as there was a chance, and undid his belt and pulled up his shirt, and showed him the scar from the eagle's talons. It was still impressive.

Howard was astounded. "And only one leg! I'd like to know how he lost the other one!"

The two boys were in the spring house taking long drinks of milk out of the bucket that stood in the trough of spring water.

Ken dipped himself up a ladleful. "Maybe he got in a fight with another eagle. Or maybe he was born one-legged."

"Aw—don't be a dope!"

"Well, calves are born with two heads! Why shouldn't eagles be born with one leg?"

Howard buried his nose in the ladle.

"Howard, those rams were as big as cows!"

"What're you giving me!"

"Well, anyway, as big as two-year-old steers. Honest, Howard—no kiddin'. And when they rammed each other they made a big BOOM like dynamite going off. Say! Maybe that's where the word rammed came from!"

"Gee, I'd like to get a mountain sheep," said Howard. "When we go I'll take the Marlin thirty."

"And we mustn't forget our fishing lines— Say! Those trout were whoppers!"

All Ken's ideas were a year larger. The waterfall fell practically from the skies. But he didn't try to describe the Thunderer or the other mountains. They still towered over his spirit and silenced him.

"Gee, I hope everything's there still when I get to see it," gloomed Howard.

They leaned against the waist-high trough, white moustaches ornamenting their upper lips, beginning to slow up on the milk drinking.

"Gosh, it's funny to be home," said Howard. "Home isn't anything like what I remembered."

"How is it funny?" demanded Ken.

"Well—you notice things you never noticed before. For instance, the very minute I got into the house I noticed the legs of the dining room table; and it gave me a funny feeling. Those legs seemed more like home than anything else. It was just a comfort to look at them."

Ken marveled about this. "What is it about the legs?" he asked.

"I can't explain, but you'll know after you go far away from home and don't even come back for week-ends or vacations."

Ken registered an intention to examine those legs closely at the first opportunity and see if *he* could get any comfort out of them. Meanwhile he questioned Howard further in the hope that he might have other peculiar ideas.

"And when I'm lying in bed in the morning," said Howard dreamily, "not exactly awake, and not exactly asleep, and I hear a kind of chug-chug-chug—and I wonder whether it's a freight train out on the track or Mother beating the batter for the hot cakes—then I remember back to when I would always be wondering that same thing in the mornings all the years I was a boy— and that makes me feel funny too."

All the years I was a boy. Ken looked at Howard in a startled manner. What was he now then? Surely not a man? Seventeen wasn't a man. But seventeen was not only tall this year, it was straight and had a firm steady walk. *There goes McLaughlin bouncing in line!* Ken looked away. That seemed long ago. Howard no longer bounced. There were times he stood and walked and even drew his brows down and frowned like his father.

All this gave Ken the feeling of the world rushing in on them there at the ranch; and as the barriers of his consciousness were pushed back, he too had a strange gripe in the pit of his stomach and felt that he was growing up.

Then with a wild leap his mind soared away to the thought of Thunderhead and the race, and he had to hang his head and bite his lips. That was the most exciting and the biggest thing of all. Not even Howard, with Bugs and Jake and football and a new military walk, had anything as big and bold as a racing stallion!

Nell lay on the outdoor couch and watched the two boys walking down from the spring house to the cowbarn. They were absorbed in what they were saying to each other. Howard so tall, Ken still a little boy—she was glad of it—there wasn't much time left when they would be boys at all. Howard looked more like his father every day—he drew down his level black brows and the blue of his eyes became more intensely cobalt. And the way his chin jutted. It was going to be a strong face. When he had got a good coat of tan on this summer he would look just like Rob. But Ken looked like *her*—would he ever learn to keep that touseled mop of hair smooth!

She began to gather up loose bits of their boyhood. The way Ken, last spring, on a cold day, had run into the kitchen and lifted one of the lids off the stove and stuck his nose down to the hot coals to get it warm!

The way he still ran upstairs on all fours.

The way he was still sure—as he always had been—that she could look at him and "read his heart." "Look at me, Mother, can you read my heart now? What does it say?"

The hay ripened early that summer and because there was going to be a heavy crop, Rob McLaughlin got a big hay crew and a cook to cook for them.

He had blasted the rocks out of the two largest meadows early in the spring, before the grass started growing, and then had filled in the holes and seeded them, and even this first year, there would be new grass there, and by next year it would be as thick and strong as anywhere on the meadow.

He wasn't able to do any blasting in the meadows during the summertime, because the tramping and hauling would ruin the grass. But he was going ahead with his plan to develop several little draws.

He explained it to the boys. "The hay is a *sure* crop. You can always be disappointed when you try to sell your horses, or beef, or sheep, for that matter. But hay can always be sold, so it's of the utmost importance."

Now that there were not so many horses, Rob had more time for other work, and the boys too.

Rob gave them one draw which they were to convert into meadowland all by themselves. A dam had been thrown across the upper end of it and irrigation ditches dug down the two sides on a level with the dam gates. Now the draw had to be grubbed out, bushes hauled up by the root, rocks blasted and the pieces taken away. They had the use of the big team, Old Tommy, the bronco-buster, and Big Joe, the Percheron, and a rock sledge, and all summer long they toiled at it.

At noon, Rob would drive the car into the meadow where the hay crew was working and give them their dinner there. Howard and Ken, up in the draw overlooking them, would see the car and drop their tools, hastily put the nose-bags of oats on the horses, then run down

309

into the meadow to get their share of the hot corn beef and cabbage and potatoes and bread and butter and pie and milk.

After dinner they had an hour's rest—Ken was supposed to make up the sleep he lost early in the morning riding Thunderhead—but this was the time they talked.

"Gee, Howard," said Ken, "I wish you could stay to see the race."

Howard lay on his back, one knee up and the other foot resting on it.

"Well I can't," he said calmly. And it made Ken remember what his father had said. "If there's something Howard wants and can't have, he's philosophical about it."

Howard flexed his arm and said contemplatively. "Gee! This rocklifting gives a fellow a wonderful development. I might let Jake and Bugs come out here next summer."

"Would they come?" asked Ken with awe.

"Sure. They'd be nuts if they didn't. This sort of work really sets a fellow up. Besides, everybody in the east wants to come out west."

"You know, Howard! Gee! Sometimes I just can't believe it."

"Can't believe what?"

"That it's all turning out to be *real* about Thunderhead."

"Real? Why you dope—what fun would it be if it wasn't real?"

"Well I dunno—"

"Were you just pretending about it all?"

"Oh, of course not!" Ken was puzzled about that. How you can be planning a thing in a real way thinking about it nearly all the time, and yet it is more of a dream than a reality, so that when it suddenly comes true and has to be geared in with actual events, hours and dates and weighing scales, and entrance fees and shipping arrangements, it is just as much of a shock as if you had never really expected it to happen.

Howard was squinting one eye, and then the other,

making a hawk that was floating high up move from one end of a cloud to the other.

"When we get to Saginaw Falls and change these heavy shoes he's wearing to light aluminum shoes they'll feel so light on his feet he'll go like the wind."

Howard held a finger in the air above his face and looked to one side of it and then the other.

"And if Charley Sargent buys Dad's surplus hay and sends it down to Saginaw Falls for the race, then Thunderhead won't have to change to a different kind of hay from what he's used to. Besides, Charley can sell it down there for fifty dollars a ton. He said so. Mountain hay is the best, and down there they'll pay anything if they think it will give their nags a better chance. *But nobody can beat Thunderhead!*" Ken went off suddenly into one of his wild bursts of joy, rolling over backwards and trying to stand on his head.

"Can't you do that?" said Howard contemptuously. He got up slowly, stood on his head with ease and nonchalance, then lay down and stretched out again.

"Gee, Howard! Do you know something?"

"What?"

"I think so much about Thunderhead that when I see my own face in the mirror I'm surprised!"

"Hah! You goof! Do you expect to look like him?"

Ken giggled. "Sure. I see him in my head all the time —that long fierce face and his nostrils going in and out snorting, and the red lining to them, and those white-ringed eyes rolling at you, and when I pass the mirror, if I saw his face in it, I don't think I'd even notice it, but when I see my own face I'm surprised and for a second I wonder who it is!"

Howard sniffed at such childishness. "Say! When shall we go down there—to the Valley of the Eagles?"

"Let's go soon. Golly, I hope that one-legged eagle is there! I'd like to pay him back for what he did to me."

"Maybe we could go this week-end."

"We won't say a thing about where we're going," said Howard. "It might worry Mother."

311

"No. Just off for a camping trip."

"Yes. But I bet Dad won't give us any time off till we've finished this draw." Howard looked at his watch. "Hour's up. We'd better hop to it."

They removed the nose-bags from Big Joe and Tommy, hitched them up to the sledge, and left them by the fence. The two horses had got used to the blasts of dynamite and watched the proceedings with interest.

Ken held the rock drill and Howard swung the sledge hammer until a deep enough hole had been drilled in the rock. Then they stuck the fuse into the stick of dynamite, tamped it into the hole with mud; then lit the end of the fuse and retreated to the far edge of the draw beside the horses and waited to hear the explosion and see the pieces of rock fly. Then they put on their heavy leather gloves, drove the team down into the center of the draw, loaded the broken rock onto the sledge and hauled it away.

By night the boys were so groggy with sleep they staggered to bed at eight o'clock.

But it was not until that draw was finished and another one as well, and all the hay put up, that Rob McLaughlin said the boys could have the rest of the summer to do as they pleased in.

Rest? There wasn't any rest. September was here, and there were only four days before the date for which Howard's return accommodations had been taken.

But four days was twice as much as they would need. So they announced that they were off for a camping trip, and Nell put up provisions for them, and Thunderhead and Flicka were hung with bags, rifles, slickers, frying pans, and the boys rode away up the Saddle Back.

Under their feet the bare rolling hills and soft burned grass—beyond, the Buckhorn Mountains, a wilderness of forests and peaks. And an infinite distance away and above, as if born up on the lower crests, a gleaming shape misted in clouds—the Thunderer—beckoning to them!

And how eagerly they answered. Not the antelope nor the jackrabbits fled more swiftly over the plains than the

312

four young things, wild with excitement and freedom, galloping south with yells and shouts and pounding hoofs, and their faces cold in a wind that was sharp and sweet with snow.

37

From the moment of leaving the ranch Thunderhead was in a state of intense excitement. And when they had climbed the Saddle Back and headed south, his wild eyes and his nostrils and his pricked ears never ceased exploring those mountains ahead of them. *His* mountains! *His* valley!—from which high fences and stern masters had kept him for a year.

He was hard to hold when the smell of the river reached them. Ken let him go and he galloped on the little trail he had made himself until they rounded the hill and the Silver Plume river came into view. While the horses watered, the boys debated whether they should stop and fish, or try to complete the trip that night; and because of Howard's limited time decided on the latter.

Thunderhead took the lead and they plunged into the mountains. He was filled with a fiery and masterful energy. He had never forgotten; and now that the way was open to his inherited destiny, he was ready and eager for it. His stallion's consciousness had come of age at last.

It was already twilight in the gorge; and under some of the overhanging cliffs and great trees the trail led into darkness. But Thunderhead went swiftly; and when the boys stopped to pause and look and exclaim at the plunge of the great waterfalls or the foaming cauldrons of whitewater, his iron shoe struck the rock impatiently, and his strident neigh tore the thunderous roar of the river.

The scent was getting stronger, and it maddened him with joy. It was the scent of a destiny, of a life, of an overwhelming emotion. For not under the saddle or running obediently around a track, but here in these mountains lay his whole existence and he had carried the flame of it in his consciousness for a year.

That evening they pitched camp in the park-like grounds not far from the base of the valley rampart.

Picketed with Flicka below the camp Thunderhead did not lie down and sleep as a young horse should. Only older horses, who no longer have growing pains, sleep standing on their feet. But Thunderhead stood all night long, his body quivering, turned to that rampart and the pass into the valley, his ears pricked to catch the faintest sound.

He knew it immediately when, in the early dawn, a group of mares and colts drifted through the pass to graze in the park here below the rampart. He nickered and started to run to them, but was pulled up by his picket rope and stood there pawing impatiently, nickering again and again.

Flicka woke up and was also seized by the excitement of meeting strangers. Thunderhead ran around the circle allowed him by his picket rope. He backed away, lowered his head and gave it a few shakes, pulling at the rope. But his training had been thorough. It was now almost a physical impossibility for him to fight a head rope. He plunged a bit, and then reared up, pawing the air. When he came down he whirled and looked at those mares again—just dark shadows in the vague gray dawn—then he dropped his muzzle to earth, placed one forefoot on the rope, with a little fling of his head got it between his teeth and bit it through as neatly as he had bitten off the leg of the eagle.

With an eager neigh he trotted off toward the mares, leaving Flicka impatient and unhappy, nickering lone-somely, but too docile to attempt escape.

Ken had been dreaming all night of the playful nickering of horses. He dreamed he was riding Thunderhead on the range in a band of yearlings, but why did they keep nickering so? What was attracting their attention? There came an uneasiness into the dream. The nickering persisted but, as if attempting to present a plausible explanation, the dream changed rapidly. Now he was riding Flicka in the brood mare bunch. And now he was riding in the corrals on the day of the weaning, for that was surely the nickering of young colts—

Ken's dreams became still more uneasy, and he sat up suddenly and saw the dawn and knew where he was and could not understand why the nickering continued even now that the dream was ended.

There was one dazed minute in which he sat there, collecting his wits, brushing the sleep and the hair out of his eyes, and then he realized that off near the rampart was a group of mares and colts with a white horse among them, and that the nickering came from them.

It was just what he had seen on his former visit to the valley except that this was only a small number of mares; and the Albino, for some reason or other, was not behaving like a sensible stallion but was rearing, squealing, whirling around to face first this one then the other, in fact was a living coil of movement and excitement.

But there was nickering closer at hand too, and suddenly Ken became anxious lest Thunderhead and Flicka should be excited by the proximity of the strange mares and break away from their picket lines. He flung back his blankets, leaped out of them and ran down stream. It brought him up sharp to see only one horse there. Flicka hardly paid any attention to his arrival. Her ears were pricked toward those strange mares, and she pawed the ground, and it was her nickering that had aroused him.

In a daze, Ken picked up the second picket rope and looked at the end of it. Bitten clean through. He dropped it and rubbed his hand through his hair. That was Thunderhead over there with the mares then, not the Albino!

No wonder he had behaved peculiarly. Thunderhead with mares at last!

Ken's mind began to labor. He must be got away from them immediately! The Albino might come out through the pass, looking for those mares. And suddenly near-panic seized Ken. The race so near! And the least injury to Thunderhead at this late date might make it impossible for him to run.

Now he thought fast. He picked up a nose-bag half full of oats and walked very quietly over toward the mares.

As he drew near, he called Thunderhead softly and held out the nose-bag and shook it. The oats made a rustling sound. That was enough, as a rule, to draw twenty horses at a run. But Thunderhead merely turned his head to glance at him, then gave his attention to the mares again. Now and then he would drop his nose to the ground and half-circle the mares—plunging at them—turning, dodging, snaking them. It looked as if he were going to round them up! Ken became more alarmed. If he rounded them up, he'd get them going and he'd go along with them, and it would be still harder to catch him!

"Here, boy! Here, Thunderhead! Come along, boy. Here's your oats— Oats, Thunderhead! OATS!"

Thunderhead paid no attention. With more determination now, he drove at the mares. He whipped around them, got them moving, drove them toward the cleft in the rampart.

Ken stood still, appalled by the realization that the horse had actually taken possession of the mares. They gave him complete obedience, as if the electric power within him had welded them all into a unit of which he was head and master.

Suddenly Ken ran forward again. "Oh, Thunderhead! Come, boy! Oats! Come get your breakfast!"

"Hey, Ken! Ken!" rang out behind him. "What's up?"

As Howard came running, Ken looked at him speechlessly. Howard saw Thunderhead driving the mares through the gap, and he too halted.

"Holy Smoke!" he exclaimed.

Thunderhead and the mares disappeared in the twistings of the passage. Ken began to trot after them and Howard followed. Ken was still calling desperately, "Come, boy! Get your oats! Here, Thunderhead! Oats!"

The passage narrowed. They were going through the keyhole, passing directly underneath the great boulder which hung over it, and the next moment there was the wide spread of the valley before them, ghostly with a faint luminescence through which the dark forms of the horses moved like shadows.

Then light flooded the heavens and shafts of rosy gold poured up from the rising sun to bathe the snow covered peaks of the Neversummer Range.

Not even the disaster of Thunderhead's rebellion could lessen the impact of this sight upon Howard.

"Holy Smoke!" he exclaimed again and stood motionless.

But Ken's agonized eyes found what they were looking for. The Albino, and his instant alert as Thunderhead entered the valley! The two stallions saw each other at the same moment. The Albino rushed forward as if for immediate attack, then turned and began to round up the far-flung band of mares and colts behind him. At a swift twisting gallop he circled them, gathered them all in and bunched them in an invisible corral. All his actions were strained and nervous.

But Thunderhead moved with exuberance and calm. His muscles flowed smoothly under his satin coat as he leisurely circled his little band of stolen mares, bunched and froze them, then trotted out in front.

The two stallions faced each other about a hundred yards apart, motionless as statues. The Albino moved forward a little, then stopped. He did this again. Thunderhead stood without a quiver, his head high, his weight forward, his hind legs stretched back.

Ken suddenly thrust the nose-bag into Howard's hands. "Hold that! They're gonna fight! I've got to get him!"

317

He ran to Thunderhead, calling his name. Thunderhead did not even twitch an ear in his direction. He was watching the Albino with a minute, comprehensive stare that penetrated the body and timed the nerve-fuses.

Ken seized the dangling halter rope and flung his weight on it. "Come away! Come away, Thunderhead!"

He hauled with all his power, trying to break the stallion's fixation, but he might as well have tried to move a rock. The stallion stared over him, immobile.

The boy burst out crying and struck at the stallion's head, jerking to and fro with all his weight. "Oh, stop it, Thunderhead! Please, Thunderhead! Come away!"

Howard dropped the nose-bag, rushed to his brother's side and seized the halter.

Ken's voice reached Thunderhead dimly but he made no response. This was his world, his inheritance. Ken had no part in it. But how to become master of it? Only by the destruction of that which barred his way.

Rearing backward, he shook loose, knocking Howard down and snapping Ken aside with a whip-lash of his head. Then, screaming his challenge, he hurtled forward as from a spring-board.

At the same instant the Albino rushed to meet him and both animals stopped short about thirty feet apart and stood tensely eyeing each other. These were two antagonists who had met before and had not forgotten the event.

Mingled with Thunderhead's desire to annihilate this obstacle before him was the satisfaction of an intense curiosity. Here at last was the great being who had overshadowed his whole life, the image of whom had hung in his blood as persistently and as challengingly as the snow-scent hung in the mountain wind.

But the Albino was confused. His feet shifted nervsouly as if taking firmer hold of the earth. His reaching nostrils expanded and contracted slowly. In his sunken eye-sockets his white-ringed eyes stared and meditated, seeing there before him, HIMSELF! His own superb and invincible youth! He was there! He was here! But the

318

strength was as one. It flowed like a current between them as if it were already creating a third horse that appeared in a misty globe between them, and in which they were both fused.

Power and fire and glory rushed through the old stallion and he trumped with ecstasy at this transmutation of himself into the shining magnificence of that vision.

He rushed forward. One will seemed to animate them both, for Thunderhead charged too, each flinging bared teeth at the other's back in passing.

The Albino drew first blood. A red stain sprang out on Thunderhead's withers and spread slowly down his shoulder.

As they passed, they whirled and reared to strike at each other with their front hoofs, reaching over the neck to land body blows that resounded like great bass drums. Short snarling grunts were jarred from them.

The Albino reached under and seized Thunderhead's throat, trying to pull back and tear out the jugular vein. But Thunderhead locked his forelegs around the Albino's neck and pressed close into those grinding jaws.

The horses staggered like wrestlers, Thunderhead forcing the Albino backwards. Then he loosed the grip of his forelegs and began to use them for attack, flailing with his hoofs on the back of the Albino, raking the flesh from the bones and striving to land a crippling blow on the kidneys.

For an instant the massive jaws crunching down on Thunderhead's jugular vein relaxed, he tore loose, both horses wheeled, plunged away, then whirled to eye each other again and to get their wind and their balance for the next charge.

There was a jagged bleeding gash in Thunderhead's throat. The Albino was laced with pulsing crimson streams. The unnatural expansion of his nostrils showed the beginning of exhaustion.

Again, as if animated by a single will, the stallions charged each other with high heads and stiff, lifted tails. Meeting, rising, swerving, sinking with indescribable coiling grace—not one motion lost—they turned their heads sideways with bared reaching teeth and thrust them forwards and under to seize the foreleg.

Each blocked this maneuver cleverly; they braced themselves against each other with locked, straining necks, and swung back first one and then the other foreleg out of reach of the darting, snake-like heads. But Thunderhead was as quick as a rattler. His muzzle thrust in and caught the lower leg of the Albino before he could withdraw it and fractured the bone with a single twisting crunch of the jaws.

The Albino gave no sign. The moment Thunderhead loosed his hold, the older horse rose to his full height. One foreleg dangled useless, but he still had that mighty right hoof with which he had nearly killed the colt two years ago. The same blow would do it now.

Thunderhead too was on his hind legs, feinting as if to strike. But he saw the blow coming. In mid-air he whirled, dropped his head and lashed out with his heels.

As the Albino came down with his killing stroke, his face received the full impact of those terrible hoofs, and both cheeks were ripped up so that the skeleton of his head was bared.

The Albino's one good foreleg hit the earth with a crashing jar. Thrown off balance by failure to land his blow, and the murderous kick, he sank to his knees. Before he could recover, Thunderhead had spun around. His right hoof shot out in one pawing stroke which crushed the bony structure of the old stallion's head and sliced off the lower part of his face.

Blood spouted from the fatal wound, mingled with the choking and bubbling breath. The Albino's eyes closed and his body sank into the earth, his head moving slowly from side to side in agony.

Thunderhead stood over him. The Albino's eyes opened once and looked up at Thunderhead. There was the vision. The shining phantom horse—oversoul of the line! To this prince of the royal blood he now bequeathed all his wisdom. He gave his knowledge of the voices of the trees and waters and the great snows and winds, so that nothing in the valley would be strange to him, no, not a single mare, nor the smallest colt nor a humming-bird nor eagle nor a blade of grass.

Thunderhead's right hoof rose and fell with lightning speed, cleaving the skull.

The Albino quivered and was still. Then one deep sigh came from him, and on it there ebbed away his life, while his blood and brains pumped slowly out to mingle with the earth of his beloved valley.

Thunderhead lifted his mighty crest and made the mountains ring with his unearthly screech of triumph.

38

"Stand, Thunderhead!"

Hardly had the echoes of Thunderhead's cry of victory ceased than a small familiar figure was beside him, commanding him.

Obediently Thunderhead stood while two hands seized the halter rope and gripped his mane. Ken vaulted onto his back.

The stallion's eyes were on the mares. All through the fight they had stood in two close bunches, watching, fascinated. Now that it was ended they began to disperse. They were confused and nervous.

Howard picked up the nose-bag of oats and started toward Thunderhead. But the stallion suddenly plunged toward the mares. Ken flung his weight back, hauling on the rope, but it was whipped out of his hands as the great white head jerked impatiently, then dropped, snaking along the ground. The stallion was not only beginning the roundup of the mares, he was taking command and making himself known to them as their new master. Ken seized handfuls of the thick, wild mane.

Thunderhead galloped faster. He swept in a huge circle, whipping the two groups of mares into one. Then, as if merely to discipline them, he bored through them, scattering them again. They dispersed over half a mile. And now he began to herd them at full gallop. Not for a moment was he straight between Ken's knees. His body was in continual undulation. Ken was riding the end of a whip-lash, twisted mercilessly. Occasional cries of pain and helplessness burst from him. The stallion was driving the mares and colts further up the valley and they were all running now, increasing speed at the furious coercion of their new master.

A black runaway mare with a little white colt at her side streaked out at an angle from the band of mares, bent on escape. Thunderhead altered his direction and took after her. Ken felt the great body underneath him knotted and gathered for a sudden turn or stop—for any one of half a dozen maneuvers; and, unable to ride with his usual free, balanced seat, clung like a monkey.

The stallion came abreast of the mare and closed in. She did not surrender.

Ken knew what was coming and flung himself back, braced for the shock. The stallion reached over the mare and seized her neck in his powerful jaws, jerking it toward him, and at the same time threw himself back on his haunches.

Ken was flung sprawling on the horse's neck.

The mare's body went over in a complete somersault and she crashed to the earth, rolling over and over.

Ken, clinging to Thunderhead's neck, was, by a miracle, still on.

The mare got shakily to her feet. Thunderhead galloped after the herd and now she followed him obediently.

He reached and passed the mares, and took the lead.

The black mare forged to the front of the band and the little white colt galloped mightily as if trying to reach the side of the stallion.

Wave after wave of nausea went over Ken. His face was deathly white. His body ached as if it had been beaten. His fingers in Thunderhead's mane clung merely because they were stiffly locked. He had lost all hope of ever getting control of his horse—the hills were sweeping past— he could not stick on any longer—the herd was thundering behind him. Where was Howard? Where was the keyhole, and safety, and Flicka? At this pace, he was leaving them far behind.

There came at last a moment of anguished exhaustion when he cared about nothing—only to be off—

He loosed his grip, flung himself flat back on Thunderhead's broad rump, at the same time swinging one leg over his withers. From this side-saddle position he slid to earth. His feet touched for a second, then he was hurled on his face.

He felt the jarring thud of the ground and lay there. The thunder of the herd roared up and over him. The ground shook. Clods of dirt and stinging gravel pelted him and abrupt blocks of light and darkness alternated over him as the big bodies of the mares lifted in the air to clear him—one after the other.

It receded into the distance—that thunder of hoofs— until at last it was not even so loud as the sound of the wind in the pines, and his own heart-broken sobbing, and the harsh faraway cry of eagles who dropped from the clouds to feast upon royal carrion.

39

The command not to cause Nell any anxiety had been disobeyed. For the boys, riding double on Flicka, hardly got home in time to hurry Howard into his clothes and pack his suitcases.

After he had gone, Ken sat down by his father's desk in the study and told the details of all that had happened.

Rob was in a very quiet mood. He sat in his square wooden chair, turned slightly toward Ken and puffed at his pipe.

"Why, in God's name!" said he at last, "did you take Thunderhead to a place where there were mares and another stallion?"

"But Dad!" exclaimed Ken woefully, "he'd been there often before! And he had his own regular place to watch them from—perfectly safe—up there on top of that rampart! He never went into the valley, not since that first time when he got the awful swat when he was a baby!"

"And so you figured he'd continue to do as he always had done. And that's where you made your mistake. After all, Thunderhead's three years old now, and in some ways, for a horse, that's grown up."

Ken's tired and dirty face turned away and his eyes wandered, then came back to his father. "But he's never done any hell-raising. And he's been trained for running and racing. You said yourself a horse will develop the way he's trained."

Rob's slight sardonic smile showed a line of white teeth beside his pipestem. "There's still nature, my boy—don't forget that—! God made horses, you know, Ken. Not domestic horses, to labor and toil for men. Not race horses —prima donnas in stable-boudoirs, with valets and ladies' maids and trainers— But *wild horses!* Stallions and mares, with intelligence to take care of themselves. He made the stallions to breed and take care of the mares, fight for them, round them up, make them obey, see that they have proper food and shelter. He made the mares to have their foals and take care of them. They drop them out on the hills. The cord tears loose, drains blood for a little while—that is as Nature intends. Then it dries up and falls off and there's never an infection. Nature takes care of it—not a veterinarian. It's all very well to call it hell-raising when Thunderhead begins to live and behave as we don't want him to—but that's Nature. And if you forget that, you've got a jolt coming."

Ken sighed deeply and wearily, nodding his head. Well he knew about Nature now.

"And between you and me, Ken," continued his father, "every horse-lover in the world has to take off his hat to *the wild horse*—a horse that acts like a horse—as God made him—not according to some cooked-up plans of men."

Ken gave perfunctory attention to what his father was saying but his mind was on one thing only. Where exactly was Thunderhead now? How exactly could he be got back?

"We hunted up there at the far end of the valley as long as we could," he said. "If Howard hadn't had to get home, we would have had more time. I wanted Howard to take Flicka and leave me up there for a while. But he wouldn't. He said we had to stick together."

"Quite right. It would have been dangerous. Besides, you had no horse. How would you have got home?"

Ken averted his eyes, ashamed to say that his father or Gus would have had to come for him. "I might have got hold of Thunderhead again."

"Ah! A pretty long chance!"

325

There was a silence while Rob sat in thought. Then he said, "Have you any idea where he took the mares?"

"Well, we went far enough up the valley to see that it went out into other valleys, and then other valleys branched off of those. There wasn't any real rampart—that volcanic wall I told you about—up at the other end—just a lot of mountains going up one behind the other, higher and higher. That left a lot of places where the horses could have gone. It just looked like a—a—labyrinth of mountains and draws and gorges and valleys—" Ken turned his head away again, oppressed by the memory of the scene—the clouds of snow, the blazing glaciers, pockets of emerald grass, the soaring grandeur of the peaks. He couldn't even try to put it into words.

"It was just hopeless. There wasn't a sign of the mares or Thunderhead. We had trailed them all the way up the valley—of course it was easy to see their tracks, especially Thunderhead's. But the last two hours it snowed. I think it snows every day up there. And it was getting dark."

"What time was it when Howard found you after you fell off Thunderhead?"

Ken thought a moment. He wasn't going to tell his father that he had lain there sobbing his heart out for an hour. "Well—I don't know exactly—I was asleep—"

"After you fell off?" Rob glinted a little, looking at his son.

Ken flushed. "Yes. I was so dead tired. And—and—I just lay there. When I felt Howard shaking me and looked up and saw him and Flicka there, I didn't know where I was or what had happened for a moment. But I think it was about noon."

Knocked cold and didn't know it, thought Rob. Aloud he said meditatively, "You sure can get yourself in the damndest predicaments! You must have as many lives as a cat! Anyone else would be dead if they'd been caught in half the jams you've been in! First with Flicka. And then the eagle got your gizzard. And now this."

Ken's head swayed in complete agreement.

326

Rob smoked for a few moments. In his mind the scene lived again. The hidden valley, the fight of the two stallions—

"God! I'd like to have seen that fight!" he exclaimed.

Ken wagged his head wearily. "You just oughta have seen it. It was like—it was like—Dad, you know those prehistoric monsters?"

"Dinosaurs and pterodactyls and mastodons?"

"Yeah. Those. Well it made you think of them. They both looked so big—as big as elephants—maybe that was because they were up on their hind legs all the time and their heads so high and their hoofs pawing. And then after Thunderhead had won, the way he stood up and screeched! Dad, if there were any monster roosters in prehistoric days, and they *crowed*—that's just the way Thunderhead was. You could have heard it on the tops of those mountains. It went right through you like something filing on glass—only as loud as a locomotive."

"And that's when you walked up to him and mounted him!"

Ken nodded with another of the deep sighs that expressed his physical exhaustion.

The mere thought of it made Rob get to his feet and walk around the room. "It's the God-damndest thing that ever was! Why, Ken! didn't it occur to you that all he had to do was throw out one paw the way he did to the Albino and it would have gone through your head like butter!"

"But he wasn't mad at me. He didn't pay any attention to me at all."

Rob dropped in his chair again. He was bursting with pride. He leaned forward and squeezed Ken's knee and in spite of himself the boy winced.

"I suppose you know that it doesn't often happen that a man rides a stallion in the act of rounding up a band of mares and lives to tell the tale."

Ken nodded his head in bewilderment. "He was awful queer. He didn't mind having me around or on his back, but just didn't seem to notice me, or hear anything I said.

And he wouldn't obey me at all any more." This last was in an aggrieved tone.

Rob shouted with laughter. "Obey you! I should say-ay-ay not! Who are you to interfere in a moment like that!"

Ken tilted his head assentingly. The joke was on him all right.

He had a look Rob had seen on him many times before —always caused by one of these soul-struggles over horses. He was white and hollow-eyed and looked as if he'd lost ten pounds.

"You look like a picked chicken," said Rob dryly. "You always manage to get yourself all run down just when it's time to go to school."

"School!"

"Yes. But I suppose we ought to be thankful that you came home all in one piece."

Something was choking in Ken's throat. School again! Just school! After all the year's hopes and the work and the planning! After having been a racing man! Owner of the wonder horse! Practically over with such childish things as school! And already possessed of his father's permission to stay out of school and go to Saginaw Falls with Charley Sargent!

Rob's eyes were running over him critically. "You look pretty sick. Aside from dirt and scratches and getting tuckered out, nothing happened to you this time, did it? No claws in your belly? No broken bones?"

Ken raised his right arm carefully and moved it about in an experimental manner.

"What happened to that arm?"

"When I slid off Thunderhead and saw I was going to land on my face I threw this arm up—gave it a crack."

Rob examined the arm and shoulder. Ken winced several times. "Nothing broken. Anything else?"

"Well, coming home on Flicka—I couldn't saddle her, my legs ached so—I had to sit side-saddle."

Rob laughed. "I've had that feeling myself. That came

328

from riding the stallion when he was snaking. It wrenched every muscle in your body."

Rob's eyes went over Ken minutely, noting the ragged, filthy clothes, the hands with dirt ground into the hastily washed scratches and abrasions, a dark bruise down one side of his face, stains of blood inside one leg of his blue-jeans.

"I did think I was a goner once," said Ken.

"When was that?"

"When I fell off Thunderhead and the mares were coming right behind."

"No horse will step on a living thing if it can be avoided. And I suppose they were pretty well scattered."

"Well—they weren't spread much—"

"If they have time to see, they'll jump."

"That's what they did. It was as if the light went on and off. It would be light over me, and then dark, and I'd get a squint of hoofs and belly—then light again. But they sure spattered me all over with dirt and gravel."

"I'll say they did. What's that blood on the inside of your pants leg?"

"That's from Thunderhead," said Ken.

"Was he much cut up?"

"A lot of bites and rips. A deep one on his side and shoulder that I got all this blood from. It was the very first wound of the battle. Then he got that bad one in his throat I told you about, but nothing seemed to bother him. He didn't act as if he even knew he was wounded."

"Probably didn't. And probably the Albino didn't know he was killed. I often think pain and death don't enter into the consciousness of horses at all. What about your friend, the one-legged eagle? No sign of him on this trip?"

"He came down. Six of them came down to eat up the Albino."

"Ah! They'll pick his bones! A true burial of the plains!" Rob's face lit up. "A great old boy! I've always had a corner in my heart for him, even if he did nearly brain me!"

Ken had forgotten this. His father showed him again the scar over his temple where the Albino's hoof had left its mark and it seemed to draw them all into a close little knot.

"What a great horse!" said Rob leaning back again. "Ken, there are outstanding individuals in the animal world as well as the human. The Albino was like Napoleon! Or like Caesar! To be close to one of those is like being close to a charge of T.N.T."

"Yes, sir," said Ken wearily.

He knew.

Rob made a little gesture with his hand. "Well! The king is dead! Long live the king!"

"You mean Thunderhead?"

"Thunderhead. The Throwback." And that took them both back to the day three years ago when the ungainly little white foal had been born and everyone had thrown at him the epithet *Throwback!*

"Dad—"

"Well?"

Ken hardly dared to say it. "Do you suppose if you took a lot of men—maybe ten or twenty—with horses and lariats up to the valley—I could show you the way—you could get him back? Because you see there's only a little more than a month before the race—"

Rob answered gravely, "It would take a regiment of cavalry—and *then* they wouldn't get him."

Ken was silent. He was not surprised. Moreover, deep within him, something revolted against the idea of taking such an expedition into his valley. The band of mares broken up, some of them killed during the roping, colts stolen, separated from their dams, coarse shouts and curses and brutal acts desecrating that remote, inviolate animal sanctuary—he'd almost rather lose his horse.

Ken lifted his white face with a look of straight-seeing courage and resignation in his eyes. "Dad," he said again, and paused. For the hundredth time in his tortured mental process he had come to the same conclusion—that

330

there was only one slim hope. "Won't he come back, Dad?"

"Of his own accord?"

"He always has before. This is his home and he's oriented. You always said he would, and he always did."

There was a little sadness in Rob's sardonic smile this time. "Ken! You know horses! He's got a band of mares now, hasn't he?"

"Yes, sir."

"Will he abandon them?"

The question needed no answer. Ken had reached that same conclusion in his own thoughts every time.

His head sank on his chest and Rob saw that the boy was trembling all over. He hadn't yet had a bath or change or a night's sleep or a solid meal.

"You go clean up now, son, and get ready for supper, or you'll be keeling over. You've had a great adventure. It didn't end the way you wanted it to, and I'm as disappointed as you are about losing Thunderhead."

"Oh, are you, Dad?" Ken raised his head and his eyes went to his father's face. Somehow it eased the pain to have his father disappointed too.

"Yes, I am. I've worked with him. And I had come to have confidence in him and his future. He's a great horse. Besides, you know, I needed the money—"

"I know!" Ken's face was almost happy.

"But we're both out of luck and we'll just have to take it."

"With fortitude," suggested Ken with a gleam in his eye.

"Exactly. No use crying over spilt milk. I can tell you this, if it'll make you feel any better—" They both got to their feet. "I'm damned proud of you!"

"Of me!"

"Of *you*. My God, Ken! *You rode a stallion at work!* No one but a fool even goes near a stallion when he's rounding up his mares—let alone tries to mount him—or could stick if he did!"

"I didn't stick."

"Sure you did—till he darned near killed you. You behaved with courage. You tried to get your colt back. You tried to master him. You got on him and rode him to hell and gone. You did something I've never done—and I'm proud as punch!"

Ken was overwhelmed. "Of course," added Rob, "I suppose all this was to be expected from a fellow who once pulled off such a stunt as to get a *zero* in English! I never did that either!"

Rob dropped a hand on his shoulder and shook it. "Now go on and get a good hot bath. Put all this out of your mind. Supper'll be ready in an hour and I want to see you eat! And I've got a surprise for you—something you'll like. I'm going to talk it over with your mother first."

Ken lay in his hot bath, luxuriating. All the sore knotted muscles eased and relaxed, and the feverish pain was drawn out of the scratches and abrasions.

He began to feel much happier. His mind was packed with vivid memories as glorious as thunder and lightning and rushing winds; and his own forever.

He measured out some of his mother's bath salts. He had heard salts helped take the ache out of your bones— it said just a tablespoon, but when you were so lame probably you needed a bigger dose—he emptied half the bottle of perfumed lilac salts into the tub, then lay back and stirred it up with his toes.

He examined and counted all his wounds, while his mind rolled forward on a fascinating tale. Thunderhead would always live in that valley with his mares, but he would yearn and grieve for Ken, and Ken would visit him now and then, and Thunderhead would be glad to see him, would even let him ride him—(though not while rounding up his mares).

He noticed that his head rested easily on the back of the tub while his toes were braced against the end. Surely that was new. He used to float uncomfortably. Ah! Maybe it was beginning now! The shooting up process!

332

All the while he heard the murmur of his parents' voices in their near-by bedroom and that made him happier still, for his father said he was going to talk it over with your mother and it was something nice.

Drying himself gingerly standing on the bathmat Ken decided that he most certainly was taller.

He got the iodine bottle from the medicine chest and attended painstakingly to his wounds. He was dotted and smeared all over when he finally sat down with slicked hair and startlingly clean fingernails to the supper of fried chicken and mashed potatoes whipped with hot cream such as only his mother could make.

And again he told and retold the story of his adventure, even to the bit about the black mare who made the dash for freedom. "She was a beauty, Dad. She reminded me of Gypsy, only she was bigger. And the white colt—he was like Thunderhead used to be. He had short legs. He scrabbled."

And at last Rob told his boy of the important thing. That none of his plans need be changed. He could still go to Saginaw Falls with Charley Sargent. He could still send a race horse of his own in Charley Sargent's express car. There would still be a Goose Bar entry in the races. The only change would be that it would be the two-year-old filly, Touch And Go, instead of the three-year-old stallion, Thunderhead.

And so when the big black Buick rolled down the mountain passes of the Wyoming Idaho highway on October eleventh there were two racehorse-owners sitting in the front seat, Charley Sargent, quite formal-looking in a black overcoat and derby hat, and Ken, feeling at least ten years older than ever before.

40

Ken's sudden aging was because of several things. The trousers of the new suit he wore were two inches longer than any he had had before. And a small Fedora hat sat upon his knees, carefully guarded against possible wear and tear.

But the greatest change was within him. It was so peculiar a feeling that he looked inside himself to inspect and name it. He decided finally that it must be fortitude. He had made acquaintance with the real article at last, and he knew it as an admixture of bitter disappointment with cheerfulness and readiness to go on and do whatever was in line. He wasn't "howling" about Thunderhead now when the worst had happened.

Several new experiences were grouped around the new state. When you were howling you could derive pleasure from nothing except the one thing you wanted which was denied you. But when you had fortitude, a great deal of pleasure could be built on top of that, even though, at the bottom, was still the deep grief. For instance, he was enjoying this ride immensely.

Riding in an automobile, people feel as if they were very busy doing something important; and that, therefore, nothing else can be demanded of them either by their own consciences or by external busy-bodies. This is a great comfort to nervous people, and since everybody is nervous, to everybody. When one is enjoying this freedom from duty and coercion one even resents being asked to turn the head to look at the outline of those hills back there. Or to move a little to see if you're not sitting on my glove. No nuance of this subtle pleasure was wasted on Ken. He felt very conscience-clear, very grown-up, and very lazy.

Ken was also enjoying Charley Sargent's company. The tall horseman seemed different somehow in these clothes. The derby hat took away some of the geniality of his humorous face and gave it a shrewd wariness instead. But when he glanced down at Ken there was much friendliness in his eyes.

"How long d'you reckon it was you sat on that stallion, Ken?"

"Oh, I dunno—long enough!"

"I'll bet! My God! Say—how many mares d'you think he had in the band?"

"I never had a chance to count 'em, but there were a lot, spread all around."

"Maybe thirty?"

"Maybe."

"Tell me about that fight, Ken, just how they went at each other."

"But I told you all that, Mr. Sargent."

"Well, I want to hear it again." And when Ken had complied, "God! What a horse!" He nudged Ken with his elbow. "And don't you forget, Appalachian was his sire!"

He would have gone on talking and hearing about the Valley of the Eagles and all that had happened there indefinitely, but Ken wanted to get information about the race track they were going to and the business of racing horses in general.

"Well, Ken—this track at Saginaw Falls is as sporty a little track as you could find anywhere. You know there are a few tracks in this country that are just run by a bunch of millionaires who like to take money away from each other. This is one of them."

"How do they take money away from each other? Betting?"

"Yes—and sellin' nags. Now listen, Ken—you're not to do any bettin', get that in your head."

"I've got five dollars," said Ken.

"Well, hang on to it. There are two ways to make money with race horses—or to lose it. One is bettin', and one is raisin' horses and sellin' 'em. The last is my line, although I place some bets too. But *you* can't be a racin' man, Ken—travelin' around the country, runnin' horses and bettin' on 'em—"

"I know I can't."

"And even if you could, I wouldn't want it for you, and neither would your Dad and your Mother—no matter how much money you made."

"I know."

"What you are is a breeder and trainer of horses. You've done a grand job with this filly, she's right on edge for a winnin' race, and she hasn't been coddled, she can run any distance—in her class, that is. And on any kind of track."

Ken felt a glow inside and looked up with a slight flush.

"I may bet on her myself," added Sargent, "she's a speeder and no foolin'. She might go right to the front and never be headed. She'll run in the event for maidens on the sixteenth—that's five days from now. She's already sharp as a tack so we won't have to give her any fast work which might reveal her speed. Nobody knows her, and odds'll be long against her. I may make our hotel bill on her." He glanced down at the boy, grinning.

"It sounds cockeyed," said Ken.

"Racin' *is* cockeyed," said Sargent, "except in the bull-rings where it's just a bunch of horses runnin' against each other and the beetle that runs the fastest gets a purse."

Ken thought that sort of race would be much more sensible. "Couldn't I sleep with my beetle in her stall instead of in the hotel?" he asked.

"You're goin' to sleep where I do. And that's not in the stables, young man."

Ken sat silently going over in his mind all that would presently happen to Touch And Go. She had been shipped from Sherman Hill four days ago with Sargent's four horses. She was at Saginaw Falls now in charge of Sargent's trainer, Perry Gunston, being exercised daily by Tommy Pratt, Sargent's exercise boy. And on October sixteenth she would run her maiden race. The Condition Book listed other races for two-year-olds on October twentieth and another on the last day of the meet following the Greenway race. With three chances, Touch And Go ought to show—if she had it in her.

"What rider do you think you'll get for Touch And Go, Mr. Sargent?"

"I'll get Dickson for her if I can. He's ridden winnin' races for me before and he's a good kid. But if I can't get him, there are a couple others just about as good—Green—Marble—"

Ken immediately made pictures in his mind of Dickson, Green and Marble. He liked Dickson the best. He could see him, in Sargent's colors, mounted on Touch And Go—out in front! Drawing away to win! And at this point Ken's heart always skipped a beat or two.

They were dropping rapidly down from the top of the Divide. The weather had been stormy and the rolling hills spreading out on either side were blown with snow that here and there let the brown earth through.

Charley Sargent drove at about eighty or eighty-five miles an hour, as most men do in the west where great distances have to be covered and there is little traffic on the roads.

They stopped every few hours at wayside stations and Ken would sit beside Charley Sargent at the counter and would have to go through an agony before he would know what to order, while Charley, in the twinkling of an eye, would have ordered a cup of coffee and a piece of pie.

They ran in and out of snow storms. You could see them ahead, far away. The air would get thicker and darker, and suddenly you would be right in that storm, you had caught up with it, presently you ran out of it again.

Everywhere were mountains. They sprang up unexpectedly not half a mile away at a sudden turn of the road, or there was a fall of miles and miles, a wide valley lying purple-dark at the bottom, and far distant ranges of mountains shining white in the sun, turning to misty blue when clouds covered the sky, vanishing altogether in mid-afternoon, and blazing out in the sunset against a sky like the inside of a furnace.

Sometimes the wind would burrow into the snow and sweep up a bunch of it into a little cyclone, and Ken would watch it spinning along the plains, turning into the shape of a waterspout, and it would remind him of the plume of snow the wind lifted from the Thunderer when he was in the mountains. And the memory of that brought a sudden emptiness inside him that made him gasp.

Thunderhead! Where was Thunderhead now? No... think of Touch And Go... think of the little filly, so bright and gentle and docile... so beautiful with her dancing step and smart style... think of her airy lightness, her extraordinary speed... think back to the day you first saw Flicka run... run away from Banner who was chasing her on the Saddle Back and she was only a yearling with a pink-blond tail and mane, and she showed Banner a clean pair of heels. ...

Touch And Go was just Flicka all over again. Ken loved her with the gentle protective love that a mother gives to her second-born when the idolized first-born has died.

His thoughts sprang to his mother. He had been wishing for a long time that a person could have fortitude for someone else. He would like to have it for his mother and give it to her, but it wasn't possible. Fortunately, she had it for herself. He had discovered that, one evening standing in the empty dining room with the door open into the kitchen. He was quiet, doing nothing but looking out the window. His mother was getting supper in the kitchen, and suddenly he heard a sound from her. There was no one in the kitchen, but she was talking out loud as if there were, and he heard the words, "Oh, will I ever be young—and slim—and quick—again!" and then a soft little moan. And he had turned quickly and looked through the door and she was leaning against the wall with her back to him, her head tilted over, one hand hanging straight down at her side with the dish towel in it. And it made him feel so bad he hurried out of the dining room and outdoors and wandered around in terrible confusion of mind until suppertime. He felt he ought to tell his father, they ought to get the doctor, something ought to be done right away. But when he went in to supper, there was his mother just like she always was, with quick smiles for all of them, and that serene look about her dark blue eyes, and a face flushed pink from the stove, and a ready laugh if there was anything funny. That was her fortitude.

Well—it wouldn't last much longer! And then she *would* be quick and slim and young again. He wished he knew just when it was going to happen. Several times he had been on the point of asking the exact breeding date but had refrained for fear it might not be considered polite.

No matter how fast Charley drove, the world was so vast it didn't sweep past them, it stayed there. There were white-faced Hereford steers and cows grazing on the barren-looking ground. Horses too—all of them with thick warm coats for winter. And now and then a close band of gray sheep, hardly visible in the gray air. They made Ken think of their own sheep. Perhaps his father was out looking them over at this very minute, talking to the Mexican herder, planning just when they would put the bucks into the band with the ewes, planning for spring lambing.

Sometimes Ken napped. When he woke again it was the same panorama of hills and plains and distant ranges, part snow, part rock, part bare brown earth, and the same Herefords and horses grazing in the foreground.

During the two-day trip to Saginaw Falls there were three passes to descend. They reached the first in a snow storm and were blocked by a truck coming in the opposite direction which had ascended the grade and slid sideways on the very summit, nearly closing the road. Behind the truck were several dozen east-bound cars trying to get up the grade.

As Sargent stopped his car and waited for the truck to get out of the way, other cars came up behind them and waited too, skidding on the snow-coated road as they put on their brakes. Sargent and Ken got out and walked forward and looked down the grade. For a mile, you could see the east-bound cars that had been held up by the jam on the summit. They were in every sort of crazy position on the road, tilted on the inner bank, or two or three of them locked together with their occupants stamping around in the snow, shouting at each other, pulling or shoving at the machines. Men in shirtsleeves, and bareheaded to save their hats from blowing away, squatted on the ground, trying to untangle their chains and put them on.

To get past the truck every west-bound car had to crawl out to the very edge of the road where it overhung the abyss, squeeze around the truck—and this could not be done too slowly because the wheels would lose traction —and then wind and slide in and out among all the stalled cars on the down-grade.

Charley knew the road well and had taken the precaution of having his chains put on at the last service station. But there was no chatting as he negotiated the pass. Ken looked at his face but did not speak to him. Now and then the boy cast a fascinated glance over the edge of the cliff to the right—that sheer drop into a dark chaos—it seemed a mile!

At the bottom of the pass they got out and Ken helped remove the chains.

"It's bad enough without snow," said Sargent as they put the chains in the back compartment and got into the car again, "those hairpin turns—now you see why I send the horses by rail instead of bringing them in vans or trailers down this highway."

"I should think," said Ken, as they hit the straightaway and Sargent increased his speed, "that cars would go over the edge of that road sometimes."

"If you look at the daily papers," said Charley, "you'll find that that's a very frequent occurrence."

Ken could see it in his imagination. The big black thing rolling over and over—bouncing—falling through sheer space—perhaps one or two tiny human forms dropping out of it and going down like dolls, head over heels—then the crash at the bottom. It made him feel sick.

"Or," said Charley, "while you're driving these roads you'll often see a break in the little fence at the edge—if there happens to be one—where someone's car has gone through. Or you'll see a tree broken. Of course the passes aren't always as bad as this one today. The first real snow catches everybody unprepared. By tomorrow the snow ploughs will have just about cleared it. They have to, otherwise the transcontinental busses couldn't keep goin'. Even in the worst storms, they keep the roads open. If they can't clear them, at least they break up the surface so that cars with chains don't have much trouble."

Ken hugged to himself the picture of Touch And Go as he had last seen her, cosy and safe in the express car with Sargent's horses, and bales of hay and sacks of oats for the journey.

"Mr. Sargent, if Touch And Go does turn out to be a winner, wouldn't you like to take her around with you to all the meets you go to and run her on shares with me?"

"Ken, I've got too many of my own already. I'm always tryin' to sell, not to buy, nor to add to my overhead. Perry can take care of only so many horses, you know, without hirin' more men. Your best bet is to sell her if you can."

Ken wondered if anyone would want to buy his filly. When it came right down to it, it didn't seem possible that someone would buy Touch And Go and give him a big check that he could take home to his father.

There were other passes, but they were running out of the snow storms as they reached the lower altitudes, and the last pass was a really thrilling sight—as if a giant mountain of granite had been split by lightning and the two sides leaned apart, and the road and foaming white river wound down between them in a lost world of stone.

Ken peered from the window. It was like the Silver Plume river. It *was* the Silver Plume—swiftly leading him away from the highway and the race track and taking him back to the gorge and the valley and the mountains and Thunderhead. . . .

"Better close that window, Ken—" Charley reached a hand over and wound up the glass.

Ken leaned back, suddenly sick with longing for his horse.

It was getting late. Sargent put on the lights and the car hurtled westward through the darkness.

41

Thunderhead lifted his nose high and searched the wind.

It was a bare craggy peak overlooking the southern end of the valley that he had chosen for his lookout. From here he could see below him where his mares were grazing. He could turn and look at the tiers of mountains behind away up to the Thunderer in his eyrie in the sky. He could see the clouds rolling around them, he could hear the deep rumble of the giants that lived underneath, the fall of every avalanche, the crack of every frozen tree; and not a bird nor animal could move without his eyes' and ears' taking note of it.

It was an uneven pinnacle of rock on which he stood, with barely room for foothold. His hind legs were braced down and apart. His body was twisted. His head, with its floating white mane and spear-pointed ears, was lifted high, his dark, white-ringed eyes filled with the wildness of the mountains and the clouds. Dangling from his black halter was a bit of rope, frayed and worn at the end.

A little below him, balked by the steepness of the last sheer ascent, a small white colt stood looking up at him. Now and then Thunderhead's glance rested on him for a second, then brushed past and up again.

A new message was on the wind this early morning. There was a heavy storm coming. The temperature was twenty below already and still falling.

The mares and colts were protected by a long thick growth of hair which they had started growing in September in preparation for this early storm. But Thunderhead was warmed only by the inner heat of the stallion. His coat was, as always, silky and shining, scarred only by patches of rough, long hair under his throat, and on his shoulders where he had been wounded.

Around the mountain peaks many storms were tossing, rolling down the slopes, colliding with each other, carried on opposing currents of air. A boiling mass of wind-cloud swept north over the valley with an eagle sailing before it. Now and then the storms united and came down in a deep white blanket, then were broken up again and, roaring, separated and moved in every direction. Gradually the smother thickened and snow fell, driving first one way, then the other.

Thunderhead reared his crest high into the storm. His mane streamed to the west. The eastern wind was strongest and would prevail. *An easterner.*

Memory tingled through him and his pawing hoof rang on the rock.

When the cold burns too deep, when there is death in the wind, take the way down the mountain. Gates are open. Mangers are full of hay. There is shelter and food and kindness for all. And the screaming whiteness cannot follow you in.

He made several abrupt movements of his head, then turned and picked his way down the crag, his tail sweeping over the white colt, who carefully followed him.

343

Thunderhead rounded up his mares and headed them north down the valley. When he had them running he took the lead, with the black mare and her white colt close behind him. His pace was carefully chosen so that the smallest colt could keep up.

What snow there was, boiled like seafoam around their feet and there was that sound in the steadying eastern wind—that unvarying roar—that would turn into a whine as the velocity increased.

They strung out single file going through the keyhole and down the river gorge. Now and then Thunderhead circled to see that there were no stragglers, giving a few nips to keep the tail-enders aware that they were on a drive and expected to keep up.

Below, on the plains, they spread out, kicking and biting, wild with the heat of their blood, and the excitement of the run, and the fierce beating of the wind and snow.

They neared the ranch in the late afternoon, Thunderhead swinging along at a canter, finding his way through the white smother with the ease of infallible instinct. He was on his own ground now, and had known every square foot of it since birth.

Reaching the crest of the Saddle Back, he halted to survey his domain and his mares crowded up around him. Nothing could be seen through the snow, but to his inner eye, every building, every fence post was visible, and as he plunged down the slope he indulged in some coltish bucks of pure joy. With those thirty handsome mares and colts behind him he could be forgiven for feeling the pride of a young heir when he brings home his bride and displays her to the family.

Down the Saddle Back they poured at a full gallop, up the County Road—the gate was open! Thunderhead made the sharp turn, the mares following close, cantered down through the Stable Pasture to the corral—again the gates were open! They poured in—

It was already full of mares and colts. All the familiar old smells! Every brood mare as comfortable to him as mother's milk! Oats and hay. The corral and stables. Banner—

Thunderhead nickered and squealed in an ecstasy of homecoming. He plunged through the mares to the feed racks and tore out a great mouthful of hay—Castle Rock Meadow hay that he had been brought up on. His mares pushed in behind him, mixing with the other mares, starting little fights and scuffles.

Banner met him in the center of the corral. The two stallions stood nose to nose, quivering and squealing, half rearing. They were filled with the excitement that goes with the meeting of old friends—and something else, too, because of these mares and colts. They turned away from each other and began to investigate. Thunderhead's approach to the Goose Bar mares was the greeting of old friends, but it was different with Banner. These strange mares were new and exciting! There were so many of them—and his own quota was incomplete. With a mere ten brood mares any self-respecting stallion is looking for more.

The mares and colts milled around, crowding the walls of the stable and the feed racks.

Banner pursued three of Thunderhead's mares that were in a little group together. His head snaked along the ground. He drove them over to a group of his own. Thunderhead tossed his head high over the crush where he was feeding at the rack and his flaring eyes caught sight of this maneuver. He dropped his muzzle to feed again. Banner continued to move Thunderhead's mares from where they were feeding over into a corner of the corral and to freeze them there.

Thunderhead wormed himself out of the jam. He pursued Banner and neighed challengingly. As the red stallion turned and faced him, they both reared and nipped, then dropped to earth and stood quivering.

In Thunderhead was all the old love for Banner, but there was another feeling too, and it was getting stronger every instant. Anger. Combativeness. A furious uprising and outpouring of energy that lifted and stiffened his tail and burst from him in squealing grunts of protest and sent him rearing and pawing into the air. It would presently find outlet in more dangerous action than that.

The two stallions plunged past each other again and this time each aimed an ugly nip in passing.

"Boss! Boss! T'underhead is here mid a big bunch of mares und colts!"

Thunderhead knew that voice. It went with the oats and the shelter and the kindness.

"Coom qvick, Boss! Dere all mixed up wid our mares —de stallions is fightin'—"

He knew the other voice too that answered from the Gorge, the deep, commanding voice with the anger in it. And he knew the two faces as they appeared through the driving flakes—the round pink face with the gray curls framing it—and the long dark face with the white teeth showing in a wind-beaten snarl— He knew the smell of them, but not this other smell of consternation—this smell of shocked horror. Nor the panic of that voice when it shouted, "Get the whips, Gus! Bring a couple of pitchforks!" Didn't know the arms that flailed him and beat him back with frenzied shouts, "Turn Banner's mares into the other corral—he'll follow them!" Even while he plunged past the man and reared again and Banner reared to face him and each aimed a smashing blow over the other's neck that landed like a dull thunder-clap, he had to take care to avoid this man who lashed his head and face with a whip, who hung, yelling, on his halter, who interfered in every possible way with his fixation, who flung his whole weight and heft against him, turning him, while the other man turned Banner. . . .

There was confusion flooding his brain . . . snow-wind blinding his eyes . . . obedience conflicting with libido. . . .

The barn. His own stall and a manger full of hay and oats. How had this happened? How had he got shut in here? He loved this stall. He dipped his head in the manger. Lifting it, he listened and pricked his ears and reached his sensitive nostrils into the air and fluttered them . . . He could smell each one of his mares and colts.

346

They were all there, around the stable, feeding at the racks...everything all right...all safe and cared for while the blizzard whined and the wind seized the barn and rattled it like a dried pod...

"Can you beat it? Thunderhead came back in the storm and brought his new harem! Habit was too strong for him."

Rob made a practice these days of hiding his temper from Nell, announcing even serious news in a careless manner.

So for a moment Nell was deceived and turned from the table where she was placing the silver for supper and looked at him with wonderment and joy.

"Thunderhead back again! Oh, Rob!"

Rob stamped across the kitchen floor to wash his hands at the sink, and it seemed to Nell that the grin he flung over his shoulder at her was more of a toothy snarl than a smile.

"Where is he now?" she asked.

"I've got him shut into the stable."

"I'd like to see him. I'll go up after supper."

"You will not!"

As he turned toward her, snatching the towel from the rack and drying his hands violently, she saw the wildness in his eyes. She said nothing more but set the supper on the table, and as Rob went to his place, he leaned over and kissed her and said contritely, "I can't let my darling be doing such reckless things as that at this late stage of the game."

Why is that reckless, thought Nell, then suddenly asked, "Where's Banner?"

The frenzied look Rob flung at her opened up to her understanding the whole scope of this predicament.

"I've got him in the east coral with his mares—and Thunderhead locked into the stable."

"Is he—is he safe there?"

"Not any too safe. You know that old stable. Horses have got out of it. Flicka beat her way through one of the

347

windows. Thunderhead broke through the top half of the door once—hope he doesn't remember it—" Rob was wolfing his supper. "The two bands of mares and colts are all mixed up in both corrals—eating me out of house and home—eighty head of horses! Gus and I'll have to spend half the night sorting them out—putting them through the chute—Banner took some of Thunderhead's mares and put them with his—"

A look of consternation dawned on Nell's face. "He did! Why, Rob! Why, that might start a fight!"

"It might and it did!" Rob reached for bread.

"Oh, Rob! What did you do?"

"We beat them apart. Just in time, too—before they really went berserker. A little later and we couldn't have done it. One of them would be dead now."

Nell was stunned into silence. Rob ate hungrily, then added more quietly, "And it wouldn't be Thunderhead."

Nell said nothing to that. No. Certainly not the powerful young creature who had overcome such an antagonist as the Albino— No—it would have been Banner—

"Rob," she said quietly a little later, "do you think they're safe now?"

"I do not." Rob shoved back his chair, went over to the stove and stood with his back to it while he filled and lit his pipe.

He took a few puffs, drew the smoke into his lungs, felt the calming effect of it, and finally took his pipe out of his mouth and held it, his eyes fixed in a brown study on the floor and said, "Banner will never be safe again."

"But—but—" stammered Nell, "we can send Thunderhead away again—he'll go back to that valley with his mares—"

"And in every storm he'll bring them home," said Rob quietly. "He's done that all his life, he'll continue to do it."

And for a while there was nothing to be heard in the cosy kitchen but the whine of the wind around the chimneys, and a sudden furious onslaught rattling the windows.

Pauly crawled out from under the stove, stretched slowly and sensuously, curling up her coral tongue, then seated herself and began a leisurely and thorough bath.

"No," said Rob again with a sharp sigh, raising his eyes to the ceiling of the room and taking a few more puffs of his pipe, "Banner will never be safe—not till Thunderhead is dead—or gelded."

A sound burst from Nell. "But Rob—*Ken!*" And at that Rob went wild again.

"I'm thinking of Ken too!" he shouted. "Do you think I like to do this? Now, when the boy has done better, achieved more, made me prouder of him than I ever have been in my life? If there were any way to get rid of that stallion—get him hundreds of miles away from here—turn him over to someone else— But who would buy him or accept him as a gift? He's no use to anyone."

Rob knocked the ashes out of his pipe, slipped it in his pocket, stamped across the kitchen to the porch and started to get himself into his outdoor rig. Woolen trousers into overshoes. Canvas trousers over both, tied at the ankles. Sheepskin-lined lumberjack, felt-lined gloves, and deep, padded Scotch winter cap. With his hand on the door knob he paused and looked back at Nell.

"I would be smart," he said slowly, "to put a bullet through him and haul him away. Ken would never know but what he was still up there in that valley."

Nell made no answer and waited for Rob to open the door and leave. But he did not leave. She looked up finally and saw that he was looking at her, waiting. There was a certain expression on his face. He was suffering. He was furious. He was stumped. He saw only one way out —he didn't want to hurt her, through Ken. He was asking her, and waiting for her answer.

Her heart gave a terrible leap, and she felt weak, and sat down at the table. He was serious about this, and he had put it up to her. She leaned her head on her hands.

Not to judge this like a sentimental woman—to judge it fairly like a judge. No, like someone who has the real responsibility and whose duty it is to find the safest way out for everybody. She could see the years stretch ahead, the constant annoyance and expense to Rob of having these wild mares and their colts brought down for feed and shelter in storms. At last they would feel that the ranch belonged to them. Thunderhead was oriented to this place, there was no way to prevent his coming, except by a sustained program of discouragement and unkindness that Rob would not be capable of, to say nothing to Ken. And lastly, the worst thing of all, it was only a matter of time before Thunderhead would kill Banner.

A deep wave of compassion for Rob went over her. What terrible decisions he had to take on himself! And such a decision as this—to shoot one of the finest young animals they had ever raised!

Help him! *Comfort* him! She rose swiftly to her feet with outstretched hands. Her face was strong and bright and smiling. "Shoot him now, Rob, and haul him away, before anything terrible happens. We just won't say anything to Ken about it. And don't feel too badly, dear, he's had a glorious life!"

Rob was bewildered. He took her gently in his arms and kissed her, looking at her wonderingly. "Will you go to bed now, my darling, and leave the dishes to me? I'll do them when I come in."

"Oh, you'll be so late—and after all that struggling to sort out the mares! I can do them! I'm not tired!"

"Please, Nell. I'll feel better if I know you're in bed up there with a book. Is there plenty of wood and coal in your box?"

"Plenty. All right, Rob, if it'll make you feel any better, I will."

Nell went to bed and sat reading, but she didn't know what the words meant, for she was listening for a shot. At last she fell asleep, and Rob came in and undressed and put out the lights without waking her.

But there had been no shot, for Rob had thought of another way—just a chance of a way—a very slim chance.

350

In the morning the storm was still raging. Rob rose early, saddled Shorty and rode over to the telegraph station to discover the state of the weather and roads westward. It was worst right here on Sherman Hill but snow ploughs were keeping the highways open and busses were running. Fifty miles to the west no snow was falling.

He rode back and explained his idea to Nell. If he could take Thunderhead in the trailer to Saginaw Falls— if he could make the trip in two days, they would arrive on October twenty-third, the day before the Greenway race. There was still time. And if Thunderhead should give a good account of himself in the race, someone would buy him and take him far away and everybody would be happy. After all, this was what he had been trained for.

"But the storm, Rob! And the roads! And those awful passes! Taking a horse down the Divide in a trailer in such weather as this!"

"Fifty miles west it's clear weather," said Rob as he threw things into his suitcase. "And, Nell—the kid deserves it. The hardest part will be getting out to the highway over the ranch road. It's up to my waist in drifts."

Gus had orders to take Shorty and spend all day, if necessary, driving those wild mares and their colts off the ranch. They would hang around for a while, but with Thunderhead gone, they would be at loose ends, and once off the ranch they would go straight back to their valley and stay there.

Thunderhead was blanketed and put in the trailer, his head tied low so that he would be helpless in case he wanted to make a bolt for freedom.

Big Joe and Tommy were hitched to the home-made snow plough, and Gus, bundled up like an Eskimo, with only a slit of storm-reddened face visible between cap and collar, forced the horses through the drifts. The car and trailer followed close behind.

351

42

Lights blazed out suddenly in the dark room, and Ken began to dream that his father was standing underneath the bright chandelier of the old-fashioned hotel bedroom, talking to Charley Sargent.

They talked about Thunderhead. Again and again Charley said, I'll be damned. It seemed so real that Ken began to tell himself that it must be true, but still he was asleep and dreaming and unable to drag himself out of the dream.

Then his father said, Don't wake him, and Ken tried to say, I'm awake! and to sit up, but instead he fell deeper into the dream, and presently it faded out entirely and he went sliding down into thick darkness.

It was just beginning to be light when he suddenly sat up. All night long the dream had been at the edge of his consciousness—was it really a dream? Charley Sargent was, as usual, snoring softly in the twin bed beside him. But Ken wasn't surprised to make out the form of someone else sleeping on the sofa across the room. It was his father.

Ken sat staring, while thoughts and speculations raced through his mind. What did it mean! Could it mean—was it possible—

He slid out of bed noiselessly and began to dress. It was barely a ten minutes' walk from hotel to the stables. Ken made it on the run.

As he saw the long lines of the stables against the faint morning light the suspense was almost unbearable. Running along under the portico of the stable in which Sargent's horses were kept, his eyes probed every dark opening, met the eyes of the quiet, brooding horses.

Long before he reached the last stall, the head of the horse standing in it had been turned in his direction. Ken's sharp thudding footsteps were as familiar as the squeak of the handle of the Goose Bar oat bucket.

A deep grunting murmur surged up through Thunderhead's chest, and the next moment the boy's arms were around his neck.

Presently Ken swung open the door and went in and closed it behind him.

Thunderhead had taught Ken to keep his distance. He had invited fondling from no one but Nell. But now, when Ken put his hands on each side of his face, the big stallion leaned forward and dropped the weight of his head against Ken.

Ken's cheeks burned as he laid them against the satin smoothness of the horse's hide. His hands ran up between the wide dark eyes, playing with the forelock, as he had often played with Flicka's. His lips whispered over and over again, "Thunderhead! Thunderhead!" and then, "You came back!"

Ken moved around him, smoothing his arched neck, tossing the mane to the right side—the proper side for Thunderhead to wear it. He ran his hand and arm down the great muscular ridges. He was filled with the secret joy and astonishment a man might feel when a desired woman suddenly turns and leans upon him. To have won the horse's love after a struggle of years—and such a horse!

Thunderhead suddenly swung his head, and nearly knocked Ken over. There was affection in the nudge—but something else too. Thunderhead wanted to get to the door. Shoving past Ken he reached his head out, pricked his ears, fastened his eyes on the farthest line of the horizon.

His wide nostrils flared and drew in the fresh morning air. They trembled as if struggling to find on the wind some other scent. And suddenly there was a movement, a turn toward Ken, a lowering and swinging of his head, a constriction of his chest that was like an inaudible neigh, and a pang shot through the boy. If Thunderhead had been able to talk, he could not more clearly have said to him, "Where are they all? Who has taken them away? You were there with me, you know that valley and those mares! We were together. Where have you hidden them? If we are friends, you will do this for me—you will give me back my mares! To whom else could I turn?"

Ken, stricken, stood back against the wall, and the stallion restlessly stepped around the stall, switching his tail, came up to Ken, gave him another shove with his nose, again reached his head out the door and watched the eastern horizon where it was brightening with the morning light. He was tense and quivering all over.

The early-morning activity around the stables was beginning. Little fires were made and breakfast pots began to steam over them. Horses were fed, and brought out by stable boys, for washing and grooming. Exercise boys trotted off on ponies, leading race horses for a slow gallop around the track.

Ken was not alone with his horse long. Perry Gunston and Tommy Pratt came to look him over and give him his morning oats, and presently others of the stablemen and trainers who had heard of the stallion gathered around. Thunderhead would not touch his oats. He nosed them, then turned his head away, standing inert and indifferent.

Gunston was disturbed. "Off his feed?" he said, looking questioningly at Ken.

Ken took some oats in his hand and held them cupped under Thunderhead's soft black muzzle. Thunderhead played with the grains, nuzzled Ken's hand, blew some of them away, then in a weary sort of manner, swung his head aside and stood quietly—waiting.

The boys began to chatter. "It's the trip upset him. When Dusky Maid was brought from Denver, she was off her feed for a week." "He might be coming down with shipping fever." To Ken, "You won't enter him, will you? If he's off his feed like this?"

"It doesn't mean he's out of condition," said Ken scornfully. "He's never out of condition. He can run faster than any other horse any time he wants to."

Gunston suggested that Ken should give the horse a run. He might be willing to eat after he'd had a bit of exercise. Dickson came running up, anxious to inspect the racer he was to ride that afternoon.

"Maybe Dickson had better ride him," suggested Ken to Gunston, "so he can get used to him."

But Gunston decided that Ken had better take him out for his first run. They saddled the horse, and Ken mounted him and moved slowly off toward the track, Dickson close beside Ken, and Gunston and Pratt following.

The jockey was firing questions at Ken. Ken answered quietly. No, he doesn't mind the whip. Sometimes you got to beat hell out of him.... No, he's not hardmouthed. You can guide him without any rein at all. He knows where you want to go.... Sure, he's got a chance to win the purse... he *can* win it, if he wants to, there just isn't any doubt about it. He can run faster than any other horse, I tell you. It's just if he wants to... Well—if he takes a notion... if he's in a bad temper... if he's got anything else on his mind—"

As he said the last words, Ken looked uneasily off at the horizon. Dickson looked anxiously at the horse.

Ken added, "Sometimes he starts bad. Don't worry about that. He might start with a rough, hard gallop. That's not his real running gait. Just beat hell out of him. Fight him. Make him mind you. He can catch up with anything once he hits his gait."

When Ken moved out to the track, there was a small crowd strung along the rail, several of them holding stop watches in their hands.

But this was not one of the times when Thunderhead "started bad." The familiarity of the light figure on his back, the well-loved voice, and those feather hands—

Thunderhead went from an easy canter without a hitch into his extraordinary floating run, and Perry Gunston's narrow, tense eyes narrowed still more. He glanced at the watch in his hand, looked at Dickson, shook his head, and put the watch away.

Dickson exploded, "Ker-r-rist! You don't *see* a horse run like that! You just dream about it!"

"Gosh Awmighty!" exclaimed one of the others, "he's got the Greenway purse in his pocket!"

"Looks like Ken's sold his horse," said Gunston.

Further down the rail old Mr. Greenway himself was out watching the morning runs. With his heavy knobbed cane assisting him in keeping his weight off his gouty left foot, and one ear studded with an acousticon like a small black boutonniere, he stood with that ear turned toward the track as if by sound as well as sight he could take the measure of these runners. He knew that one of them would be his before night. He was curious to know which one.

It was not until Ken sat down for breakfast with his father in the grill room of the Club House that he learned all the details of Thunderhead's return. It seemed to him more dreadful even than he had thought. The stallion had not just come home alone, as he often had before, he had returned with the entire band of mares and colts—his most cherished possessions—and had trustfully put them in the keeping of the Goose Bar corrals. And now, if his own plans went through, and his father's plans, Thunderhead would never see his mares again.

With head down and eyes on his plate, Ken fiddled with his fried eggs.

"Where do you think they all went—the mares and colts?" he asked after a moment.

"Back to their valley," said Rob. "That's their home. They would drift back there—and—" he broke off.

"And—?" prompted Ken, raising his eyes.

"I was going to say," said Rob, "wait for Thunderhead. They'd be expecting him to come back, of course, and take care of them. Why aren't you eating your breakfast?"

Ken ceased all pretence, laid his fork down and leaned

back. It was rather a garbled speech that poured out—about Thunderhead's new affection for him. His trust. And the way he was so terribly lonely for his mares and his valley, and right now when, for the first time, the horse had accepted him and turned toward him as if he was a friend—right now, Ken was playing the part of an enemy to him—not a friend at all.

Rob listened with an impassive face, eating his hearty breakfast with zest, buttering his toast, filling his cup with more hot coffee, glancing around the room, his head cocked as if he was hearing all that was going on as well as the words that came hesitatingly from Ken.

He flashed one lightning glance at his boy. He saw the shadowed eyes, and the pallor and the thin drawn lips that had become familiar signs of Ken's heartache.

Finally he said sharply, "You've been moving heaven and earth for three years to make a racer out of this horse and now you're changing your mind. Can't you stay put? Why in hell do you have to wobble about like that?"

Ken thought that if his father could only see the pictures that moved slowly behind each other in his own mind, he wouldn't ask such things. Right now Ken was seeing the picture of the way Thunderhead had—so trustingly—laid his head against him and placed his whole misery and longing in Ken's hands to straighten out for him.

Ken spoke hesitatingly. "I guess it's just—what you always say yourself, Dad—what we do to horses when we make them do what *we* want, instead of what they were naturally meant to do."

A flashing glance of Rob's fierce blue eyes paid tribute to Ken for this sign of understanding and honesty. "All the same, Ken, we're committed to this and we can't turn back. Neither can Thunderhead turn back. It's too late. Remember, too, how much depends on this."

"What?"

"Have you forgotten all the things you were going to get for your mother?"

Ken winced.

"Right now, with hospital expenses facing us, believe me, if there's any money in Thunderhead, we need it."

Ken's mind began to turn and twist, looking in every direction for some escape for Thunderhead. Touch And Go had run in two races and had not shown in either, although she had nearly been in the money in the second race. She had one more chance, in the race which would follow the Greenway race that afternoon. But certainly she was nothing to count on now.

"And," went on Rob, "remember the things you were going to do for the ranch. Wooden fences. Clear off the debts."

"I know."

"Are you going to turn tail and be a quitter now at the last moment just because Thunderhead is mooning for his mares?"

"But Dad—it's just because—because—well, he never was like this to me before. He always stared at me, and did things to me, aimed a kick or bite at me, you know. I always had to watch him. But he's changed. He was *glad* to see me this morning—*glad!* He—he—"

"What did he do?"

"Well he just put his head in my arms and leaned against me the way he always did with Mother, as if I was the only friend he had in the world—and gave a kind of a little mumbling grunt, you know the sound, as if it comes right out of his heart."

Rob was silent and could not raise his eyes to look at his boy.

At last he said, "Ken, you've got a divided loyalty here. And there's nothing tougher than that. Whichever way you turn you hurt yourself and someone else too. This happens to people often and it'll be a good experience for you. Are you going to stick to your plan to make money for the ranch and for all our needs—your own too, don't forget that—the money that's needed for your education and Howard's— Are you going to carry on with what you've started—what we've all worked for for three

358

years? Or are you going to—well, not exactly quit, but be deflected from your aim at the last moment?"

"Would that be wrong, Dad?"

"It would not be strong, Ken. I could not admire such behavior. It wouldn't be manly. Sometimes, in life, you have to choose a course that is right and pursue it even if it hurts some innocent party."

Ken did not answer. Rob finished his breakfast, laid down knife and fork and pushed his plate away. "When Dickson gets on that horse this afternoon I want you to be pulling for them both with all your heart and soul."

Ken's face began to burn. Visualizing Thunderhead prancing out with Dickson on his back, he couldn't do anything *but* pull for him! The idea of any other horse beating Thunderhead!

"And remember this, Ken, although right now Thunderhead's got his mind on other things than racing, and he's sulking, yet he's been trained for a race horse. It's in his blood now. And after a little of it, this life will become his true life."

Ken's eyes lifted to his father's with a deep probing question. "Honestly, Dad? As much as his wild life would be?"

Rod hedged. "Well, Ken, you know how I feel about horses. I always have the regret that when we take them for our own ends and make artificial lives for them, we deprive them of their true and natural and self-sufficient lives. But those would not always be necessarily *better* lives, in terms of the horse's well-being and happiness."

This made Ken thoughtful. Rob was getting impatient. He called the waiter and paid the check. A glance at Ken showed him that the boy was still in a state of indecision. He leaned across the table.

"Listen!"

Ken looked up. There was a different tone in his father's voice and a different look on his face.

"You're going to make your decision right now, Ken, and then stick to it."

"Me?"

"Yes. Be a man. It's your horse. If you want him taken away from the race course without making a try, why it's up to you!"

"Is it, really, Dad?"

"Sure it is." But there was a sharp, contemptuous look in Rob's eyes. "Make your choice!" He leaned back and took out his pipe and lit it, then looked around as if he had no further interest in the subject.

The decision leaped up in Ken, ready-made. He said, suddenly, "He'll run. And he'll win."

The words went through Rob like the twang of a string and caused him the emotion he always felt when one of his boys took a stride toward manhood.

His hand came down on Ken's arm and squeezed it. The other hand reached for his hat. "Come on, son! We'll go out and see to getting Thunderhead's shoes changed."

They walked out to the stables together, and if anything more had been necessary to crystallize Ken's determination, it was the remark his father made as they reached Thunderhead's stall. "Of course, Ken, if he doesn't win, and if we have to take him back, you realize I can't have him around the ranch any more. I'll have to sell him for anything I can get—and that means gelding him first."

Ken came to a dead stop. "But Dad! I'd get him off the ranch. He'd go back to his valley!"

"But he wouldn't stay," said Rob simply, "and sooner or later he'd get in a fight with Banner—and, well—you know what that means. You saw—"

43

Thunderhead did not like Dickson, and came out of the stall fighting.

The rest of the field were off and away on the two-mile race while Dickson was still trying to shake the bit out of Thunderhead's teeth and head him in the right direction.

The ordinary, run-of-the-mill excitement of race tracks which flares up, climaxes, and dies with every race that is run, is as nothing to the excitement that is generated when something really out of the ordinary happens; when the horses—one or more of them—take the game into their own hands, disregard the plans made for them by man, and stage a show all of their own devising. Then you really see such movement in the grandstands that you think of a river bursting its dam.

As when, at Hialeah in 1933 the two bay mares, Merryweather and Driftway, who had a feud of several years standing, proved the exception to the rule that mares never fight and threw their jockeys and fought it out, biting, squealing and lashing each other all the way down the home stretch.

As when Dinkybird of the Hawthorne stables took a fall at Jamaica, got up and was mounted again by his jockey, but started running in the wrong direction and could not be stopped.

It was this kind of excitement that Thunderhead of the Goose Bar stables provided for the onlookers at Saginaw Falls on the afternoon of October twenty-fourth.

Ken, standing close against the fence in front of the grandstand, leaned down and thrust his head between the bars. The blood came up into his face as he saw the fight Thunderhead was putting up. The field was way ahead already, Staghorn and Bravura, the two likeliest winners, running in the lead, five others bunched against the rail behind them, and three outclassed contenders trailing hopelessly. Thunderhead stood in the same place, whirling and plunging. Dickson lashed him unmercifully, and, as always, the fury engendered in the horse by this conflict mounted and finally exploded, releasing him from the complex of his inhibitions and flinging him into his smooth running gait.

Ken straightened up, drenched in the sweat of relief. But the field was already sweeping around the turn into the back stretch. The grandstand fell into a sudden breath-holding silence as the white stallion hit his pace, running, as it always seemed with Thunderhead, in the air, propelled by one lightning-quick hoof-thrust after the other, the unbelievable power of which kept him hurtling forward at a speed which was rapidly diminishing the distance between himself and the rest of the field.

Dickson rode with mouth open and a look of dumb amazement, and as Ken glanced around him, he saw this expression mirrored on a hundred faces.

The horses swept around the track.

Thunderhead passed the tail-enders, gradually overtook the next group and at the head of the home stretch passed them too. At that, the grandstand came out of its stupor and a low, sustained sound burst from it. Thunderhead was pulling up on the leaders, then was abreast of them, then passed them. At this, the grandstand rose, swayed, and burst into a roar, fluttering hands and programs and hats.

Thunderhead wavered and stopped, his flaring, white-ringed eyes and sharply pricked ears turned nervously to this strange heaving mountain to the right of him. At Dickson's yell and the shaking of the bit in his mouth, the stallion went up onto his hind legs.

Bravura and Staghorn rushed past, beginning the second lap of the race.

"Whip him, Dickson! Beat hell out of him!" Ken's voice, cracking with strain, reached Dickson from the crowd. Dickson cast one hopeless glance toward Ken as Thunderhead whirled and plunged, and a wave of the jockey's empty right hand showed that he had lost his whip.

Ken's open mouth closed without another sound and his face paled. Dickson pulled off his cap and beat it from side to side on Thunderhead's neck. Other horses passed him, streaming along the rail. Suddenly Thunderhead plunged forward, and again Ken was weak with relief. He unclenched his fingers slowly. Little bleeding scars were in the palms of his hands. It was all right now—Thunderhead had passed them once, he could do it again.

But Thunderhead had no intention of doing it. All he wanted, apparently, was a good spot in which to show everyone what he was going to do to this rider whom he didn't want on his back. Angling across the empty track, he floated over the inner rail, galloped to the center, leaped into the air, corkscrewing, came down with feet like four steel pistons—rocked a couple of times, and had no need to do more. For Dickson was making one of those slow curves through the air that Ken had made, times without number.

Free of his rider, Thunderhead decided to join the race. He floated over the rail again—and the beautiful easy leap drew a gasp from the grandstand—and then he started to overtake the field. Again it grew like an orchestral crescendo—the roar of the grandstand—until the white horse closed the distance between himself and the rest of the field.

Thunderhead did not know when to stop. He floated on when the race was over and the winner proclaimed and the other horses were walking back into the paddock. Attendants ran out on the track and tried to stop him. That angered him. He dodged them, sailed over the outer rail and away into the distance, the little stirrups dangling and tapping at his sides.

When Thunderhead vanished beyond the grove of willows south of the race track, Ken fought through the crowd behind him, under the grandstand out at the back and around the west end of the track. He ran as fast as he could, keeping his eye on that little dip in the willows through which Thunderhead had disappeared.

He felt in his pocket. The whistle was there. If he could get within earshot of the stallion he could call him with the whistle. He fought his way through a dense patch of undergrowth, emerged, and stood for a moment searching the country before him, his scarlet face streaming with sweat, the wild mop of his hair tangled with bits of leaves and bark.

Half a mile away the white stallion stood quietly. When Ken whistled for him, he turned his head, then trotted toward his young master.

As he came up, Ken looked at him bitterly. "You fool! You've thrown away the only chance you had in the world!"

Thunderhead stopped, recognizing something other than approval in Ken's voice.

"You *could* have done it! Easy as pie! And now you've spoiled everything!" There was a tremor in Ken's voice as he finished, and he said nothing more, but mounted the horse and rode him slowly back, circling the track to reach the stables.

As he did so, he heard by the roar from the grandstand that another race was in progress, and drew rein on a little elevation and turned in the saddle just in time to see the horses flash over the finish line—a bright golden sorrel with blond tail a good length in the lead.

Touch And Go! He had entirely forgotten that she was running! And now she had won! A flood of joy alternated with the feeling that it could not possibly be true.

Ken galloped Thunderhead to the stables, not dismounting to open gates, but jumping every one. He put the stallion in his stall, called to one of the stable boys to attend to him, and ran back to the race track.

He was in time to hear the announcement over the loud-speaker. "Winner, Touch And Go, of the Goose Bar stables. Owner, Kenneth McLaughlin."

Ken stood still a moment. This was what victory felt like— Then he dashed forward. He wanted to get his hands on Touch And Go and see if she was really still herself.

Perry Gunston had her in the paddock. A blanket had been thrown over her, and around her was a crowd of men. Rob McLaughlin was talking to old Mr. Greenway, and he called Ken to him and said, "I want you to meet Mr. Greenway. This is my son, Mr. Greenway, the owner and trainer of the filly."

As Ken put out his hand he heard an eager little whinny behind him.

Mr. Greenway exclaimed, "You don't say! You don't say! And I hear you trained the white stallion too. But you'll never have any luck with him, my boy, too undependable."

The whinny came again and Ken longed to go to her.

"Mr. Greenway has just bought Touch And Go, Ken."

"Bought her!"

"I'm a collector of fine horses, my boy. That's the second one I've acquired this afternoon. Hop up on her now, son, and ride her over to my stables."

Mr. Greenway limped over to the filly. Rob caught Ken's arm and showed him the check. It was made out to Kenneth McLaughlin, and the amount was five thousand dollars.

Ken looked up at his father. Rob McLaughlin's big white teeth were flashing in a wide and joyful grin. "That does it, Ken!" he exclaimed. But Ken could only stare at his father's face, then at the check, and feel dazed.

Greenway called to Ken, "Take a last ride on her, son."

Touch And Go's face was turned eagerly toward Ken as he walked to her. A sudden reluctance made his feet heavy—*last ride!*

He smoothed her face. His father and Greenway stood beside her, talking. "Good girl," murmured Ken, "you did it, baby."

It was a marvel, certainly, what she had done. Without any fuss about it, she had just always done as she was taught to do and done it with all her heart. And she had it in her, that speed and power, as if she had been Flicka— Flicka with the four beautiful legs she had had before he, Ken McLaughlin, had brought her in off the range and lamed her—but, too, with the sweetness and docility that she had only acquired through her suffering.

"Good girl," he muttered again, and turned his face down against the filly's head that was gently shoving at him. Then he put it into Swedish, "my *flicka*—"

Perry Gunston drew the blanket off, Ken mounted her and rode her slowly toward the Greenway stables.

"Are you awake, Thunderhead?" It was a soft whisper from Ken, who had spent the night on a blanket at the edge of Thunderhead's stall.

The stallion did not move. He was standing with his head out the upper half of the stable door. But one ear flicked back and Ken rose to his feet and went to the door and folded his arms over the top of it close by Thunderhead's neck. Outside, the light grew stronger. It was nearly day.

Ken thought over all that had happened and all that was going to happen. He and his father and Thunderhead were starting back to the ranch this day. Then Thunderhead would be gelded—plenty of money now to have Doc Hicks come to the ranch and do it—and then he would be sold to the Army for a band horse. They brought the most money of all, his father had said, more than the Army paid for ordinary horses. He might bring as much as three hundred dollars. White horses for cavalry bands were not easy to find.

Ken stared out at the dim shapes of stables and trees while he thought of Thunderhead carrying a bandsman in a band. He had seen those bands in the parades at the

366

post. Thunderhead was a big husky—he might carry the kettledrums.

Kettledrums! Cavalry bands! The drummer's arms and big sticks weaving a crisscross over Thunderhead's back —pounding the drums—putting on a clown act. And the huge glittering horns, the fancy uniforms, the smart drum major, the deafening blare of band music! Thunderhead—the big show-off—prancing in the middle of it!

Ken thought suddenly of getting on Thunderhead and running away with him. Turning him loose somewhere. Giving him away—

When they were getting ready to load the stallion, Ken asked, "Dad, is the reason you've got to geld him because you can't get rid of him unless you do?"

"Bright boy!" said Rob sarcastically. Then he put his hand on Ken's shoulder. "It's not the money, Ken—not any more, although three hundred dollars isn't to be sneezed at. But it's really because there's no other way to save Banner and to save myself, incidentally, from having to adopt about thirty wild mares."

Before eight o'clock they had the stallion in the trailer and had started the long drive back to the ranch.

44

The eagle headed into the strong westerly wind and hung on motionless wings high over the valley.

The "easterner" had blown itself out and no sign of it remained except for patches of snow under the trees and in the depressions of the hills. Here was summer again. Indian summer, with the quakin'-asp a riot of crimson and ochre and the cottonwoods shedding golden leaves on the surface of the river.

The eagle saw the mares and colts grazing, saw something large and white moving through the pass in the rampart and slipped sideways to poise himself directly over it.

Ken McLaughlin was leading his stallion through the keyhole. As they emerged on the threshold of the valley they halted. The horse was saddled with the small horsehair saddle Ken had made himself. Underneath the bridle was a heavy chain halter and lead, and over his eyes a blindfold, but in spite of this he knew where he was and his body was tense, and fierce snorting breaths came from his nostrils.

He pawed the earth.

With one hand Ken uncinched the girth, lifted the saddle off and dropped it on the ground. The glint of the sun on steel stirrups struck the eagle's eyes, and a sudden lift of his body registered the reaction. Again he spread his wings wide, circled and centered over the pass.

Ken undid the latch of the throat strap, talking softly to his horse. "You don't know it, Thunderhead . . . but this is good-by . . . you've got to go to your mares and take care of them and live a stallion's life . . . you're a true throwback, Thunderhead . . . you're not a race horse though you can go like the wind when you want to . . . and you're not an Army band horse prancing around carrying a kettledrum . . . you've got to go back . . . and I've got to go to school and do a lot of other things . . . so . . . . we . . . can't be together any more . . . ."

Thunderhead's hoof dug impatiently at the earth. Ken slid his arm up underneath the stallion's neck and laid his own head against it. His voice went on while his fingers drew off the bridle, the chain halter, and at last the blindfold. "Don't forget me, Thunderhead . . . I won't forget you . . . never, Thunderhead. . . ."

Ken stepped back, the stallion was free, and he knew it. He took a step forward, switching his tail. His head was high, his ears alert, his eyes roved over the valley. It was as if he counted every mare and colt grazing there a quarter mile or so away. But he seemed in no hurry to join them. They were all his, and now there was no one to dispute him.

He turned toward Ken again, poked out his head and gave the boy an affectionate shove. Ken slipped his arm around the stallion's nose. "But you've got to go, Thunderhead... those are your mares... I think you do know it's good-by..."

Thunderhead lifted his head and again examined the mares. Ken tossed the bridle and halter to the ground; and as he did so something that came plummeting down from the sky startled him and made him look up. It leveled off and curved upward again but the shadow of the broad wings slid across the pass and Ken was surprised to see the stallion give a violent start and then half-crouch.

"Why, Thunderhead!" he exclaimed and put out his hand to reassure him.

But the recoil was only a second. Thunderhead straightened up and threw back his head, snorting out that hated scent.

The eagle circled and came at them again, this time lower, leaning back, his one talon thrust out and his great wings humped forward to break his speed. Thunderhead leaped to meet him, reared to his full height, and delivered half a dozen furious pawing strokes.

The eagle slid over them, just out of reach, leaned into the wind again, and a few lazy wingbeats sent him spiraling upward. It was as if he served notice that he was the guardian of the pass and had something to say about this valley. Would it be Thunderhead who would get the eagle under his feet and cut him to pieces, or the eagle who would swoop down to pick the stallion's bones?

This encounter had attracted the attention of the mares. There came trotting out from the band the black mare with the white colt, her ears pricked inquiringly at Thunderhead. She neighed. He answered. He left Ken and went to meet her, lowering his head, curving and wagging it from side to side. His tail lifted, flared wide, and streamed behind him. And now all the mares were staring. They recognized him and rushed to meet him.

The little white colt was the first to reach Thunderhead. It sniffed him, bared its little teeth and nibbled at him in affection, then whirled and thumped him with its heels. This, while Thunderhead and the mare were greeting each other ardently, pressing their faces together, nuzzling each other, finally rising lightly on their hind legs to embrace each other.

Now Thunderhead greeted the rest of his harem. They milled around him, kicking and nipping each other in the excited jealousy of having him back. Finally they settled down to the real business of life, which was grazing.

Ken watched it all with a smile on his face. At last he picked up the equipment he had dropped on the ground and went back through the keyhole to finish the business. He had spent hours with drill and sledge hammer working on the rock around and underneath that monster boulder which formed the roof of the keyhole. He had studied where each stick of dynamite should go. He did not intend that there should be a single one of those small slips or miscalculations which brought so many of his good intentions to nought. The dynamite was tamped into the holes, the fuses attached.

Now he lit the fuses, turned and ran. He didn't stop running until he reached the place he had picketed Flicka. He slipped his arm up underneath her head and held it against him so she would not be startled, and, standing so, waited for the explosion.

It came. The pile of boulders around and above the keyhole rose with a dull boom. The earth under Ken's feet seemed to heave. There was a frightened chattering of birds, and small animals scurried out of the rocks. A cloud of dust floated up from the passage. And as earth and rocks settled back again, the valley was filled with detonations caroming back from the hills. Last of all came a deep rumble from the Thunderer.

After some minutes Ken entered the passage to see exactly what had happened to the keyhole. It no longer existed. Just as he had planned, the support for the boulder had been blasted away, and with its fall, all the other boulders had found a new position. There were some crannies a cat or a small dog could have crawled through, but for Thunderhead the passage was closed for all time.

Ken retraced his steps, ran along under the rampart until he came to the place Thunderhead had made the trail to the summit, and climbed up.

There was excitement amongst the mares over the blasting. Thunderhead was nowhere to be seen. Ken lay down, hanging his head over the edge, certain that the horse was below there, pawing at those stones, investigating every cranny, discovering that there would be no more going in and out of the valley. At least, thought Ken, not from this end. You might be able to find a way out the other end, old fellow, through those valleys and mountain passes and glaciers, but it would be a hundred miles around for you to get home, and all of it strange going—no—I think you'll stay in—

And then it was as if his father's fiery, commanding eyes were suddenly looking into his, and he spoke to them, "I've done it, Dad. He won't come back to bother you any more. Or to kill Banner. . . ."

His father! It was a warm and happy thing to remember how his father had looked at him and spoken to him and squeezed his shoulder even at that moment of disturbance getting ready to take his mother to the hospital. And the friendly words, "If you think you can do it, son, I'll leave it to you. I don't want to shoot your horse or geld him." And his mother had slipped her arm around his neck and kissed him and said, "Keep your fingers crossed, darling, we want a little *flicka*, don't we? And Ken—thanks to you and Touch And Go, I'm going away without the slightest worry about expenses—and I shall send out from the hospital and order a new negligée! Velvet! With feathers!"

Thunderhead came out from under the rampart at a gallop and rushed back to his mares. Ken leaped to his feet. What would he do now? What did he think about the blocked passage?

Thunderhead was heading away from this end of the valley as if that gunpowder were behind him. He began to round up his mares.

Ken watched it for the last time . . . the weaving in and out, the snaking head, the plunges of the mares as they felt the stallion's teeth in their haunches. . . .

The daylight was fading. Ken had to strain his eyes to see how every mare and colt was gathered up and swept into that rushing charge of pounding bodies and sweeping hair and flying limbs.

Wild exultation filled the boy. He had done it, after all! He had given back the mares to his horse! And this round-up! And a thousand others like it—and the valley and the snow peaks and the river—

That other life he had tried to give Thunderhead—the life of a race horse—how desperately he had prayed for it! He felt almost bewildered. For all his prayers had been denied and all his efforts frustrated, and yet this— *this*—was the answer.

The boy's head lifted and his eyes flashed from crest to crest.

All the world was beginning to glow with the sunset. Three cream-colored antelopes were drinking at the edge of the river. The river was emerald green and turquoise blue and rose pink and there was a big golden star in it. Yellow light swept eastward from the sunset in long level shafts. A half moon, lying on its back, began to glow like a lamp.

All this for Thunderhead!

Thunderhead floated past the band of mares that now, in the gathering darkness, seemed like a swift-moving blot of shadow, and took the lead.

Ken strained his eyes to see the last of that rushing white form. Here it was, now, the parting. He put up his hand and brushed warm tears from his cheeks, surprised to find them there, because, in spite of the loneliness and the sense of bitter loss, it was as if the beauty of the valley and the gloriousness of Thunderhead's freedom were inside him too.

And now they were gone.

In the deep breath that Ken drew, there was the wideness and the emptiness of the world.

With startling suddenness, day fled from the valley. The golden spears were withdrawn, the pink clouds faded. Shadows seemed to rise from the earth, and, floating on this sea of darkness, the encircling snow peaks turned to ghostly silver. The ice-blue slopes of the Thunderer, marked with triangles and bars of deeper blue, glittered here and there as if strung with diamonds. Its jagged outline lay sharp as crystal against the emerald sky.

It was time, and more than time, for Ken to go. Flicka was waiting. Once again it was just himself and Flicka, as it had been before Thunderhead, before Touch And Go. He ran down the trail, packed up, mounted, and was off.

The eagle hung in the sky where the daylight still lingered, watching all that the boy did. When he had gone, the great bird dropped slowly down over that pile of boulders which had suddenly changed its shape.

He hovered, examining, estimating, the difference. At last he swept up into the sky again, and his harsh, lonely cry, "Kark!—Kark!—Kark!" floated out on the sound waves that played across the valley, spending themselves in inaudible ripples against the mountainsides.

By the year 2000, 2 out of 3 Americans could be illiterate.

It's true.

Today, 75 million adults...about one American in three, can't read adequately. And by the year 2000, U.S. News & World Report envisions an America with a literacy rate of only 30%.

Before that America comes to be, you can stop it...by joining the fight against illiteracy today.

Call the Coalition for Literacy at toll-free **1-800-228-8813** and volunteer.

**Volunteer
Against Illiteracy.
The only degree you need
is a degree of caring.**

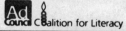

Ad Council Coalition for Literacy